Praise for

THE ALCHEMIST'S DAUGHTER

"Set during the twilight years of Henry VIII with vibrant characters, a compelling plot and accurate historical depictions, *The Alchemist's Daughter* brings the darkness and danger of Tudor London vividly to life as it weaves its suspenseful tale. This beautifully written addition to the medieval mystery genre is sure to delight all fans of the period."
—Sandra Worth, author of *Pale Rose of England*

"A smart, scientific sleuth . . . Lawrence uses her enthusiasm for Elizabethan England to create a historical novel within a mystery."
—*Portland Monthly*

"The writing is terrific, with great period details. There are lots of red herrings and a surprising amount of action that will keep readers engaged until the very last page."
—*San Francisco Book Review*

"I absolutely loved *The Alchemist's Daughter*—the characters, the authentic feel of the period, and of course the richly drawn story."
—Dorothy Cannell, author of *Murder at Mullings*

"Lawrence proves herself to be an excellent storyteller with this grim tale of murder, mayhem and medicine."
—*CentralMaine.com*

Please turn the page for more outstanding praise for Mary Lawrence and her Bianca Goddard mysteries!

The Alchemist of Lost Souls

Books by Mary Lawrence

THE ALCHEMIST'S DAUGHTER

DEATH OF AN ALCHEMIST

DEATH AT ST. VEDAST

THE ALCHEMIST OF LOST SOULS

Published by Kensington Publishing Corporation

The Alchemist of Lost Souls

MARY LAWRENCE

KENSINGTON BOOKS
www.kensingtonbooks.com

KENSINGTON BOOKS are published by

Kensington Publishing Corp.
119 West 40th Street
New York, NY 10018

All Kensington titles, imprints, and distributed lines are available at special quantity discounts for bulk purchases for sales promotion, premiums, fund-raising, educational, or institutional use.

Special book excerpts or customized printings can also be created to fit specific needs. For details, write or phone the office of the Kensington Sales Manager: Kensington Publishing Corp., 119 West 40th Street, New York, NY 10018. Attn. Sales Department. Phone: 1-800-221-2647.

Kensington and the K logo Reg. U.S. Pat. & TM Off.

ISBN-13: 978-1-4967-1532-6 (ebook)
ISBN-10: 1-4967-1532-2 (ebook)
Kensington Electronic Edition: May 2019

ISBN-13: 978-1-4967-1531-9
ISBN-10: 1-4967-1531-4
First Kensington Trade Paperback Edition: May 2019

10 9 8 7 6 5 4 3 2 1

Printed in the United States of America

For Lacey, Theo, and Jasper

The cost of friendship is loyalty.

CHAPTER 1

London, spring of 1544

This tale begins with a rascally lad and a disgraced alchemist. One sought allowance with a group of puckish boys, and the other wished forgiveness from his petulant king. The two crossed paths one spring day when the air puffed warm against their cheeks, calling to mind the hope of renewal that comes with the lengthening days and appearance of green tips on trees.

Albern Goddard wore his best woolen gown, one he'd bought from a fripperer back when he was in the king's good graces. The clothes dealer had gotten it from the widow of a barrister who had been stabbed in the back—a fitting end to any lawyer, thought Albern. The rip had been mended and the bloodstain scrubbed clean. No one was the wiser, and he himself barely remembered the gown's tainted history as he strode triumphantly down Thames Street.

His coif did not hide the lift of his chin; the scholarly garb accentuated his proud posture—for here was a man basking in the ticklish glow of divine favor. A smile strained the muscles around his mouth; his usual expression was one of stoic indifference. And that was on a good day.

He may not have discovered the philosopher's stone—the coveted agent of transmutation capable of turning base metal into gold; instead, he had discovered a substance of unplumbed worth. Of this he was certain. Months of collecting and fermenting the golden stream—*his* golden stream in urns stinking up his alchemy room—had eventually wrought a substance so astonishing, so exceptional, that he could hardly keep from whooping and dancing down the street.

However, unbridled enthusiasm can easily turn a man into a fool. The alchemist knew this; he had eaten from fate's fickle hand before. So, he quashed the smile on his face, replacing a cheerful expression with one more solemn. Ahead of him lay several days of careful analysis to prove his discovery's importance.

Meanwhile, on the street ahead, there lay an ambush in the form of a gaggle of gamins. Their winter boredom had festered, so that this day of sun and warmth was like a needle to their boil, releasing the hellions to run free.

What boy can resist the call of his friends' mischief? After a winter of trudging through cold, wet lanes, lugging home bundles of sticks for his mother's fire, of being cooped up with his siblings like chickens kept from wolves, of listening to the constant wails of younger kin, what lad of any spirit could suffer another moment staring at four cracked and soot-grimed walls? So it was that on this day, a boy with threadbare britches and raggedly hair wandered farther than was his usual habit.

He hitched himself to a group of boys kicking a pig's bladder stuffed with hay. Other stragglers left their chores to join in, and soon there was a mob of exuberant, yelling imps tripping over one another and upsetting geese, pushcarts, and pedestrians. They raced around, calling each other "lead-legged" and "beetle-brained buzzards." They ran down Bread Street and exited onto Thames Street just as Albern Goddard was crossing it. The ball rolled to a stop inches from the alchemist's shoe.

His serious face drew the boys to a scritching halt. They stared wide-eyed at the person standing before them. Deeply set gray eyes glared back, unamused. The man's exceptional gown bespoke a person of import, but when they ran their eyes down his august garb, down his black netherhose to his shoes, they found a pair of leathers as haggard and as somber as he.

The alchemist looked down his nose at them. He picked up the bladder ball and turned it over in his hands, still studying the unruly herd of boys. Not until every eye had met his did the alchemist release the ball, turning and throwing it back in the direction he had come. Like a sorcerer he released them from his spell and the boys ran after the bladder, hooting and yelling.

But a handful of boys remained where they were. The novelty of the sport had worn off in favor of this odd person now striding down the street. These boys did not suspect that the man was an alchemist. They didn't know what he was about, but they saw an opportunity to antagonize the pretentious man just the same.

They fell into line a safe distance behind, imitating the alchemist's heron-like stride. His long legs jutted out as if they bent forward at the knees. A few citizens paused to titter at the boys' mockery, and this only emboldened them to exaggerate their gestures. They mimicked wearing the sweeping gowns of learned professionals and dismissively flicked their wrists to discount any who looked their way. The lads deserved a good cuffing about the ears.

One of them crept closer to Albern and brazenly threw a rock. The missile sailed within inches of the alchemist's ear. Though he must have heard it, he seemed not to notice. His pace never slowed, his head never turned. However, ignoring the boys only provoked them further. They made obscene gestures. They called him a rooster, laughing. They *cock-a-doodle-dooed* louder than the squeaks of cart wheels and the clopping of horses—but their mockery had no effect. Goddard's focus stayed on his single-minded purpose.

Some of the boys became discouraged and abandoned their efforts. When their quarry was waylaid by a conversation with another man, the remaining scamps grew bored and ran off to find trouble elsewhere. All except one.

* * *

Timothy Browne ducked behind the support poles of a produce stand and watched. From where he stood, he could hear the puff-cock address the other man in a patronizing tone. Even though Timothy was a simple boy of nine and was unsophisticated in the nuances of adult conversation, he sensed the condescending quality of the fellow's reaction to the inquiry of the other and took exception to it; for the man to whom the fellow was speaking was his father.

Dikson Browne was an alchemist, one who'd fallen on rough times—but then, to Timothy's knowledge, his father had never known good ones. Like most alchemists, he had squandered his family's resources and they always seemed to be living on the edge of despair. Timothy noticed his father stiffen as he spoke.

That this other fellow seemed smug was obvious to the boy.

"I sense that I am delaying you, Goddard. Have you discovered the stone?"

Timothy caught the man's name and remembered his father's barbed comments about the fellow on more than one occasion.

"Nay, I shall leave that pursuit to others more inclined." Goddard tilted his head. "Dikson, why do I have the fortune of chance meeting you? Who is watching your latest chemistries?"

"Oh," said Timothy's father, straining geniality. "I am at a stage where the projection must rest." But Timothy thought the only thing that rested in their home was his father after too much drink.

Goddard attempted a smile. "Well, my good sir, I wish you every success. A fair day." And with that, he tucked his chin, stepped aside, and sallied on, leaving Dikson Browne gawping after.

Timothy Browne, watching the curt exchange, felt sorry for his father but quickly turned his back when Dikson stopped glaring after Albern and glanced his way. Pretending interest in hay-stippled fleeces, Timothy waited until his father had moved on, then searched the road for the arrogant alchemist. He caught sight of Goddard—the man's height easily setting him apart from others—and scurried down the lane after.

Thames Street happened to be the longest thoroughfare in

London. The boy had never explored its entire length stretching from St. Andrew's Hill all the way to the Tower. This morning, his mother was keen to be rid of him and, as long as he returned in time for supper, he could do as he pleased. He followed Albern Goddard past the old church of All Hallows the Great, where the beseeching left hand of a stone carving of Charity had been lopped at her wrist. All Hallows the Less stood a few yards beyond, living up to its name, abandoned and home to vagrants. A young dog trotted cheerfully beside him, and he threw sticks for the pup until a butcher cart en route to market led it astray. Then Timothy ran ahead, looking for the tall alchemist, spotted him, and fell back to stalking.

Eventually the man turned into an area of warehouses near Billingsgate, with its merchant vessels bobbing at the wharf. He twisted through a warren of rubble stone buildings to an area of derelict ones made of wood. At one of these leaning structures, Albern Goddard stopped. He worked a padlock held with a rusty chain, and after a moment the heavy impediment fell away and he slipped inside.

Timothy cautiously approached. Looking left and then right, he hesitated opposite the door and leaned an ear against it. No sounds ranged within, but when the door suddenly shook from the weight of a deadbolt being secured, he let out a yelp and fled around the corner.

The door rattled open. There was a pause, a slam. Timothy blew out his breath. Listening at the door would be risky; the man might skin him like a rabbit and no one would know the better what happened to him.

The lad considered going home, and had taken a step in that direction when a loud creak issued overhead. A pole pushed open a high window that resisted being prodded. He crouched behind a barrel as it fell shut, then finally was gotten under control and propped open.

Boys have the curiosity of cats but lack a feline's guarded stealth. Timothy noticed he shared the cramped alley with an abundance of discarded crates and barrels. The smell of rotting wood and mildew permeated the air. However, if he could properly stack them, he could scale a ramshackle tower and have a look inside the alchemist's room.

Testing several barrels, Timothy found one strong enough to support his weight and rolled it under the window. The crates took more effort to arrange, requiring him to balance on the remains of those less sturdy while placing one atop the other. Soon he had built a tottering structure that could withstand his climbing it.

The construction wobbled and threatened collapse as the boy picked his way to the summit. Once there, he stood upon his toes and, careful not to disturb the support pole, poked his head under the window frame to peer inside.

As his forehead rose above the sill, the first thing he spied was a set of fierce-looking teeth. It says something of the child's background that he did not flinch upon seeing such a sight, as most boys would have at least lost their balance. Timothy, though, searched beyond the glinting enamels to the desiccated remains of a creature hovering at eye level and suspended from the rafters. A crocodile. A layer of grime covered its scaly green-gray hide, turning it into a less formidable creature, dangling with writhled skin, dull with dust. He had, after all, seen one before.

His own father's room of alchemy was a garret from which pigeons were shooed in the uppermost reaches of his family's rent. On the rare occasion that Timothy had seen inside, he found a room a quarter of the size of this, and not nearly so well stocked. The boy marveled at the array of bottles and bowls lining the shelves in this room of alchemy. A variety of furnaces, one he recognized as a fusory furnace for melting metals, sat against an exterior wall, where a smaller window provided some escape for the caustic fumes that spewed when it was stoked. Large, pelican-shaped, still heads balanced atop copper cucurbits. Clay pots and urns littered the floor, and wavering plumes of smelly smoke escaped lit tallows. This was a proper alchemy room, not the sad imitation in which his father toiled.

At first he did not see the alchemist unlocking a cabinet against a wall. The man had removed his scholarly gown; his brown jerkin and dark hose blended into the drab palette of the room's interior. Presently, the cabinet door fell open.

If he had not witnessed it for himself, Timothy would have sworn that a lantern had been left burning inside the cupboard. A brilliant white light illuminated the alchemist's face, emphasizing his lengthy, thin nose and wiry eyebrows. It was not a lantern of any type with which the boy was familiar. No metal housing encased it; rather the light filled a bulbous-bottomed flask. The boy blinked. How could it not have burned down the room? Timothy leaned forward. What was this strange spectacle?

The alchemist smiled as he withdrew the flask glowing bright with the luminous intensity of a full moon. His eyes widened as he lifted the vessel and admired it.

Astounded, Timothy drew back, bumping his head on the window. The pole wiggled free, balancing in midair for a moment before he grabbed it. With a trembling hand, he repositioned the prop against the window, holding his breath until he was sure the alchemist had not noticed.

He need not have worried. Enthralled (or perhaps blinded) by the light, Albern Goddard set the flask on a tripod and pulled up a stool to sit. Neither candle nor lantern, this light did not flicker but remained a steady, robust glow.

The boy did not know how long the two of them gazed at the flask. He was sure he was witnessing something unique, perhaps even magical. At one point, the alchemist adjusted the cork. Eventually, though, the brilliance faded and the glow diminished. It changed to an eerie green, then vanished, snuffed like a candle.

The alchemist stirred, rubbed his neck, stretched his limbs. He fetched a pair of tongs off a nearby furnace, set them on the table next to him, twisted out the cork, and laid it on the board.

Immediately a crackle and spark erupted inside the flask. The crackling grew, sounding like ice shattering on a puddle. Flames began spewing from the flask. The alchemist shoved the stopper back in the opening and nearly dropped the vessel on the table. He yowled and cursed, Timothy thought, from being burned.

After a few minutes, the fire lost its strength; its dance diminished to a gentle ruffling of flames, then died.

Timothy frowned. Removing the stopper had freed and restored its vigor—much like the boys who had been released from their winter captivity. Stoppering the end of the flask had tamed it.

What could one do with such a thing? Timothy began pondering the possibilities, all of them having to do with making money and garnering awe. It didn't seem right that this toffish prig of a puffer should enjoy the fame that might come from its possession. *His* family would be better served.

Goddard crossed the room to his shelves and surveyed the collection of bottles, some with labels, most without. His head dipped, then rose, like a strange bird assessing a beetle. He gripped the neck of a plump-bottomed decanter and removed its plug to sniff its contents. Satisfied, he cradled it back to his work area and poured a small amount into a cup.

Timothy watched as the alchemist again removed the cork. Taking hold of the tongs, he tilted the vessel to work them through the narrow opening. The crackling began and sparks flew up the neck of the vessel. The alchemist worked quickly, fishing around until he withdrew a piece of material the size of a pea and dropped it in the cup.

Albern hurriedly replaced the cork, giving it a forceful twist, and the glow in the flask continued for a bit, then eventually faded. The lump in the cup, however, did nothing. The alchemist sat on his stool and stared at it. He poked it with his tongs.

Timothy, unimpressed, grew bored. His stomach told him dinner was nigh upon him, and if he did not return by the time his mother called for him he'd suffer more than just going to bed hungry. The sun was somewhere beyond Bridewell and soon the starlings would be lining the eaves of St. Martin Vintry. He was ready to end his covert surveillance when he smelled a strong odor of garlic. He rocked onto his toes and peered back inside.

Smoke billowed from the table, nearly obscuring the alchemist on his stool. It quickly grew into a cloud, doubling in size. Timothy could hear the man coughing and even he could not keep from gagging over the pungent smell wafting past his nose. He didn't worry that the alchemist would hear him; the man was cursing and trying to fan away the encroaching storm, trying to find the little lump and do something with it.

Sparks pierced the swelling cumulus, reminding Timothy of a fireworks display he once saw over Hampton Court Palace. No celebration here. An orange flame shot up from the table and he glimpsed a look of fear on the alchemist's face as it singed the man's beard and lit it on fire.

Frightened, Timothy jumped back. His head knocked against the window and sent the pole toppling. He hardly had time to care before his tower gave way under his shifting weight, and with a terrified shriek he rode the bumpy slope down to the ground, landing in a heap next to a pile of splintered crates and barrels. Rubbing his bruised bum, he glanced up at the smoke pouring out of the high window.

Timothy sprang to his feet. What became of the alchemist or this sorry row of warehouses wasn't his concern. He imagined his mother's voice calling, her bellow echoing through the streets of Queenhithe Ward, through Romeland, reaching him in this dank alley behind an alchemist's room. God help him if he was late.

CHAPTER 2

On the opposite bank of the Thames, the marshy fields of South-wark had also noticed winter's passing. Thriving on consistent days of warmth, the grounds beyond Paris Garden and the bull-baiting venue had erupted in a carpet of wildflowers, none more impressive than meadowsweet. By right the queen of the meadow reigned supreme in this patch of competitors. At the end of star-tling red stalks her delicate flowers bowed to the breeze, rippling like tatting on Katherine Parr's sleeve. Fie on anyone who dared mention she was common. She was no dropwort, so mundane and undignified.

Beyond that field was another plot of ground with more martial purpose. Archery butts lined one end of it, the mounds savagely stabbed with arrows. At the other end, some two hundred yards opposite, fifty men of military age gathered, waiting instructions. All of them held bows of some fashion, either of yew (for those more serious and of some money) or of wych elm (for the rest).

On his way to join them was John Grunt, Bianca Goddard's husband.

The king's law required that every man between sixteen and

sixty years must possess a warbow and practice his archery skills (though if a man were to achieve that ripe age he would need a cart to haul him to a field of battle). One never knew when their foe (namely, the French) might invade and try to seize their fair isle. No matter that Henry was the more likely instigator of any clash between the two realms. With His Majesty keen to relive the glory days of his youth and with the season for war drawing near, a summons had been ordered for the men of Southwark to congregate beyond Broadwall for the evaluation of their archery skills.

John loped at a pace commensurate with his lack of enthusiasm. He cared not a sliver that he was late—his inability to locate his bow had assured it. First impressions made little difference to him. Once the officers had noticed his strength, he was as good as gone. Years of working as an apprentice to a coiner had plumped up his muscles, and his above-average height would make him a desirable asset.

"It will do you no service if you miss the butts," said Bianca, walking beside him. "And do not dawdle on my account. I can keep stride with you."

John glanced over and his eyes fell to her stomach. A worried look came over his face. "I should shoot myself in the foot."

"And pretend it an accident?" Bianca lifted the hem of her kirtle as she picked through a soggy stretch of road. "Do you think that I cannot fend for myself?"

"Nay, it isn't that."

"You think I will do something foolish and lose our child?"

John's reticence was her answer. She looked away, biting her tongue to keep from using it to argue.

"I worry that I cannot help if I am away spearing Frenchmen. If I broke an arm I'd be of no use to the army."

"If you broke an arm you'd be of no use to Boisvert, or to me for that matter. Prithee, what would you do to 'help' as you say? Birthing is not a man's chore."

"I could send for a midwife."

Bianca looked askance at him.

"Bianca," said John in response. "If I should be conscripted, I might not live to see our child."

"John, if you broke your arm you might not live. Worrying will not prevent us from knowing sorrow. Why color today with black thoughts? The future will bring what it will."

And indeed, it had; her pregnancy had come as a surprise to both of them. Bianca had taken "precautions" that she did not openly discuss, not even with John. After all, one should not thwart God's purpose for a woman. Doing so was a sin. However, she was not the only one to use herbs to try to prevent God from getting His way.

Her mother often chewed handfuls of wild carrot seeds during a gibbous moon. "To prevent the abdomen swelling," Bianca was told. When Bianca's own "time" had come, her mother fashioned a plug out of bog moss and explained the finer points of a woman's expected function, then told her in sworn confidence how to prevent it. It was not lost on Bianca that this education was probably necessitated by her mother's desire to prevent her from suffering a similar fate. Her parents' marriage was not an amiable one.

It was not Bianca's nature to wonder whether her mother regretted birthing her. Instead, she saw the inconvenience motherhood might pose in her own life. She would have preferred to postpone the responsibility. John had not finished his apprenticeship, and they relied on Bianca's earnings from medicinals to help feed them. Besides, Bianca was not ready to set aside her curiosity to care for a child. But the future had brought its own will to bear upon their lives, and Bianca had no choice but to accept it.

"I can't remember the last time I shot an arrow," said John, plucking the string of his bow. Then, remembering he'd forgotten his bracer and finger guard, stopped in his tracks and swore. "I'll turn my arm into minced meat."

Bianca reached into the pocket of her apron and handed him the leather guards. "I pray you make an effort to impress them. It is far more dangerous to be a billman."

A horn blew and the gathering turned their attention to a mounted nobleman—a captain splendidly dressed, wearing a bonnet with a red-dyed plume and a satin white jacket shimmering in the morning sun. He was accompanied by several soldiers, a gentleman pensioner, and a sheriff, each riding their own fine horses, though the sheriff's was a little less fine. The captain forwent any introduction, assuming, wrongly, that his name was known, and divided the men into three groups behind a scored line.

"You'd better get on," said Bianca, urging John ahead. "Shoot well."

John took a step, then turned and held Bianca close, seizing a hearty kiss before trotting off; a sure sign the lust for competition was coursing through his veins.

Bianca watched him fall into line with the others, then joined the company of spectators. From where she stood, she could see John had settled himself. He stood nearly a head taller than most. Chin level, John knew how to exude confidence, or at least affect it. There was no use in pretending incompetence because failing would only land him in a worse position. Archers had the benefit of distance in battle. They had pike and billmen to go before them.

The captain shouted instructions to the first row of archers while a soldier dispensed a quiver of arrows to the first in each row. To start, they were to shoot two arrows on command. Each man would have his opportunity; then they would be tested for speed and accuracy.

Onlookers quieted as the first group selected their arrows. The captain waited until the archers squared, then shouted, "Nock!" His voice carried over the murmuring crowd and screech of seagulls circling over the mudflats. The archers set their arrows on the string.

"Draw," commanded the captain, and the men raised their bows, pointing the arrowheads at the sky and pulling the string to maximum.

"Loose!"

A bevy of arrows arced down the field toward the waiting butts. Only two of the men managed the distance, their arrows hitting the earthen mounds with a solid *thwack* that sent puffs of dust into the air.

The captain and his cohorts looked at the targets. Results were recorded in a log as the captain looked back at the archers. "Again!"

With each successive archer, each "nock, draw, and loose" order, the mood of the crowd grew increasingly somber as each man's fate became clear. There were those who shook from their toes up and whose arrows flew wild because of it. Others could have hit the target standing on one leg. Bianca watched John move up in line. To his benefit he had physical strength and composure under duress. To his detriment—his negligence in practicing.

As Bianca waited for the archers to cycle through their turns, she mused on the man she had married. He had been her husband less than a year, but they had known each other since they were twelve. A mischievous childhood defined them—neither had been curbed by doting parents and John was an orphan. Both had learned to survive by their wits. By the time they met, Bianca was an effective cutpurse and John excelled in scavenging through barrels of rubbish, though neither of them performed their knavery with absolute success. If Bianca had not been caught filching sausage from a butcher's stall, their paths might never have crossed—or rather, their paths might have taken longer to curl through the streets and back alleys of London and eventually meet.

John had saved Bianca from the sweaty hands of an odious constable eager to make an example of her by whacking off one of her fingers. The constable had gripped her ear and John had stared at her until her eyes found his; what passed between them in that brief exchange went deeper than any vow of trust. They understood one another.

John had darted forward and delivered a sharp kick to the officer's shin. The man doubled over and let go of Bianca. The two ran until they couldn't, exchanging an ugly fate for one more hopeful.

Bianca wondered if their mutual loyalty sprang from being unwanted children. The only affection she'd gotten came occasionally from her mother. Mostly, Bianca had spent their shared time running errands or performing chores. Her mother was less cold in character than her father, but she was not a content woman. Bianca had learned at a young age not to depend on other people for love and approval. She would learn to find peace from within. And she would find that peace pursuing what she loved—which included her chemistries and, now, loving John.

When she was old enough to carry a pot of boiling water without spilling it, her father had enlisted her help in his room of alchemy. There she became fascinated with the instruments of her father's science. She could have hated fetching ingredients from apothecaries and gnarled-fingered white witches. She could have resented sitting in the noxious fumes of her father's projections. Instead, her curiosity found a home. And through observation she had learned the secret language of alchemy.

The crowd of onlookers suddenly burst into cheers as one of the bowmen hit the target twice, the second arrow nearly splitting the shaft of the first. Bianca looked at the archers and thought for a grand second it was John who had impressed the spectators. But no, John was to follow the exemplary archer.

As the skilled bowman received back slaps of congratulations, Bianca felt a rill of apprehension watching John step forward to his mark. Even if it seemed a folly to his ministers and to his people, the king was determined to relive the successful campaigns of his youth during his final years on earth. Henry needed men for his ships and army, and no matter how John performed, she expected he would likely be conscripted.

Then adding to her worry was John's warbow. It could barely be called such. He had found the thing on Finsbury Field, and that is where he should have left it. John took the fraught semblance of a bow to a bowyer who deemed it inferior, made of black cherry, with a pin knot on the back of the stave.

"I only deal in bows made of yew," declared the man. But with some cajoling the man grudgingly sold him a string of good condition and said it might compensate a bit for the wood's poor quality. John had lost interest in archery soon after, but because it was the law to own a bow he dutifully toted it about through two moves, to Aldersgate Ward and back to Southwark, and regularly saved it from a cat that filed its claws on the wood.

The crowd settled as John and two others chose their arrows and prepared their stance. Following the best archer on the field would have been difficult for anyone.

The captain on his handsome destrier cast a dubious look at John and his bow. Bianca thought she saw his mouth turn up in skepticism. With a visible intake of breath, he gave the command to nock.

John placed his arrow.

"Draw . . ."

With forearms straining, John pulled back the string and Bianca held her breath.

"Loose!"

The men leaned back, aimed, and released. The trio of shafts whistled through the air and arced down the field. To his astonishment, John's hit the earthen mound with a solid thud, placing better than the other two. Bianca blew out her breath. He'd hit the target.

From where she stood, Bianca saw the officer's brow lift in surprise and he appraised John more keenly. "Again!" he bellowed.

The men selected their second arrow, and again the crowd quieted. Bianca took another breath as the officer's horse snuffled and the command came to draw. John pulled the string and his bow bent with tension.

However, this time, the captain slightly hesitated before shouting "Loose!"

A loud crack issued from John's bow as it snapped in two. The arrow released, careening to one side, straight toward the captain on his mount.

Unfortunately, the officer could not turn his horse fast enough. The crowd gasped as the arrow lodged in the horse's flank. The magnificent warhorse reared and the captain tightened his grip on the reins, struggling to control his steed. He leaned forward into its arching neck as it shimmied and bucked. Men shouted, adding to the confusion, while the spectators exchanged stunned looks.

The captain's bonnet tipped and fell to the ground. A moment later he followed.

An archer ran forward and grabbed hold of the bridle, pulling the balking horse away from the fallen lord, flat on the field and not moving. Others circled the horse, trying to steady it while one of them reached for the embedded arrow. John dropped his splintered bow and ran to the downed officer.

Bianca's heart sank seeing the captain injured because of John. From where she stood, she couldn't be sure if the man was not dead. But neither could the spectators tell if he was just knocked unconscious.

Bianca ran forward close enough to get within earshot as two soldiers got the captain to sitting.

At least he was not dead.

"Idiot. Your treachery will undo you," he spat at John upon being uprighted.

John apologized like a blibbering lunatic, then pointed to where he had dropped the defective warbow. "My lord, it is the bow. Look there, see it in two?" An archer picked the pieces off the ground and held them up for all to see.

The captain groused as he gathered himself and was helped to stand. "Bring me that bow so that I might use it to flog him."

John should have invited the beating rather than try to explain. Bianca winced that he overstepped his bounds.

"It is of inferior wood," said John, attempting to reason.

"Does he describe the warbow or his head?" asked the captain of a soldier brushing off his cap and handing it back.

"My lord, this was an accident. I meant you no harm." John cursed himself for not taking the king's law seriously enough to have gotten himself a decent weapon. His indifference had landed him in a plight worse than the momentary loss of a few coins in his pocket.

"Away! Be gone from my sight." The officer turned his back and cursed as his horse led a string of men on a chase through the fields of Southwark. "Put a mark next to his name."

Dejected, John slunk back to the gathered candidates, who offered sympathetic glances but then quickly distanced themselves. A soldier caught up with him and marked John's name with a flourish. "He won't forget ye," said the soldier. "That is his favorite mount."

"I wish I'd shot myself instead."

The soldier smirked, glad he had not been the one to displease his commander.

"I won't try to cheer you," said Bianca when John made his way over. "But an ale at the Dim Dragon with friends will smooth your brow."

Off Bermondsey Street on a less traveled lane, the sign hanging over the entrance of a neighborhood boozing ken looked natty with a fresh coat of paint. The Dim Dragon was no longer so dim. The beast looked resplendent touched up with vibrant blue-green skin and carefully defined scales. The original artist had painted a whimsical dragon with human attributes, but those had gone ignored under dull, peeling paint. The creature now assumed its original impertinence, leaning back and resting an elbow on the roof such as the one before them. One eye winked conspiratorially as the dragon sipped an ale held to its gaping maw. The conspicuous sign was in sharp contrast to its namesake's weathered entry door and drab daub exterior. But Bianca appreciated the inn's attempt to improve its looks.

"A sign fit for the likes of Aldersgate, I'd say." She had tried to cheer John and he was having no part in it. The diversion of a newly painted placard proved too brief.

"It is overly grand and frivolous. A waste of coin. If they want to attract more customers they should spend their money procuring better ale instead. That would draw them in."

Bianca pulled open the door and let John through. She preferred that he take the brunt of everyone's stares, not her. Besides, woe is he who enters the Dim Dragon Inn looking demoralized.

The usual clutch of mudlarks and laborers manned the benches, drinking the sludge they called ale and belching up bits of kidney pie. Bianca's stomach rolled from the earthy pong of river bottom and perspiration. Her sense of smell had always been acute, but her condition had heightened her sensitivity so that she became queasy from odors that never used to bother her. She pressed a hand against her stomach to steady it and followed John to a table.

Less than a year ago, Bianca had taken her chances going to the ken alone to fish for information about various miscreants about whom she needed to know more information. More often than not, her probing had to do with a murder. Any young woman with clear eyes and smooth skin stirred the interest of the inn's patrons, and she had endured her share of snide comments and attempted groping. But since marrying John, and often accompanying him here, the leering and untoward comments had ceased and she had become just another ale-gulping customer.

John took a spot next to the portly curber Mackney and his partner, Smythe. The two had had a good day of it and were in high spirits. Mackney moved his hook (used to lift valuables from open windows and folded to look like a walking stick) to make room for them.

"How now, John?" said Mackney, and nodded to Bianca.

"Well enough." John looked about for the serving wench. Not finding her, he leaned his cheek against his fist.

"Methinks not so well. Your knitted brow tells a different story." He elbowed John in jest. "Come now, what is in you?"

Bianca settled beside John and answered for him. "He's come from the archery field."

"The View of Arms?" asked skinny Smythe.

"Ye should make yeself scarce, Smyttie. Why did ye not go?" Mackney's upper lip lifted in something close to disdain.

"Helping you, I was; or is yer recollection as piteous as yer face?"

The thief harrumphed. "I should like to stab a Frenchman. Methinks their flesh is soft as jelly." He held an imaginary dagger and poked the air in front of him. He glanced at John. "Where is yer warbow, lad? Did ye leave it?"

John dropped his fist from his cheek. "It be kindling now. But I wouldn't trust it to burn without incident. Filthy, foul stick of wood."

"It is a fierce opinion of a branch."

"Deservedly so, sir," said Bianca.

The serving wench appeared from the back toting forth six pots, her fingers linked through the handles. John waved, then stood and waved more vigorously until she acknowledged him.

"A new serving wench," said Bianca. "When did she come?"

"Only two days back," said Smythe. His gaze clung to the maid in a manner in which he clearly wished his hands.

Mackney smacked the lad's cheek to bring him round. "Ye just skirted yer duty to the king, ye fool. Think on how to remedy that. Lay low if ye must, but if they find ye they'll set you in stocks at the very kindest."

Now there were two sullen men of military age sitting at the table.

Still curious, the malmsey-nosed crook pecked at John like a hen. "So, if ye didn't impress with yer archery skills, they'd still want a strappy lad of yer height. It is to yer advantage as a pikeman."

Bianca shifted uncomfortably hearing Mackney voice what she'd been thinking.

His opinion did nothing to cheer John. He groaned and glared at the kitchen trull, who was busy prattling on with the group of men she'd just served. "What could be so important that she should ignore us so?"

"John, would you have me so impatient watching you do your work at Boisvert's? She saw us."

Perhaps the maid sensed their frustration, for she finished with her customers and wound her way between the benches. She arrived at their table wearing a pleasant smile. A lock of autumn red hair had escaped her head wrap, and her cheeks bore the ruddy lash of windburn and sun. "A pottle pot for me lady and her lord?"

Bianca lifted an eyebrow at the wench's tart address. She stiffened, aping the superior manner of the upper class. "Aye that," she replied. "And see that the pot has no floaters. I dislike swallowing bits of bug." But really she didn't care.

"I shall rinse it in the rain barrel first. I'll be but a moment." She made away and John called her back.

"Bring three pottle pots."

The wench's eyes flicked over to Bianca, who shrugged.

"I don't fancy waiting for my second," muttered John under his breath.

Once the wench turned, Mackney admonished, "Why so foul a mood? In matters of war, the hand-to-hand combat of a pike or billman is more honorable."

"I care not for chivalry. I care more to live." John noticed the two thieves exchanging looks. "There, call me cowardly, but I do not wish to lose my life for our wastrel king."

Mackney shushed John, casting about for signs of anyone overhearing. "Defending the realm is a noble cause, lad. Think, too, of the money earned from a campaign. Ye might secure a cruck house with it."

"If ye don't drink or gamble it away," sniped Smythe.

John glanced at Bianca, then shook his head. "Those thoughts are like dreams. They vanish in the light of day . . . and by the king's will."

Bianca pretended interest in another table. There was a time when the two had tried living in Aldersgate, a wealthy ward north of St. Paul's. John's master, the French silversmith Boisvert, endeavored to marry a wealthy French widow and vacated his quarters to share her lavish residence. John and Bianca moved into his rent to watch his shop and prevent it from being burgled; however, the free accommodations had come with a price. Bianca had been wrenched from her chemistries, and Boisvert had been thrown in Newgate Prison for poisoning his bride. Ultimately, all had been resolved and the solution had returned them to their former tenancy in Southwark, in Gull Hole.

"I am not sure what it would take to move Bianca again. She prefers clucking chickens to the bells of St. Leonard's."

"There is no accounting for preference," said Mackney.

The serving wench returned with their ales and dispensed them round.

"I've not seen you before," said Bianca.

"Aye, ye haven't," said the maid. "I've come from Dartford." She introduced herself as Cammy Dawney.

"You're brave to take up in Southwark." Bianca took a sip of ale. "Why do you not cross the river? It is a wealthier clientele."

"Mayhap I will. But there is a place for me here." The girl rested her fists on her hips. She was of sturdy build with a strong back, a maid accustomed to hauling buckets of water on a yoke and birthing calves. Bianca wondered how long the girl would tolerate being pent inside this stagnant ken. Not for long, she concluded, once she'd had a certain fill of it.

The door swung open and a boisterous group of men entered, their warbows slung over their shoulders. They slapped one another's backs, exchanged gibes, dug their elbows into each other's ribs. John grumbled and stared into his pottle pot.

"Cammy," called one. The fellow edged his way through the tables and caught her up in his arms, engulfing her in a lusty embrace. Her head linen fell askew and her hair came tumbling out. The patrons of the Dim Dragon began pounding the tables with their hands and whooting.

"I have made the Royal Guard of the king's army," he announced. "Such good fortune should not go unheeded."

The patrons cheered. "A round of ales for the king's most valiant," called a man from across the room.

John slunk down and stared into his tankard as the exuberant archer recounted his success in detail. When he finished, the archer looked round at the table, then recognizing John, exclaimed, "Three pottle pots to drown a single sorrow?" He gestured to John, who looked up, chagrined. "Or rather, a single arrow?" He grinned, enjoying his pithy wit. "Take solace, man, there is no greater honor than wielding a pike to protect a king's archer."

"Oh, it is he!" exclaimed another from the proficient tribe. He ambled over to add to the discussion, and to John's misery.

Others craned to glimpse John's pinking complexion.

"The target is downfield, sirrah," said the man when he reached their table. "They are called butts, but they are of earthen build. Not the fur butt of his Lord's horse." The men erupted in raucous guffaws and knee slapping. "But," said he, holding up a finger to garner attention, "methinks a butt is a butt whether furred or nay. But then, would a butt by any other name be *but* the same?"

John tipped his tankard and drank long from it, setting it down with a thud. An arrow can only hit its target if it is first pulled backward and remembering this, he opened his mouth to reply.

Bianca touched his arm and cut him a hard stare. "Stay you," she mouthed.

John rolled his eyes but obliged and clamped his mouth. He took up the second tankard to muffle his mutterings.

The archers, having loosed their barbed arrows and willfully punctured John's pride, looked elsewhere for a target when they failed to provoke a reply. "Come now, we have duly pricked his hide so that he shall weep until he is conscripted as a billman. Let us take up a table and leave him to lick his wounds."

Hand to shoulder they filed past to a table in the room's corner. The tavern wench noted John's sullen glare. "He means no harm," she said, brushing past. She stopped and then said over her shoulder, "Not everyone can be an archer. There is a great need for those who cannot master the skill." She said this in innocence and continued to make her way to the men.

Bianca leaned over and touched John's arm. "It is meant in kind assurance. Let us leave."

John slapped his hand palm down on the table, drawing attention. "My bow snapped. Else I would be as satisfied as that haughty cockerel." He looked at Cammy, who turned to hear him address her. "Humiliation is a cruel reward for bad fortune," he said. "Why must fate depend on gerful luck?"

Cammy, having unwittingly kindled her customer's ire, came back and attempted to soften his hurt. "You must not take his innocent jabs to heart."

"Innocent jabs? By what measure do you judge them innocent when they pierce like a knife? Why do you defend him? Is he yours?"

"As I am his."

"You call him husband?"

"I call him Roger."

Bianca met Cammy's eyes. She sensed the girl had greater hopes, but perhaps it was not a mutual feeling.

John snorted and received a swift kick to his shin under the table.

"Come along, Smythe," said Mackney, rising from the board and collecting his hook. "Let us disappear. We can ill afford your being discovered shirking your duty. Do not look on the group of archers as we pass, and hide your blameful face."

As they watched the pair skulk toward the door, Bianca was overcome with an ill feeling, which Cammy noticed.

"You do not look well. If I weren't familiar with the green look of morning sickness I would think ye ate a frog."

Bianca put a hand to her brow and wiped away the beads of sweat forming there. "You are observant," she said. "And correct."

"I have not experienced the sickness," said Cammy. "But my sisters suffered from it. Wait here." She hurried off to the kitchen and quickly returned with a clove pinched between two fingers. "Take this and bite on it until the nausea passes."

Bianca lightly bit the clove, numbing her tongue. "Methinks its pungency is a distraction."

The kitchen wench agreed. "A distraction a woman does well to learn."

Seeing Bianca ill, John roused from his self-absorption. "We should take our leave," he said. "We both need air. These quarters are cramped." He took hold of her arm and Cammy took the other, helping her to her feet.

"I can manage. I am not an invalid," said Bianca.

"Still, you need steadying," said Cammy. "Have you a midwife when the time comes?"

"It is a long way off. I have not thought so far ahead."

"I know something about it. I've helped in a few births."

John cut her off. "I am certain that when the time comes we can manage."

Cammy Dawney let go of Bianca's arm and watched John lead her to the door. "Be you so sure?" she said under her breath. "A fool learns too late his sad folly."

Chapter 3

Two days later . . .

Spring is a trickster. A stage monkey with a churlish disposition. One day she unrolls a rug of verdant clover laden with buttered poms bending with bees; then the next, she rolls up the carpet like a cartographer with his map; spoiling a glorious display with cloud piss and cold. The weather was not the only thing to succumb to a return of wintry temper. Albern Goddard had, too.

His scholarly gown had been replaced with a more practical knee-length version of moth-eaten wool liberally dotted with stains from his chemistries. His beard had lost its length and was trimmed close to his chin. He stared at the ground just beyond his feet, consumed in thought, and turned onto Thames Street. He might have been run over by a wagon and would never have realized it.

No clutch of brats interfered with his determined stride. This was not a day for loitering or making merry. Business was business and Albern Goddard had serious matters on his mind.

Chief among them was his daughter, Bianca.

He'd never been to her room of "Medicinals and Physickes," as she preferred to call it. The corner of his mouth turned up. How presumptuous. But in fairness, it would not do for her to label it a room of alchemy. That would land her in a vat of boiling oil, for no woman would dare undertake the dark art without fear of retribution.

So let her call it this contrived name. It was but the same in his mind.

In his mind . . .

He viewed Bianca in terms of her usefulness to him. True, she had saved him from an untimely death, but he expected nothing less from her. She owed him her loyalty as a daughter.

Even though he'd never been to her nest in Gull Hole he knew he would be able to find it. The area was home to brothels and a myriad of low-lifes, each lane leading to another area even more deplorable. It did not bother Albern Goddard that his daughter should live in squalor. She could have waited to become a servant in a fine home, she certainly had the intelligence. Instead, she had struck out on her own, living amongst those of strange perversions and wanton inclinations, preferring to pursue her passion— a shameful endeavor for a woman.

Goddard crossed under the gate onto the narrow span of bridge. On such a bleak and drizzly day, no sunshine filtered between buildings to light his passage. Albern glanced up at the overhanging stories filled with rich merchants and their families. These were the most desired addresses in all of London. The only benefit to living there, thought he, was that the privies opened into the river.

A few buildings, mainly those with attached shops, had lit lanterns by their doors, which cast his ghoulish shadow to dance beside him as he passed. Despite the poor weather, patrons bustled about, intent on commerce, barrows lumbered and creaked, a boy chased a squealing pig dodging obstacles—but just barely.

Albern reached the drawbridge section and found the undulating water beneath the trusses discomfiting. A step was not so solid with the water moving silkily below him. He lifted his eyes to focus on the building opposite to steady his stride.

A fleeting thought sailed through his conscious mind and he stopped suddenly, drawn to look down at the water folding in the dark recess beneath him. Perhaps it was more of a feeling than a thought; an unsettling premonition that pressed his breath from his lungs and felt like a hand taking hold of his heart and squeezing it. Was that a cat staring at him from the starlings below, its eyes glowing eerily like his newfound element? He angled his head for a better look. Nay, his mind was toying with him. Albern looked out at the river, at the few wherries near the Bishop's House in Southwark appearing and disappearing in the tenebrous fog. The façades of stews and boozing kens peeped at him from the south bank's shore. A lone church steeple skewered the thick brume creeping past. Albern Goddard moved on, hurrying his step over the final length of drawbridge.

And how would he find this room of Medicinals and Physickes? Like any good alchemist, he would use his nose.

So it was that another alchemist used his.

Beneath the bridge, the wraith of the Thames devoured the last of his breakfast. He spit a rat's tail into the water and was picking the gristle from his teeth when he caught a whiff of the metallic scent of alchemy. His eyes flicked around, searching. He licked the saporous air, tasted antimony and milk of lime on his tongue. A memory woke from within and he looked up through the trestles.

On the bridge, a man stopped a moment as if disoriented, and their eyes locked. The man shuddered as if shaking himself free— of some thought? Some tigerish notion? Then he walked on.

Ho, thought the Rat Man, recognizing Albern Goddard, the ignoble alchemist. The alchemist was making a rare visit to Southwark. The wraith looked toward Gull Hole, where Bianca lived, and he listened.

For years the Rat Man had lived on the edge of people's imagination. Only drunks and madmen swore to his existence, those being the only souls who might chance to see him when he made his rounds. To others, the wraith was a phantom of grotesque invention conjured out of a dark seed of memory from a time long ago. A time when the Black Death scourged the king's good land, killing a third of its people and condemning the others to a living hell.

For he, too, had once been an alchemist. And, aye, he was wrought from that bleak time of ineffable suffering.

Nearly two hundred years ago, he had conducted his alchemy in a room similar to Goddard's. And, like Goddard, he had desired to create the philosopher's stone, the agent of transmutation capable of changing base metal into the father of perfection—gold. He, too, had been licensed by his king to practice the dark art. The king required him to report his successes so that he could not solely benefit from them. Every sovereign requires wealth to subdue threats to his crown, whether internal or from foreign forces. King Edward was no different.

However, there came a force more catastrophic, more evil than any single person or foreign power could ever conjure alone. A force that rattled King Edward's world and devastated the population of his fair isle.

On a late summer day when shadows stretched long toward the horizon, two ships moored near Melcombe. Riding in one from Gascony was a man whose blood carried the filth of pestilence from the continent. In port the man took intimacy with a doxy most fair. Neither suspected that the cove's body was beginning to rot from the inside out. A few days later, a lump appeared under his skin. He hid the bubo beneath his jerkin and continued to take his pleasure. But dismissing and ignoring its warning would not make it disappear. His skin became riddled with purple buboes impossible to hide. And so, from a common sailor, the great plague found the Elysian Fields of England to its liking and danced a galliard of death.

The Black Death seized the good king's people. Its black lips kissed theirs with infection. It breathed on babies and licked children's innocent cheeks. Weeping mothers collapsed on their graves. A raft of doors painted with red crosses warned others away. If one survived the forty days of quarantine he was released to resume his life. But what was that life without his loved ones?

The alchemist watched helplessly as his own daughter and wife were placed upon the body collector's cart. He shook his fist at God. His wise and merciful God. His silent God.

Collectors rang their bells and their carts continued to creak by his door. The reek from purging fires permeated the air and filled his lungs with its tragedy. There was no escaping the constant reminder of his loss. What was the purpose of living if all he knew was death?

Could nothing be done?

Just when his grief had nearly consumed him, a kernel of hope fell on fertile ground. He cast off his despair and threw down his cup of remorse. He rejected his selfish pursuit of gold. Instead, he would use his knowledge to help his fellow man.

The philosopher's stone had two forms: one could transmute base metal into gold; the other could grant immortality. It was the second form to which he now aspired.

Proceeding with the twelve gates of projection, he traveled through calcination, separation, conjunction, through to sublimation. Each stage required focused attention to technique and method. Each stage built upon the previous one. Kerotakis in hand, he patiently sublimated the coveted *caput corvi*—head of the crow—until a thin trickle of nacreous liquid coursed down the side of a flask and pooled in the bottom.

The liquid did not glow. It did not dazzle. More sublime was its attraction.

An intoxicating scent of roses, the holy virgin's breath, filled his room of alchemy. Was this the elusive elixir?

His hopeful heart could not imagine otherwise. What ill effect could result from a concoction so sweet?

The alchemist considered what to do. Should he dribble the liquid upon a dying man's tongue and watch the result? If the man recovered (which the alchemist believed would certainly happen), should he then take his test one step further? Should he cut out the man's heart and see if he lived?

Such a drastic move would verify his discovery, but the alchemist had not the mettle to commit such a deed. What if it was not the elusive elixir?

However, there was nothing left in this world for *him* to miss. His wife and daughter were gone. The wails of grieving citizens filled his head so completely that he found no solace, no assurance that this world would endure or even survive its current suffering. He saw no beauty in the sun's ceaseless rising. Nothing soothed, nothing offered promise, save for this elixir that carried the sweet smell of the Virgin Mary's love.

As the scourge raged, as the plague pits filled with victims, as the sound of parish bells dolefully echoed off St. Paul's Cathedral, the alchemist made his peace—then tipped the flask of elixir to his lips and drank.

No real or imagined hell could equal the one he'd just unleashed.

The succubus of elixir had seduced and made a fool of him. She careened down his throat on a sled of fire, burning and dissolving his flesh. The alchemist dropped to his knees and clutched his throat. He puked. Caustic fumes rose from his vomit and burned his eyes.

His pounding heart writhed in his chest; it somersaulted and crashed against his ribs. It inched up his throat. His body burned from within and he threw open his door and ran to the river to throw himself in it. But at the water's edge, he stopped. Again the urge to vomit overwhelmed, and this time his heart landed on the bank, pulsing and steaming.

This was not the philter of immortality he had envisioned. This was evil's worst. He dropped to his knees and his ears filled with the surreal screeching of a choir of demons. They circled him. They stripped away his skin. They stomped his bones into dust.

Though his intent was one of compassion, the cosmos railed

against him. Who was he to tinker with life and death and the natural order? We are the stuff of stars, but we do not rule them.

As the alchemist's life drained from his body, he cursed God one last time. His screams rose to the heavens and reached the depths of hell. Both angels and demons crept to their office portals and stuck their heads out to listen.

The sorrow of those who'd died of the plague, whose lives had been taken too soon, poured into his mouth and filled him with their anguished cries. Their lost potential, their despondent souls, found shelter in his wretched carcass.

The result of his transmutation had been neither to live nor to die, but to exist in a purgatory of his own making. Doomed to the banks of London's lifeblood—the Thames—he would forever ply her waters and dispense with the vectors of the Black Death.

Days turned into nights and then turned into years—this was his reality. He was doomed to watch over London for all of eternity.

This semblance of a body with gray skin stretched over bone, and spindly fingers with nails like claws, with eyes slit like a cat's, this costume covered the torment that lay within. His black woolen cape sucked away the light of reflection so that he folded into the fog and dark with the surety of a raven in the night. He dwelled beneath the bridge in its caverns, floating in his skiff, waiting for descending night to attend his duty.

But still within his being lurked the desire for redemption. He longed to end this purgatory and be cast either to heaven or to hell. What he desired was finality. He sought his end.

And with him to his final rest, and theirs, would go the victims of an unkind plague.

The Rat Man listened to Albern Goddard's fading footfall. He glanced in the direction of Southwark and listened.

CHAPTER 4

Per request from Meddybemps—street peddler, lascivious gadder, but, most importantly, friend—Bianca minced ingredients for a remedy to ease the symptoms of ague. Her brisk chopping made a rhythmic tapping on the board and she had to stop to push Hobs out of danger. It wasn't the movement that attracted the cat, but the intoxicating smell of *Nepeta*. He cruised near the catwort, then flopped on top of her hands, risking his whiskers, and nose to the blade of her knife.

Still mumpish from his poor showing at the View of Arms, John stood in front of the food cupboard, staring at a shelf of shriveled mushrumps and mummified cheese. He seemed rooted there, and Bianca glanced at him a couple of times before speaking.

"Why don't you go to market if there is nothing here to please you?"

John remained staring at the near-empty shelf.

Bianca knew he had heard her. She left him to his brooding and went back to chopping her herbs.

Eventually John would shake off his foul mood. She knew him well enough to know that thoughts often ran through his mind like the scenes of a play and his eyes would glaze over as if watching them. Bianca left him to ponder the shelf while removing a determined Hobs and dropped him on the floor. The thud stirred John from his rumination.

"I haven't time," he said, though his response came so late that it sounded as if he was answering a question tumbling around in his head and not Bianca. "Boisvert is expecting me."

He paused by the table as she chopped the herbs, then scraped the leaves and stems together and chopped them in the opposite direction. Bianca sensed his thoughts were still elsewhere, and she let him be.

It occurred to her that companionship exists in these small moments. Moments spent in thought, isolated, secret, and silent. They string together and make a lifetime of partnership. But this moment evaporated when the neighbor's chickens announced an intruder. She heard the sound of their wings flapping and boisterous squawking outside their door.

Few braved the pungent smell of chicken droppings to venture down their alley in Gull Hole, a decrepit area in an already neglected borough. Its low-lying land was nearly always spongy, except in a particularly frigid month when the ground might freeze. Bianca had grown accustomed to the noisome odors so that she hardly noticed them. Unfortunately, John had not reached that level of indifference.

The door shook from a resolute knocking. Such determined rapping was always cause for alarm. Bianca signaled to John to answer while she moved from behind the table, keeping her knife at the ready. They rarely received unexpected inquiries so early in the morn.

John opened the door and peeped through the crack.

"Fie upon it! God's flesh, do you not see who I am? Give way or I shall knock you over and not think twice of it."

John hardly had time to stand back before the door stubbed his toe. Albern Goddard breezed into Bianca's room of Medicinals and Physickes with a proprietorial air and patent look of disgust. He took quick measure of his daughter's quarters, started to speak, when his eyes settled on Bianca's knife.

"Is that how you welcome your father?"

Bianca lowered her weapon. "I should wish you might greet my husband more kindly."

Albern swung around and studied John. "He is, granted, your husband, but no more to me."

"Do you think so little of me that you would treat my husband so poorly?"

"I think of you as my daughter—your intimacies do not interest me." His colorless eyes made his point, then wandered over the accoutrements decorating her small room. A calcinatory furnace sat near a rear door, a practical choice if one could afford only a single furnace. An array of bottles lined a few shelves, but she was in need of more storage. A copper distillation apparatus sat on a table against a back wall, dented, but serviceable.

Annoyed, Bianca said, "There may come a time when you might have greater use for him. Do not take him for granted."

"The man is a staple in your life. As dependable as the sun. If I take him for granted, I mean it as a compliment."

As disagreeable as John found Bianca's father, he forgot his hunger and delayed leaving in order to see what the man wanted. It wasn't every day that Albern paid a visit. In fact, John wondered how he had found them. "What brings you to Southwark?" he asked, attempting to be cordial.

Albern glanced at him, then looked at Bianca to answer. "I have a matter of importance to discuss," he said. He strolled over to the table where Bianca had been working and picked up a sprig of mint to sniff. Overhead, a shadow caught his eye and he looked up at the dangling stems. "I don't see what this fascination with plants and chemistries will beget. Perhaps you should aspire to be an apothecary." Albern dropped the sprig of mint on the table. "But then you are of the wrong . . . sex."

Bianca swept the catwort into a bowl and found a cruet of rape oil to pour over it. "I suppose I am an apothecary in a matter of sorts. However, I doubt that you troubled to come here only to insult me. Come, Father, be quick of it and then be gone."

John's eyes grew round as his father-in-law's narrowed. Such terse words from a daughter were parlous indeed.

Without a word, Albern turned away and examined a shelf of ingredients. He removed a jar and lifted the lid to view the contents. Looking over the bottles, he moved one over to take its place, rearranging Bianca's lineup as if his preference mattered more than hers. His face remained passive. He seemed not to sense or care that Bianca grew increasingly annoyed. He took his time going through her crucibles and canisters, held up a pair of tongs and clacked their metal pincers together.

Bianca returned to her work. She'd learned long ago that her father would do as he pleased, speak when he pleased, leave when he pleased. Irritation was met with cynical amusement and a cold war of attrition. The best way to annoy *him*, and to move him, was to ignore him.

It worked.

Albern finished his perusal and pulled out the bench next to their table. He took off his cap and sat.

"Ale, sir?" asked John, since Bianca hadn't bothered to offer him any.

"Of course."

Bianca covered her bowl of macerated leaves and set it by. She was tying together some loose herbs when her father began to speak.

"I've made an important discovery," he began, accepting the ale from John and wetting his lips.

"Can you hang this, John?" Bianca handed him the clump and pointed to where she wanted it placed.

"You may not be interested in what I've done, but you should lend your ear to it."

"Can you wind it about the nail and bring it up? I fear your hair will strip its leaves clean if you bump it."

"When did you plan to tell us?"

Bianca stopped fussing and faced her father, who tipped his chin toward her belly.

"Or did you hope to keep it a secret?" The corner of Albern's mouth lifted.

"I am not far enough to speak of it," said Bianca.

"You are far enough for me to notice that your face is more round and your complexion is not so pale." He took another sip of ale and wiped his lips with the back of his hand. "Your free hand rests upon your stomach as if supporting it."

"Perhaps we both keep secrets," said Bianca, referring to a weeping wound on his hand. "You've burned yourself and the skin on your nose is red and peeling."

Albern lightly touched his nose almost self-consciously.

"Also, your beard is not so evenly trimmed." She took a step forward, her eyes analyzing his facial hair. "I might say it appears singed on one side."

"I suppose I must suffer bodily harm before I warrant your interest."

Bianca sighed. "Mayhap you might dispense with your contempt and simply tell me why you are here."

Albern opened his palm, gesturing her to sit. She did.

"For years I've given myself to the practice of alchemy. My accomplishments have been many and others used to look to me for guidance. Even the king believed my skills were worthy of his patronage." He paused and a shadow of regret fell across his face. "No other master of the dark art was so esteemed and admired."

Bianca thought otherwise, having witnessed his fall from grace. But she saw no point in reminding him. She allowed him to trumpet his accomplishments, which in her mind were of scant value and, at best, amounted to expert chicanery.

"There are four elements to which we subscribe: air, earth, fire, and water. In any given substance, we strive to understand the proportions of each element relative to the others. Our goal is to manipulate those ratios and propel a substance toward perfection. And, as you well know, that perfection of the inanimate is gold.

"The processes we use are as diverse and varied as the men who practice the dark art. The journey is fraught with failure. One cannot succeed without introspection of spirit and respect for the mysteries of nature. The practice is discouraging and the path is long. When we fail, we question our faith, our process, our technique. Forsooth, we may even question our sanity!" Albern pinned Bianca with a prescient stare.

"For those who have devoted their lives in pursuit of the stone, there will be discoveries that will intrigue, but whose portent cannot be imagined. Whose value will remain undeciphered. Some of these discoveries will be lost to time, their page burned in the fire of neglect, their ashes carried away by the winds of change. Some discoveries will never be understood. Some may never be duplicated."

Bianca stifled a yawn. Her stomach began to sour and she couldn't be sure whether it stemmed from her physical condition or from listening to her father blathering on about alchemy.

Hobs leapt upon the table and paraded between the two, inciting Albern's irritation.

"It should not do for you to keep a cat," he said, distracted from his discourse.

"He earns his keep," answered Bianca. "Besides, he is a cat like no other." She declined to tell her father that Hobs once belonged to Ferris Stannum, an alchemist whom she held in great esteem, an alchemist who had earned her admiration. In fact, she had found Stannum's murderer. She refrained from telling him that she believed Hobs was immortal. Doing so would undoubtedly have elicited Albern's skepticism and perhaps even a petulant desire to prove her wrong. She simply wished to avoid more conflict and have her father get to the point of his visit. "As you were saying?" Bianca set Hobs on the floor again.

Albern took another drink of ale, then continued. "An alchemist desires to transmute imperfect metal into gold. Discovering the agent of change, the philosopher's stone, is our ultimate goal.

"But as I said before, there are other discoveries, diversions that occur perhaps by chance, that have possibilities worth exploring."

Albern straightened his spine and glanced at John, who had just tossed Hobs out the door. "You have grown restless waiting for me to tell you." He paused, tapped a finger on the rim of his drink, waited.

Bianca sighed. She propped her chin upon her fist and lifted an eyebrow.

Albern looked at her and then John. Seeing that he had their full attention, he continued. "I have discovered an element like no other. Never has there been a substance such as this."

"Why do you think it is like nothing else?"

Albern's lips pinched, as if his declaration was proof enough that it should be true. "Since you seem distracted with other matters," he said, his eyes flicking toward her belly, "I will merely describe it, then tell you why I am here."

Bianca tilted her head, waiting.

"I have discovered an amalgam of earth and fire. It is as solid as the ground that we walk on, but it can also spontaneously combust."

"Is that how you burned yourself?" asked Bianca.

Albern continued without answering her question. "At the end of a long and painstaking process, a shining liquid collected into a glass vesicle, then solidified into a waxy lump. If pearls could melt and turn to liquid I would describe it as such. I found a cork and stoppered it. To my amazement, it became a luminescent white, as if it were glowing like a flame the color of milk. But the light was markedly brighter and more radiant than any candle I've ever seen.

"After a while, the glow dissipated, turning a goose-turd green."

"And did the color last very long?" John's interest was piqued and he sat down beside Bianca.

This time Albern acknowledged his presence by directly answering him. "Not long. It faded."

"Hmm," said Bianca. "It glows and fades. It appears solid like the earth, then inexplicably turns to fire."

Albern nodded. "I removed the cork from the flask to smell the contents."

"Did it have a smell?"

"It smelled like garlic. After a few moments, sparks began to fly and it smoked. A fire erupted, and flames began shooting from the neck of the flask. I quickly shoved the cork back into the opening, hoping to contain the fire."

"And the burn on your hand?" asked Bianca.

"I got it from touching the stone."

"Is it the philosopher's stone?" asked John.

Albern shook his head. "I know it resembles a stone. Therefore, I shall call it one. But I do not know if it is, in fact, *the* philosopher's stone." He finished off his ale and set the empty mug back on the board with a defining thud. "I am unable to determine if it is the special stone because I am no longer in possession of it."

Bianca and John exchanged looks. "What happened? If you do not have it, then who does?"

"That is what I want you to find out." Albern's gray eyes settled on Bianca's blue. "It is a substance of unknown potential. I have told you what I observed of its behavior and characteristics. But as you can see, my knowledge is incomplete. It is cursory. I did not intend to tell anyone of the discovery until I had thoroughly understood its nature."

Bianca was well aware of an alchemist's secrecy, but she was curious whether or not her father could recreate his discovery. "And did you record how you created it?"

Albern snorted. He tapped his head.

"It sounds like a dangerous element," said John. "It should not take long to find something so volatile." He turned to Bianca. "Perhaps, though, we should not bother."

Albern objected. "It might have qualities that are beneficial."

"Imagine if one no longer needed to use a flint to start a fire," said Bianca, already intuiting its worth. "We could dispense with the huffing and puffing, the damp kindling . . ."

"The amount of smoke it creates is voluminous," added Albern. "It yields a blinding, choking smoke. Only a tiny piece would be needed for that purpose. The stone is easy to divide."

"What good is there in creating smoke?" asked John.

"My boy, think on what advantage a man might have if he could move and not be seen." Albern's voice rose with excitement. "The king seeks to invade France. Smoke could screen his army from the enemy and give us the advantage."

Neither Bianca nor John mentioned it, but their thoughts went to John's likely conscription. The sudden necessity of recovering this volatile element grew as voluminous as the purported cloud of smoke a piece of it could make.

"I shudder to think about this being used against anyone," she said.

"Then you need to find it," said Albern. "You must put your mind to preventing the deaths of many, instead of finding the murderer of a few as has been your habit of late."

"I'll see what I can learn. Such things do not stay a secret forever. If you suspect someone, then you must tell me."

Albern closed his eyes and inhaled. The blue veins in his forehead were noticeable even in the subdued light of Bianca's room of Medicinals and Physickes. He blew out his breath in a controlled exhale and opened his eyes. "I believe you must start with your mother."

Bianca tutted. "Mother? Why would she have cause to take it? She despises everything about the dark art."

"I believe she knows of the stone's whereabouts but will not say."

"Is this speculation, or do you have proof?"

"This is not conjecture. Last night I stirred from my sleep and she was not beside me in bed. She often rises in the night to check the fire, or to relieve herself. I do not trouble myself with what she does. I woke as usual, had porridge, and dressed. All was well until I went to unlock my room of alchemy. I reached into the pocket of my jerkin and did not find my key. Thinking I'd gotten a hole in it and the key might have slipped between my smock and my jerkin, I patted my front, feeling for it. I found it in the wrong pocket. This puzzled me. I always put it into my left chest pocket."

"Could you have been distracted? Perhaps you mistakenly put the key in your other pocket."

Albern gazed on his daughter with a look of staid annoyance. "I favor my right hand. It is sensible that I lock a door thusly"—he mimed turning a key—"then replace the key across my chest into a pocket on my left side," he concluded, demonstrating his habit.

"Do you keep anything in your right pocket?"

"Coins, a half crown, pennies. If I must work at wrangling them from my pocket, I will think more about spending it. But you are questioning the obvious. Your mother has a hand in this. Of that I am cert."

"You are quick to conclude such."

"It falls to reason that she is the only person with knowledge of the element."

"You confided in her?" asked John, a bit surprised given the level of indifference between his in-laws. He was late to Boisvert's, but he couldn't drag himself away.

Albern tapped the rim of his mug again. "Your mother has a nattering way of chittering on about finance. All the time she is telling me about our lack of coin. We haven't bread, we haven't ale, but we do have oil of vitriol and sal ammoniac. She is of a simple mind and hasn't the ability to understand the significance of my work."

Bianca listened with half an ear, sympathizing with her mother and letting her father run on until he'd run out.

"This discovery is my opportunity to win back Henry's good grace. There is much that a king could do with such a discovery."

"Then," said Bianca, "if the element should be in her possession it might be easy enough to find, especially if she removed it from the flask. It would smoke if not properly stored."

"The flask *and* the stone are missing. Whoever has the stone knows about its dangerous properties. That is why I believe your mother has knowledge of its disappearance."

Bianca's face colored a surprising shade of green and she removed herself from the table and ran for the door. She flung it open and a waiting chicken ran inside while she rid herself of the contents of her tetchy stomach. When she was done, John met her on the threshold with the feathered intruder and tossed it into the street. He wrapped his arm around her waist and helped her back to the bench.

"With all of these"—Albern gazed at the long row of drying herbs tacked to the rafter—"plants . . . I would think there is some tonic you might concoct that would settle your woozy constitution."

John set a small bowl of ale before her, and Bianca drank enough to clear her mouth. "I suppose," she said.

Albern rose from the table and placed his hat on his head. "No doubt this is a woman's affectation to garner attention. John, you should be wary of a woman's wiles."

"Sir, Bianca is not seeking attention. Her ill health is no pretense." John rubbed his wife's back. "She can hardly keep any food down." He took a breath to chastise the man for thinking so little of his daughter when Albern interrupted.

"Bianca, you must speak with your mother forthwith. I shall send her to visit you. Obviously you need her advice about these . . . female matters."

Albern strolled to the door and turned with one final request. "See what you can find out from her regarding my element," he said. "Then inform me."

CHAPTER 5

Where dreams cause fitful sleep and leave their print of unease upon one's heart, so did Bianca wake similarly etched. She had stirred once in the night with the heavy feeling of drowning, the terror of being pulled down and thrashing for a gulp of air. All around was the brown murk of churned water and a faint sense of "up," where she would find the surface. She woke in a sweat, her smock sticking to her body like a second skin. John slept beside her, oblivious to her confusion, while Hobs napped, curled between his legs. The black tiger lifted his head and blinked awake.

Bianca removed her drenched smock and dropped it on the floor beside the bed. For a moment she sat with her arms wrapped around her drawn-up knees. Her father's request had stirred a heated discussion between them, with John asking her to refuse to carry out Albern's bidding. He argued that this was a matter that did not concern her. She did not disagree with him; it did appear that if this white stone were lost, or if another alchemist claimed the discovery as his own, it would relieve her of the need for involvement. Besides, her father's unsavory dealings had nearly gotten her killed two years before. The incident had been the impetus for leaving her parents' home in London and finding a place in Southwark, well away from them.

Bianca lay back, crooking an arm under her pillow. The murmurs, the scuffling and slithering of creatures in the alley out their door, lulled her back into a restless sleep until dawn's insistent light coaxed her awake. That, and the smell of food.

John ate from a steaming bowl of barley and milk, and watched Bianca sit up in bed. His wood spoon stopped midair and he raised his eyebrows at the sight of her with nary a stitch on.

"You rise," he said.

Bianca saw his face pink. "You, as well," she quipped, collecting the damp smock from off the floor. She retrieved a dry one from a chest.

John adjusted himself beneath the table. "You rival the sun in accomplishing that."

Bianca dropped the smock over her head, stretched her limbs, then settled a hand on her lower back to support it. "Dressed so soon?"

"Boisvert expects me early. I've time to make up for him. With the View of Arms and your father's visit . . ." His voice trailed off remembering their argument. He stuffed another spoonful of porridge into his mouth.

"I've no intention of finding this stone," said Bianca, addressing the silence that gaped between them. "Though I admit I am curious about its qualities." She went to a pail of collected rainwater and splashed it on her face. "I see no benefit to my father possessing such a thing."

"Then you agree with me," said John, cheerfully resuming his meal.

"I agree with you," said Bianca. "Though not entirely."

John stopped chewing. "Mean you what?"

"I warrant that I should not involve myself in finding the stone and returning it to my father. However, if I should happen upon this exceptional element I would not throw it in the Thames. But neither would I return it."

John lowered his spoon. "God's breath, Bianca! I see nothing good about a fire-inducing stone. If you were to find it and start experimenting, you could burn yourself like your father obviously did." He gestured to their living quarters. "Fear me, one misstep and you could burn down this room of Medicinals and Physickes. Forsooth, you could set all the borough alight! Have you no concern for your own well-being and that of our unborn child?"

"John, I shall only give cursory involvement to my father." Bianca ran a comb through her hair. The teeth snagged on a thick black tangle, which she concentrated on trying to unsnarl. After several yanks, she gave up and tossed the comb on the table. "If my mother should come calling, I *will* ask her about the key. But I shall not seek her out with an accusation on my tongue just because my father asks it of me."

"Between doing your father's bidding and maintaining your distance from him is a thin line."

"It is one I can walk."

John shook his head and pushed his bowl aside. "By that measure, mayhap your mother will come here and simply confess. Neither possibility is likely." He rose from the table and looked around at the jumble of equipment and ingredients that took up most of their room. He equated the mess to the confusion their life together in Gull Hole had become. They had returned to Bianca's favored hovel in Southwark after having enjoyed a brief stay in a wealthy neighborhood. He sniffed. Well, *he* had had enjoyment of it. Bianca never warmed to Aldersgate Ward, and he could not convince her to stay and look for a better rent, where the two might at least be able to turn around twice and still have room for her chemistries. At least she had agreed not to keep rats while she was with child. Until he completely finished his apprenticeship with Boisvert and became his own master, all they could afford was this rent within the putrid bloom of Morgan Stream and the River Thames.

John found his flatcap and put it on. "Anon," he said, "think on the decoction for Meddybemps. There lies the better use of your time." He kissed her forehead, a chaste kiss; he'd lost the desire to meet her lips for fear of what she might use them to say.

Another willful declaration of her desires would only further aggravate him.

Bianca spent the morning washing their smocks and hanging them on a rope she strung across the back alley. By the time she retrieved the chopped herbs covered with oil and started a small fire in her furnace, the sun had started its downward arc. With the spring season came an increase in ague and its symptoms. It was a malady common among those inhabiting low-lying areas, where the air was thick and damp. Headaches accompanied sweats and chills. Even sleep offered no relief, for a victim's dreams were vivid torments.

Bianca had witnessed a man's chills lessen when given a potable septwort concoction. To soothe a bumptious stomach, she added catmint. She thought the combination might be the beginning of a remedy for the malady; at least Meddybemps could dispense the syrup for some profit until she had figured out a better combination of herbs. She was fanning the dried grass in her stove when she heard a familiar voice call through the window.

"Hey ho!"

Bianca looked up at a straw hat bouncing just outside the sill.

"Must I climb through the window?"

"Mother," said Bianca, opening the door and welcoming her inside. "You must have knocked while I was in the alley."

Malva stepped into her quarters, wearing a mustard-yellow kirtle that brought the cheerful warmth of the sun in with her. She wore a frayed straw hat tied with a jaunty bow under her chin. She had only been there a minute before her lighthearted expression fell like a baby robin from its nest. Malva looked around and grew quiet. The look on her face was not one of interest, but dismay. Her brown eyes widened as she stared at Bianca's still heads and alembics, so like her husband's. "You still have a man's obsession with metals, I see," she said at last. "Have you learned nothing from me?" She untied the bow at her neck and tossed her hat on the table. "Men are such fools. When will you learn no good will come from practicing alchemy?"

"Mother, I am not an alchemist."

"Then what is this nonsense I see?" She pointed to the bizarre-looking instruments and paraphernalia of Bianca's room.

"I do not practice the dark art. But some of its methods are useful."

Her mother rounded on her. "Hmm?" Her expression had turned defensive. "And pray tell me what do you find that makes it useful, for I have seen nothing come of an alchemist's rattle-brained quest except empty pockets and the ash of ruined dreams."

Bianca shouldered past her mother. "Look here," she said, pointing to her distillation apparatus. "This extracts the essence of septwort and catmint. I shall use the purified spirit in a remedy to help with fevers and chills."

Her mother ran a mistrustful eye down the elaborate coils and long tubes ending like a mole's snout. "Why so many twists to arrive at something so simple?"

"The length is needed to cool the vapors. The vapor condenses on the surface and turns to liquid."

"Paa," her mother said with a dismissive wave of her hand. "But then you were never one to make life easy on yourself."

Bianca moved away from the convoluted piece of equipment and realized she could not change her mother's mind. Instead, she changed the subject. "How did you find my room of Medicinals and Physickes?"

"Is that what this is?" Her mother tossed a pouch on the table. She chuckled. "I didn't raise ye for eighteen years and not learn how ye think. But ho, your father described your whereabouts. He told me to walk with the river to my left toward Morgan Stream, turn in front of a cleared area that looked perpetually squishy, then follow my nose to the overwhelming smell of chicken turd."

She eased herself onto the bench and began fanning her face with the brim of her hat. She was taller than Bianca and of heavier bone. Their physical similarities stopped at their round faces and almond-shaped eyes; Malva's were brown instead of blue like Bianca's. "Have ye an ale to offer?" Her mother removed her coif, revealing coiled braids of dark hair like Bianca's, only streaked with silver strands, but there was no doubt which parent Bianca favored.

Bianca filled a mug from their store of ale from the Dim Dragon.

"I've never seen such cloudy dreck," said Malva, peering into the cup suspiciously.

"It is a feature of Southwark swill."

Her mother's brows knit and she took a small taste. She deemed it potable and finished it off, punctuating her last swallow with a loud "aah." She set the mug on the board. "When were you going to tell me of your condition? Or were you?"

"Methinks Father and you mewl too much. I am not far enough along that it should be for certain."

"He says ye have some sickness of it."

"I do, but it is not a concern."

Malva patted the pouch on the table. "This be some red raspberry leaf for a tea. I've found it helps with the first woozy days." Malva leaned back to gaze upon the row of herbs drying overhead. She pointed to a bundle. "Peppermint. Ha! Ye didn't ignore me completely. No room of 'medicinals and techniques' can be complete without peppermint."

"Physickes, Mother. It is a room of Medicinals and Physickes."

"Pish. I care not what you call it." She took another drink. "I combine peppermint with equal parts red raspberry leaves and chopped dandelion root. Have you dandelion root?"

"I do."

"Of course it is important to include the barbs of a goose feather in the brew."

"Pray you?"

"To help with padding your womb so the fetus doesn't rock."

"Mother, your logic confounds me."

"This is sensible advice and I have found it effective. The softness lines your womb much like a bird lines its nest with plucked feathers. It is the fitful sleep of the child inside of you that unsettles your stomach so."

"I agree with using peppermint and perhaps raspberry leaves and will be happy to try it. But you'll not find me chasing a goose for its feather."

"Nay, there is no need to." Malva opened her purse and produced a long plume. "I took care of it for you." She laid the feather on the table and finished off her ale.

The smell of goose attracted Hobs, who jumped to the bench beside Malva, then stepped onto the board. He took hold of the feather in his tiny teeth and started off with it. "What is this?" exclaimed Malva. "You keep a cat?"

"He keeps me," said Bianca, teasing the feather from his mouth and sticking it behind her ear.

"You should not share company with the likes of a feline. It will drink the soul from a sleeping babe."

Bianca did not respond. She remembered why she preferred a hovel in Southwark to living with her parents.

Malva got to her feet and perused the dangling herbs and sawed the string releasing the peppermint. She collected a few other herbs for good measure. Bianca's attempts at organizing her stock now lay in several heaps on the table.

"I'll make you a decoction for your early sickness. Sit and rest yourself. That is what you need most."

Bianca dutifully watched her mother gather the necessary bowls and told her where to find the dandelion root. Albern's latest discovery came to mind, and while watching her mother chop the leaves she mentioned it.

"Nothing good will come of his discovery," said Malva. "Your father believes he will redeem himself with the king. But I tell him to keep away from old Mouldwarp and his scheming courtiers. Albern had his time in that den of rawgabbits." She stopped chopping and looked toward the window. "He nearly got the whole lot of us hanged," she said, lowering her voice. "I'll not forgive him for that." She leaned in and pointed the blade at Bianca. "No one comes by here, do they? The alleys don't creep with ears."

"Nay, there is better entertainment in Southwark than our conversation."

Bianca's mother stared a second, then laughed, catching her meaning. Southwark did have a tenuous reputation. Malva scraped the leaves into a bowl. "Blessed fig's end."

"Have you seen Father's miraculous stone?" asked Bianca. "He says it can combust without prompt and glow bright, then fade to an eerie green."

"I've not seen the thing. I've no interest."

Her mother laid down her knife and went to Bianca's calcinating stove. She bent over and looked inside at the small fire wheezing there. "You haven't got sticks or dung?"

"On the floor next to you." Bianca spun her mother's knife on the table in bored amusement and watched Malva throw a dung patty on the flame. "Then you haven't been to Father's alchemy room of late?" she asked as her mother blew into the fuel box.

"What would I want with going there? I'm glad for every moment the man is gone." She huffed a few times and cursed the flame with a few oaths.

"Do you ever borrow some of his ingredients?"

"What does he have that I could use?" Malva pointed to a pan of water sitting on top of the stove. "Is this water?"

"Aye." Bianca began spinning the knife in the opposite direction, her cheek propped in her palm.

Her mother dumped the bowl of herbs into the pan, garnering a scowl from Bianca. "I might have been wanting to use that," she said.

"The river is nearly outside your door."

"I don't use river water for my concoctions. I use rain." Bianca flicked the handle of the knife and watched it spin as she thought how to word what she needed to say. She knew her mother would take it as an accusation, but she saw no way around it. "This wondrous element of his," she ventured, "has gone missing."

Malva set the pan on the tripod and fiddled with starting a fire as if the news came as no surprise. "I'd say that it's probably for the best."

Bianca pushed a little further. "Father says the key to his alchemy room was in the wrong pocket."

"Did he now?" said Malva, only half listening.

Bianca didn't give an explanation. She waited for her mother to offer one.

"Oh, aye," said Malva, catching Bianca's intent and straightening. She faced her daughter. "He thinks I took the key and stole his precious stone."

Bianca neither confirmed nor denied the claim.

"Blessed fig's end. Your father pins his hopes to this devilish rock and thinks he shall find his lost favor by presenting it to the king. Your father is almost giddy with thoughts of pardon and the glory he expects will be showered on him." Malva snatched her knife off the table and tucked it in her belt. "He has lost his good sense over it. There are times that he cannot remember to eat! His distraction is complete, and now he dares to accuse me of misdemeanor. Well, I shall tell you once, and then you can tell him, for I am certain he put you to ask it of me—I did not steal his fool stone!"

"Mother, those were not his words."

"Then what were they?" Malva stared, her eyes intent as if she could see the heat radiating from Bianca's cheeks.

Bianca's throat caught with the shame that she would do her father's bidding. Her mother had always defended her. She could think of no way to soften her words or take them back. In spite of this, she persisted, unable to keep herself from knowing more. "He noticed that you were not by his side when he woke the night before last."

"A woman my age cannot keep a full bladder through the night. You'll find that out soon enough."

"He said he unlocked the door, entered his room of alchemy, and discovered the element was gone." Bianca met her mother's eyes.

"And he sees fit to blame me for that?" Malva dipped a spoon into the pan of boiling leaves and gave it a vigorous stir. She came back to the table and sat down.

Bianca shook her head. "I am only relaying what he said to me."

"And he cannot tell me this himself? He goes through you?"

Bianca toyed with the comb she'd thrown on the table. They might have sat staring at one another for a time but the smell of burning herbs prompted Bianca to hurry to the rain barrel in the alley. She came back with a pail, slopping water on the floor as she tipped it over the dry pan, dousing the burnt leaves and creating a billow of steam.

"That is lost," she said, peering into the scorched pan of brown juice.

"Nonsense. I've done worse." Malva pulled the pan off the heat and looked for a way to strain the mixture. Unable to find a piece of cloth, she held a spoon against the leaves and poured the brew into a mug. She set it before Bianca.

"Here, drink. It will ease your queasy stomach."

The strong smell of peppermint managed to mask the possible charred aftertaste, and Bianca sipped cautiously while her mother began cleaning her mess.

"Meadowsweet is in bloom in the field near Paris Garden," said Bianca, hoping to smooth over their rift and talk about herbs. "Did you know?"

Malva stood looking around for a place to put the dirty bowl and pan as if she did not hear Bianca's question.

"Set them on that shelf," said Bianca, pointing to a space no different from another.

"I heard tell," answered Malva, making room on a shelf packed with unwashed crockery.

"Meadowsweet leaves help stiff joints, I've found."

"The flowers help calm fevers and chills," added Malva. She settled on the bench opposite Bianca. "It is good for strewing about. Keeps down the lice and fleas." Her eyes drifted to Bianca's scalp. "You're not wearing your coif."

"I don't wear it inside."

Malva took up her straw hat. "It is almost dark and I have a mind to pick some before heading home." She plopped the hat upon her head and watched Bianca drink the concoction. "Save some of that and set it by. You may need it again."

"If it works I can make more."

"Paa! If it works." Malva rolled her eyes. "*If* it works. It *will* work."

"You've given me a thought," said Bianca, brightening. "What if I combine septwort with flowers of meadowsweet?"

"I see no harm in it."

"The two might balance each other and help with the symptoms of ague."

Malva considered it for a moment. "There is the visitation of evil dreams that comes with the fever sleep."

"I don't know what I might use to allay them."

"Tie a dead cricket dipped in goat blood to a stick of hornbeam and have them sleep with it against their right side."

"I should think that would induce such dreams, not prevent them."

"In these matters, you should heed my word." Malva rose from the table and ambled toward the door. "And that includes leaving off with your father's foolishness. Let him dither with the likes of it. You're with child now."

CHAPTER 6

If one seeks to skirt London's city government and its fickly en-
forced rules of conduct, one looks to the other side. The other
side of the river, that is. Squatting on the opposite bank is Southwark, with its warren of brothels tucked in side lanes, its venues
of bear-baiting and bull-baiting, its ignominious collection of pleasures and vices designed to tease those with coin to willingly part
with it.

And for those seeking vulnerable sots from which to wangle
that coin, there is no better place to be than Southwark.

With husband engrossed in his latest projection and son tucked
peacefully in bed, Leadith Browne slipped out the door of her
meager rent and hurried down Trinity Lane. She would take a
wherry, untroubled that the fare and night out might consume her
savings. If all went well, she would have enough for a month of
fares. "God's foot!" she said, drawing a frown from a passerby. She
would have enough to buy her own boat if she wanted!

A bawdy tavern song buzzed from her lips as she made her way
to the landing near Queenhithe. Never had she been in such high
spirits. It had been a long time since she'd known the goose-bump

thrill of hope. Nine years to be exact. As old as her son, Timothy, whose birth, she finally conceded, might have been worth the misery after all.

Tonight she would fill her purse with coin. She stopped a moment and checked its seams for holes. She didn't want to lose a single crown or penny. Walking on, she ticked off the items she would buy with her newfound wealth—a new kirtle, perhaps an overcoat lined with fur for the winter. Oooo, what kind of fur, she wondered? Might she have a gown lined with squirrel? Nay, she wanted coney. But what if she could afford ermine?

Then, too, she would set herself above the mud with a smart pair of wooden pattens carved out in tiger paws with real claws to grip the slippery muck. Leadith's giddy mood was tamped by the first sprinkle of rain hitting her low neckline beneath her light cape. She looked out at the gray sky encroaching from the south. The cloud bank brought with it a humid air, but she thought she might make it across the river before her hopes were washed away by a downpour. Besides, she might never have this opportunity again.

At the water's edge she found a ferryman willing to take her across.

It had been several years since she had last crossed the Thames onboard a wherry. There was no comfort, no money in being married to an alchemist. Especially one who had lost his patron, a wealthy merchant who owned a tin mine. This mistake of a marriage and life of poverty, she had not expected.

At first, she had been impressed with Dikson's knowledge and his mysterious ways. He wore a fine doublet of black say and supple leather boots that covered his knees like a horseman. A dapper flatcap crowned his head of russet hair, and he kept a pheasant quill and a bottle of ink tucked beneath his doublet should he suddenly become inspired and need to write down an idea for his alchemy. Nay, he was not a handsome man, but his allure had held her fast.

Upon spying him at market, she had made up her mind to win him. And she did. She had thought herself clever to have won the affection of a man destined for greater riches than she could ever imagine. He spoke to her about creating the philosopher's stone and said that once he had accomplished what no other alchemist had ever done, he would make his patron, and her, very wealthy indeed.

But two years into their marriage Browne's patron had grown impatient. When asked for proof of an accomplishment, of some progress toward his goal, Dikson had resorted to trickery, hoping to allay and fool his patron into continuing his stipend. He did not expect to be exposed for the mountebank and babbler that he was. His funding had come to an abrupt and ugly end.

To Leadith, his downward spiral seemed never ending. They had moved to a derelict rent on Trinity Lane with walls and wood trusses punky with rot. Every night Dikson escaped to the uppermost reaches, to a garret under the eaves so cramped he had to stoop to stand. It was just as well, thought Leadith. Let him disappear into the attic and drink himself silly; she didn't want to look at him.

The ferryman steadied the boat as she stepped into it and settled on a seat of wood. No padding on this sad conveyance. A strange smell arose from the hull, of what she did not know and it was too dark to see. Perhaps it was the stink of the river itself, she thought, as a bloated fish floated belly up off the starboard side; or perhaps the source of the smell was the stagnant water pooling by her feet, sloshing back and forth with the rocking boat.

In a voice so soft she thought she might have imagined it, the boatman told her to leave her fare in a cup nailed to the gunwale, but this was all he said, nothing more. The night was warm enough that she wondered why he wore a thick, woolen cape with the hood up. But by the thin wrist she glimpsed when he poled the wherry out into the current, she assumed he was older than most ferriers, and she knew how the elderly could sometimes feel cold when it wasn't.

She turned her sights to Southwark as they crossed the river, singing in a husky voice to the twinkling lights of bawdy houses and inns on the water—

"Tis sweeter far than sugar fine
And pleasanter than Muscadine.
And if you please fair maid to stay . . ."

The storm clouds billowed toward the unsuspecting borough
and a warm wind lifted her coif, threatening to dump it in the
drink. She pressed a hand to her head and with the other held on
to the seat as the waves began kicking the boat.

Not many boaters were plying the waters; she saw perhaps one
other farther upstream. For a fleeting second she worried that perhaps she might not be able to return to London if she made a late
night of it. She dismissed the idea. If it should rain very hard she
could always find a room. With all the money she would be making, it would not be a problem.

The ferryman landed at Bank End Stairs and braced the boat as
she endeavored to leave it. As she hurried up the steps she thought
to ask him if he might be available for her return ride. She turned
to call to him, but when she searched the landing he had already
disappeared into the night.

The sprinkles changed to heavy drops. Lights winked from
taverns and ordinaries near the bridge, inviting her to join others
seeking their pleasures and opportunities. She had just reached
the area when the rain fell like slanting arrows driven by a gusty
wind. Leadith turned down the first street she came to with over-
hangs that might shield her. A sign with a beguiling dragon sipping an ale swung in the wind overhead. She hauled open the door
and scuttled inside.

Boozing kens always benefit from poor weather, and the Dim
Dragon was no exception. Leadith didn't take long studying where
to sit. Nearly every table was crammed with laborers except for
one near the back. Instead of rough woolen jerkins and dirty fin-
gernails, these men wore the tailored doublets of the professional
and merchant class. Obviously they were men of greater means,
and Leadith wasted no time in getting to them.

Though of lower social standing, she bore a pleasant face (or so she thought, based on her memory of it some ten years previous). Time had relaxed the skin under her chin and had rearranged her curves. She was no longer buxom, but boxy. Her manner was no longer perceived as coquettish, but crude. When she smiled, the black gap of a missing canine startled, and she wondered why a man would suddenly become cold. She'd forgotten she'd lost that tooth years before.

Leadith reached the table and sat at one end, forcing the men to scooch down and make way. She looked round at them and nodded. "Gentle sirs," she said, in her throaty timbre.

The men did not grimace long, for while she was of average countenance, when she shed her thin cape, her ample brisket more than kept their interest.

The gentleman next to her had a very good view and leaned over farther than was necessary to summon the serving wench. Cammy Dawney arrived and noticed the men's eagerness to order the woman an ale.

"The sky began spitting. I found myself at this ordinary's door," said Leadith once Cammy moved on.

"Ha," said the gent across from her. "Let the sky rain turnips! For sit we here, cozy and content, dry until we choose it not." His eyes were already seeing more than two of her and her assets were quickly multiplying. He envisioned laying his head upon those soft pillows, drowning in them, but oh, it was too fleet a vision.

Leadith settled herself and checked the narrow ruffle of her smock along her bodice's edge to be sure that she revealed a little, but not too much, creamy soft skin. However, she had no sense of what was too much since her cleavage was as long and deep as a Scottish loch.

A gentleman sitting near mopped the last of his stew and watched the men around him make fools of themselves. He finished his end of bread and dabbed a napkin to his tiny mouth, which was surrounded by an impeccably trimmed straw-colored beard. Indifferent to her arrival, he continued his conversation with the man across from him, an apothecary.

Cammy Dawney returned with an ale for Leadith and was sent back for several more. The men directly around her were in rollicking good cheer.

Leadith, enjoying the attention being lavished upon her, was not content with the interest of just a few. Several bunches of lacy white flowers lay next to the men who were ignoring her, so she interrupted their conversation to ask about them.

An apothecary spoke first, laying his hand upon the bundle. "Goodwife, this is meadowsweet. The leaves help those with stiff knees and fingers. They are useful in several of my remedies. I come here every spring to pick them."

"Ah," she said. "An apothecary. We have a common interest. I, too, make remedies." Certain that he must be impressed, she continued. "And when do you know to come for the meadowsweet? Do people speak of it?"

"A fellow tells me when they bloom into a sea of frothy white-caps."

"A memorable sight," said Leadith. She aimed to engage every man at her table; for who could know which of them would want what she had to offer?

"And you, sir," she said, addressing the patron with the close-cropped beard. "Why do you gather the herb?"

The man's pale eyes appraised her. He looked reluctant to answer, but he did. "I use them to scent my candles."

"Ho," said she, after finishing off her ale. "I've never smelled a sweet candle. But what can mask the smell of rendered tallow? Nothing I know can curb that foul odor."

"I do not deal in tallow candles," he said curtly, apparently insulted.

"He is a chandler of beeswax," said the apothecary.

Thinking the difference must matter since it was mentioned, Leadith accepted being corrected, though she thought the chandler prickly about being lumped together with tallow chandlers. What did it matter? They both dipped candles. She let the matter be.

The fellow next to her ordered up another ale and grinned lasciviously. He kept running his eyes up and down her throat and bodice.

Across from her, a man with more rimples than a snake's face only wished light conversation. He asked why she was about on such a night. Despite her stating otherwise, he assumed she was from a neighboring stew, though he thought she might be a madam of the game given her maturity. But it had been many years since he'd taken pleasure with the ladies and his eyesight was failing.

The Dim Dragon's rotgut loosened Leadith's tongue. Basking in the attention of all the men at her table, she addressed them archly, "Sirs, I have on my person something so wondrous . . ."

The man next to her thought he knew what she meant and reached a hand under the table to give it a squeeze.

Leadith shoved him away. She had not yet lost her good sense—though on another day she might have welcomed such a man.

Cammy arrived with more tankards and the alchemist's wife took another long quaff, letting the men at her table speculate for a moment. She finished the drink before continuing.

"Kind sirs, I do not live in this crooked borough, I've only come to visit." Leadith felt a pleasant warmth from the brew. "My purpose is for business."

A couple men exchanged looks. Leadith shoved the man next to her a second time.

She straightened and continued. "My husband is an alchemist," she said. "And he has made a wondrous discovery. One of great potential."

"Then why do you sit here telling us?" asked the apothecary.

"Because I have come to sell it to the man who wants it the most." Her face softened into a smile. "I mean to settle our debt since my husband hasn't the wherewithal to do it."

"Perhaps the king might be interested," suggested one, wondering why she was bothering with the likes of them.

"Nay, I haven't the time to seek that hulchy hedgepig." The words hung in the air like the rank smell of fish; then she clapped her hand over her mouth.

Heads swiveled to see if anyone had overheard. But since they were the closest things to gentry at the Dim Dragon, no one else seemed to mind.

"Ha. What is this discovery so fantastical? And what would any of us want with such a thing?" asked the apothecary.

Leadith's shrewd instinct prevailed. "You will look on it, and then you shall make yourselves silly outbidding each other."

The man next to her slammed his hand on the table, making her jump. "God's nails, stop mooning about and show us this thing!"

"As you will," said Leadith. "Give me room to work." She shoved the man next to her for good measure. Returning her audience's gaze, she reached below the table and brought up a clenched fist.

The men stared at her closed hand.

"Aye, well?" said one.

"Goodwife, you waste our time," said another.

The men started to shake their heads and naysay.

"Wait!" said the chandler. "Light shines from between her fingers."

The men stared, leaning forward.

"Open your hand," said a man opposite. He reached across to grab her wrist, but Leadith was quick to withdraw it.

"Stop that, ye fool man." And with a coy smile she clutched it next to her bosom. She made sure every eye was trained on her, then slowly opened her hand.

There in her palm was a small glass vial that glowed brilliantly.

Some of the men put up their hands as if blinded and shied away. The elder man crossed himself. "What manner of conjury is this?" he cried.

Their reaction caused a stir and soon Leadith had the interest of half the tavern.

Leadith covered the vial and, like extinguishing a fire, smothered the light. "Get on, you men of no money," she said, waving off the muckrakers and men with worn jerkins who had come over to witness the odd spectacle. "This is not for your eyes nor your pleasure."

The men grumbled, but Leadith refused to open her hand. She refused everyone, until the men grew bored and troubled themselves with more drink. But her rebuke didn't stop them from gawking when she wasn't looking.

"Let me see this," said the chandler, reaching across.

Leadith clutched the vial tight against her. "No one touches it until they pay my price."

"'Tis a trick. The vial contains the bulbs of a hundred fireflies. I've seen it before," said one of the men opposite. "Tsk. Poor bugs."

"Do you think me simple?" Leadith's face colored as much from the ale as from her indignation. "Stay back. I will show you wonderfulness."

The men groused, but then quieted when the alchemist's wife uncorked the vial and tapped a bean-sized stone onto the board.

"It does not impress," said the chandler, staring at the white lump.

"Wait!" said Leadith, holding up a finger.

The chandler grumbled. "Methinks the lady is counterfeit."

The words had no sooner escaped his lips when the little stone began spewing gray smoke. In a matter of seconds, the cloud quickly doubled, then tripled in size. There was no preventing the whole of the Dim Dragon from noticing and soon the table was again surrounded by excited onlookers, each clambering for a better look, though half the tavern feared a fire and fell over themselves to escape.

"The smoke shall choke us dead! Open the door!"

"It blows a mighty wind for such a little bean," said the apothecary, too fascinated to flee.

As people frantically fanned the smoke, sparks crackled at the surface of the stone.

"What is it doing?" cried one of the patrons.

The sparks rippled for a moment, then burst into flames. Shouts of "fire" rang through the ken. Even Leadith grew alarmed.

The table caught like a bed of kindling, and the man sitting next to her threw his hat on the flames trying to smother them—

but it caught fire and created even more commotion. If not for a quick-thinking patron one table over who sacrificed his pitcher of ale to douse the blaze, the night could have ended very differently. The fire sizzled out.

While half the patrons fanned the smoke out the door, Leadith sighed with relief and pinched the little stone to put it back in the vial. But she didn't expect something so small could still be so hot. With a yelp, she dropped the little stone like a hot coal and stuck her finger in her mouth.

In a matter of seconds, sparks rippled across the surface again and it threatened to burst into flame.

"Give me this," said the man next to her. He grabbed the vial out of her hand to scoop up the bean, then jammed the cork in the end and gave it a twist. The fire faded, then snuffed out, leaving behind two pebbles that glowed a brilliant white.

Leadith snatched at the vial, but he held it out of reach.

"Methinks you need to be protected from this," he said. "But the brilliance does astonish. What causes it to shine so?"

Again, Leadith grabbed at the vial like a child being teased from her favorite toy. The man kept her away, enjoying Leadith's breasts mashed against his face; after all, he'd sacrificed his hat and believed he deserved something in exchange.

"Such things are not of this world," said one of the patrons, settling down to his ale. "It is a stone wrought from hell's evil fire. A conjuration."

"Perish that!" said Leadith, still swiping at the vial. The man finally gave it over, while groping one of her breasts. She shoved him off. "This is no conjuration," said she, straightening her coif. "These stones were got by alchemy." She wanted no part in the mention of sorcery and witchery. "And alchemy is not conjuring. The king licenses it."

"Let me see this vial," said the apothecary. The men had settled back in their places. He reached out his hand, imploring Leadith. "I swear by God's truth I shall give it back. I want to look on this more closely."

Leadith shook her head adamantly. Now that she'd gotten her vial back she wasn't keen to part with it again.

The apothecary frowned. "If you should want money for this, then you must trust the buyer to examine the goods," he reasoned.

The alchemist's wife bit her bottom lip and shook her head no.

"Goodwife, no one will buy your vial if he cannot hold it in his own hand. We are reputable businessmen," he said. "We only wish to confirm that these stones are not trickery."

Leadith's face grew more red. "You just saw what they are capable of. It is no conjuration or trick that makes them behave thus."

"Then you must look elsewhere for a taker." And the men around the table nodded in agreement.

Leadith realized she risked losing their interest if she did not consent to their examining the vial. She looked round at the men, wondering if she could trust them. They were of some money and because of it Leadith assumed they were probably honorable. Surely if one were to abscond with the vial, the others would stop him. These were men who could not abide another man's deceitful gain. Her eyes traveled back to the apothecary. Reluctantly, she handed over the vial. "Only you may touch it."

The vial illuminated the man's face, which beheld a childlike fascination, except that his bulbous nose looked like the red bottom of a baboon.

"Does your husband know how to make more?" he inquired.

Leadith's eyes slid away. "This is all there is."

The chandler leaned in to inspect the vial, his mind filling with possibilities. If no one else could see the value in this little glowing vial, then he might have it for a song. "How much do you want?" he asked, eliciting a hard look from the apothecary, who handed the vial back to the alchemist's wife.

"Well now," said she, feeling the air shift in her favor. She cocked her head to the side and started high. "Two . . . gold . . . sovereigns."

The candlemaker stared at her with flat, humorless eyes. "My lady, you should be glad to get what you can. This is a dangerous substance. Do you believe you have the means to prevent it from causing harm to others? I suggest that you rid yourself of this hazardous object—before you find yourself in trouble."

"I want what I deserve," said Leadith. "I undertook a great deal of risk bringing it here."

The apothecary resented the chandler's sudden interest in the stones. He quickly made an offer, hoping to persuade Leadith that he was the more serious. "I shall offer you one gold sovereign," he said. "It is a fair price given the nature of this thing."

Leadith perked to hear the offer even though it was less. Still, one sovereign was a good starting point; more than she ever dreamed possible. "Well now. I've got a player." She lifted her chin, feeling more assured. "Sir," she said, facing the chandler. "Would you care to counter?"

In truth, the light produced by this little stone interested the chandler greatly. What if it could be used as a source of light to replace candles? However, the smoke was a detriment, worse than tallows even. He wasn't sure he knew how to control it. Still, the opportunities outweighed the inconvenience. Once he had the element in his possession he would be able to test and understand its nature.

"A sovereign is more than a servant makes in an entire year," he said. Insulting her would not win her, but the woman needed to be set down. Expectations had to be tamped.

But Leadith didn't even flinch. Her brows remained lifted, expectant. A single sovereign would do nicely if he was not willing to counter.

The chandler caved. "One, plus two and six," said he, though it pained him to say it.

Nettled that the chandler would outbid him, the apothecary bid a sum slightly higher.

A third man entered in, just for the joy of pushing up the price.

There began a lively exchange of ever-increasing offers until finally the apothecary literally threw in his hat. The brown topper skidded across the table. "That is it, I can do no more," he said, conceding defeat.

Leadith nodded and glanced round at the men. "Any more offers?" she asked.

She was met with head shaking and a few softly spoken nays.

"Well then, you shall have possession." She held out her hand to the chandler.

"Goodwife," said he. "A man does not carry such sums on his person. This borough is rife with thieves, especially at night. Tell me where you live and I shall have it to you the day after tomorrow."

"Two days!" exclaimed Leadith. "I did not bargain to wait."

"If you desire such a price, then you must exercise patience to get it."

Leadith grumbled, then sighed in resignation. "I will grant you two days. But if you do not come I shall find another taker. I will not wait."

The chandler rose from the table and tucked his chin in deference. "Goodwife," he said. "If our business is done I can escort you to the stairs. We could share a boat back to London."

"Nay," said Leadith, not entirely trusting the likes of him. Besides, she was ready to celebrate her success and waved over the serving wench.

"As you will," he said. "Then inform me where we shall meet?"

Leadith followed him from the table and spoke in confidence, securing the details of their future meeting.

The men round their table watched, as did the patrons of the Dim Dragon Inn. All returned to their revel; all except one.

CHAPTER 7

The apothecary watched the alchemist's wife return to the table. With the chandler gone and another ale about to gurgle in the woman's gut, he might be able to convince her to part with that vial of glowing pebbles. He may not possess the monetary resources of the chandler, but he could appeal to her humanity. Though he wasn't sure she had any.

She *was* a white witch, or so she claimed. The sorry lot of them knew scarce little about disease or the human condition, had never heard of Paracelsus—the great healer—and certainly had no working knowledge of balancing a person's humors in order to bring about healing. Most of these women were nothing more than windbags capable of strident gabbling tailored to persuade peasants into believing that their mole butter or bottled breath of grasshopper would heal the tetters or an arthritic knee.

In his experience, a white witch's survival was tenuous at best. They cared for the poor and took their pay in barter. It was an economy of desperation—though it did serve its purpose. The church no longer had the means to help the destitute; they could barely survive themselves after Henry and his chief minister, Cromwell, closed the monasteries and appropriated all their wealth. Not only did this woman subsist by peddling a kind of false hope, but she shared her life with a master of delusion—an alchemist.

Nye Standish had decided long ago that alchemists were desperate men. He found most of them scatty-eyed and strange. They clung to their superstitions, their compulsive behaviors, thinking that the discovery of the stone came from strict adherence to a surreptitious method usually of their own making with no basis in fact. If there was one thing that all alchemists had in common, it was their ability to deceive.

Sometimes an alchemist would wander into his shop and ask for cormorant's blood, or lead fume. At first, he welcomed their business and thought nothing of cultivating the trust of almost any man who walked through his door. In time he'd learned, unfortunately by mistake, not to extend credit to these fraudsters, and now he could pick them out as swiftly as a terrier could rout out a rat.

For all of their wasted noodling, occasionally one of them might genuinely discover something useful. Perhaps these glowing pebbles might actually be the rudiments of a wondrous medicine. Well, thought Standish, watching the woman settle in at the table and order up another pottle pot, perhaps he might appeal to her better nature.

"Goodwife," he began. "I expect that you want the full amount the chandler has promised. However, what say you to a lesser amount . . . now? Think on it. You have the convenience of money in your pocket with no delay."

Leadith took up the ale the serving trull set before her. Her eyes fixed on the apothecary as she tipped the tankard to her lips and were still on him when she set it down. "By lesser amount, how much do ye mean?" she asked, entertaining the idea.

"A crown and two shilling," said Standish, laying his purse upon the table and keeping his hand on it. "Accepting my offer would be an act of charity. For I believe I can make an exceptional medicine from these little beans."

Leadith studied him as best she could.

Standish noticed the slight sway of her body, the compulsive blinking him into focus that comes from too much drink. "My work will benefit humanity, and if you resist your greed for money it would serve your soul. Verily, you might avoid purgatory altogether."

"God's blood!" said Leadith, boldly dispelling the notion, then covering her mouth. She quickly made the sign of the cross with her other hand.

"You may not have the funds to afford prayers of intercession, but God looks kindly on those who seek to help their fellow man."

The men at the table perked to hear this battle of conscience. Not many of them thought the apothecary had anything in mind but his own self-interest. They'd seen him clench his jaw as the chandler outbid his best offer. However, he was a clever man appealing to the woman's higher nature. He might secure the glowing beans at an affordable price, her soul be damned.

But Leadith Browne had lived with God's unpredictable reward system for too long to think that life after death would be any better than what she already knew. She was of a mind that "God helps those who help themselves," and wasn't this a prime example?

"Ye have to do better than that for me to bite," she said.

The men at the table looked from Leadith to the apothecary, their heads swiveling as if they were watching bandy ball in Spitalfields.

Nye Standish took off his shoe and from it produced one penny more.

The corner of Leadith's mouth turned up in condescension. "Ye do no better?"

"This is all I have," he said, hating that she should mock him so. He'd never met a more duplicitous creature.

"It isn't good enough." And with a dismissive lift of her nose she pushed the purse and penny back to Nye Standish.

The apothecary glared at Leadith. He swiped up his purse and cinched it tight. "Very well, Goodwife. I've done my best." He rose from the board. "May God have mercy on your covetous soul."

* * *

"Methinks ye insulted the man," said a table mate to Leadith as they watched the apothecary stalk out the door.

"Why should I sell for a loss?" Leadith waved the air in front of her face like she was batting away a nigglesome fly. "So I wait another day." She leaned over and nearly toppled doing so. "I deserve my due."

The alchemist's wife uprighted herself and returned to her ale, nursing it while listening to men talk about the king's plans to invade France and his efforts to subjugate the wily Scots in the North. She hardly noticed the blister forming on her finger from touching the hot stone. Her attention wandered and she leaned back to gaze around the room. It was a pleasant enough boozing ken, though the place smelled of spilled ale and stale farts.

Her arm went up to wave over the serving wench when a discomfited look came over her face. She got to her feet. It took some effort to do so, but she managed to wend through the maze of tables—which seemed many more than when she had first arrived—then pulled open the door. Outside, the night air hung about her heavy and lifeless, sodden from the recent rain. She took a moment to locate the direction of the Thames and to see where the building ended and where she might find a discreet spot to sprinkle.

No one passed on the lane and she could have crouched where she stood, but even in her squiffy state she remained prudish, wanting her privacy. With a concerted effort she followed the profile of the building, crabbing down its length and around its corner.

A cat leapt from a barrel and brushed against her as it escaped. The space could not be called an alley; it was merely a gap between two buildings—a rare occurrence in this warren of rents and establishments one abutting the other.

Finishing her business, she arranged her skirt and tucked her hair back under her coif. She hoped she could hail a wherry to take her home at this late hour. A measly coin rattled in her purse, but she was glad to have it, thanks be to the silly men who willingly bought her ale. Peeking out from the corner of the Dim Dragon, she saw that no one had followed her. She stepped into the lane and launched herself in the direction of the river and a ferry ride home.

Leadith thought of the money she would soon have, and as she lumbered down the road she congratulated herself for being so clever. "Cunning, I is!" she said to a rat feeding on a pile of rubbish. "Indeed, that is I!" A dog ran up to sniff her and she pointed to herself. "Sooooo . . . wily, am I!" She gave the dog a swift boot, then giggled. Her giggles turned into a hearty laugh.

She stopped a moment and looked around. Was her mind playing tricks on her? Had she heard someone cough? If only the street would just hold still. She wobbled where she stood, squinting and closing one eye and then the other. The lane appeared empty as far as she could tell. Leadith patted the vial of glowing stones in her purse, wishing the road was not so dark. "Why don't ye hang out lamps to light the way?" she asked the buildings. "They do it in London," she complained. She stumbled on, shrugging off her fear of the dark—when a thought occurred to her. Why not light her own way? Congratulating herself for yet another clever idea, she fumbled with her purse and pulled out the vial.

The small vial illuminated better than a lantern and she happily followed its bright glow as she wove a sinuous path down the lane. As she neared the end of the street she heard the heavy tread and breath of someone splashing through puddles behind her. Leadith hardly had time to react. She whirled around, but the distance had already been closed. Someone seized her arm and yanked her into an alley.

Leadith recognized who grabbed her. At least she had the sense to hold on to the vial and valiantly resisted having it prized from her hand. In spite of her sozzled state, her grip did not falter. She held her ground, but a slap across the face made her reel. The sting spread across her cheek and she staggered backward. "You'll not get this," she hissed, catching her balance. "It is mine!"

Her defiance was suitably rewarded.

A punch to her jaw lifted her off her feet. Down she went, hitting the ground as hard as a falling tree. For a moment, she lay still. Her whimpers sounded faint to her ears, becoming distant and disconnected. Beneath her bruised cheek the cobbles made a harsh pillow. Her head throbbed against them—unforgiving and wet. She couldn't tell if she lay in a puddle or in blood.

It would have been easy to give in to the pain; to lie there and let the cool drops of rain soak her skin. The rain grew louder and she began to drift, feeling herself dissolve into oblivion.

But a sudden crushing weight forced the air from her lungs. Her eyes flew open and she gasped. She struggled for breath against a sharp knee pressed in her ribs. Gulping, she screamed with every last ounce of strength she possessed.

A hand dropped over her mouth and covered her nostrils.

Leadith grabbed hold of the wrist and her other hand resisted the vial being wrenched from her grasp. But the hand slid to her throat and tightened its grip. A thumb dug into her windpipe and she desperately tried to pry the fingers off. She thought she was surely finished, when a sudden surge of vigor coursed through her body. With an ear-piercing scream, she bucked free of her assailant and rolled out from under him.

Leadith attempted scrambling out of reach, but her knees caught on her kirtle. She grabbed hold of her dress, still clinging to the precious element. But just as she gathered her skirt, a sickening tug on her ankle yanked her backward and she clawed at the cobbles while being dragged.

In the scuffle, the cork fell out of the vial and the stones spilled on the ground.

They both saw it. One stone skittered away, landing in a puddle. Its light snuffed and disappeared. The glow from the other stone faded in the damp, but Leadith trained her eyes to where it fell. She dared not blink for fear she would lose sight of it. Her vision danced from too much ale, and the wisp of light doubled and began spinning. She dove where she thought the stone might be, scrabbling after it.

Barely missing an angry lunge, she snatched up the stone and got to her feet. Victorious, Leadith peeked at the luminescent treasure and remembered the apothecary's intent to use it in a medicine. It would come out the other end in a day or two, and so Leadith put the stone in her mouth.

With a defiant glint in her eyes, she swallowed.

"Coads nigs! Ye stupid calf!"

And again, Leadith felt the ground beneath her cheek.

With every punishing blow Leadith lost her ability to fight. For however wet and slimy she found that dank alley, she clung to its unforgiving cobbles, dug her fingers into the crevices between pavers as blood ran from her mouth. She could do little more than curl into a ball and wish it over.

Her mind emptied of thought. Time became irrelevant as the pummeling continued and she began to lose consciousness. She could no longer distinguish between the dark of the alley and the dark of her dreams.

But from somewhere came a familiar voice. Who? Who was it? Leadith heard feet hitting the earth, splatting through mud in a run. A moment later a hand took hold of her arm and shook her. She blinked, trying to see.

The face did not comfort.

Leadith pulled away and cursed. "Don't ye touch me, ye lecher. I'd rather die in this alley than be saved by you." She got to her knees and sat back on her haunches. "Leave me or I shall scream and bring all of this stinking borough to running."

"You are confused. Let me help you."

"There's no help that is worth your company for even a pissing moment. Get away or I will scream."

"Fool woman. You don't even know what is good for you."

"Good for me? Ha! You're a fine one to advise. Get out and leave me be. I am warning you." Leadith staggered to her feet, swaying. An arm draped over her shoulders and encouraged her to lean in for support.

But she wanted none of this. With a vicious growl she pushed herself free. She tripped over her own feet and stumbled backward. "Get away! I'll not have you touch me."

"You idiot woman."

Incensed, Leadith loosed a scream that flushed mice from their hidey-holes.

"Clamp your mouth or I shall stuff it."

"Do your worst," dared Leadith.

Fool woman. Earlier that evening, she had asked that she get what she rightly deserved.

And she did.

CHAPTER 8

Bianca suffered through another restless night of sleep, where phantom dreams lurked in the corners of her mind and taunted her with whispers of fire and death. She sat up drenched from a febrile sweat, her hair damp against her head, elflocked from tossing this last hour. If she had stayed up all night she might have felt more rested.

She saw no hint of John across the room or lying in her bed. Then she vaguely recalled him getting up and kissing her goodbye. "Sleep," he had said. "You need your rest."

Once her mind had cleared, she dressed, then sat at the board chewing on a stale end of bread and sipping the last of her ale. She heard a knock at the door and nearly stepped on Hobs as he ran across her path on her way to answer it.

Cammy Dawney looked as surprised to see Bianca as Bianca was to see her.

"How now, Cammy? This is unexpected. How did you find me?"

The girl's eyes were wide with what Bianca assumed was alarm. Looking beyond Bianca, she sidled past and stepped into the rent.

"Goodwife Frye told me where to find you. She pointed me in the right direction and said to turn at a smelly pen of chickens. I wouldn't trouble you if it wasn't important. There's been a murder in an alley near the Dim Dragon. A woman has been stabbed."

"It is not unusual for someone to end at the point of a knife here in Southwark."

"She was at the Dim Dragon last night. I served her table."

"Granted, that is upsetting, but why seek me? You should tell the constable."

"He's been summoned, but Goodwife Frye wants you. She said you have more sense than any bleating, brazen-faced beck. She worries the Dim Dragon will be needlessly dragged through the muck."

The side of Bianca's mouth turned up in a crooked smile. "I fear it is too late for that. The Dragon's reputation is not the most honorable." She pulled on her stockings and shoes and let Hobs out to terrorize the neighborhood. "Still, if the Goodwife has asked for me, I will oblige."

As the two walked to the Dim Dragon Inn, Cammy talked about the woman's brash behavior and what she had seen the night before. "She had a glass vial that glowed as bright as a room of lit candles. Never have I witnessed anything so unusual. She had the attention of nearly every person in the ken." Cammy pulled the container out of her pocket and handed it over.

Bianca stopped to examine the vial. She ran it under her nose but didn't detect a smell. Nor did she see any remnants of glowing beans.

"Was this on her person?"

"It lay near her body."

Bianca offered it back.

"I don't want it," said Cammy.

"What was she doing with the vial?"

"She was trying to sell whatever was in it. I don't know if she did. The patrons kept me busy. But the men at her table kept buying her ale. And to her foolish heart, she didn't stop them."

"What was her name?"

"I do not know. It seems she came from London. She'd never been to the Dim Dragon before."

They angled down a lane past a bawd house, silent and still in the morning hours as if sleeping off a crapulous night.

"When did you learn of her death? Who discovered her body?"

"One of the cooks happened on her. Webster was coming in this morning when he needed to piss. He ducked into an alley and found her. He'd barely made himself decent before barging through the door of the Dragon blaring like a set of wailing bagpipes.

"'Someone did her!' he shrieked. 'Someone finished that woman from last night!'" Cammy shuddered. "I don't like knives," she said. "Maybe ye learn to expect that folks will end badly in Southwark. There's plenty of destitute drabs who will find their grave at Cross Bones without anyone to utter a prayer to speed their soul. But it chills my blood seeing a woman slit by a man's blade."

"You believe a man stabbed her?" asked Bianca.

"What kind of woman stabs another woman?" said Cammy. "I've never seen or heard of it. Have you?"

Bianca ran through her collective memory of murders. "I regret to say that I have." Women poisoned other women, women cheered at executions and threw buckets of rotten table scraps on the accused. And yes, the mutilation of flesh, by knife—that masculine weapon—was not a crime reserved for men.

"He took Tendle—the kitchen boy—and me to the alley. There she was, on the cobblestones like she was sleeping. Lying in a pool of blood."

"No one has moved her?"

"Nay, Goodwife Frye wanted you to see her first. She's set Tendle and Webster to keep an eye out."

The two turned down the lane where the Dim Dragon was and Cammy showed Bianca the narrow alley where the body lay. A couple of neighbors took exception when Webster and Tendle let the two women through while they had to stay back.

As it was, the alley was as black as a plague pit. Its angle refused the morning light so that Bianca had to send Tendle for a lantern. She laid her hand on Cammy's back, letting the girl lead her to the body.

"Here," said Cammy, pointing.

After a moment, Bianca's eyes adjusted to the dark. The dim shape of a woman lay on the cobbles. Her coif and hair rail were askew, her tumble of hair covered her cheek and mouth. Bianca knelt beside the body and lifted the hair off her face. The woman's cheek bulged and Bianca could faintly make out the woman's mouth, open and crammed with what appeared to be grass.

"Someone has stuffed her mouth."

Cammy squat down beside her. "To keep her from screaming?"

"Possibly." After studying the position of the woman's body, Bianca gently rolled her over. The dark prevented her from seeing details, but she felt the woman's bodice and traced the blood with her fingertips to the wound. "She's been stabbed in the liver." She pushed her fingers through the tear in the kirtle and felt the length of the laceration. "The killer took time to cut her."

"A simple stab was not enough?" asked Cammy.

"She might have fought back. The killer wasn't content to just puncture her."

Cammy took the purse dangling from the woman's belt and felt a small weight inside. Its only contents was a ha' penny.

By now, word of the woman's death had made its rounds through the neighborhood and a small crowd had gathered at the end of the alley. Several shouted, asking after the victim.

"She's not from Southwark," yelled Cammy. "She was from London. We don't know her name."

A few of the onlookers lost interest and moved on. If it didn't concern one of their own, then they had no use for it.

While they waited for Tendle to return, Bianca scanned the ground for signs of the glowing element. Nothing caught her eye. There were plenty of puddles, and if a stone had fallen into one she would not see it. She would have to return to the alley later when she could search without anyone watching.

As Cammy discussed what she had observed about the woman,

the bystanders took exception to being jostled by a brassy-tongued authority demanding that they give way. Tendle appeared first, his wide eyes fully illuminated by the lantern, and fast on his heels was a visibly vexed constable.

"Give us leave!" he shouted, as if it was a massive crowd he needed to get through.

Bianca got to her feet and cursed under her breath.

"Who is he?" asked Cammy in a low voice.

Bianca turned her back toward the approaching lawman. "You'll soon find out."

The constable shouldered past the last of the spectators and took a moment to brush off his popingay blue velvet doublet with polished brass buttons. He adjusted the flatcap on his head and straightened his exceptionally large codpiece.

"Wells now," says he. "What have we here?"

Instead of his eyes resting on the dead woman lying at his feet (which one would normally expect for a man of his position), they came to rest on Bianca. It was *not* the corpse to which he was referring.

Bianca nodded in slight acknowledgment. "Constable Patch."

"Last I knew ye was mangling with goldsmiths and such." He appeared delighted to see that this was no longer the case.

"Sirrah, you must remember how that ended? I am glad to return to Southwark and have John's master installed in his former home on Foster Lane instead of Newgate Prison. All is as it should be. Except it makes me wonder why you are not in your ward across the river?"

Constable Patch's mouth twisted as if the words had trouble finding their way out. "It seems the fellow who took over the ward here in Southwark was unceremoniously mauled by one of the bears at the baiting garden. I am told there is some confusion over how it happened. They claim he crawled into the cage on a bet." Patch rolled his weaselly brown eyes. "But methinks he was probably placed there. Someone liked him not."

"So you have been assigned to Southwark?"

"Temporarily!" Patch emphasized. "Until they find someone with the prowess to handle this knotty ward. It is a tall order."

Bianca was certain there was some truth to this. She doubted anyone knew when to look the other way better than he.

Bianca noticed Patch eyeing Cammy. From the look on his face, he had taken an instant dislike to her, if only because Cammy's shoulders were broader than his, mused Bianca. "Cammy is a serving wench at the Dim Dragon," she said by way of introduction. "Apparently the victim was well plied with ale when she left the inn last night."

Patch's eyes lingered on Cammy, deciding whether the girl could be trusted.

Bianca continued. "The victim has a sizable laceration. Whoever ended her life made sure she would die." Constable Patch reluctantly turned his attention to Bianca while she surmised, "Either this person harbors a personal hatred for this woman, or he can't control a fiendish impulse to inflict suffering on his victim."

Patch's eyebrows raised. He pulled Tendle over and positioned the lantern, then bent over the body to look at it. He suddenly straightened as something occurred to him. "I suppose it pleases ye to crawl"—and here he mimed the act of crawling with his hands—"into a murderer's mind and presume to know how he thinks." Patch pinched back a mocking smile. "But I see no purpose to congitate with evil."

"Do you mean cogitate?" asked Cammy, brightly.

Patch's smug expression fell. "Suppose one of ye tells me what happened last night?"

Cammy launched into an account of the woman showing off a vial of glowing beans. Patch had no interest in studying the body of a woman who probably could have crushed his thigh bones if she'd sat in his lap. Instead, he listened with surprising attentiveness to Cammy telling her tale. The glowing beans intrigued him. He asked for Cammy to repeat her story about the smoke and sparks and fire.

The light from the lantern began to dwindle. Bianca quietly listened to Cammy talk and tried to commit the dead woman's face to memory before they were back in the dark. She noted darkened bruising about her neck but didn't interrupt Cammy to mention it.

Despite Patch's excitement over the glowing element, Bianca kept her father's part in this to herself. Constable Patch's memory was long and he knew about Albern Goddard's ignoble reputation. It was this fact alone that kept Bianca forever on her guard when dealing with him.

"What is in her mouth?" asked Patch, finally noticing.

"It looks to be grass," said Bianca. She kneeled and carefully removed the wad from the victim's mouth. Fingering a wilted flower, she sniffed its leaves. "I am wrong. It is meadowsweet."

"God's bones!" exclaimed Cammy, pointing at the woman's face.

At first Bianca didn't see what she was looking at. Then, in the still-dim light of the alley, she saw an eerie green vapor hovering over the woman's mouth.

"Jesu!" cried Patch, stepping backward. "What manner of evil have ye wrought?"

"I've not done anything," said Bianca. "I simply removed the plug in her mouth."

Cammy took a step back. "What would cause such a thing?"

In a matter of seconds the emanation vanished.

"Ye saw it?" cried Patch, rubbing his eyes and wondering what sort of humbuggery he'd just been party to.

"Aye," said Bianca, taking the lantern and trying to see into the woman's mouth, without success.

"It was her soul departing," said Patch. He made the sign of the cross but remained skittish.

"I smell garlic," said Bianca, and looked up at Cammy.

"Wells," said the constable. He thumped Tendle on the chest and the boy winced. "Get the sexton at St. Saviour and tell him he's got a body. You," he said, pointing a finger in Cammy's face, "stay with the body until they return. And you"—he then jabbed his finger in Bianca's face—"are coming with me to the Dim Dragon."

* * *

The boozing ken burred with the sound of neighbors speculating about the woman's murder. Once word had spread about the strange glowing vial, the Dim Dragon filled with familiar faces and not so familiar, all yammering, postulating as to who the victim was, where had she gotten the fiery stones, and who sliced her.

Constable Patch stood inside the door with Bianca behind him and immediately grew agitated with all the commotion. He walked up to a bench and ordered an elderly man to slide over. When the fellow didn't move fast enough he stepped on the man's hand as he got up on the table.

"Silence!" Patch glared round at the room and puffed out his chest. He waited until he had everyone's attention. "It seems there has been an unfortunate murder associated with this ken," he began. He didn't bother to introduce himself. Apparently he assumed everyone knew who he was. A few patrons did remember, and his name was repeated in low murmurs to confused clientele.

"Now, I'd likes to take care of this in as deficient a manner as possible." He looked down at the bewildered faces staring up at him. "First offs. Does anyone know the victim's name?"

"Leadith," called a man from the back.

"Leadith," repeated Constable Patch. He scanned the room looking for the fellow who spoke. "Does Leadith have a surname?"

"Browne," said the man, getting to his feet.

"Brun?" echoed Patch.

"He's Scottish!" yelled a second man.

Patch blinked.

"Browne," shouted a third man.

"And does anyone know where Leadith . . . Browne is from?"

"She's a white witch by Trintery Lane," offered the Scot.

Patch tugged his scraggy chin hair, thinking.

"He means Trinity Lane."

"Her husband is a metal cheat," the man continued.

"An alchemist," interpreted Bianca.

"And ye is?" asked Patch.

"William Thomson."

Constable Patch nodded and continued to finger his scarce beard. "So's how do ye knows this?"

"I've bought her remedies."

"Did anyone else speak to the wench?"

Not a single hand raised or waved for attention. Constable Patch frowned as he ran his eyes over the clientele. "Not a ones of you?"

A more astute lawman would have realized that the ken, or for that matter, any ken in slithery Southwark, was filled with thieves, criminals, and malcontents. These sorts were the least likely to tattle about anything they might or might not have seen, be the constable respectable or not. They kept their counsel and remained faces in a crowd. On some level, some very reptilian-brained level, Constable Patch knew this. He sought the Scot with the incomprehensible accent. "And William Thomson," he said, "what more can ye tell us?"

The Scot's posture was impressive. His shoulders were as broad as the portcullis at South Gate, and his assured manner elicited a certain amount of respect even for a resident alien. "I dinnae know. I only overheard a bit. I was playing Pope Joan with me table."

Constable Patch stared at the Scot, waiting for him to continue. When Thomson did not, he turned to Bianca, who shrugged.

"We knows she hads some wondrous stones she was trying to sell." Patch looked around at the faces staring up at him. "Does anyone know who entertained buying them?"

No one offered a name. This group kept its tongue in a box.

Patch grumbled, which only assured a complete lack of cooperation. "Wells, if any of ye knows anything else of importance," he said, realizing he was getting nowhere, "anything ye think might be useful, ye needs to tell me. A woman from London has been murdered in a not so subtle way." He ran his eyes around the room one last time, then climbed off the table.

"Ye see what else ye might learn," he said to Bianca. "I'm going to Queenhithe Ward to find this alchemist named Browne and tell him his wife is done."

CHAPTER 9

After Constable Patch left the Dim Dragon Inn, another wave of nausea made Bianca's stomach sour. She hurried back to her room of Medicinals and Physickes to finish off the remainder of her mother's concoction and to make new. Hobs caught sight of her at the corner and left his spot in the sun to follow her home.

She was busy chopping mint and raspberry leaves when Meddybemps called through the open door. "How now, my soldier?" he said, dipping his head to clear the lintel.

He walked over to the table and dropped a bundle of flowers next to her.

"What is this?" she said, stopping her work, knowing full well exactly what the flowers were.

"Meadowsweet for my sweet!" said the street peddler, bowing low and sweeping off his red cap in a grand gesture.

"Why are you giving them to me?"

"It is in bloom," he said. His one eye veered away from center as was its habit, especially when the streetseller had cause to wonder. "You can use them in your remedies." Then, noting the tepid reception to his gift, he added, "Or so I thought." Meddybemps wiped his forehead on his sleeve. His sparse hair sprouted from his scalp like the points on a nautical star.

"Where did you get it?"

"In the fields near Broadwall. Are you not pleased?"

Bianca resumed chopping her herbs.

Puzzled by her reaction, Meddybemps tried cajoling her out of silence. "What are you making?" The girl had a generous helping of black bile coursing through her veins at any given time, and the best way to squelch its influence was to get her to talk about her latest experiment.

"This isn't for market. It is for me."

"You? I daresay you rarely need your remedies."

"I do now."

Meddybemps tipped his head. "What secret do you keep? Prithee, what ails?"

With the blade of her knife, Bianca swept the herbs into a pan. "It is no illness, but a condition. One that shall pass in time."

Her hint fed his curiosity and the iris of his errant eye appeared to skip. Taking a moment to study her, he asked, "Are you with child?"

Bianca checked the firebox of her stove and scraped out the ashes.

"Go to!" said Meddybemps. He danced a little jig, his bony elbows and knees jutting all akimbo like a skeleton. He took hold of Bianca's hands and danced her around the room, twirling her once and making her smile. He looked so foolish, how could she not?

> "With a hey and a ho,
> The gentle spring knows,
> That a babe doth bloom
> in a young maid's womb.
>
> And the pink of her cheek
> Did the lucky John seek
> To rival the blush of a rose?

With a nod and a wink
This rogue does think
That while birds build their nests and sing—

These lovers so fair, this lady so fine,
Gave her dearly beloved his best Valentine.
With a hey and a ho,
The gentle wind blows and
Ding a ding ding the birds doth sing."

Pleased to see his prodigy smile, he sat her down on the bench and got her an ale.

"Nay," said Bianca, waving it away. "I do not want it. This is what I need." She held up the pan of herbs. "A recipe of Mother's."

Meddybemps settled opposite his young charge and, since she had rejected his offering, helped himself to the brew. He took a sip, happy to think of Bianca becoming a mother. But her complexion appeared off. "What might I do to help? You look as green as the pilings at Molestrand Dock."

Bianca absently ran a finger through the mound of meadowsweet. "Meddy, have you knowledge of a woman named Leadith Browne?"

"Why do you ask?"

"I asked you first."

Meddybemps took a drink of ale. "Nay, I do not."

"Nay, you do not know anything of her? Or nay, you have not met her?"

"Aye."

"Aye . . . what?"

The streetseller looked into his drink and swirled the dregs of ale. "The name is not familiar."

Bianca scowled as she studied him. "She was stabbed in an alley near the Dim Dragon last night."

"A not so gentle end."

"Her mouth was stuffed with meadowsweet."

"How inventive. I daresay someone found the need to stop her mouth."

"Indeed," mused Bianca, propping her chin in her hand. "Apparently she was a neighborhood white witch."

"Where?"

"Queenhithe Ward. Not far from Lambeth Hill."

"Near your childhood home," said Meddybemps, stating the obvious. He scratched a stain on the table with a fingernail.

Bianca debated whether to tell him about her father's discovery. She decided not to mention it.

"Something exceptional happened when I pulled the meadowsweet out of her mouth," continued Bianca, looking up at him. "The air glowed green."

Meddybemps' lazy eye swerved. "Glowed green?" He scratched his balding pate. "The air—where—glowed green?"

"The air over her mouth. Just above it."

"I've never seen nor heard of such a spectacle," Meddybemps said in wonderment. "How long did this miracle last?"

"Only a few seconds. I wasn't the only one who saw it."

"What would cause such a thing?"

Bianca pushed out the bench and stood. "I cannot imagine." She carried the pan of herbs to the stove.

"Are you involving yourself in this murder?" Not getting a response, he chided, "What does your intrepid warrior husband say about this? He worries after you so, and now with a child to think of . . ."

"He likes it not." Bianca ladled some water into her pan. "I'm only asking a few questions because Goodwife Frye asked it of me."

Meddybemps finished his drink and gave a small snort. Bianca irritably set about starting a fire. She had just got it sparked when a distraction arrived in the form of Constable Patch.

"Wells now," he said, entering without invitation. He looked around at the clutter that Bianca called her room of Medicinals and Physickes and the end of his thin nose flared. He did not care for the smells that lingered, or rather festered, there. He recalled a time, just over a year ago, when her board was laid out with dissected rats. The gristle had dangled from her wiry black locks, making her look as dotty as an inmate at Bedlam on the night of a full moon.

Adding to his disapproval was Bianca's questionable taste in company. He drew up short at the sight of Meddybemps with his unnatural eyeball lolling about. He threw back his shoulders when he realized the two of them were staring at him with something less than respect in their eyes.

"I have come from Leadith Browne's residence and have spoken to the husband. He calls himself Dikson . . . Browne." Patch tugged down the edge of his doublet, which only drew attention to his codpiece fashioned in stiff leather overly stuffed with bombast. In his opposite hand he held a bundle of cloth. "As ye know, Browne is an alchemist." The constable watched Bianca fiddle with the fire in her small stove. "I am not so sure," said he, "that this man is altogether truthful."

"What makes you think that?" asked Bianca, still more interested in her stove than in whatever he had to say.

"He denied knowing anything about his wife's death. And he showed a lack of surprise when I tolds him she'd been shanked."

"Mayhap the man was relieved," suggested Meddybemps.

Patch eyed him curiously. "Relieved?"

Always the advocate for staying free of marriage's tethers, the street peddler gave a droll smile. "Some men are glad to be rid of an ungrateful wench. Once bound, their contract *is* until death do thee part."

Patch's eyes shifted to Bianca, who seemed untroubled by her acquaintance's insolent remark. He thought of his own wife berating him for having to return to Southwark and a tatty rent next to a butcher, where the squeal of pigs being slaughtered woke her in the morning. He had honestly thought she might appreciate the convenience of not having to walk far for her pork. "What I be saying is I thinks the man is covering the truth. And I can't begin to decipher his twisted mind—especially he bein' a puffer." He waited for Bianca to respond. When she didn't, he said, "That's what I want ye for, Bianca Goddard. Ye understand the way these types work. I want ye to come with me to listen to his story."

Bianca had just got the fire going and was watching the bubbles collect on the bottom of her pan. She knew that if she refused Patch he would continue to hound her. For a small investment in time she could appease him and avoid subjecting herself to his endless pestering. "I'll finish this, then I will come."

Satisfied, Patch wittered on about the fiery stones and the green glow emanating from the victim's mouth. Bianca snuck a peek at Meddybemps. She had purposely failed to bring up the glowing stones, thinking the streetseller might mention them and thus prove that he knew something about what had happened. But his expression gave nothing away.

Instead, they both listened to Patch speculate about the evil emanation, putting forth his superstitious explanations (of which there were several). Having nearly worn them both out, Meddybemps finally interrupted.

"Constable, the lady's death is certainly troubling, and these stones of which you speak are like nothing I've heard of. But, what do you carry in that bundle? What is it that you must bind so tightly in cloth?"

Patch blinked, having completely forgotten what he had so carefully transported across Southwark. "Oh! This," he remembered, unswaddling his bundle on the table. "This . . . is the murder weapon." With the last fold of increasingly stained cloth he uncovered a knife still tacky with blood.

Bianca's breath caught in her throat. "Where was it found?" she asked. Her voice sounded small.

Patch's gaze shifted between Bianca and Meddybemps. "It was in a barrel behind the Dim Dragon Inn."

Meddybemps balked. "A barrel? That is of no relevance. How can you be sure it is the murder weapon?"

"By matter of interference, of course." Patch explained his theory. "It's got bloods on it." He picked up the knife and showed the blade, holding it to within an inch of Bianca's nose and then Meddybemps's.

"It doesn't mean that the blood is Leadith Browne's," said Bianca.

Patch looked dubious. "If not hers, then whose?" He sighed as if his patience were being tested by children.

Bianca spoke. "It *was* in the back of an inn. The cook might have lost it in his scraps when he dumped them."

"What's the likelihood of thats?" asked Patch. "No one recognized it when I asked."

"Well," said Meddybemps. "What fool would claim it if they know that a murder had just happened?"

"Be that as it may," said Patch, "this would be a useless knife in a kitchen. Not something to be used to filet fish or hack meat."

"May I see it?" asked Bianca. She carried it to the light of the open door and studied the carved handle, turning it over. It was remarkably similar to the one her mother used to chop raspberry leaves the day before.

"If you will excuse me," said Meddybemps, putting on his cap and nodding to them both. "I must be away to ply my wares. Bianca," he said, catching her eye and nodding farewell as he edged past.

Patch watched the streetseller exit. "Methinks the man is squeamish about knives."

Chapter 10

Constable Patch hailed a wherry near St. Mary Overie within yards of London Bridge. The tide flowed upriver and Bianca sat in the bow as the boatman pushed them into the current. They rode across with the sun blazing on their cheeks, gilding the water, reminding them that the long days of summer were not so far away.

Remnants of last night's rain had burned off in the sun's strong rays so that when Patch and Bianca climbed the stairs on the opposite shore the streets were only slightly tacky with mud.

They headed up Salt Wharf past cranes used to hoist barrels of goods from ships, and followed Thames Street to St. Michael Queenhithe, where, inside, the monuments were defaced—looking like statues dunked in flour. At Trinity Lane they trod up the hill until Patch stopped at a tenement opposite the failing parish church of Holy Trinity. He rapped on the door while Bianca gazed at the stilts and props supporting the building, now in serious danger of toppling. In a moment, the door opened.

"Is ye father in?" asked Patch of a young boy.

Without a word, the lad let them in. It did not seem to Bianca that he needed to ask permission and it soon became clear why.

Dikson Browne lay sprawled on top of a table, passed out from too much drink, an empty flask on the floor beside him. His belly rose and fell in time with his rattling snores, and the king's cavalry could have driven through his kitchen without him noticing.

Grumbling to find the man in such a condition, Patch leaned close to the offender's ear. "Hie, thy misery has not yet begun, ye stink-breathed, slovenly scoundrel! Ye's as fat as a toad filled with bugs. Get up, ye worthless rascal, or I shall beat yer nose 'til it is level with yer cheeks."

Patch's shrill reprimand tore through Dikson Browne to the part of his brain that was still semiconscious. His eyes shot open, his snores snuffled, and he sat bolt upright as if Gabriel's trumpet had just tooted in his ear.

"That's better, ye addle-brained conniver. I is not done with yous." Patch reveled in his office, especially when he had the upper hand. "Now thens," Patch went on, once Browne had struggled to sit at the edge of the board. "I've a few more questions."

Dikson Browne rubbed his face, trying to make sense of where he was and who these people were standing before him. He was too befuddled to object.

"Was ye or was ye not in Southwark last night?" Patch's voice had not lost any of its bluster.

"I was not," said Browne, finding it difficult to keep from swaying.

"Ye said ye were before. Now which is it?" said Patch.

Browne's attention settled on the constable and he eyed him suspiciously. Had he really incriminated himself? He tried to remember their previous conversation.

"Yer son said ye was missing for a good part of the night," said Patch.

Bianca watched the boy, who was cleaning out the hearth. His sweeping slowed. He didn't turn to face his father or them. She couldn't be sure whether Patch planted this idea to get a reaction from Dikson.

Angered, the alchemist defended himself. "The lad sleeps like the dead. You cannot take a boy's word for what he likely dreamed."

Patch chuckled. "It does not matter if the boy told me the truth. I have conflagration."

Browne's confusion doubled. His face contorted while his mind tried grasping the constable's meaning.

"I has it on good faith that you was seen skulking about the vicinity of the Dim Dragon last night." It wasn't beneath Patch to weave a lie in order to get a rise out of a man. He had no proof of Browne's whereabouts, but he sensed the man's sodden state might be linked to something the man wanted to forget.

"Who?" Browne demanded. "By troth, I slept soundly in my bed. I heard the town watch call one in the night and I looked upon the sheet beside me. My ungrateful, cuckolding wife was not upon it." Browne's second chin wobbled. "She goes where she doth please herself."

"Be that so," said Patch. He pinched his mangy chin hair, delighted to be antagonizing the man. "Have ye done yer duty by her?"

Bianca glanced at the young boy. There was nothing delicate about Constable Patch's questioning.

If Dikson Browne was riled before, he now rose to a new level of outrage. "If, sirrah, you desire to know my business in my marriage bed, then tell me by what authority you ask it?"

"Paa," said Patch, dismissively. "I care not whether ye dock yer goose or stuff her with plum pudding. What I wants to know is, how often did ye beat her?"

Dikson Browne looked at Patch suspiciously, then realized he needn't be offended by the question. "Why, as much as the next man, of course. I did not shirk my responsibility."

The willingness of men to treat their wives and children like property had never set well with Bianca. She'd witnessed her own father's harsh handling of her mother and had, on occasion, been the recipient of her father's discipline. All in the name of making a woman behave since she was by nature and by the devil's hand wanton and sinful. Bianca thought, with gratitude, of John and his reluctance to follow suit. Perhaps some of his restraint came from not having a proper home with a mother and father leading by example—though he had seen plenty living in a barrel behind an inn on Olde Fish Street Hill.

"And dids ye beat her last night?" asked Patch.

The alchemist's eyes bulged, a symptom of his thumping heart.

"Out with it!" Patch shouted. And Bianca startled along with Browne and his son. "Have ye not learned that I will not be trifled with? I'll have ye dragged to the Clink and ye shall suffer the not so gentle prodding of Horace the heathen. I knows him well and he would relish thrashing an alchemist like yeself."

For as unkind as Dikson Browne was to others, he did possess a mote of kindness—but only toward himself. The idea of being incarcerated in the Clink did not appeal to him.

"God's nails, I beat her! I followed her to Bankside and saw her at the Dim Dragon Inn. When she started for home, I dragged her into an alley and I trounced her for her insolence. It is what a man does when he has been so wronged." Lest he be accused of remorse, he added, "She got what she deserved."

Alarmed, Bianca spoke. "Did you, sir, then stab her?"

"That, I did not! Do you take me for a murderer?" He sat up straight, indignant. "By God's own blood, I did not stab her."

"You say she got what she deserved," Bianca insisted.

"Aye, she did! I beat her as is my privilege and God-given right. But if God sees fit to have her finished, then I do not question His wisdom. But I am not a murderer. I swear that I did not finish her."

"And did you, sirrah, know that she had in her possession glowing stones?" asked Bianca.

From the filthy pit of Browne's vindictive heart, a voice warned him to stay his tongue. His sense of self-preservation had not been completely muddled by drink. "Hear me, I believe she sought comradery." It took humility to admit this, but better to pretend it for a fleeting second. "She planted a tree of schemes and finally tasted the fruit of all her evils."

"You might ask to see his knife," said Bianca quietly to Patch. She looked over at the alchemist's son near the hearth. His back remained turned and he leaned on the stick of the broom, his head hanging. She regretted the young boy being privy to their questioning, but the fact that he had lost his mother bothered her more. One could not tread lightly in such a matter. The boy was living with a possible murderer. Still, if he should end on the street as an orphan, what purpose had they served?

Constable Patch agreed. He still had the suspected murder weapon on his person, swaddled in a length of cloth. "Dikson Browne, do ye carry upon yer person a knife?"

"Of course. Who does not?"

"I would like to sees it."

"Why?" objected the alchemist. "It is the only one I own. A man cannot navigate these streets at night without protection!"

Bianca realized the confusion and intervened. "Sir, we only wish to examine your knife. We will give it back."

Browne looked from Bianca to the constable. He leaned over to search the floor for his weapon and came dangerously close to falling off the table. On the other side of the room he spied the belt he had unbuckled in an attempt to get comfortable. It lay half buried in the rushes, having missed its hook on the wall. "Timothy, fetch him my belt," he demanded.

The boy did as he was told.

"This is what ye wear about yer person?" Patch took the belt from the boy.

"Aye," said the alchemist, whose weaving upper body circled as if the room were spinning at a greater speed than before.

Patch looked sharply at the boy for confirmation, and the boy gave it. The constable unhooked the fastening strap and withdrew the dirk from its leather sheath. It was a bullock dagger, one with the hilt carved to mimic the testicles of a bull. The added adornment amused Patch and he couldn't conceal a snide grin. "Such a brutish choice of weapon," he said, securing it back in its guard and crossing the room to hang it on the hook. "And did ye have yer knife with ye last night?"

The alchemist's brows knit in thought. His recollection of the expedition into Southwark was spotty at best. "I would not go across the river without it." He sat a moment with his chin resting on his chest when suddenly his eyebrows parted and a look came over his face as if something else just occurred to him. "When I was disciplining my wife, someone interrupted."

"Aah. So someone saw ye beat her," said Patch.

"A voice came out of nowhere. Yelling. I didn't know if it was a constable or a rascal. I didn't stay to find out."

For a man to run instead of rail revealed cowardice that most men would be ashamed to admit. Bianca and Patch exchanged glances.

"What else? Did ye notice anything about this person?"

Browne rubbed his temple, remembering. "He wore a red cap."

"I thought you ran," said Bianca.

"Well," wavered the alchemist. "I got a look at him."

"Was it not dark in the alley?" asked Bianca. "Be you sure of its color?"

"He was on the street and lit by a lantern. For cert it was red. And the whites of the cozen's eyes shone bright." He scowled and shook his head. "Was strange."

A cold feeling crept down the back of Bianca's neck like a trickle of February rain.

The two left the alchemist's residence, and while Patch commented on the poor condition of the street and Browne's rent, Bianca trundled down Trinity Lane in silence. A witness remembered for the whites of his eyes and a red cap called to mind the only person Bianca knew who might fit that description. She wondered if Patch was thinking of the same person.

If Patch *was* considering Meddybemps, he did not mention it. Instead, the constable complained that he was hungry, and as the two parted ways Bianca left him with the assurance that she would try to find out more. Patch accepted this and ambled off down the road to find an ordinary serving meat pie.

Her parents' rent on Lambeth Hill was only a few streets over. It was late enough in the day that her father would probably be at his alchemy room. Bianca took the opportunity to speak with her mother without him present.

As she made her way there, Bianca considered the possibility of Meddybemps interrupting Leadith's beating. Was it mere coincidence that her mother had been in Southwark just hours before and that the knife in Constable Patch's possession looked identical to her mother's?

Then there was the meadowsweet Meddybemps had brought her hours before. The same herb that had been stuffed in the victim's mouth.

Bianca slogged up Lambeth Hill, thinking on what to say. As she neared her parents' rent, she dawdled, delaying what she believed would be a distressing conversation. What if she sensed her mother was lying? Bianca stood a moment outside the door. She took a breath and knocked.

The door cracked open. "The last time ye visited it was about some fool book and that elixir of death," said her mother, ushering her inside. Her sleeves were rolled to her elbows and she hadn't put on her coif yet. A loose braid reached the middle of her back, needing to be replaited.

"Elixir of immortality," corrected Bianca.

"Whatever the piffling word for it is."

"There is some difference." Bianca looked around and saw that the rent had not changed since the last time she had visited. A cupboard staked claim to the covey where she used to sleep, where she had lain awake at night listening to the mice chew inside the walls and scamper across the rafters. Rows of herbs, tied with string, hung from beams and from pegs driven into walls. Malva's concoctions were simpler than Bianca's and required only pans and basic carrier oils.

"Father is gone?"

"Aye that." Malva was readying a basket of soiled shifts and netherhose. On a day such as this, the sun lured women from their homes to properly wash a winter's collection of soiled wears. The sun could take the sting out of a stream's cold water and make the task less onerous. "And to what do I owe your company?" Malva riffled through a chest of clothing.

"I was near the area."

Her mother responded with a grunt as she removed dirty aprons and shirts and dropped them in the hamper. Bianca couldn't be sure if it was in response to her, or to the plentiful stash of dirty clothing. A particularly soiled apron caught Bianca's eye. "What happened there?" she asked, smelling the iron tang of blood.

"Turner gave me a goose for taking care of his piles. The goose did not go softly." She wadded the garment into a ball and pitched it into her basket. Malva looked up. "How be the remedy for your sickness?"

"Well enough." Bianca pulled over a stool and sat. After a moment her gaze drifted to the herbs overhead. She looked for meadowsweet but did not see any. In as casual a manner as she could manage, she asked her mother whether she had picked the plant while in Southwark.

"Aye, I managed to get there before dark."

"You haven't hung it yet?"

"I gave it to a fellow who needed it."

"You gave it away? You specifically wanted to pick some for yourself."

"I'm not concerned. I can get more." Malva let the lid of the chest drop. "Where is that John of yours?"

Bianca was slow to answer her mother's deft change of topic. "He's at his master's on Foster Lane."

"When is he finishing his apprenticeship?"

"I don't know anymore. It may be delayed."

Her mother lifted the basket to her hip and rested her arm across the dirty laundry. "Delayed? How so?"

"He was summoned to a View of Arms. He may be chosen for the king's army."

"Pish! To fight the French?"

"Mayhap. Though they are not the only ones Henry wants to trounce."

"The king is so fat I pity the horse beneath him." She crossed the room and set the laundry on the table. Her brow lifted, and for the first time since Bianca arrived she looked at her daughter square on. "You're worried if he should go he may not come back."

As much as Bianca tried not to think about it, the possibility stalked her in the quiet hours of the night when her mind could not settle. She blamed her troubled dreams on her fear of losing him. However, with her father's request to find the missing stones and an unfortunate murder to occupy her mind, she had, for the most part, been able to set aside her concerns, at least during the day. But what if John were conscripted and never returned, leaving her alone with a baby to care for?

Bianca broke her mother's gaze. "I can't allow myself to be afraid of what might not be. I will manage." Her words sounded braver than she felt. Perhaps saying them might prepare her for that bleak possibility. Besides, she had no say in the matter.

Apparently, neither mother nor daughter cared to discuss what the other one asked about. Still, Bianca persisted.

"Did you stop at the Dim Dragon to have an ale before you left Southwark?"

Malva's head turned slightly while her eyes stayed on her daughter. Bianca noticed her hesitation before speaking. "I stopped at an inn for an ale," said Malva. "Was it the Dim Dragon? Perchance it was. They serve ale, that is true."

"A sign hangs over the door. A blue-green dragon hoisting a tankard," Bianca prompted.

The corners of Malva's mouth pulled down as a shoulder jerked up in a shrug.

"Did you see Meddybemps last night?"

"Ha! Meddybemps?" said Malva. "Odd you should ask." She put her fists on her hips and looked about the room. "Where did I put the wash soap?" Finally spying it on a shelf near the back door, she went and got it.

Bianca waited for her answer.

"I did see him," said Malva, dropping the soap on top of the clothing. "Purely by chance it was."

"Did you speak?" Bianca's stomach became unsettled.

"We did." Malva nodded slightly but did not offer more.

"It's been a while since you've seen him."

"Aye."

There had been a time in the not so distant past when Meddybemps had taken an unseemly interest in her mother. By then, Bianca had gotten used to Meddybemps's licentious behavior and had simply chosen to ignore it. She'd known him since she was old enough to snitch sausage, and she owed him a measure of gratitude for watching out for her at market when she was keen to cut purses. She'd grown to rely on him and he'd protected her like the daughter he'd never had. But even though Meddybemps kept an eye (albeit a wavering one) on those who might do her harm, Meddy rarely curbed his randy inclinations, even in her presence.

He directed his charms toward older women, to widows and the unhappy wives of men who took their pleasure elsewhere—outside the marriage bed. Trysts, he said, were a kind of "service." He dispensed attention and affection to women he believed were in "need." Bianca was wise enough to see through his farce, but she didn't think less of him for it. At least not until his interest settled on her own mother.

She loved them both, but not as a couple.

"What did you talk about?" asked Bianca.

Malva waved her hand as though she was brushing away the question—or at least the importance of it. "Oh, we bid each other a good eve." She glanced about and found a bundle of rope in the corner and a batlet for beating the clothes. "Sometimes I might be able to string a line. The clothes dry in half the time." Taking a short knife from off the table, she measured a length and sawed through the stiff fibers. She replaced the blade in the empty sheath on her belt.

"Where's the knife you had when you visited me?"

"What knife?"

"The one you used at my house to chop herbs for the remedy you made."

"I used your knife."

"Nay, you used yours. It had a blade about yay long"—Bianca gestured—"a short, stocky blade."

"Oh—that knife. I must have lost it between Southwark and home. I haven't seen it."

Bianca's eyes dropped to the sheath on her mother's belt. It didn't appear that a knife would go anywhere if her mother had properly secured it. Despite her alarm, Bianca persisted. "Mother, perchance do you know a woman named Leadith Browne?"

Malva was folding the length of rope and at the mention of Leadith stopped.

"She is practiced in herbals, I hear," Bianca added.

Malva finished looping the rope and dropped it on top of her laundry. "She did deal in remedies. But I would not call her 'practiced.' She could tell a good story and con the dead to try her potions."

Bianca noticed her mother referred to the woman as if she were no longer alive. A blop of acid hit her stomach, but she continued to chink away at her mother's wall of resistance. "Leadith lives a few streets over on Trinity Lane."

"Aye."

"So you know her?"

Hoisting the laundry basket to her hip, Malva carried it to the door and set it down. "Aye, Bianca," she said, returning to stand opposite her daughter. "The woman has a jealousy of me. She is not so fine a healer. I do not say this to gloat, but many people have been hurt by her remedies and they end up coming to see me instead."

Bianca nodded. She wondered, by comparison, how many people had been hurt by her mother's advice. Plenty, she thought, remembering a particularly odious toothache cure. *Take a rusty nail, rub it over your gums, then drive it into the wall behind your bed.*

"Her body was found behind the Dim Dragon Inn this morning."

Malva revealed no amazement or curiosity at the news. "I won't say that I am sorry to hear it. The woman had a meanness about her."

Most people were curious to know how others died. Bianca expected her mother to ask how Leadith succumbed to an untimely death. However, Bianca might have waited until the end of the world for all the interest her mother showed in her neighbor's demise.

"Aren't you wondering how she met her end?"

Malva shook her head. "Nay, but I suppose you want to tell me."

"She was stabbed."

"It does not come as a surprise," said Malva. "If she was stabbed in the back it would only be fitting."

Chapter 11

The chat with her mother had so fully occupied Bianca's mind that she walked almost to her father's room of alchemy before realizing where she was. But before she could meet with him she needed more time to sort her thoughts. The tide had turned, so she caught a ferry at Botolph's Wharf and rode back to Southwark on the opposite side of the bridge from where she'd come.

The bridge loomed beside her; the sun angled such that the span's upper stories threw an ominous shadow over the wherry befitting her black mood.

Several issues troubled her, each more worrisome than the last. It was poor enough that Dikson Browne had got her thinking about Meddybemps in all this, but after visiting her mother she felt even more disheartened.

Had Meddybemps recognized the knife as Malva's? Was that the reason for his sudden departure during Patch's visit? Meddybemps nursed a robust dislike of the constable stemming from Patch's accusation against her the previous year in a matter concerning the death of a close friend. As much as she'd like to forget the memory of Meddybemps's affair with her mother and pretend it never happened, their meeting last night made her wonder whether it truly was a chance encounter. The two would be more careful to hide the truth now that she was a couple of years older and certainly more aware.

The boat passed dangerously close to the bridge supports, and the rough current rocked the wherry, forcing the ferrier to angle the bow to keep from hitting a wave broadside. They broached a curl of water and Bianca became airborne before landing hard on her seat. This jarred her from her pensive thoughts and she grabbed on to the gunwale. The dark underbelly of the bridge hulked uncomfortably close.

"Codso, man! Do you think I want to swim?" Bianca shouted as the water sloshed over the side.

Most people portaged the rough water rather than trust their lives to the uncertain skill of an unknown water man. But "shooting the bridge" was not necessary for this ride, and Bianca resented the ferrier traveling so close to the starlings.

The boatman said nothing and deftly steered them into calmer water.

After a minute, Bianca's pulse returned to normal. An oversized cloak and hood hid the boatman's face and body, and she realized she had been so preoccupied that she had barely looked at him, nor had she spoken. Men who worked on the river were a different breed, she concluded. It took a strong stomach to breathe the mawky smell of dead fish and refuse day in and day out. If they ever fell into the water, the weight of their clothes would drag them under before anyone could help.

But looking across the stretch of river, she saw that they would land near Gull Hole, and for that small convenience she was grateful. For the rest of her ride, though, she kept one eye on the man's steering and tried to ignore the fetid water sloshing at her feet.

Arriving at the stone steps, Bianca decided to detour away from Gull Hole and went to the Dim Dragon Inn instead. Her mind could not settle until several questions had been answered.

Bianca hoped for a moment to talk with Cammy, but once inside, she saw the wench focused on the patrons surrounding the tables ordering their evening meals and ale. Though the day's light was lengthening with the advent of summer, most stomachs knew the hour of dinner and growled accordingly. The ken hummed with loud conversation, which included talk about the woman stabbed in the alley. The story would enjoy a long life of speculation and thorough discussion at the boozing ken, or at least would last until a new scandal replaced the tired tale.

Bianca waved to Cammy, then wended through the trestles to where she was tending her customers.

"I need to ask you a few questions about last night."

Cammy handed her a couple of empty tankards. "First help me pour ale."

Bianca followed her to a back room lined with barrels, their stop cocks glinting in a faint lantern light. "Have you learned anything more about Leadith Browne's murder?" asked Cammy, sticking a tankard under a dripping tap.

Bianca thought how best to avoid discussing her mother's and Meddybemps's possible involvement, though she needed to know whether Cammy had noticed either of them at the Dim Dragon.

"Apparently Dikson Browne, Leadith's husband, swears he did not stab her," said Bianca. "He admits to beating her, but claims a man with a red cap and strange eyes scared him off."

"Strange eyes?" repeated Cammy. "What, prithee, does that mean?"

Bianca positioned a mug under a barrel and opened the stopcock. "Methinks Browne meant that the man's eyes were memorable." She adjusted the flow of ale, inching it to the rim of the tankard.

"Hmm." Cammy finished filling a mug and set it aside while she got another. "What makes a man's eyes memorable?"

"Perhaps they made an impression on him. When one is caught in a misdeed, their recollection might not be accurate."

"I see plenty of men with yellow eyes, or red. But nothing particularly different."

Obviously Cammy had never seen Meddybemps. The peddler's eyes were as odd as a fish glued to a forehead. His eyes set the standard for memorable.

"Then, too, the man wore a red cap." Bianca hoped to spur Cammy's memory of Meddybemps, if indeed Meddybemps had been there.

"Well, that is of puny help," said Cammy, pouring another ale. "I see plenty of red caps. Red caps, brown caps, black caps . . . I pay no mind."

"Think on last night," said Bianca. "Mayhap one stood apart?"

Cammy scowled, trying to remember. She set down the tankard and scratched her head. "I don't remember seeing any red cap. And even if I did, a red cap isn't important enough to catch in my mind."

Bianca filled another tankard. She still wondered if Cammy might have seen her mother and thought how to ask it without divulging her mother's identity. "There are fewer women in the Dim Dragon than men. Mayhap *they* might catch in your mind?"

Cammy thought and her face brightened. "That, I do remember. I am always glad of it to see a woman. There are far too many men. And rude ones at that."

"So you remember Leadith Browne?"

"Aye that. But I told you everything I know about her carrying on."

"Might you remember any other women?"

Cammy thought a minute. "I remember a woman wearing a marigold kirtle," she said.

"Ah," said Bianca, remembering the yellow kirtle her mother wore the day she visited. "Can you describe her?"

"She had a pleasant face, a handsome nose, well favored. She kept to herself."

"Did you see anything distinguishing about her?"

Cammy frowned. "Like what?"

"Did she possess an olive complexion?" In Bianca's eagerness to confirm if this was indeed Malva, she forgot her caution. "If in a certain light, did you notice a small scar like an indentation on a forehead . . . ?"

"That is a specific feature. Have you someone in mind?"

Bianca privately chided herself for being obvious, and pretended indifference. "Well then," she ventured, nonchalantly. "Was she older than us?"

"Old enough to be someone you know?" Cammy glanced at Bianca from the corner of her eye. "Mayhap, your mother?" She smiled. "I do remember such a wench. She kept apart from the others. She drank her ale, then left."

"Did she have an interest in Leadith Browne's glowing stones?"

"If she did, she kept her interest to herself. She didn't try for a better look."

"Did you see her talk with anyone?"

"Bianca, I can just manage to remember who gets pie or bread. A woman in yellow is not my interest any further than getting her an ale to sip."

The two gathered the full tankards.

"Might you point out the men who were interested in the glowing stones?"

Cammy waited for Bianca to shift the tankards so that she could carry them all. "Indeed. I can point them out to you."

Despite the worrisome coincidences that incriminated Meddybemps and her mother, Bianca reminded herself that she had not talked to, nor had she learned the names of, the other men interested in her father's element. She hoped against hope that she would find someone else with a more heated desire to stab Leadith Browne. However, the connections could not help but weigh upon her mind.

"One last question," said Bianca as they headed out of the taproom. "Did you notice if the woman in the marigold kirtle had any meadowsweet?"

Cammy stopped walking and turned to face Bianca. "I do remember seeing a pile of stems next to her."

Bianca had trouble keeping the tankards from spilling as she carried them to the waiting patrons. Presuming that Meddybemps was the man who had intervened and stopped Dikson Browne from beating his wife, why, then, did Meddybemps not tell her he had done so? What was he hiding?

The men accepted their mugs and tried teasing Bianca out of her somber-faced service. When they saw she remained oblivious to their gibes they dismissed her as an odd lass and let her alone.

Lost in thought, Bianca absently followed Cammy as the maid collected empty tankards and filled her arms with them. She wondered if Malva had met Meddybemps outside and had asked him to get the stones back from Leadith?

But why would he kill her? The thought of Meddybemps stabbing a woman ran counter to her belief in him. Not that he would never commit murder. Meddybemps had a dark side about him, one she rarely saw or wanted to acknowledge or hear about. But, killing a woman? And not just stabbing her, but brutally cutting her?

Surviving in the sinister streets of London and Southwark took wiliness. Meddybemps had that and more. A man didn't reach the ripe age of forty without knowing how to skirt trouble.

"Bianca, are you well?" asked Cammy after leading Bianca back to the kitchen. "Is it your stomach again?"

"Oh, aye," said Bianca, startling out of her gloom. "I shall be glad when I am far enough along so that it settles."

Cammy put her arm around Bianca's shoulders and gave her a reassuring smile. "N'er you worry, my friend. In time, your ill ease shall pass."

True, thought Bianca. In time, *everything* shall pass. "I think I need to take my leave," she said.

"You wanted me to point out others who were interested in the glowing stones," reminded Cammy.

"Aye," said Bianca, remembering. "Is anyone here?"

Cammy looked around. "Not at the moment. But if you come back later there might be."

Before returning to her room of Medicinals and Physickes, Bianca passed the alley where Leadith Browne's body had been

discovered that morning. A usually dark ginnel, the sinking sun-
light fell at an angle to illuminate an area of cobbles that Bianca
had had trouble seeing during her initial search. Bianca slipped
down the alley to take advantage of the lengthened day and low-
setting light.

A few puddles remained from the previous night's rain and
she bent down to run her hand through one, feeling for stones
the size of her father's element. She fished out a few pebbles,
rubbed the mud off of them, looking for the tell-tale opalescent
white nacre of the glowing stone. Finding nothing that appeared
remotely like her father's lost element, she moved on to another
puddle. She looked like an odd maid crouched in the alley, swish-
ing her hand through stagnant pools, surrounded by the leavings
of both man and animal. In her sensitive state the foul odors made
her queasy and Bianca hurried her search.

For her efforts, she found nothing but useless rocks, a penny
(which she slipped into her pouch), an aiglet (perhaps from someone's doublet), and what she thought at first to be a perfectly round
stone. But as she rubbed off the dirt she noticed indentations—
parallel lines in a raised circle. She stood and held the sphere in
better light. What she thought was a perfectly round stone (finding one in nature was exceedingly rare) instead turned out to be a
deliberate carving.

Bianca dug a fingernail between a pair of lines and removed
the grit to better see the emerging pattern. Raised circles abutted
raised circles, each containing rows of either parallel or perpendic-
ular lines. She bent down and tried rinsing the ball, but the turbid
water was of little help. The sphere had a weight to it, heavier than
what she would think a stone its size would normally be. There
were no more puddles and from the looks of it, no more spheres.
She dropped it in her purse and cinched the strings closed. She
would study it later.

CHAPTER 12

The dependable, if not mundane, assurance of wedlock would be taken for granted if it wasn't for life's occasional, unpredictable test. Or, in the case of Bianca and John's marriage—tests. The View of Arms had thrown John into a morose state of denial these past few days. He spent an inordinate amount of time at Boisvert's working at his apprenticeship. Part of his all-consuming dedication was to keep his mind occupied and from dwelling on leaving Bianca in her current condition. It was perhaps odd that he found it painful to be in the same room with her. Thus had the realization of separation and death diddled with John's sensibilities.

Bianca had noticed his long work days and, for as insensitive and impervious as she often appeared to be, she knew better than John the reason why. She did not question him or broach the subject; she knew he would work through his worries in his own way. Just as she was working through hers.

So that when John dragged himself through the door that evening, Bianca simply kissed him on the cheek in greeting and warmed some porridge for his meal. Hobs seemed to think the bowl was for him and was unceremoniously removed from the table.

Bianca waited for John's shoulders to relax before asking him about his day. She saw his neck tense, but he remained calm in answering.

"They announced the assignments from the View of Arms," he said, focusing on the porridge.

Bianca had been collecting the dirty crockery and stacking it to rinse. She waited for him to finish.

"I am to be a pikeman."

She knew John was too strong *not* to be conscripted. It was only a matter of time before he would be tapped to fight in Henry's next risky and ill-advised incursion. The clack of pottery gave away Bianca's distress.

There was no misunderstanding on the part of the officers. John's poor showing and the incident with the captain and his horse conspired against him. Bianca wished she had insisted that John practice his archery every Sunday as the king decreed. Plenty of able-bodied men of age gathered at Finsbury Fields, shot a few arrows, then wandered off to lawn bowl or flex their muscles lifting ales at a local ken. John had done none of that. Instead, he had spent his days working with Boisvert or, on occasion, convincing Bianca to take a stroll with him.

"When do you leave?" Bianca lowered herself on a stool and ignored Hobs rubbing against her legs.

"The day after tomorrow," muttered John into his bowl.

Bianca's heart missed a beat. It was hardly enough time to sort through one's life and ready oneself for the arduous task ahead, much less prepare others for a long absence. Not even two days to say goodbye.

"And where shall you go?" asked Bianca. "France?"

"It seems likely. Though there are other matters the king cares about."

"Where else might you go if not there?"

John mopped the inside of the bowl with his bread, working it around to sop up every bit of porridge. "I do not know all of our king's frivolous fixations; they number many."

"But will you be able to send word to me? I want to know where you are."

John swallowed the bread and washed it down with the cloudy dregs of their remaining ale. "Bianca," he said. "It matters not. Being gone is the same, whether I am sailing to France or marching to a border."

"Still, I would want to know."

"Why? So you can imagine me dying at the hand of which foe? Whether I perish on a Frenchman's sword, or a Spaniard's halberd, or a Scot's bill, I suffer no less by one or the other."

"It is a sad day that you would speak to me so."

Taken aback, John realized his sarcasm only aggravated their already fragile heartstrings. Regretting his careless words, he rose from the table and went to her. Her eyes never failed to pierce his soul, and taking her hands in his he felt the tension in his body begin to ebb. He could not apologize for being angry, for being scared, and he knew that she didn't expect him to. He raised her hands to his lips and kissed her fingers, stained from plants. "I would slay a thousand French in a day if I knew that it would bring me speedily home. But I am not my own man in this world. I am the king's pawn. I can never know otherwise."

"*We* can never know otherwise," said Bianca. She laid her head against his chest and closed her eyes. The time was coming when the sound of his heart would be just a memory.

The next morning they lingered in bed with Hobs sprawled in between. John mussed the fur on the cat's stomach while cradling Bianca. John and Hobs had come to an agreement of sorts. As long as the feline responded to John's attention with purrs of content, then John spoke well of him.

"He will keep you good company while I am gone."

Bianca rolled to face her husband. "He'll cause enough trouble to keep me occupied." She teased the cat and drew several nips and lethargic kicks from his hind legs. Indignant that he should have his reverie interrupted, he got to his feet and marched across

Bianca like she was a lumpy rug, and jumped to the floor. Bianca rolled onto her back and stared up at the ceiling.

"Is something troubling you?" John asked. "Other than the obvious."

"Nay," she said breezily.

"I noticed you did not sleep."

"I don't seem to get comfortable these days."

John studied her a moment. "Something is on your mind. I can tell. You're not just worried about me leaving."

Bianca shook her head and made a face.

"Did you speak with Albern again? That would set anyone in a mood."

"I have not spoken to him, but he will want to know what I've learned."

"Which is not much," said John.

Bianca had not told him that a woman's body had been found behind the Dim Dragon or that the murder was connected to Albern's missing stones. To have talked about it last night would have diminished the gravity of John's leaving. But if John were to find out that Constable Patch had solicited her help, she would be accused of keeping secrets. Even worse, John would have accused her of being careless. With that in mind, Bianca told him what happened.

The news was met without enthusiasm.

"Firstly," said John, "what is Patch doing back in Southwark?"

"His position is only until a replacement is found."

"Then you need to inform Meddybemps so he can look out for you while I am gone. I don't trust Patch to care about your health and safety."

Bianca nodded, agreed that she would. She had not mentioned her concerns about Malva and Meddybemps, only that Leadith Browne had in her possession what sounded like her father's element. She couldn't be sure how John would react if he knew that her only source of income was possibly at risk.

"Secondly, why must he involve you?"

"Patch only consults me if he thinks I might be able to decipher what he cannot explain. It suits him to let everyone think he can outwit any lawman in the realm." She wove her fingers through John's. "I'll keep a perfunctory role in assisting Patch. Besides, it appears the woman may have swallowed the stones."

"She ate the stones?"

"The air glowed over her body."

"Say again?"

"Queer, I know." Any other time she would have offered several theories about what happened and why. Rumors about glowing air were bound to find his ears, and Bianca thought it best to stem exaggerated accounts before he heard them. "I can't see that the incident will amount to anything more than simple theft."

"Then, you believe the stones killed her?"

"I think they could have. However, it appears she was stabbed." She purposely couched the findings as commonplace and affected disinterest. "Probably her husband is to blame."

"So, your father's discovery has resulted in someone's death." John thought a moment. "I see nothing redemptive about these stones—these *lapis mortem*."

Bianca closed her eyes. The gravity of Albern's creation pressed against her like the lid of a sarcophagus.

"You don't think your father found out she had his stones and murdered her to get them back?"

John's words felt as if he had pinched her. "I doubt it. I don't think he knows about Leadith's death." She then rolled on top of John and pinned his hands above his head. "Now, sir, let us not spend our remaining time speaking of murder."

Their intimacy aside, Bianca took her time dressing while John walked over to alewife Guilford's, whose third mash was better than most, and replenished their supply of morning ale. He even bought freshly churned butter and the two ate bread slathered with mounds of it until they felt happily full. They gazed at one another as two lovers were wont to do, and they spoke of hopes for their future, and whether their child would be a boy or a girl, and which they preferred, but really it did not matter so long as the child had ten fingers and toes.

"I won't be so long today," said John, after he had delayed his apprenticeship for the better part of the morning. He had enjoyed the brief respite from his preoccupation about wielding a pike, but he was already late and Boisvert would have something to say about it.

"He will miss you," remarked Bianca, referring to the silver-smith as she walked him to the door. "How shall he manage without your help?"

"Boisvert is able to manage as well as he did before I came along."

"He was younger then," said Bianca, and she pulled down some dried sage and ran it under her nose. "And older now."

"I agree that his time in Newgate Prison aged him."

"Then, too, losing the love of Odile," added Bianca.

"Aye, but he will survive. He's lived in London all these years suffering the insults of *les rosbifs*. He shall not be easily defeated."

Bianca smiled at the silversmith's name for Englishmen. "Not everyone can sharpen their wit from life's misfortunes."

"It is his clever disposition that sustains him."

The two parted, and Bianca stood at the door watching John round the corner. These were her last precious hours with him; she would never get them back. She shut the door and her stomach began gnawing—this time with resentment. How could Meddybemps and her mother be so foolish? And the thought of spending more time doing her father's bidding did not set well with her. Still, if she did not seek out Albern and report her findings, he would seek her out; and the last thing Bianca wanted was for her father to disrupt any time she had left with John.

CHAPTER 13

William Thomson blinked up at the ceiling of his room in the Bishop of Hereford's Inn, a once-grand and ancient house built of stone and timber now ruinated through neglect and turned into cheap housing. Unfortunately, it was all the Scot could afford. The sheets on which he lay felt damp against his skin. Several hours of chills, then a fever that seemed interminable, had left him drenched along with his bed linens. The symptoms of his ague had finally begun to subside, leaving him with a throbbing head. In a day it might lessen enough for him to nearly forget how miserable he had been.

He put his arm over his face, knowing that the cycle would only repeat itself.

With Leadith Browne dead, he needed to find someone else who could make a remedy to ease the ill effects of his disease. Nye Standish came to mind, as he was the only apothecary Thomson even vaguely knew. He hoped the man's medicines weren't prohibitively expensive.

With no small amount of effort, he brought himself to sitting and sat until the pounding in his head lessened, then got out of bed and changed his smock. A man of routine, he opened the shutters to take a piss out the window. The daylight, albeit that of a typical gray day, momentarily blinded him and he aimed his manhood at a dog crouched in the lane below. Alas, his malady had left him parched and he hardly had a dribble in him—which was just as well, because now once he could see properly the dog had transformed itself into Mrs. Lynn, a kindly widow who did not deserve to be sprinkled upon.

The need for sustenance had reached a critical juncture; he finished dressing and got himself to his favorite place of comradery, the Dim Dragon Inn. He had no sooner ordered up a bowl of porridge and ale when the new serving wench cheerfully impinged upon his personal space a second time, bringing with her a doleful maid with scintillating blue eyes, the same one who'd accompanied that peacock of a constable yesterday morning.

"Ye was with that oaf, weren't ye, lassie?" he said in greeting.

"I am not *with* him, sir," she said with a detectable hint of irritation.

"Ye two arrived together. It seemed ye left together."

"Unfortunately, Constable Patch knows my history. He uses it to his advantage."

"Ot, does he?" This piqued his interest.

"May I ask you some questions?"

"Are the answers for him?"

"Not anymore. They are for me."

"And who is me?"

"My name is Bianca Goddard."

He motioned for her to sit. "As ye will."

Bianca sat on the bench and pulled herself down the table until she was opposite him. "You were here when Leadith Browne was soliciting offers for her glowing stones."

"Aye." The nidorous odor of wet wool rose from his chestnut-colored jerkin. It momentarily distracted him, realizing his coat had not dried since he had gotten caught in the rain the other night.

"Can you tell me who lent an ear to her story?"

"Is she a friend of yours?"

"I have no interest in Leadith Browne except to prove my friend's whereabouts on the night she was murdered. That is all."

"Who be your friend?"

"Sir, I will not answer that, except to say that the person may be wrongly accused."

"Is it Leadith Browne's husband?"

"It is not my practice to share what I know before the perpetrator is determined. But I recall that you offered Leadith's name and told us where she lived. How did you know this?"

"I've gotten remedies from her. I cannae afford the physicians in London." He situated his belt, took time smoothing the fur of a sporran with a badger head closure. "I suppose I'll haf to find another to make my remedies now."

A patron shuffled past, a dark-skinned Egyptian who hid his brown hide beneath a layer of ceruse to avoid obvious notice. The man made his coin reading the squiggles on a person's palm and did a fair business flattering conceited men of money. He made his way past, eyeing Thomson's guest, and the Scot nodded in kind, warning him off with a quick furrowed brow. "Several men took an interest in Leadith," he continued. "But there were two in particular. One was a chandler."

"Do you know his name?"

"Nay, I dinnae know him."

"Had you ever seen the chandler here before?"

"A few times. But he doesn't mingle with the likes of me. So, I ignore him."

"Who else wanted the stones?"

"Nye Standish, an apothecary."

"An apothecary?" Her brows drew together. "Can you tell me what happened that night?"

William Thomson took off his cap and laid it on the table, wondering what harm there would be in giving this lass a bit of chops to chew on. "I'd never seen Leadith behave more saucily. She swaggered in, teasing she's got a secret we'd all want. Ye cannae come into a ken in this borough spewin' that kind of codswallop and not expect to get a bristle." He smiled salaciously and wiped his nose to hide his sneer. "She had plenty of cozens gawpmouthed after her."

"I do not doubt you. But tell me about the apothecary and the chandler."

"I was playing cards, and paid no real mind until the entire place got lively over the vial of glowing beans. She was looking to sell them and the chandler won the bid. He and Leadith were to meet in two days to settle up. Leadith took exception having to wait, but she gots herself so soused she didn't know what she'd agreed to by the end of the night."

"And the apothecary?"

Thomson snorted derisively. "He comes here a bit. He can't resist what the South Bank has to offer."

The ale arrived and with it a bowl of barley soup. The food and drink took precedence and he drank down his tankard in a couple of long pulls before continuing with his story between mouthfuls of soup. "Once the chandler left, Standish tried to persuade Leadith to sell to him. He said it should not be a matter of money when it comes to saving souls."

"You heard him say this?"

"I did."

"How does one save souls with glowing rocks?"

"I wondered tha' meself." He set down the bowl, then wiped his mouth with the back of his hand. "I took him to mean that the glowing stones might be used to heal people. Though, anyone seein' the stones—with them smoking and fuming—would not think them mild. It would take a wise hand to tame such brimstone."

"Do you know where Nye Standish keeps his shop?"

"By way off Cheapside on Bucklersbury."

"What was Leadith's reaction to his offer?"

"She rejected it." He waved Cammy over and ordered another ale. "Who would blame her? She stood to make some money. Standish left soon after."

"And that is all you saw of him?"

"I saw him later. His clothes were disheveled. He looked upset."

"Where was this?"

"Here."

"Do you know why he was upset?"

"'Tis not me business."

"By chance did you notice a woman wearing a yellow kirtle?"

He thought a moment and noticed her watching him with an intensity that unsettled him. "Aye, there be a wench in a dark yellow kirtle," he said, searching her face. "She seemed ill at ease. But then, women wander in for an ale without knowing anyone. They grow uncomfortable, then leave." Mayhap she might do the same, he hoped.

"Was she here while Leadith Browne showed off the vial of glowing stones?"

"Ach! I don't watch everyone come and go."

"Well met. But sometimes folks remember when specifically asked."

"I suppose she might have been there."

"And when you left, do you recall seeing anyone you might have cause to remember?"

"Like who?"

"Do you remember a man with a red cap? He would be tall and thin and his eyes might have struck you as . . . noticeable."

"There are plenty of odd ones around here. But none more so than the other." He needed to take a piss. He was about to excuse himself when it occurred to him he'd seen her there with her husband. "Didnae your husband get tapped to fight for the king?"

Bianca ignored the question. She slid down the bench and got to her feet. "If you think of anything else, tell Cammy. She knows where to find me."

A cloud of mayflies harassed the mudlarks combing the tidal flats, so Bianca chose to cross the bridge rather than take a wherry and subject herself to the swarming beasts. She passed under South Gate and glanced at the new collection of impaled heads rimming the battlement. In spite of its grim decorations, the bridge was home to London's most desirable addresses. The dreary day made for a dark passage through the sections lined with shops and wealthy residences. Upper stories canted toward one another, some nearly touching. If a tailor wanted a ribbon or bead, he need only lean out his upper window to get one from a haberdasher across the way.

On the other side, she emerged onto Thames Street and followed it to the warehouse district to her father's room of alchemy. She found the room easily enough, having spent so much of her youth there. The buildings looked more ramshackle than she'd remembered. No one had bothered to improve or secure them. No doubt, determined thieves could break in without much effort. A wagon loaded with crates creaked by, the driver ogling as he passed.

Bianca knocked and called to her father, who answered and ushered her inside. A pungent smell of urine percolated in a barrel against a wall. Her squint-eyed look of distaste made him snicker. "I collect it for use in creating the element."

"Your element comes from urine?"

"It is the stuff of magic."

Man's fascination with piss. Physicians sniffed it; they dropped it on their tongues to taste. Alchemists believed the philosopher's stone could be projected from the dross. "Be that as it may, why not set it outside to fester if that is your intent?" she asked.

"It is too valuable. I won't chance the barrel getting overturned in the alley."

Bianca moved away from the offensive odor and found a stool on the opposite side of the room. A crucible simmered in a bain-marie, chattering softly in the bath, a sound that Bianca always found soothing. Her father might be creating a substance of evil import for all she knew, but the familiar clatter of ceramic against a metal pan calmed her.

"Tell me what you have learned of my element," prompted Albern, impatiently.

"Some events appear possibly connected." Bianca straightened, which relieved a cramp in her stomach. "A woman named Leadith Browne took merry at the Dim Dragon in Southwark two nights ago. She made much of a vial of glowing stones. She removed one and set the pebble on the table. It lay there peaceably, long enough to disappoint her prospects, then a billowing cloud of smoke filled the room to the rafters."

"It is my element. She has it!" Albern's expression became hopeful. To Bianca, his guileless joy at learning news about his discovery squelched any thoughts that he might have been the murderer.

"Alas, the story does not end well," said Bianca, muzzling her father's excitement. "There were some who were interested in buying the glowing pebbles and she came to an agreement with one."

"Who? Out upon it!" demanded Albern, unable to wait for Bianca to tell him.

"A chandler offered her the most money and they agreed to meet in two days."

"That would be today! Who is this knave? I shall forestall his undeserved profit."

"There is little advantage to learning his name. The woman was found stabbed in an alley not long after their bargain was made."

"And the stones? Were they recovered?"

It did not surprise Bianca that her father was less concerned about Leadith's murder than in the whereabouts of his precious *lapis mortem*. "No, Father. They were not."

"Someone stole them!"

"It is not certain. They may have been lost."

"Have you talked with this chandler who wanted the stones? He might have laid in wait, then stabbed her so he would not have to pay for them."

"It is possible he is the culprit, but I have not followed up."

"You must seek him out! What is this chandler's name?"

"I do not know it."

"Well then, you must learn it! Likely he is guilty."

"It is also possible that the stones were lost," she repeated.

"They cannot have been lost, unless they landed in a puddle and were snuffed like a wick on a candle." Albern grew agitated. "But if they are dry—they will smoke. Such copious plumes would be impossible to ignore."

"I searched through the puddles in the alley and I did not find your element. There was nothing remotely like it. However, I did find this." She reached into her pouch and pulled out the small stone ball.

Albern took it near the high window for better light. "It is a button," he declared, unimpressed, and handed it back.

Bianca pocketed her finding. "So you have no familiarity with Leadith Browne?"

Albern's eyes rolled under his lids as he thought. "Browne, you say?"

"Aye," said Bianca, tucking her partlet into her bodice, where it had come loose.

"Was she the wife of Dikson Browne—an alchemist?"

"You know the man?"

"Regrettably, I do. He is a scoundrel of the highest order. A sot and a prevaricator. A man of substantial folly and even greater falsehoods." Albern's eyes narrowed, assuming a conspiracy. "And have you asked your mother what her part is in all of this?"

Bianca feigned nonchalance. "I find no cause for you to think her involved. This room could easily have been broken into." Bianca's gaze lifted to the high window overhead. "For one, that window is not secure."

"A thief would have broken his neck jumping from that height."

"He might not have jumped. One could descend by rope."

Albern's lips thinned as he studied his daughter instead of the window. "I see what you are about," he said. "You seek to deflect your mother's involvement. I am not so gullible, my dear. I shall learn the truth if you will not."

Bianca riled at his charge. She was as much irritated that her father should think her mother complicit as she was angry that her father should see through her attempt to mislead him. "Have you seen evidence of Mother profiting?" asked Bianca. "Has she bought herself a new kirtle or smock? Does she eat oranges and drink Spanish sack? Nay, she does not. Mother may not have wanted you to take your discovered element to the king, but she did not prevent you from doing so."

Albern grumbled and turned away. "She had a part in this. I am certain of it."

"Father, the likely culprits are the Brownes."

"If Leadith is dead, then Dikson Browne must be to blame."

"A moment ago you believed it was the chandler."

"It could be either one of them!"

"I am not sure that Dikson is responsible for Leadith's murder or for the element's disappearance," said Bianca. She avoided telling him about Dikson's vehement claim of innocence regarding his wife's murder. "Unfortunately, I do not know what happened to your stones. I have found no evidence of anyone taking them. Others are listening for word of them surfacing and they will tell me. But there is strong cause for me to believe your element is lost forever. And not because someone stole it and has it in their possession."

"How now?" Albern did not follow her line of reasoning.

"What would happen if a person swallowed your element?"

"One's throat would burn. It would not be pleasant."

"Could the stones continue to glow?"

"Sitting inside one's stomach?"

Bianca nodded, knowing it sounded absurd.

Albern made a face to dismiss the idea. "Why would anyone do such a thing?"

"Perhaps to prevent another from taking it."

Albern took a ewer and brought up the level of water in the pan of the bain-marie. "It is a severe measure to ingest something that is inherently dangerous."

"Perhaps she was ignorant of the level of peril."

"Are you suggesting that she swallowed my element?"

"I am."

"Why, say you? What reason have you to think this?"

"Someone stuffed Leadith's mouth with meadowsweet. When I removed it, the air glowed green above her." Bianca read the disbelief in her father's expression. "It was the glow of which you described the first time you told me about the element."

"Tilly vally! Being with child has affected your good sense as well as your sight."

"I was not the only one to see it."

Albern set the ewer down, thinking. "If it is true and she swallowed the stones, then she was as witless as pounded sand and deserves a knife in her gut."

"It makes me wonder which she died of first," said Bianca. "Was she stabbed because someone thought she had the stones on her person? Or did the element kill her and then someone tried to retrieve the stones from her gut?" Bianca got a distant look in her eye and mumbled, "Then again, maybe her murder had not much to do with the element."

Albern fixated on Leadith swallowing the element. "The element may still be in her body."

Bianca juddered out of her rumination.

Albern's unruly eyebrows fluttered. "Where at does Dikson Browne live?"

Bianca wondered if Albern would take matters into his own hands. If that was the reason for his asking, then she might do better to remind him of the consequences, though she knew he was not ignorant in matters of criminal misconduct.

She studied his face, attempting to discern his intent. Was he thinking of going to the parish church to retrieve the stones from Leadith Browne's stomach? Bianca recoiled envisioning it, yet her father was as determined as he was capable. Realistically, though, such a task would require more than one person—and one would have to be mad to risk getting caught.

With a sigh, Bianca realized her father could find out Dikson

Browne's address nearly as fast as she could tell him. Sadly, Bianca harbored an indifference for her father that equaled his own disregard for her. "He lives on Trinity Lane," she answered. And concluding that her father had plans for some sort of treachery, added, "With his impressionable young son."

CHAPTER 14

Nye Standish swept down Bucklersbury Lane past the cluster of grocers and apothecary shops crowding the west end of the street, en route to his own establishment in the converted Bucklers Mansion now known as the Old Barge. He regretted leaving his shop and losing business while procuring needed supplies, but he had run out of candles, and during the unpredictable spring weather with its rain and dreary days he could not work without them. One of his regular customers exited a competitor's shop and sneaked by with his eyes averted, setting Standish in a peevish temper. It took longer than normal for him to unlock his door; he lacked the usual finesse turning the padlock's rusty wards.

At last the encumbrance yielded and he stepped into his herbarium, relishing the relief that came from inhaling the robust smells in his modest shop. A collection of jars crammed with crushed herbs and bins of dried plants lined a wall of shelving at the back. In front of this, a long table stretched nearly the width of the room, organized with scoops, a balance with neatly lined weights in a row, and a myriad of mortars and pestles in several sizes. A stuffed lizard mounted on a block of wood sat at one end, nailed to the table in a permanent pose of quirky grandeur.

Like alchemists, most apothecaries displayed an alligator swinging from a rafter to advertise their trade's exotic and exclusive practice. Standish preferred his stocky lizard with its spiny tail, and had acquired it alive from a Spanish Moor who was desperate for burdock to soothe a case of sloughy skin. Unfortunately, London's dank climate took a toll on the creature along with the apothecary's ignorance on how to properly care for the poor beast. Still, he had grown fond of his lizard in the short time it had lived, and once it expired, he had taken it to a taxidermist to be preserved for posterity.

Standish tossed his parcel of candles onto the table and patted the head of his scaly friend, whose eyes still retained a glossy, lacquered shine. The reptile was mounted with its mouth open to reveal a set of sharp, tiny teeth, but its ferocity was diminished by this permanent pose. Not even a tiger looked fierce showing all its teeth in perpetuity. For a beast to retain its dignity it must hide its gnashers and occasionally show them with a snarl. Still, patting his lizard was a soothing habit the apothecary never forgot.

There were other habits the apothecary never neglected. It could almost be said of Nye Standish that he possessed the superstitious reverence for his trade that an alchemist reserved for his dark art. For instance, Standish would never collect herbs unless the position of the moon benefited their effectiveness. An almanac calculating the rising and setting dates of the planets sat in a place of honor on his shelf, consulted and pored over to correctly dispense, with care and insight, the proper therapy for whatever ailed his client.

Perspiration formed at his temples, and Standish shed his gown from his outing, then unwrapped the candles Jacoby Nimble had sold him. He'd sought the chandler out, not only to purchase needed light for his shop, but to see up close what the man was about. Today, after all, was the day Jacoby Nimble had agreed to meet Leadith Browne.

He had found the chandler busy clipping wicks, and the man showed no hint of surprise upon seeing him. Perhaps the man assumed everyone he met would be drawn to try his candles on the pretense of his refined and confident manner alone. Standish could not care less where or from whom he bought his sticks; he'd seen little difference in quality from one maker to another.

Nimble was pleasant enough attending to his needs. When asked if he had met with Leadith yet, Nimble answered that he had not. A moment of silence followed where Standish thought the chandler might continue the conversation, perhaps express enthusiasm about the mysterious pebbles. But Nimble remained reticent, oddly quiet. Perhaps the chandler was having second thoughts. But if this was true, then why not admit it? For as convincing and eloquent as Nimble appeared two nights ago at the Dim Dragon, he now seemed, to Standish, almost a different man. Could it be attributed to an insecurity that he did not have the necessary skills to handle the stones? Or was he one of those silent types who superstitiously refused to talk about his good fortune?

To the apothecary's disappointment, he had been unable to tease any more information out of the chandler. He couldn't imagine what a candlemaker would want with the stones and, despite his carefully couched probing, Nimble resolutely stayed his tongue.

Standish dispensed with a stump of wax in a pricket candle holder on his workbench and replaced it with one of Nimble's sticks. From a smoldering brazier he teased an ember to flare and lit his new purchase. The flame smoothly licked the wax and burned steadily.

The lizard's eyes glinted in the yellow light and he gave his mascot another pat on the head for good measure. He had told Leadith he wanted the stones for a possible medicine, and he had reiterated that intention to Jacoby Nimble. There was always the possibility that the chandler might reconsider and sell them to him. Whatever Nimble had planned for the stones it could not possibly match the apothecary's desire to benefit mankind. Of this he was sure. And he had made certain that Jacoby Nimble understood.

William Thomson had seen Standish's shop once on his way to having a shoe mended, and found it easily enough. A bell tinkled upon his entering, eliciting the apothecary from a back room.

"A good day, sir," said Standish, cordially. He recognized Thomson's face from the Dim Dragon Inn and asked him what brought him up from Southwark.

Thomson plunked a gathered bunch of meadowsweet on the counter. "I'm having bouts with the fever. I need a tisane for ague."

Standish stared at the pile of wilted flowers and stems without touching it. "What is this?"

"'Tis meadowsweet."

"I know it is meadowsweet," said Nye Standish, annoyed. "But it is useless."

"Ach! Where I be from it is used to calm the fever."

"I've not heard it used for that. When was it picked?"

William Thomson shrugged. "Does it matter? It works the same." Then, seeing he must convince the man of his need, he explained his illness. "Ague be a cursed malady," he said. "I'll be of merry content when stealthily the chills do come." His head still throbbed and this, combined with the dread of another bout of chills and fever, made him more irritable than normal, and more insistent. "The shakes begin in me jaw and sets me teeth to chatter. I cannae clench it away but must give over to its endless clatter. Then comes the fever and me head aches so fierce that I would beg Henry's black executor to cleave it from me neck just to be done." The Scot flattened his hand and dramatically swiped it across his neck. Then, seeing Standish unmoved, said, "This is a remedy in my country for fevers."

"I do not subscribe to a peasant's recipe," said Standish.

"Do you call me a peasant?" exclaimed Thomson. "If the recipe works, why should it matter whether it be from a poor man or an apothecary?" The Scot caught himself, realizing his desperation was making him testy. A more subdued approach might be better received. He closed his eyes and took a breath. He started over. "I know ye are not familiar with the lore of me land. But, and I mean no impertinence, what do ye care, so long as I pay ye and it pleases me?"

Standish pulled a flower from the pile and examined the limp stalk like he was holding a disgusting fly by its wings. "It matters when these were picked," he said. "A remedy is ineffective if the ingredients are plucked haphazardly. They must be gathered during a waxing moon and it is now waning."

The Scot was tired of making nice. "Ye professionals are a pernickety lot. Why wouldnae reap some boon?"

"Because you cannot gather plants whenever you want and expect them to work! *I* am schooled in the intricacies of my trade, not you!" said Standish.

The Scot's jaw lowered at the apothecary's sudden rebuke. It was for *him* to feel irritable, not the shopkeeper. *He* was the one sick with the fever.

But Standish would not be stopped once he'd started. He continued in a world-weary voice. "I grow so tired of every woozy, ailing pillock telling me how to conduct my labors." He turned away from William Thomson and snatched a bottle off his shelf, popped the cork, and tilted his head back. His throat worked up and down, swallowing whatever was in the bottle. Then, with a truculent harrumph, he pushed the cork back in, gave it a vigorous twist, and returned it to the shelf. He glared at his customer.

For a moment, Thomson didn't know what to say. In Duns it didn't matter a sheep's teat when you picked a plant. These Southrons were a techy breed. He'd never liked London and people marked him a carl from the North as soon as he opened his mouth. Then, too, it was here that he contracted this miserable disease in the first place. He blamed his fevers on the squalid river that bred nettlesome insects and on the city's unwholesome, polluted air redolent of putrefying waste.

But he needed his tisane, and despite Standish's petulance, Thomson was not inclined to look elsewhere to find a willing apothecary. "I shall pay you well and it will benefit me regardless of whether you think it will or not. I haven't the desire to keep looking for someone to help me." He impressed upon the apothecary his humane duty to help those in need and Nye Standish, worn down by the Scot's plea, reluctantly acquiesced.

"As long as you do not fault my efforts if the remedy fails," he said, still skeptical. He did not want his reputation and good name besmirched by producing an inferior medicine.

Thomson assured him he would preserve the apothecary's reputation even if the tea turned him into a newt.

On the opposite side of London, Bianca left her father's room of alchemy, regretting telling her father about Dikson Browne. What would he do with the knowledge that Leadith may have swallowed his precious element? A normal man would conclude that the stones were gone and that he must begin anew to recreate his lost discovery. But her father was not a normal man.

Traipsing down lengthy Thames Street gave Bianca time to think. Nye Standish, the apothecary, lived a fair distance away off Cheapside. She wanted to pay him a visit in the hopes that he— and not her mother or Meddybemps—had something to do with Leadith Browne's death.

Barring any proof to make her think otherwise, Bianca believed that her father's element was probably lost. And if the stones *were* lost, then Bianca only needed to make sure that Meddybemps and her mother were seen as innocent in Browne's death.

Bianca turned onto Bucklersbury Lane. She wondered if she had misunderstood the Scot's directions when she looked about and saw nothing but a cobbler's shop and grocers. Bianca lingered in the pleasant smell of leather, slowing to stroll and to watch men cutting hides and sewing through open doors. She wondered how much it would cost to repair her own poor stampers and determined she would have to make do with patches of thick wool basted haphazardly in place—a temporary mend that, to date, seemed permanent.

Near the west end of the lane she saw a cluster of apothecary shops. The rich smell of hide faded and a fragrant melange of herbs exuberantly scented the air. Here gathered the best apothecaries in London. Well-kept exteriors and tidy shops declared their success in business. Bianca looked for some indication of Nye Standish's place and found it after walking to the end of the lane, then retracing her steps back toward the cobblers. A discreet nameplate tacked above a closed door had escaped her notice on the first pass. After peering through a window and seeing no one, she saw no reason to tarry and entered the shop.

The pure smell of herbs untainted by the sometimes offensive odors of chemistry enthralled Bianca to the point that she forgot herself. Her eyes fluttered shut and she stood stark-still, cataloging the various scents, identifying gentian, sorrel, sage, thyme, and the unpleasant whiff of valerian.

"A good day," said the apothecary, entering from a back room.

Bianca blinked. "Aye, it is," she agreed with a smile. She looked at the generous selection of herbs and display of bottles. "I am in no haste; prithee, finish what you were doing."

"I'll be but a moment." The proprietor disappeared and Bianca occupied herself with sniffing the air. The stuffed lizard caught her eye and she was staring at it when Standish returned. He weighed a measure of sage and she noted his attention to detail, removing with small pincers the tiniest flake from his scale until the instrument balanced perfectly.

Expecting to create a medicine or weigh an ingredient, he looked puzzled when she responded that she only wished to speak with him.

"Were you at the Dim Dragon in Southwark the night before last?" she asked.

Standish's brow furrowed. "I am usually consulted on what is the best tincture for wet lungs or whether one might take garlic and mugwort with no ill effect." He neatened the counter, brushing loose herbs off the table into his hand, then depositing them out the front door into the lane. "I wonder why you ask?" He closed the door.

Bianca waited until he returned to his workbench and faced

her. "I have been sent by the constable to speak with you." This was not entirely true. However, it was an opportunity to disprove her fears about Malva and Meddybemps while satisfying her obligation to Patch. She sensed that this was a man who would respond to official inquiry.

Standish lightly placed his hands upon the worktable and tipped his head. "You have been sent? Why, pray tell, are *you* being required to undertake this task?"

"If you will, sir, I have earned the constable's . . . trust. I grant it is uncommon for a woman to do what is usually reserved for an agent of the law, but I believe you would prefer to speak with me if you met the constable in charge." She expected Standish might think he could deceive her more easily than an official. Bianca prepared for this eventuality and continued. "Shall I conclude that you were at the Dim Dragon Inn?"

The apothecary appeared bemused. "You may . . . but you haven't told me what this is about?"

"I was told that you expressed interest in some unusual stones."

Standish responded with a slight tilt of his head in the other direction. His eyes scanned Bianca's face before answering. "There were several who expressed interest. Do you ask this on behalf of the constable of Southwark?"

"I do, sir," answered Bianca. She got back to her questioning. "However, you were not successful in convincing Leadith Browne to accept your offer to buy these stones."

"I was not." Standish adjusted the position of his balance on the table, angled it slightly. "I was outbid by Jacoby Nimble, the chandler on St. Laurence Lane."

His answer saved Bianca from having to wheedle the chandler's name and whereabouts out of him. "So Jacoby Nimble bought the stones."

"That is his intention as far as I know."

"I was told that after the chandler left, you tried to convince Leadith Browne to change her mind and accept an offer from you."

"I thought the woman might take less money just to have coin in her pocket and be done with them. She did not agree."

"And you appealed to her better nature to help mankind?"

Standish looked up from the balance. "Who told you this?"

"Sir, the Dim Dragon was not empty when you made your offer."

The apothecary snuffed. "I grant you that, however . . ."

"However, you were disappointed that she rejected you. It was reported that you left."

"There was no point in belaboring trying to convince her."

"Where did you go after the Dim Dragon?"

Standish straightened the weights in front of his balance before answering. "I walked to the waterfront to catch a ferry."

"And you caught a boat straightaway?"

"Aye," said Standish.

"That is curious because I was told that you came back to the Dim Dragon after being gone for a time."

The apothecary frowned. "Why are you questioning me if you already know what I did and did not do?"

"Sir, I am simply trying to understand when people came and went that night."

"Is the woman with the stones the victim of some misfortune?"

Bianca thought she saw something of a glint in his eye. She wondered about his sincerity. "It is not some misfortune, sir. It is the worst misfortune. Leadith Browne was murdered."

The apothecary nodded. "She seemed a common filch capitalizing on her husband's efforts. Assuredly, within her lie crimes worth a stretch on Henry's board. Deceit begets more of the same."

Bianca couldn't be sure whether it was the man's nature to remain stolid in the face of dour news, or whether Leadith's death might already have been known to him. "Might you answer my question? Did you return to the Dim Dragon after having previously left?"

Nye Standish lifted his chin. "In my disappointment I realized that I had forgotten my meadowsweet. I walked back to the Dim Dragon to retrieve it."

"Why risk the hazardous streets of Southwark at night by returning? Is the plant so important to you?"

"Waiting another night would have diminished its potency." His tone was slightly arrogant, as if this should have been obvious.

"And so you collected your meadowsweet and returned to the river."

Standish shook his head. "Unfortunately, my meadowsweet was not there. I searched the floor and table where I had been sitting, but I did not find it."

"I wonder who would take it when it is so abundantly available?"

"I do not know."

"Yet I see a posy of the recently picked plant hanging in your collection of drying herbs." Bianca pointed to a beam where a bunch was suspended. "The bunch is still wilting and limp."

"I was given that."

Bianca perked, hopeful that her mother had told her the truth. Perhaps Standish was the 'man in need' of whom she spoke. And if that were true, perhaps it was Standish who stuffed Leadith's mouth with it. "Sir, who gave you the meadowsweet?"

"A client who wishes me to make him a remedy."

Bianca felt a prick of disappointment. If there was anything she'd learned, though, it was that information rarely fell into her lap. But perhaps Standish's client was the mysterious 'man in need.' And if that were true, then she'd have another possibility to follow. "Who is this client?"

Standish pressed his lips together. "Apothecaries do not divulge the names of those who seek our help."

Irritated, Bianca then sought to learn more about the apothecary's night in Southwark. "I was told that you looked upset upon returning to the Dim Dragon."

"I was upset! My purpose for coming to Southwark was to pick meadowsweet while the moon was in phase. And someone took it."

"Did you ask whether someone threw it out?"

"I did, and no one had knowledge of it."

"Perchance, did a woman offer you her meadowsweet?"

The apothecary shook his head. "A woman? There were no women in the Dim Dragon, save for Goodwife Frye and the serving wenches." He snorted as though the thought of women at the Dim Dragon was ridiculous. "Oh!" he said, holding up a finger. "There was one the other night, but she kept to herself unlike the gaumless alchemist's wife. Women don't frequent the ken at night. Occasionally one ventures in by accident."

"This woman you saw. Can you describe her?"

"She was of some age. She had a round face."

"Do you remember what she wore?"

"I cannot be certain given the dim interior, but I believe she wore a saffron-colored kirtle. She had a straw hat."

"When you returned, was she still there?"

"Nay, she was not."

So Malva had already gone by the time Standish returned.

The apothecary inclined his head. "Have the stones been recovered?"

"They have not been found, sir."

The apothecary's eyes drifted.

"We believe they are lost."

"Lost?" Standish's mouth drew down, considering this. "You think they were not thieved?"

"It seems unlikely." Bianca paused, noting the look of disbelief on his face. "You have some doubt?"

"There were several men interested in those stones."

"Then, do you care to speculate as to who is the likely culprit?"

"That is for you and your constable to sort out, is it not?" A flash of a smile made his point. "But if you should find the glowing stones, I'd be interested in buying them."

Bianca nodded while her eyes surveyed the interior of his shop. At the least, Standish had confirmed Malva's presence at the Dim Dragon Inn that night. He also claimed he did not have the stones—a claim Bianca wasn't sure she believed. There was one last thing that Bianca wanted to ask of the apothecary. She dug into her purse and pulled out the round stone with indentations. "I wonder if you might have seen this before?"

The apothecary picked it out of her palm and examined the piece. "It is a weight that a chandler might use to keep the wicks straight while he pours the wax."

"An elaborate bauble for such an ordinary purpose."

Standish handed it back. "I doubt a tallowmaker would bother with pieces so fanciful, but certainly a candlemaker with some money might indulge in such an embellishment."

"What do you suppose is the meaning of the design?"

"Meaning?" said Standish. He snatched the sphere out of her hand to study it a second time. "There is no meaning, only purpose. One wraps the string between these grooves and its weight straightens the string and holds it taut." He demonstrated, pointing to the gap between the carved circles. "The wick would not slip."

Having exhausted her questions and her welcome, Bianca pocketed the round stone and wished the apothecary a good day. Her eyes settled on the mounted lizard, then flicked over to meet Standish's defensive glare.

"Most men of your profession display their lizards less prominently," she said.

"Goodwife, I am not like most men of my profession."

CHAPTER 15

Dikson Browne removed the rag from under his chin and gently touched a finger to his wound. The cut had finally stopped bleeding. He wadded up the saturated cloth and threw it in the hearth, watching the fire snap and curl its edge. As long as he was careful for a day, he could tolerate the slight oozing until the cut began to heal.

He changed out of his ruined smock and slipped into a dirty one, but at least it wasn't stained with blood. If Leadith were around he would have made her do the wash; the neglected pile kept growing and loath was he to do a woman's chore. Something had to be done about the laundry before he completely ran out of a change of clothes.

"God rot that boy," he said, cursing his son under his breath. At least he had sent the boy on an errand instead of throttling him for letting that pompous puffer into their rent. "A man is here to speak with you," Timothy had called from the second-floor landing, and thinking the matter was of a fiscal nature, he had hurried to the ground floor from his enclave in the rafters.

He hadn't expected to find a livid Albern Goddard in his

kitchen. The audacity of the man coming to his home and threatening him. And to do it in front of his son! The brass of Goddard only made Browne despise him more.

Goddard had demanded his fool stones. But Browne didn't have them, nor did he know that it was from Goddard that his wife had gotten them. How was he expected to know every misdeed Leadith had committed? He'd given up watching her years ago.

But the pursed-lipped cove refused to believe him. Before he knew it, Goddard had pushed him up against a wall and was pinning him there by the point of a dagger.

Now as Dikson ambled toward the flimsy stairs of his decrepit rent, a second inquiry summoned him at the door.

Browne turned to see that the door Albern Goddard had so thoroughly slammed had not latched as he had thought. Outside on the stoop was an impressively groomed man with steady gray eyes and a concerned look on his face.

"I beg your pardon," inquired the man. "It is not my wish to trouble you. However, I am to meet Leadith Browne. Is she home?"

"Not anymore," gruffed Dikson. He stumped over to the door. "She be dead."

The man blinked and pulled his ear, surprised. "I just spoke with her nary two days ago. That was sudden."

"Murder always is," said Browne.

"Murder?" repeated the man. "God's nails, what happened?"

"If we knew, I could say. But since she is the victim of someone's frenetic blade, it remains unknown." Browne tired from having to explain himself yet again. "Sir, if your business with Leadith does not concern me, I beg that you leave so that I might properly grieve for my dead wife." He started to close the door—and this time he would bolt it. Timothy could spend the day making mischief on the street for all he cared.

But the man stuck his finely clad foot in the door. "If I may, good fellow." He glanced over his shoulder, then lowered his voice. "I had agreed to pay good coin to your wife for a vial of glowing stones. We were to make the exchange here, today." The man's face turned generous. "I am still willing to pay for the vial, if you are willing to part with it."

Dikson Browne thought a moment about what a full purse could buy. Never mind that his lease was in arrears and that without Leadith he would now have to find a way to put food on the table for himself as well as Timothy. Besides the basics, he would be able to afford a replacement gown for his worn, scratchy one. People respected a well-dressed man, and it had been a long time since he'd known the quiet adulation that came from looking well attired. Alas, he sighed, he did not have the glowing stones. His idiot wife had swallowed them.

"I do not have them . . ." He paused, waiting for his visitor to provide his name.

"Jacoby Nimble," said the man.

"Very well. Tell me, Jacoby Nimble, what is it that you do?"

"I am a chandler."

"A chandler," said the alchemist, surprised. "I would not think a man of your trade would be interested in fanciful stones."

Jacoby Nimble feigned humility. "A man is not always defined by his work. There is more to life than dipping and selling candles."

"Your interest, then, is one of curiosity?"

"I collect oddities. It is a pastime of mine."

"And you are willing to pay for this indulgence?"

"I am, sir." The chandler smiled.

Dikson Browne's brain whirred with possibilities. This was a man he could play. True, he did not have the stones, but he could sell Jacoby Nimble the expectation of acquiring them.

"Unfortunately, the glowing stones have been lost. But, if you would like to buy some, I can make more for you. It will take a mote of time and it would require some money to buy the required ingredients. Alas, I do not have the resources to purchase what is needed. I invested everything I had into creating those stones." Here, he pretended a brave and sacrificial face.

Nimble asked to come inside and discuss the details and Dikson Browne, remembering his earlier altercation with Goddard, hesitated. But this man was willing to give *him* money and since there was nothing of any value for the fellow to take, Browne threw aside his misgivings and let him in.

"Where do you practice your noble art?" asked the chandler, surveying the interior. Not a single cucurbit or still head was in sight.

"I have a space dedicated to my work."

"Ah. In separate quarters?"

Browne snorted and he glanced behind him. "In a matter of sorts," he said.

Jacoby Nimble's gaze followed Browne's to the set of stairs at the rear of the rent. "And you can repeat your earlier success?" he asked.

"Most certainly. But as I told you, it takes time to go through the projections."

"How long will it take? When can I expect results?"

The oily machinations of Dickson Browne's nature slithered into action. "Well, sir, you see it depends on whether I can produce a ferocious hellfire in my stove. Into which I put a *caput corvi* which shall be made to roast to a powder of pewter gray . . ." When the alchemist finished unraveling his knotty tale, not only had he succeeded in thoroughly confusing the chandler, but if asked to explain in greater detail any of the methods he had just tangentially mentioned, he did not think he had an ounce of blabber left to construe.

It was with great relief for Dikson Browne that Jacoby Nimble nodded. "Then how much do you require to begin?" he asked.

The alchemist calculated the cost of two months back payments on rent, plus two more, plus a sufficient stipend to allow himself enough ale to keep comfortably sozzled. "Two and six," he said. T'would be a good start.

"A half crown," the chandler confirmed, hesitating long enough to worry the alchemist into thinking he'd asked for too much.

Browne beamed when the chandler handed over the money and they shook hands.

"I expect to hear about your progress when next I call."

"You have no need for worry," enthused Dikson Browne. "I shall begin the process immediately."

Having riled the impertinent, slubbering dog known as Dikson Browne, Albern Goddard made his way to the parish church at the end of the street. At least he had found out from the squeaking cur where his wife's body had been taken. The woman hadn't been dead very long before the man had nearly put her out of his memory.

Albern had already searched the alley where she had been discovered and, like Bianca, had not found the stones. Though he'd asked her to help him ferret out his element, he remained skeptical that she would actually follow through. Her indifference was obvious, and though he tried to impress upon her the importance of finding his missing element, he suspected she would only marginally commit herself.

Rather than depend on his daughter, whose temperament had become even more mercurial now she was with child, Albern took it upon himself to view dead Leadith Browne and see what could be done. He stepped into the nave of St. Michael, a slightly better-preserved church than the one in shambles up the street. After creeping past the silent and solemn chancel, he wandered into a separate area, where he found an office and a parish clerk busy at his ledger. He stood a moment in the doorway, then cleared his throat.

The clerk looked up.

"A good day, sir. My name is Albern Goddard. I have reason to believe Leadith Browne's body is in your care." He stepped inside.

The clerk placed a ribbon in his book and closed it. "Her body is here awaiting burial."

"She may have something on her person that is rightly mine."

"That being?" queried the clerk.

Albern saw no reason to be vague. "I am an alchemist. I believe she stole a discovery of mine."

"Sir, her clothing has been removed and returned to her husband. I suggest you inquire there." He flipped open his log to return to his figures.

Albern was not easily put off. "I have already questioned her husband. The item was not found."

The clerk looked up, puzzled. "What is it that you seek? I do not see how I can help you."

Albern removed his cap. He turned it around in his hands before answering. "If I may, I should like to search her."

The clerk stared. For a moment he seemed at a loss for words. Whether the man was surprised or disgusted was difficult to say. His face bore a blank expression as unreadable as the sanctuary's whitewashed wall. "I'm not sure I understand," he said. "There is nothing *on* her to search."

"I heard you the first time," said Albern. "I wish to examine her body."

The resulting weighty silence would have shamed most to see the error in their ways, but Albern thought his request was perfectly justified. His self-interest was as profound as it was complete.

The clerk got to his feet and his face colored a plummy shade of purple. "Sir, I do not presume to understand, nor do I wish to be informed about what, exactly, it is that you want me to agree."

Albern, certain he'd been misunderstood, explained. "The woman was sliced. I believe it was an attempt to remove something inside of her. I would like to penetrate her."

The clerk rattled like an old cart. "What you imply is revolting." He came around his desk and stood within inches of Albern Goddard, looking as though he might pop. "This is sacred ground!" he challenged. "And might I remind you that necromancy is a sin of abominable proportion!"

Goddard could hardly believe the bad turn this had taken. The clerk's reaction further confirmed his low opinion of the clergy's intelligence. "You misunderstand me. I want to use my finger."

The clerk clenched his fists and leaned forward. "Perhaps I have not made myself clear. Remove yourself forthwith and may God have mercy on your soul!"

The silence of the church worked against Albern, for there soon appeared a sexton of considerable heft. He shuffled into the room, accessed the situation, and laid a meaty paw on the alchemist's shoulder.

It was a hand that would broach no quarrel.

Albern swallowed, grudgingly accepted the verdict, and was roughly escorted to an exit.

On the street, he arranged his jerkin and gown. He put his cap upon his head. There was no amount of explaining or reasoning with religious men. He brushed off the shoulder of his gown, removing the memory of his poor treatment, as well as the last fleck of dirt from the sexton's grubby hand.

He had no choice but to accept that his element was gone. He would have to start over.

Chapter 16

Dikson Browne paused to ponder life's inexplicable curves. A turn of fortune cheered the alchemist, whose purse now tugged heavily at his belt. He enjoyed the feel of extra weight against his groin, of money sluggishly bouncing with every step. It had been a long time since he'd enjoyed the pleasure of so much coin and it made him greedy for more.

He felt a new lease on life strolling down Thames Street from the warehouse district. He'd hurried out and bought himself a buttery yellow doublet from a fripperer. Afterward, he decided he needed a gown to top it off, so he doled out money for one of enviable quality. His feet barely touched the ground as he imagined women staring and wishing to stroke the gown's rich walnut brown velvet. Without his complaining wife to berate his every move, he felt as light as a flower petal twirling on a breeze.

However, dainty flower petals were the last thing that came to mind for those he passed on the street.

The man's portly abdomen struck an ungainly profile and even though his upper attire indicated a man of wealth and good taste, his lower attire shouted the opposite. His worn and shapeless hosen hung loosely about his legs, calling attention to his calves' scrawny anatomy, unexpected given the girth of his paunch. Browne was no Henry the VIII in the matter of handsome calves. But if there was one thing that Browne and his now-deceased wife, Leadith, had in common, it was their inability to fathom the unkind toll that years had taken on their bodies.

He had been careful to remove his new gown before positioning a ladder he'd filched from outside a warehouse near Albern Goddard's room of alchemy—a fortuitous find. Despite missing its lower rungs, he was able to boost himself to the middle boards by scrambling up a pile of debris.

With a mind for stealth, the alchemist ascended the shaky ladder and cautiously raised his head to peer through a high window. At first he did not see Goddard and he grew anxious wondering if his nemesis was on his way and might catch him skulking about. Then, as his eyes adjusted to the dim light of the interior, he saw Albern working on his latest projection. Dikson wondered if he was making more glowing stones. He watched as long as he was able, reflecting on what he was seeing, figuring how soon Goddard might finish making his valuable element.

Browne did not know for certain what exactly Albern Goddard was attempting to project, but he was heartened to see the puffer industriously at work. He left with the intention of keeping an eye on his progress, and when the time was ripe . . .

Having also visited his landlord and paid his arrears, Dikson Browne now felt the urge to celebrate his good fortune. In spite of the day beginning in an unpleasant row, it had ended with him feeling smugly victorious. Odd how the course of one day could both break and make a man. This elevated mood called for celebration and he gaily followed his whim.

Barreling through the door of his favorite boozing ken, the Royal Poke, he proceeded to waste an afternoon quaffing tankards and leering at the serving wenches scurrying about. The effects of the brew soon had him thinking where *he* might find a "poke" since he no longer had Leadith to do her wifely duty. Unfortunately for him, he would have had better results if he had gone to Southwark, but weighing sleep against rumpy pumpy he had to admit he preferred, when it came right down to it, the seductive allure of a good night's repose. He was, after all, getting older.

The alchemist turned his tankard upside down over a squinted eye. Not a drop to trickle. He rose from the trestle and gave the tavern wench an arse squeeze in appreciation, and after dramatically donning his new gown, staggered out the door. He remembered where he lived after a long tour of Queenhithe Ward, wandering up and down the lanes looking for his familiar one, and eventually he staggered up the crooked stoop to his wretched rent.

For once the boy's forgetfulness to bolt the door was to his convenience. Without the irritation of waiting for Timothy to let him in, Dikson shouldered it open, further straining its crooked hinge, and stumbled inside.

Timothy looked up from his sweeping.

The boy, he decided, favored Leadith far too much. He had her eyes—those mingy, needy eyes. And he had her way of watching him as if he were a rat in a grain bin. "Be gone," he said, shooing him away with both hands. "Before I beat you into dust."

But the boy did not waver. Confound him anyway.

"What is it you want?" he spewed. He tried meeting the boy's stare and essayed his fiercest glare, a difficult feat given all the ales numbing his face.

"I am to tell you," said Timothy, hawing and stuttering, a pathetic sight. Surely this spawn was never his. If Leadith were around, he would have smacked her one.

"What? What must you tell me?" *Spit it out, boy*, he thought. *I haven't the grit to beat you, but I'm getting there.*

"Jacoby Nimble was here. He wanted to buy some glowing stones."

"Aye, he was!" confirmed Dikson Browne.

Timothy's brows danced and he appeared uncertain. "He knocked on the door and I answered."

Dikson Browne repeated the boy's words inside his head. Inside his head a voice reminded him that he'd already spoken with Jacoby Nimble earlier in the day. What did Timothy mean *he* answered the door?

"What? Who, say you?" He felt his features twist and he must have finally managed to look fearsome because Timothy's stutters started sounding like the rapid chattering of a bird's beak against a window. "Come now, boy. Explain yourself."

"You were gone. I answered the door and a man asked for Mother."

"A man asked for Leadith?" Heat began traveling up Dikson's neck. He felt the warmth flush his skin. "And *what* name did he give?"

"Jacoby Nimble, he was."

"The chandler?"

Timothy nodded vehemently.

"Be you certain?"

Timothy nodded anew.

"And what, pray tell, did Jacoby Nimble want? Tell me again." He turned, pointing his good ear so it could rightly hear.

Timothy repeated the man's request.

This made no sense to Dikson Browne. Why would the man come back so soon? He had explained in detail how the element required special ingredients and a modicum of time in order to create it. Regrettably, as was often true for the alchemist, too much drink muddled his reasoning. A rational conclusion was dismissed for a suspicious one.

"Do you seek to make me a fool, boy?" He stalked forward and grabbed the broom away from his son. "You want to play a trick on me?" He swung the broom and clobbered the boy on the head.

Timothy reacted too late to fend off the blow. He shook his head vigorously and denied the charge. The boy knew his father would not stop until he had soundly beaten him. It was an outcome Timothy expected; but while years had been unkind to his father, they were now to the boy's advantage. His muscles were not so reedy and his reasoning was not so naïve. Besides, he no longer had his mother, and while her treatment of him was often just as poor, she had been the parent he relied on. She had been the one who put food on the table.

Timothy grabbed the broom away from his father. He made a move to hit his old man while he had the opportunity. However, the gentle part of Timothy that had not been corrupted by growing up cautioned him against lashing out at the only person whose roof he shared. He was not ready to run away forever. But he was ready to run away for a while.

The door slammed and Dikson Browne spit on the floor in disgust. "Run, you little scut. Run while you still have the legs God gave you. Because if you come back too soon, I'll cut them off and use them for kindling. Ungrateful nidget."

Browne slumped onto his palliasse and stared at the empty pillow beside him. "I blame you," he said to the innocent bolster. And then he took a long nap, having passed out.

Boisvert lived on Foster Lane a short walk from Charing Cross. With enough skulduggery for one day, Bianca turned her thoughts to John's departure. Perhaps she could convince the silversmith to let him leave early. She wanted to spend their remaining time together, enjoying each other's company instead of avoiding it.

On Foster Lane, Bianca stopped beside St. Vedast Church, its door boarded, its roof caved in from an unfortunate accident a few months prior. Being open to London's foul weather, the structure had suffered even more damage than it had already endured from the king's campaign to disenfranchise parish churches from their supporting monastery and strip them of their wealth. Her eyes ran up the height of the building to where the steeple used to be, now gone and leaving a gaping hole in the roof. St. Vedast was the site of much unhappiness for the silversmith, and Bianca wondered how Boisvert managed to live under its shadow—a constant reminder of his lost love, Odile, and his time spent in Newgate Prison. But, as John had said, the man's wit sustained him, and the fellow was not the sort to easily accept defeat.

At Boisvert's shop, Bianca found John finishing his work, polishing the angels that would soon benefit the king's coffers. "These are the coins that will pay your way to wage war," she said, noting the irony in John's task. John took his foot off the polishing wheel as Bianca gave him a kiss. "As I've said before, I am not my own man."

Bianca smiled wistfully and rested her chin on his shoulder. "Where is Boisvert?"

"He's gone to market. A matter of some importance, he said."

"I was hoping to wrest you away. I want to spend our last night making fond memories."

John's ears pinked. "Know't, I wish it so."

Bianca planted a kiss on his teasing brow and his business of polishing was abandoned until they heard the master silversmith rattling the door latch.

"It is the Bianca," said Boisvert, as he clomped over the threshold, gripping a limp chicken by the neck. A wheel of cheddar cheese was pressed against his chest with a loaf of bread on top. Bianca took the bread and Boisvert kissed the air on either side of her cheek. "To what do we owe your company?"

"I was hoping you would let John leave early. It is our last night together."

"Say no more. But you must not think it is your last night together." He handed her the cheese and patted her cheek with affection. "You will stay for dinner. This was for John," he said, holding up the chicken. "*Mais puisque vous êtes ici*, I will save you the chore of cooking it and you will stay for dinner."

Bianca cheered at not having to cook and followed Boisvert up the stairs, leaving John to finish his work.

The master silversmith removed his doublet, draping it on a chest in front of a wall mural of the fields in Provence, and contently worked in his smock and hosen. He stoked the hearth and set about heating a kettle of water for scalding the chicken. A bottle of wine was opened for basting (both the chicken and the cook), which he generously shared with Bianca.

Boisvert sipped from a silver goblet and rearranged pots, moving them from one hook to another while singing a bouncy tune in his native tongue. Bianca busied herself with slicing wedges of bread and cheese and listening to Boisvert's voice warble in French. She guessed it was a happy tune, for his head bobbed enthusiastically with every repeated chorus.

At last the water simmered and the Frenchman grabbed the chicken by its feet and dunked it in the kettle. After a couple of dips he tried plucking a feather and frowned at the result. "A few more dips, *un, deux, trois . . .*" A second try resulted in a satisfying pop as the feather gave way. "Voilà!"

Bianca ducked as he slung the bird onto the board, just missing her head by a fly's nose.

"Eh? You will help? It goes the faster with the two." He poured another splash of wine for them. "To fortify us," he reasoned.

"Did you think not to include me?" said John, appearing at the top of the stairs. Their giggling had left him feeling lonely and he'd hurried to finish the last of his chores.

"There is plenty left to pluck," said Boisvert, waving him over. "I think, though, that you should pour some wine and watch."

"There are more feathers in Bianca's hair than on that bird. I'll pour a goblet and pluck my lady instead."

Boisvert guffawed. "*Elle est ton oiseau à farcir*," he said, waggling his eyebrows.

John flushed, responding, "*Et j'ai une grosse carotte*," and they both burst out laughing. Bianca blithely kept plucking the bird and ignored them both.

And so, on their last evening together the three made merry and basked in the glow of friendship forged from years of collective history and love. There were no clashes of personality, no words spoken in regret, only good cheer and the smell of roast chicken in the air. With their bellies full and their hearts warm with wine, the evening passed companionably. Finally, when the night watchman called late the hour, they realized that the morrow was fast upon them. John's impending departure sat in the air like a malevolent spectre, but Boisvert did not indulge its daunting pall. The silversmith vanquished the shade by refusing to mention it.

Even when Boisvert opened the door and they all stood in maudlin silence looking out at the stars with the steeple of St.

Leonard piercing the sky, the Frenchman refused to let their fears ruin the night. He threw his arms around John and held him like a son. *"Je vais tu voir bientôt,"* he said, but his eyes held a painful sentiment. Then, with a final proud look, he sent the young couple into an uncertain night, their hearts large with love.

When at last Dikson Browne came to, he blinked into the early evening hours and listened for his son. Disappointed that Timothy had not returned to make him dinner, he rolled to sitting and rubbed his temple. Perhaps he had been overly harsh with the boy. He thought of Albern Goddard's room of alchemy and the high window there. When the time came, he needed his son's help to get inside.

"Bullocks," he groused, getting to his feet. "Bullocks and teats," he said upon realizing he'd slept in his new velvet gown. He shrugged out of it and tried smoothing the rumpled creases, then draped it across a chest. Handsome cloaks should only be worn on occasion. He donned his familiar shopworn doublet and stood in the doorway tucking in his smock and fastening the doublet's buttons. Outside, the shadows stretched long from the sinking sun.

Despite his throbbing temples and pounding head, Dikson Browne set off to find young Timothy and bring him home.

CHAPTER 17

"At least let me walk with you to the water," said Bianca the next morning. She had cooked a filling breakfast of bacon and boiled eggs, and had spared no expense for their last meal together. While he slept, Bianca had dressed, then woken their neighbor to trade muscle liniment for a dozen eggs. She walked down the lane for a loaf of bread, then returned to unwrap a flitch of bacon they'd been nibbling at for months. Despite the inconvenience that spattered grease would pose the next time she worked on her medicines (unexpected fires), she withstood the smoke and burns from cooking and presented John with a substantial and (John could not deny it) delicious meal.

Their time together, however, was at an end.

John preferred to say goodbye in their rent and forgo an emotional public display in front of other poor wretches similarly conscripted. But Bianca didn't care a cobbler's cuss what others thought and, despite John's objections, she accompanied him to the waterfront. Perched on her shoulder with his cheek against hers rode Hobs.

The feline must have sensed something amiss and followed

his people out of Gull Hole onto Tooley Street where Bianca feared he might get in a tangle with a roaming dog. He ignored their admonishments to return home; it was easier just to let him come. In fact, John felt touched that Hobs was so determined to follow.

The two spoke very little on the way there. They held hands and occasionally John lifted Bianca's to his lips. Rarely did the couple show affection in public, but today their usual reserve seemed a silly and wasted pretense.

Ahead, a parade of somber couples meandered toward the waiting barges at Paris Garden. Some had children in tow, others a companion dog that would be abandoned once its master boarded. As the recruited men approached the crowd of bystanders, their spines straightened and their jaws leveled. Sometimes it took the company of others to steel a man to his fate.

The boats would take the men across to Bridewell, where they would disembark and march to the Strand, expecting to camp at St. Martin's Fields. A fair number of men carried warbows and a quiver of arrows—a badge of their coveted status. John carried nothing. A bill or a pike would be supplied later, and he'd be given some cursory training on how to handle the cumbersome weapon. He wondered how long they'd be at the field practicing weaponry and drilling before being dispatched to their assigned guard.

John pulled Bianca off to the side and they watched an officer at a table tick off names as inductees filed past. Once accounted for, the recruits climbed aboard a barge and squeezed in next to one another. A brazen few made light of their situation—as much to fraternize as to mask an underlying dread. John kept an anxious eye on the dwindling line, but his focus remained on Bianca. He was in no hurry to start his new life as a soldier.

John tipped Bianca's chin to face him. "Promise me that you will love our child?"

"You need not ask." She rested her hand on her stomach. "I cherish this baby as much as you."

A wistful smile clouded John's face and he looked away. "If I should not return," he said, turning back to Bianca, and she put a finger on his lips.

"Nay," she said. "Do not speak it."

John caught her wrist. "I do not know when I will see you again. Or even *if* I will see you again. War may change me in ways neither of us can predict. But know that until my dying breath it is you who I see in my dreams. That will never change."

Bianca had no words to equal his. Though her affection for John was steadfast, she had always struggled expressing it. However much she tried, she could not effectively convey her devotion. In a sense, a part of her was broken—she lacked the warmth and ease that came so easily to him and to others. Perhaps her parents' indifference had damaged her irrevocably. She hoped she would not make the same mistakes raising her child.

But today, she managed to say what she felt. "You understand my heart," she said, fixing him with her vivid stare. "It is a grace for which I am ever grateful."

John smiled. "Content yourself, my love. I am not yet dead." And he took her face in his hands and kissed her.

A shout from an officer broke their final embrace.

"Now go to, John," said Bianca, motioning with her chin to join the others. "I will be here when you return."

He gave a final pat to Hobs, wishing that, if the cat was indeed immortal, then some of his longevity would rub off on him.

Bianca watched John with the officer, then saw him take a place on the barge. She was not the only one reluctant to leave; those gathered saw their fathers, lovers, and husbands depart for an unknown future. Her eyes found John's and they held each other's gaze for as long as they could. Gulls circled overhead, calling as if announcing the inevitable departure. The oars pointed to the sky as the barge drifted into the current, then on order they dipped into the water and stroked in unison, pulling the craft smoothly across the river. The sun reflected off the water like liquid mercury, and Bianca followed John until his silhouette grew indistinct, then became indistinguishable.

"A king's pawn," said Bianca softly. "Be well, my love."

* * *

Bianca and Hobs started back to Gull Hole. The road stretched before them like the day, waiting to be tread upon, waiting to be used. At the corner near the chicken pen, Hobs leapt from her shoulder and began stalking baby chicks, upsetting the hens. He couldn't get through the elaborate fortress the neighbor had built, so Bianca let him be. She, too, saw the need to distract herself and keep from dwelling on John's absence. Little could be accomplished fretting over his welfare. His fate was out of her hands.

Once inside the door to her room of Medicinals and Physickes, the sight of John's empty plate tore at her heart. She picked up his tankard and could still smell his breath. Her tongue caught the last dribble of ale pooled in the bottom but it did not satisfy her dry mouth.

She cleared the place setting, wiped off the plate, and set it on a shelf, her fingers lingering to trace its curve, then set the tankard on top. Through the open window, a breeze set her herbs bristling, spinning from nails and snags in the rafters, tangling their strings. Bianca moved a bench and released the sprigs of meadowsweet. She ran the flowers under her nose and rubbed a leaf between her fingers.

Working on a concoction would help to calm her; besides, she needed to earn some money. Bianca absently tapped the meadowsweet on the table. What if Meddybemps was guilty and convicted of murder? Who would sell her remedies and keep her confidence? No one. The answer was—no one.

Bianca sighed and looked around at her hovel as if seeing it for the first time. The space appeared smaller than usual, even with John gone. Cracks ran through the walls, exposing horse hair and hay to keep out drafts. A tower of alembics and pelican retorts occupied one corner and the floor rushes needed to be replaced. Despite its poor appearance, this was her home, this was her life, and she was not inclined to change her circumstances. They'd been changed enough already.

With John gone, she realized just how much she depended on Meddybemps for her own survival. For whatever deceit her mother and he had been party to, she hadn't the heart to learn more. Perhaps she should dissect Nye Standish's combative interview. Perhaps she should seek out Jacoby Nimble, the chandler, and learn more about him. Her shoulders slumped with weariness. No, for now, she would abandon the search for Leadith's murderer and hope the whole affair about her father's element would just fade with neglect.

She stared at the shelves lined with remedies for wet lungs, cough, and shallow wounds. Working on a remedy for ague using meadowsweet would give her something to think about other than an uncertain future. Her spirits began to lift as she prepared for her next medicine. The idea of trying a new combination of herbs to see if it would calm the fevers associated with the malady quickly consumed her.

She set about chopping, and once she had a sizable mound she put the herbs aside. In spite of what promised to be an unusually warm spring day, Bianca started a fire in her stove to boil her concoction. With the pot upon the tripod, she went to the window to remove the boards that partially blocked the breeze. One fell into the lane and she went outside to retrieve it.

If she'd known she'd meet Constable Patch loping up the lane, she would have bolted her door and pretended to be gone. But it was too late to avoid the lawman, who caught sight of her and called.

"Bianca Goddards!" He held up his arm so that she could distinguish him, she guessed, from the chickens. "We needs to talk."

Hobs slunk down, his hair on end as the constable passed and neared his mistress.

Patch glanced at the board in her hand and took a step back in case she decided to swing it at him.

"Come inside," she said. "I've got to keep an eye on a pot."

The constable dutifully followed, walking under the low lintel without having to duck, and made himself comfortable at the table while Bianca checked her stove and added water to her pot.

"What are ye brewing?" he asked, sniffing the air—for once the odor wasn't objectionable.

"I'm making a remedy for ague."

"Ye can't prevent people from taking exception," said Patch. "It's human nature."

Bianca eyed him curiously. "I've seen nothing that proves that it is . . ." She then realized Patch thought she was making a potion for arguments. "Constable Patch, I am working on a remedy for the illness. Ague is not a trait of human character." She turned back to her boiling herbs so he couldn't see her roll her eyes.

"Ohhh . . . ague," he said. "Ha, well, so it is." He mumbled something incomprehensible under his breath.

Bianca wished to be rid of the feckless lawman. She wanted to return to a routine of making medicines; she needed the distraction of that routine, but she knew Patch had come to pester her. She would know no peace until she learned why he was there. "You said you wished to speak to me, Constable."

"Aye. This murder of Leadith Browne is becoming twisty." Patch picked up a jar and examined it. He took a sniff, closed one eye, and set it down.

Bianca didn't ask why the murder was becoming more convoluted. She kept on working, waiting for him to explain.

Patch straightened with self-importance. "Dikson Browne's residence has been ransacked."

"He lives in a pitiable rent in a not so desirable area."

Patch snorted. "Odd for you to say it so." He motioned to his surroundings.

"Where I live serves its purpose," said Bianca. "However, I am not surprised that Browne's rent was looted. Unless you have a specific reason as to why, I will assume this is just a matter of course on Trinity Lane."

"Ha!" said Patch, as if he'd caught her out. "Browne claims this has never happened before."

Bianca turned back to the stove and jabbed the fire with a long stick. "Do you have reason to think this is relevant to his wife's murder?"

Patch replied indignantly. "It proves he did not kill his wife!"

"How do you conclude that? I fail to follow your reasoning."

Patch grumbled. "What man would stage a thorough looting of his own quarters after going through the throes of losing his wife and being accused of her murder?"

"I'd say the kind of man who is guilty and who hopes to discourage people from thinking him so."

Constable Patch huffed. "That is outrageous."

"Are you defending him?"

"Decidedly not! But ye've no proof it was Browne."

"And you have proof that it wasn't?"

Patch's eyes glinted with sarky intent. "As a matter of facts," said he, "Dikson Browne says your father made threatening overtures to him."

"My father sought Browne out?" Bianca stopped stirring.

"So sayeth Dikson Browne."

Without comment, Bianca gave her herbs a vigorous stir.

"It seems your father has an interest in this." He tugged his scraggly beard and kept his eyes on Bianca's back. "Albern Goddard, the alchemist once accused of trying to poison the king." He waited for Bianca to protest. When she did not, he prodded, "Methinks ye might not be tellin' me all that ye might know, Bianca Goddard."

Bianca sighed. She saw no way to avoid telling Patch the truth. To further skirt the issue or color it differently would only work against her if he were to find out later. "Constable, I shall tell you what I know. I swear by God's blood that Leadith Browne's wondrous stones were my father's discovery. He came to me saying that they had been stolen and asked that I find them. Never did he suspect the Brownes of theft. You came to me after Leadith was found murdered, and I told my father, after the fact, that Leadith had tried selling his element at the Dim Dragon Inn but was killed later that night. I also told him that I believed the element was lost—that apparently she had swallowed them."

"Browne said your father accused him of stealing his wondrous stones," said Patch, a smug expression causing his upper lip to tremble. "But Browne swears he did not."

"I am not defending my father, but he is angry that he was

robbed of his discovery. Why should he not suspect Dikson Browne? The man is a failed alchemist and he was married to Leadith. Is it so unexpected that he would threaten him? Might not you have reacted the same?"

Patch shrugged. "But Dikson Browne has never been accused of a heinous crime."

"My father was accused," said Bianca pointedly. "Not convicted."

Patch pushed out his lips in a skeptical gesture.

"Constable, my father knew the stones were valuable. He even thought they might be dangerous, but they were stolen before he had the chance to study them and know their nature. Do you honestly think Dikson Browne, a blundering tosspot, had the ability to make something so extraordinary?"

"So's ye saying the stones were your father's and Dikson Browne stole them?"

Bianca sighed, exasperated by the constable's slow grasp. "I am saying either Dikson or Leadith stole them." Bianca avoided mentioning that her father suspected Malva was involved and so softened her accusation. "It may not matter *who* exactly stole them, except that Leadith ended up with them. And that is where the stones ultimately ended—inside her stomach."

Patch considered this for a moment. "Then," he said, "your father killed Leadith."

"Patch, did you not hear me? My father sought my help finding the stones and never once mentioned the Brownes. He did not suspect Leadith or Dikson of stealing his element." Patch was succeeding in making her dotty. She'd learned before that the constable's reasoning was three parts goading and one part misinterpretation of fact. It was a matter of course that she spend an inordinate amount of time trying to explain anything to him. And here she was, again, simplifying the facts. Still, she persisted in bolstering her argument. "My father was stunned, he was surprised, when I told him Leadith was trying to sell his stones and that her body was found later in an alley." Bianca removed the pot off the stove and put it on the table. "And he is a man who cannot fake surprise."

Patch ran a tongue around the inside of his cheek while thinking. "Maybes he thinks Dikson might still have the beans."

Bianca shook her head and searched her shelves for something to strain her brew. "The beans are gone, Patch. I searched for them in the alley and found nothing. Leadith swallowed them." She'd had enough of Patch and if she could have booted him out she would have.

Patch straightened as a thought occurred to him. "Maybes your father wasn't the one looking for the beans. Maybes someone else thinks Browne still has them. There were, after all, more than one stone."

Bianca took a piece of cloth and scraped it clean of dried herbs. She laid it over a bowl and tied it with a piece of cord.

"I have more to tells ye," said Patch. "An apothecary named Nye Standish said he was at the Dim Dragon the night of Leadith's murder. He says that Jacoby Nimble left the Dim Dragon Inn before he did. And he says Nimble wanted to walk Leadith Browne to the water and share a ferry with her, but she refused and stayed on."

"I know that," said Bianca. "It is not news."

"How do ye know that?"

"I've already spoken to Standish. I got his name from one of the patrons of the Dim Dragon."

Patch looked a little perturbed that Bianca was one step ahead of him. He continued. "Wells, when Standish finally gets to the water and the boat is a distance from the stairs, he sees Jacoby Nimble arrive after him."

"So Jacoby Nimble was waylaid in Southwark. That is not notable. He did not leave the Dim Dragon to go straight home."

"Except he wanted Leadith to leave with him. And she did not."

"We know she stayed on," said Bianca. "Several people have confirmed that. But how does Standish know it was the chandler who arrived late? The river is dark and he was a distance from shore. How could he have known it was Jacoby Nimble?"

"Ah!" Patch gloated as if he'd caught her in his coils. "Standish saw the chandler's face clear as day. Nimble held a lantern that gave off a brilliant light."

"A light so bright that he could be identified from a boat on the river?"

Patch nodded. "Not just a normal light. Not like a usual lantern. An especially brilliant light, so says he."

Bianca puzzled over an explanation that didn't include the glowing stones. "Nimble *is* a chandler, after all. Mayhap a good one who knows how to create a proper candle for a lantern."

"Naw, no," said Patch. "Standish insists the light was exceptionally bright. Like a beacon it was." Patch rubbed his eyes. They began to itch and water and he looked up at the row of herbs, wondering which might be the offending weed. He felt the need to quit this place for a breath of outside air. "There was something else of note." He sneezed, spraying spittle across the board. "Dikson Browne received a visit from the chandler earlier in the day. The same day that his room was ransacked."

"Then why do you think my father did the pilfering? It appears the chandler should be considered in this."

"Exceptin' that Dikson's son claimed the chandler showed up a second time asking for the glowing beans."

"Ah. So Nimble didn't believe Browne and decided to try asking the boy for the element?"

"Maybes. But maybes he was looking over the room thinking he might search it."

"Or, maybe the second chandler was not who he said he was," said Bianca, stopping to think.

"I tolds ye this was gettin' twistier and twistier." Patch puffed out his chest and his brass buttons caught the sun shining through the window.

Bianca wondered why the chandler would visit Browne twice in a day. Perhaps he, or someone else posing as him, thought Leadith did not swallow all the stones. A rap at the doorjamb interrupted her thoughts.

"How now?" called Meddybemps as he stepped into the rent, crouching to avoid hitting his head. His red cap prominently appeared before he removed it in greeting. "Good day, Constable," he said as though he meant it. "We meet again." Bianca marveled at his polite manner that seemed sincere.

"Aye, well. I was just taking to leave." Patch stood, tugged the hem of his doublet to straighten and draw attention to it.

Bianca looked from Meddybemps to Patch. Her chest tightened wondering if the constable had noticed the flagrant red head wear that Dikson Browne had described? She hoped Meddybemps had the sense to keep quiet and not engage Patch before she ushered him out the door.

"We need to find out more about this Jacoby Nimble," she said, reassuring the constable if only to be rid of him. By doing so, she unwittingly committed herself to continuing the investigation, or at least to the pretense of continuing it.

As she stuffed Constable Patch out the door, she realized, with a sinking heart, that Leadith Browne's murder was not going to fade in people's memories, especially his. The glowing stones were too unusual, too remarkable for that to happen.

She glanced over her shoulder at Meddybemps, wearing a snide smile on his face—a supercilious and insincere smile. He'd probably noticed her sudden effort to hurry Patch along.

Bianca ignored her friend, keeping her hand on the door latch a moment before facing him. Patch had just handed her a lead to possibly link the chandler to Leadith's murder. Her first priority was to protect Meddybemps and her mother, and Patch might have just given her the opportunity to prove them innocent.

Bianca could almost hear John scolding her for becoming involved again. But, she reasoned, as she stood a moment thinking, her promise to John was that first she would take care of their child. And, in order to do that, she had to survive. And to survive meant that she needed both her mother's and Meddybemps's help.

Bianca turned to her friend, whose expression fell as he read the concern on her face.

"What troubles you, my prodigy? Is that beef-witted gudgeon meddling where he should not?"

"He is doing his duty, I suppose." She rubbed the back of her neck and her hand dropped protectively to her belly. Her muscles ached with tension. "What brings you by?" She sought a stool for herself and sat.

"Have you any salve or medicines for me to sell? I have nearly sold through what I have. People are clamoring for your spring purgative. Their sap is running with the warming days." He placed a pouch of coins on the table. "Your portion from market. I hope you are pleased."

"It will be helpful." Bianca didn't bother to count how much was there. Instead, she kept her eyes on the streetseller. "Meddy, I need for you to be honest with me."

The vendor raised his eyebrows as if this was an unnecessary request. "You are ill at ease," he said. "What troubles you?"

Bianca smiled faintly. "What do you know about Leadith Browne's murder?"

"What do *I* know?" he repeated, as if there was no reason for her to ask. Meddybemps tugged his earlobe before answering. "I know that she was found dead in an alley near the Dim Dragon. You told me so the last time I was here."

"And you were evasive when I asked if you knew Leadith Browne."

"She was not a pleasant woman."

"So, you *did* know her."

"I do not deny it."

"How did you know her?" Bianca resented having to pry answers out of him. Why could he not be more forthcoming?

"If you must know, we once enjoyed each other's company." He would have stopped there, but Bianca's expectant stare bore into him. "I know how much you dislike hearing about my carousing," he reminded her.

Bianca could have guessed. Meddybemps left a trail of widows and wives in his wake like crumbs from crackers. There was scarce a woman whom he had not charmed, and fewer still who had escaped his notice. She preferred avoiding the sordid details of Meddybemps's relations—she did not approve of his reck-lessness. He tread a thin line of adultery, and his ill-considered entanglements never failed to put someone in danger. A man com-mitting adultery was given greater leniency when accused, but a cuckolded husband was often paraded through the streets to the jeering throngs of onlookers. A man was a limp-hinged washcloth if he failed to control and sate his wife's wanton inklings, as it was expected that women needed discipline to prevent succumbing to their libidinous nature. Bianca hoped this particular predicament was not because Meddybemps had taken up with her mother again. "When were you last . . . with . . . Leadith?" asked Bianca, insinuating more than just the simple question.

"It has been years, my dear."

"Her husband said someone with a red cap prevented him from giving her a proper beating. The description sounds like you."

"It sounds like me because it *was* me."

"Why did you not say it so?"

He lowered his voice. "Do you think my wit so small that I would confess to such in front of Patch?" Meddybemps glanced over his shoulder, looking toward the door and window. "The man does not understand subtlety. If I should have told him I inter-vened, do you think I would be standing here now? I would be dangling from wall manacles in the Clink."

"Tell me what happened," Bianca insisted.

Meddybemps sighed and dragged a stool to sit opposite. "I was on my way to the Dim Dragon Inn when I heard shouting and the sounds of a scuffle. When a woman is being beaten I am not one to ignore it. So I shouted at the man and he ran off. I tried to help Leadith." Meddybemps searched Bianca's face for empathy, but she revealed no indication of judgment one way or the other. "She had been soundly trounced, with cuts on her face. I didn't recog-nize her at first. She was silly with drink and refused my help."

"Why would she refuse you?"

"Alas, she does not care for me."

"What turned her against you so?"

"I shall not tell you the intimate details of my dalliances."

"Except that I need to know if it is relevant."

Meddybemps's lips drew into a tight line. He would not confide such details. She was like a daughter to him and over the years he had learned there was a boundary to what he could share with her. Much to his regret, he had not been careful to protect her innocence when she was younger, and now that she was older the boundary he'd constructed as a result of this was not one he could easily transgress. "It is not relevant, but apparently she still holds a grudge against me. I can only suppose that she preferred no one helping her, to my help."

"Then, did you respect her wishes and leave?"

"I did. I chose not to argue with the woman."

"And where does my mother become involved?"

"That night, I happened into her near the Dim Dragon."

"You did not agree to meet beforehand?"

"My dear," said Meddybemps with a chuckle, "I respect your wishes of more than a year ago and have left your mother alone."

Bianca scanned his face for deceit. Hobs jumped onto the sill and, seeing the two of them, rubbed his chin on the edge of the window and started purring.

"Aw, the immortal cat returns from squiring about," said Meddybemps, strolling over to scratch his head.

Bianca bit her lip as she considered Malva's account of that night and Constable Patch's previous visit. "I recall that when Patch showed me the discovered murder weapon you did not linger."

"Puzzling over knives does not interest me." Meddybemps kept petting Hobs. He moved a finger in front of the cat's face to taunt him into trying to bite him.

"It looked like my mother's," continued Bianca. "And she said she had lost it that night."

The vendor stroked Hob's head, then faced Bianca. "I also recognized it."

Cold sweat traveled down Bianca's spine.

"However," continued Meddybemps, "I would urge caution associating it with Leadith Browne's murder. It may not be the murder weapon. And to assume that your mother must therefore be the murderer is a leap of logic I expect from Constable Patch, but not from you."

"Mayhap my mother was not the murderer," she said. "Someone else could have used her knife." Bianca caught the subtle insinuation of his words. She searched his eyes. "Was it you?"

Meddybemps met her stare. He answered in a firm and grave voice, forgoing his usual quip to lighten the serious nature of the moment. "It was not."

"Meddy, if you are lying to me, then tell me. I did not know Leadith Browne and her death does not upset me. If you murdered her, I can persuade Constable Patch to look elsewhere if he should accuse either you or my mother. It isn't necessary for me to understand why you did it. Only that you did."

Meddybemps put on his cap, locking eyes with Bianca. "I have told you what I know."

"And you tell me true?"

"I swear on my mother's grave," said the streetseller.

Bianca wondered if Meddy even knew his mother. Still, it was his sworn word. He often circumvented answering direct questions, but never had he blatantly lied to her.

Some of the anguish that had built up in Bianca released its stubborn hold and the knot in her stomach lessened. "On now, let me be about my chemistries."

CHAPTER 18

After Meddybemps left, Bianca worked on her remedy for ague. This time, however, the peace she usually found in her experimentation eluded her. The more she tried convincing herself that Meddybemps was telling her the truth, the more she began to doubt his answers. Being a prudent observer prevented her from taking the word of anyone (even those she loved) as truth without some sort of substantiating proof. When had she become so distrustful?

With the final jar filled and sealed, Bianca headed in the direction of Guildhall to find Jacoby Nimble, the wax chandler.

The long walk gave her the chance to sort her thoughts and think on how best to approach him. Questioning men as an associate of Patch had resulted in more animosity than cooperation. It also didn't help that she was a woman. Rather than face the possibility of even more ridicule, Bianca decided to try a different tack.

She found the chandler's shop on St. Laurence Lane as Nye Standish had said. The lane was a slightly curving one of maintained residences with a bakery at one end and a chandler at the other. This, she assumed, was Jacoby Nimble's chandlery, as there were no other such establishments along its length. A tasteful sign hung beside the door confirmed it.

A row of nearly identical candles hung in the lead-mullioned windows. Bianca could see that the man was skilled and took care that each taper was perfect. The glow from candles reflected in the beveled glass, creating a tessellation of prisms visible in the shadowy lane. Upon entering, Bianca noted the heavy odor of wax, but her acute sense of smell caught a whiff of something sweet. A man with flaxen-colored hair and a closely trimmed beard looked up, distracting her from identifying the smell. He held a handful of candles and continued binding them with twine. From the carved walnut paneling to the numerous standing holders of forged iron, pewter, and silver, some displaying candles, some lit, some not, nothing suggested that this wax chandler had suffered a loss of business from the king's religious reforms, the mainstays of most wax chandlers' orders.

"Good day," he said, nodding.

Bianca returned the greeting in kind.

"Purchasing candles for your master?" He presumed Bianca to be a servant and her purpose was obvious. She did look the part dressed in her common kirtle and dark brown apron.

"Nay, I seek Jacoby Nimble."

"Then you have found him."

"Ah," said Bianca. She gazed around the room and admired a particularly grand candle holder cast in silver sitting on a table. "My husband is an apprentice to a silversmith. He would appreciate this piece."

"It is one of my better holders," said Nimble. "Who is your husband's master?"

"Boisvert, a French silversmith on Foster Lane."

"I know of him."

"Do you?" Bianca wondered what exactly the chandler knew of Boisvert, but that was not the purpose of her visit. "I have something and I wonder if you might recognize what it is?" She removed the carved sphere from her purse and showed it to him.

The chandler pinched it between his fingers and examined it

closely. "A decorative ball I'd say. Perhaps it is used in gaming, like dice. Or, mayhap it is a rosary bead." He handed it back.

"Then it is not used to weight a wick for dipping?"

"Rings are preferred." He showed her a long pole on which he tied the strings to dip and pointed to the iron weights he used to straighten the wicks. "Tying them on is more reliable. They don't end in the bottom of the kettle."

Bianca noticed a large vat positioned in a hearth with a proper chimney. Nimble also had a kind of metal trough caked with residue of dried beeswax on its sides. A wooden frame with slats running crosswise on which to tie wicks for shorter candles was suspended overhead. She noticed a bundle of meadowsweet drying near the hearth—the source of the fragrant smell that had caught her attention.

"You must do a good business," said Bianca, gazing at the bins of bundled product.

"My work is steady."

"For what purpose do you keep meadowsweet?"

The chandler followed her gaze to the drying herb. "I use it to scent candles when I can find it."

"There is a field of it in Southwark. It is in bloom now."

"That is where I got it."

"You went there to pick it?"

"I did."

Bianca studied his face and believed Nimble had answered honestly. What did it matter to him whether he picked the meadowsweet or was given it from her mother? He had no cause to lie about that.

"There is less call for tapers to light the saints these days," Bianca commented. Ten years ago, wax chandlers relied on churches to buy their candles to illuminate their alcoves, their chanceries, their statues. With the surfeit of statues removed per Thomas Cromwell's orders, Bianca wondered how wax chandlers made up their loss in income.

"Aye, but there are more and more merchants with money. I

supply many noblemen and an increasing number of professionals who do not care for the stink of burning tallow."

"You never suffered a thin year?"

"At first, certainly. But I have recovered." Nimble set the pack of candles aside and gathered together a second group.

Bianca sensed he didn't mind chatting and so continued cordially. "The quality of your candles must be your greatest asset."

"I like to think it so. Still, a chandler must work hard to stay successful. I am always looking for ways to improve what I offer."

"You are keen to find other methods to produce light?"

"I am. The continent is experimenting with various oils."

"And do they make a brighter lamp?"

"Not brighter, but longer lasting."

"Have you tried any of these oils?"

"A few," said Nimble. "I've used fish oil, castor, and flax."

"My father is an alchemist and has discovered a brilliant element that throws off a generous light. A light that is astonishingly bright."

"Ah!" said Jacoby Nimble. "I should like to speak with him. Who is your father?"

"Dikson Browne," answered Bianca.

The chandler's eyes widened. He searched her face. "You are his daughter?" he asked.

"Aye. Do you know him?"

Jacoby Nimble returned to his work. He finished tying off the bundle of gathered candles. "I don't believe I've met him." He placed the candles in a box and reached for more. "Where might I find him?"

Bianca lowered her voice to tell him in confidence. "It is not information that I readily give. But I can see you are well-spoken and a man of integrity. Your shop is profitable and you might wish to consult him—the two of you might profit from doing business together. He lives on Trinity Lane."

"Off of Thames Street?"

"In Queenhithe Ward."

Nimble nodded slightly and measured another length of cord, snipped it with a pair of large scissors. Bianca found it interesting that he did not ask if Dikson was the husband of Leadith Browne. If she had not known better, she would have thought the chandler knew nothing about Leadith, the glowing stones, or her murder. The man was good at lying as she was.

"Why have you sought me out?" asked Nimble. There was no trace of suspicion in his voice.

"I visited my husband and I happened on this lane. The residences are handsome and the road is swept clean. Your window display caught my eye. And since I'd been told the little sphere was a chandler's weight, I thought I'd ask, thinking you might like to buy it. But now I know it isn't anything you could use." Bianca could feign sincerity when she needed to. "Would you like me to tell my father that you are interested in his discovery?"

Nimble gathered up another handful of tapers, scowling instead of seeming glad for the invitation. "I see no need to mention it," he said, applying himself to vigorously winding the string around the candles. "If you will excuse me, this order must be finished. But I shall consider visiting him."

"His rent is directly across from Holy Trinity Church. Do you know the street?"

"I might have been down it once."

On the other side of town, a man and his young son ducked behind a pile of splintered crates as Albern Goddard walked by. They had spent the greater part of the afternoon sitting amid the rubbish in the alley, eating soft apples left over from their winter supply and waiting for the alchemist to leave his workroom. There was no guarantee that Albern would leave anytime soon, and the only way to be sure of his absence was to bide their time until he left.

Dikson peeked around the corner. Likely, Albern was on his way home to eat a fine meal of anything cooked by a woman, he thought irritably. Seeing no sign of his return, the two hurried to stack the wood crates so they could reach the building's high window.

All had been forgiven between the two and the young boy was eager to prove his loyalty. The father was all too willing to exploit this youthful devotion to serve his own crooked purpose. Timothy scampered up the makeshift tower and waited for his father to crawl up beside him.

Dikson Brown nearly toppled the entire structure but managed to climb up its rickety face and grab hold of the window sill while sending a shower of loose boards raining down. The unsecured window gave way with an easy push, and the alchemist let out a rope and tied the loose end around his waist. He then peered into the alchemy room below.

"Open all the cabinets. Look for anything with an unnatural glow. Lift every lid, seek every corner. Leave nothing untouched." He gave his son a boost to the window and Timothy grabbed hold of the rope, easing himself over the sill.

The boy rappelled the length of the wall, avoiding upsetting the shelves lined with jars. Dikson appreciated his son's skill—the boy hardly weighed but a few stone; still, he attributed his son's ability to his own superior child-rearing. He watched with pride as Timothy deftly reached the floor and let go of the rope.

The light from the window dimly lit the interior and Timothy waited a moment for his eyes to adjust. His father hissed impatiently from above, "What are ye waiting for?"

"I can't see!"

"Then all the better to find a glowing stone."

Timothy crept forward, surveying the room for signs of the element. He moved carefully to the cabinet where Albern Goddard had removed the flask of glowing material just days before. Goddard had felt for a key on top of the cabinet and so Timothy moved a stool in front and scrambled up. He ran a hand along the dusty wood until it touched cold metal.

"I found the key!" he called excitedly.

"Then get to. And don't drop it!" warned Dikson.

Timothy felt down the face of the cabinet to the lock, inserted the key, turned it, and heard a gratifying click of success. The cabinet door swung open.

No flask of material glowed from within. The cabinet was empty.

"There is nothing here!" called Timothy to his father.

Dikson Browne leaned over the window sill. "Keep looking! You haven't been through the entire room yet."

Timothy glanced around, wondering where to start. The shelves lined with jars and flasks towered over him, and he reluctantly began at the bottom and worked his way through the numerous vessels. He lifted glass bottles and saw a tangle of worms, bloated and stinking in one, saw nothing but mice feet in another. Some of the contents burned his nostrils and made him cough, others made him gag. By the time he had gone through every single jar, his squeamish stomach could take no more.

"I've not found it," he said, disappointed, but a pleading tone tinged his voice. "He hasn't made any more. Can I come up now?"

His father stuck his upper body through the window and pointed to several barrels lined against a wall. "Look in those," he ordered.

Timothy dejectedly stumped over to three barrels next to the door. He missed his mother, even though she beat him nearly every day. He wondered if his father would be making him do this if his mother were still alive? Timothy lifted a lid and the putrid smell of standing urine hit him full-on. He slammed down the cover and puked.

"What now?" shouted Dikson Browne. "Ye've got to mop your sick!"

"With what?"

"Find a broom."

Timothy rubbed his protesting stomach and wandered around the periphery, searching for a broom. "He doesn't have one."

"God rot, boy, we cannot leave a puddle. He'll know someone was here."

Timothy went over and sullenly kicked some loose rush to cover the mess. "Can I come up now?"

"God rot," cursed Dikson Browne, a second time. He removed his head and Timothy could hear a muffled torrent of swearing. The window creaked open again and Dikson stuck his face back inside. "Come up, come up. And mind that you don't disturb anything."

Before returning to Southwark, Bianca walked to Trinity Lane. She was curious to talk with Dikson Browne again, though she wasn't sure what sort of reception she might get with her father having threatened him. Then, too, it might be worth a talk with Timothy to find out more about his visit from the chandler.

She stood outside their rent, knocking and calling, until a neighbor opened her door and said the pair had left a while ago. The neighbor didn't know when they would be returning.

Resolving to visit young Timothy the next day, Bianca headed across London Bridge, and once back in Southwark she stopped at the Dim Dragon Inn for a bowl of stew and ale. She shared a table with Mackney and Smythe, the pair of curbers enjoying the spoils of a fruitful day of picking. Cammy sauntered over and asked if Leadith's murderer had been found.

"It is not so simple," said Bianca. "Is Goodwife Frye asking?"

Cammy shook her head. "She hasn't mentioned it today. It made for some lively scandal mongering at first, but the speculation about the wench's glowing pebbles has gotten more interest than her murder."

"A sad statement, that." Bianca stuffed a thick black coil of hair back under her coif.

"You are alone," commented Cammy. She sensed Bianca's melancholy.

"John left this morning."

Mackney, who was listening, said, "So, the army took him. Dare I ask?"

"They've made him a pikeman or mayhap a billman. His archery did not impress."

"I am sorry, that," said Cammy. "Roger is gone, too."

"Well, a bit less for you to worry on—his being an archer."

"There is never less to worry over when a man is sent to fight. One of our patrons heard that they are being sent North. There was quite a lively discussion about it."

"North, to the border?"

"The king wants Scotland to bow down. They rejected his treaty and he fears the Auld Alliance."

"He has to keep the French and Scots separated," said Mackney. "They do make strange bedfellows. I'd like it not if we had to eat trotters and snouts from a sheep's stomach."

"Methinks you know nothing of country life," said Cammy. "Every piece of meat is used. Nothing goes to waste."

Mackney visibly winced, and Smythe scrunched his nose.

Bianca addressed Cammy. "Know you when they might leave?"

Cammy shrugged. "Once they've been trained. The king won't waste any time inflicting his will."

CHAPTER 19

Jacoby Nimble stared at the windows of the Crooked Cork watching the rain run down and pool at the lead joints, then spill over in a rush like a river overrunning its banks in the spring. He paid no attention to the boisterous nattering going on around him. The sudden downpour had filled the tavern with anyone who happened to be nearby, who wished to escape becoming drenched. Men of higher station congregated around the cleanest table, but the chandler ignored the class divisions and sat glum and disconsolately at an open space next to a laborer after ordering up stew and ale.

The morning had been a waste of time and his afternoon even more so. A knock at his door did not bring the steward from Clyfton Grey's Manor to collect his order of candles. Instead, three coarsely shaven and attired men insisted he accompany them back to Southwark for questioning. When asked in regards to what, he was met with a spit on his wood plank floor and a shove to turn around and have his wrists bound.

As a sole proprietor, no one witnessed his rough treatment and no one would be watching for his return. The head cullion did allow him to lock his door after he insisted that if so much as a single taper was stolen, he would have Henry himself crack their every bone. (This was a lie, as Nimble held no sway with the king, but *they*, being the low-born proxies that they were, certainly didn't know that.)

They took him by wherry to Southwark and marched him to a sad building where a weaselly-looking constable awaited his arrival. He could have sworn he saw Dikson Browne's daughter on his way there. Nevertheless, Nimble was struck by the constable's presumption as evidenced by his dazzling blue doublet—an item more common to men higher born; though, *they* would not pair it with homespun hose that sagged. The constable's appearance offered a dichotomy of taste and if he hoped the doublet would impress or deflect notice from his shoddy bottoms, then he was sorely remiss. But more likely, thought the chandler, the man was unaware of the mixed signals his attire advertised.

The entourage shoved Nimble before the constable, whose upper lip trembled with sniveling pleasure.

"Jacoby Nimble," said the constable, whom Jacoby learned was named Patch. The man sat behind a large desk that nearly swallowed him, so runty was he by comparison. "Ye was present at the Dim Dragon Inn the night Leadith Browne met her end. I have it on good words that ye was interested in her wondrous stones."

"I do not deny they intrigued me."

"Intriguing enough to want them," said Patch. "I understand ye won a bid between yeself and an apothecary."

"We were the only two seriously interested."

"Ye won," said Patch, growing impatient. "But ye didn't have the money to pay her. So's ye made plans to meet two days hence and give her the full amount."

"That is true."

Patch leaned back in his chair. "Supposins ye tell me what happened that night?"

Jacoby Nimble considered what he should say; then he took his time saying it. Careful to remain respectful, the chandler told his story, embellishing points that didn't need explanation and omitting others that could be misconstrued by dullards. By the time he had finished, he'd delivered a neatly packaged account of his whereabouts and intentions, amiably told.

Patch processed the tale, his lips pinched and circled as he gave thought to the chandler's words. Finally, his lips parted. "Dids ye offer to walk Leadith Browne to the stairs that night?"

Nimble saw no reason to deny it and confirmed that he had.

"But she refused ye and she stayed on at the Dim Dragon. Ye say ye went to a friend's to secure more money. Who was this friend?"

"Are you questioning my word?"

"It is me duty to question," said Patch.

Nimble acknowledged the obvious. "My friend's name is Poncé de Lyon."

"And he gave ye what ye required?"

"Indeed."

"And ye met him in the ward?"

"I did."

"Then that explains why Nye Standish saw you arrive at the water's edge after him." Patch drummed his fingers on the massive plain of wood and looked at Nimble for confirmation.

"The apothecary?" Nimble thought quickly. "Why, I saw him exit an alley after I went back to the Dim Dragon with the extra coin. He looked disheveled and shaken I thought."

"Did he see you?"

"I believe that he did, though he did not acknowledge me. I attributed his rude manner to poor sportsmanship, having lost the bid for the lady's glowing stones. But perhaps he did not see me. He looked in a hurry." Nimble could almost see Patch's brain piecing together these tidbits. "After I got the money I thought that if Leadith was still at the Dim Dragon I would settle our business rather than having to meet her later. But alas, she had already left."

Patch frowned in thought. "So, you arrived to the river after Standish?"

"It is possible. In truth I did not pay him any more mind and do not know when he caught a ferry home."

"And you did not ask why he was rumpled?"

"His business is not for me to judge. I took his incivility to mean he wished to avoid me."

Patch scratched his scalp and fidgeted in his chair. "I was told that ye had a brilliantly glowing light. It is how ye was recognized."

"I am a chandler by trade, sir. I carry on my person the best candles in the event that I must find my way."

"Standish says it was a light more brilliant than any he'd ever seen."

"I don't suppose an apothecary would know any more about illumination than I would about salves for scrumpox," said Nimble dismissively.

Patch's upper lip twitched. "Suppose ye tell me when ye learned Leadith Browne had been murdered?" he asked.

"I learned of her untimely demise when I went to her home to pay her for the stones as we had agreed."

"Ye wasn't eager to settle with her the next day because ye had the money on yer person?"

"Granted, it would have saved time. However, once I saw that she was no longer at the Dim Dragon I left well enough alone. I've learned that patience serves those who can master it."

Constable Patch rubbed his chin between a thin thumb and finger and studied the chandler. He appeared to be thinking, but the man could just as easily have been concentrating on an itch. Nimble shifted his weight. He had just spoken about tempering one's patience, but in truth he found it difficult to stand still while this feeble-minded lawman anatomized him.

"Constable, another thought comes to mind," he said. "As I was returning to the Dim Dragon with the extra money, I remember hearing an argument in an alley. I distinctly heard someone say, 'Clamp your mouth or I shall stuff it.'"

Patch's eyebrows jumped. "You did not linger to see what it was about?"

"Sir, I mind my own interests. I'll not involve myself in other people's disputes."

"And ye heard this before ye saw Standish leave the alley?"

"I did."

Patch leaned forward in his chair and folded his hands on his desk. "One final question, then I shall let ye go. What use is a glowing stone to a chandler? Ye, of all people, never have need for light."

It took no time for Jacoby Nimble to ready an answer. "I must stay relevant, sir. If I could procure and contain such a wondrous source of illumination, I would be a very rich man."

He then left the constable to sit behind his boat of a desk to ponder the residue of their chat for truth and twaddle. Jacoby Nimble knew that people believed a good story more readily than the God-sworn truth. This simple tenet had served him well and, as he sat at the Crooked Cork scanning its lead windows for leaks, he began to relax, confident that he had sufficiently mended his explanation to deflect interest off of him and to adequately raise doubt in another.

By the time the serving wench brought him his meal, his dark mood had lifted and he heartily devoured his food while listening in on other people's conversations. At last the downpour ceased and streaks of sun pushed through the windows, refracting through the clinging raindrops to scatter glittering prisms of light across the trestles. Gladdened faces turned to view the welcome sun and became mottled with the show of light through rain.

As he enjoyed his last sip of drink, it dawned on Jacoby Nimble that his shop had been untended for several hours and his day had gotten away from him. He silently cursed his apprentice for being out ill and leaving the chandlery vulnerable. With the need to attend to his livelihood, Nimble ventured from the warm conviviality of the Crooked Cork and made his way through streets riddled with puddles and mud, back to his shop on St. Laurence Lane.

He sloshed through the puddles that he could not skirt and trundled across the wooden boards lining the streets, already so heavily trod upon that the thick mud collecting on top was not much better than just walking through it on the road. St. Laurence Lane was significantly improved, being mostly cobble.

Upon entering his shop, all appeared as he had left it except for a pool of water on the floor beneath the window. In the confusion he had neglected to latch it before leaving. He ran his hand along the wet casing and figured the blustering storm had leaked through the loose closure. The snuffed candles sat in the dim interior and the surface on the vat of wax had hardened with no fire in the hearth to keep it warm. He then went to his storage and stood on the balls of his feet, teasing a box from the uppermost shelf with the tips of his fingers and carrying it to his table.

With a look out his window for passersby and seeing none, he returned to the box and pushed out the hook that held it closed. He carefully opened the lid, expecting to see a spreading light. Its glow would warm his face. But nothing shined from within. Perhaps it had faded? Perhaps it had died out? He flipped open the lid.

Nay, the stone was gone!

Jacoby Nimble blinked into the empty box. A sick feeling burned in the pit of his stomach.

He slammed down the lid and cursed. "Who?" he asked of his silent shop. He stared accusingly at the stacked candles and rolls of wick. Who entered his locked chandlery and thieved the hidden stone? He whirled around, looking for signs of entry and wondered if the window had been pushed open, then closed. But who would know where to look? He had stood across the room more than a dozen times, from different angles and from different heights to gaze upon this lofty repository, assuring himself that the box would not be noticed. No light had seeped from its corners or lid.

The idea that someone had searched his shop while he was gone galled him; forsooth, it didn't just gall him, he felt violated! Worried that the thief had confiscated his money, he rushed to his strong box. After a few apprehensive moments, he got it open and counted his coins. Nothing had been taken. Money had not been what the rascal wanted.

The chandler lit some candles to better see, and a thought occurred to him as minacious as the dark retreating into the corners. Had someone been watching him? And if that was true, for how long? He whirled about and glared out the window, scrutinizing a young boy happening by.

If he hadn't seen for himself the condition of his apprentice, he would have blamed him first. But the lad had a fever that rouged his cheeks and his mother wore the worry on her brow; he'd seen it for himself. Dikson looked around the shop and thought. Had that knavish alchemist, Dikson Browne, suspected his secret? The man seemed a typical mountebank with nothing more in his head than making money. Nimble cursed; had he underestimated the man's intelligence? Was Browne biding time to take advantage of him?

Then there was Nye Standish, that meddling apothecary, telling the constable he'd arrived afterward illuminated by a brilliant light.

The chandler's anger bubbled and boiled. He kicked the vat of congealed wax and stubbed his toe. In frustration, he snatched a fire rod from the hearth and hurled it across the room. His anguish came spewing forth in all its ugliness. If anyone had spied through the window they would have been cowed by his tantrum. He had just begun snapping his tapers when a calm like a halcyon breeze suddenly gentled him. Reason replaced rage. He looked down at the ruined candles—candles he had spent hours making. Destroying his hard work would not solve his loss. This unexpected setback required prudence and clear thinking.

Nimble stared round at his shop as if in a trance. An interruption at the door further distanced him from his outrage. A claviger from the Worshipful Company of Haberdashers wanted to purchase candles. Well, mused Nimble as he tended to the Company's needs, enterprise *is* the best cure for rage.

With an order just filled and a drift of ruined tapers littering the floor, his supply was now seriously depleted. He had just succeeded in creating more work for himself. As much as he'd like to pluck them down like fruit, candles did not grow on trees. His temper snuffed like the flame on one of his products, and the chandler laid a fire under his vat of wax to spend the next hour dipping wicks and thinking what to do.

CHAPTER 20

Bianca changed out of her wet clothes and put on dry. She hung her sodden smock and kirtle from the rafters and removed her shoes, preferring bare feet to squishing around in soggy leathers. The storm had come on suddenly and she had been out in it long enough to get entirely soaked.

After visiting the Dim Dragon, Patch had alerted her that he was sending for Jacoby Nimble, and in spite of him wanting her present during the questioning, she declined. They both agreed that Nye Standish's account of the evening of Leadith's death had turned their suspicions upon the chandler, but now, after hearing his questioning, she wasn't so convinced.

She'd passed Patch's minions leading Jacoby Nimble to the ward office, a blunder, and had circled around to stand outside the door within earshot of the conversation.

Bianca wanted to confirm the apothecary's description of the exceptionally bright light that allowed him to identify Nimble on the waterfront. She thought it unlikely that Patch could get the chandler to say anything incriminating about what he had carried to light his way. Afterward, she'd gone to the waterfront to question wherriers and had gotten nowhere. She was unable to find the boatman who had ferried Standish or Nimble the night of Leadith's murder.

Thinking back, she found it telling when Nimble had said that a successful chandler must stay relevant in his profession. Discovering a new source of light would decidedly improve his standing and his purse. Bianca poured herself an ale from her fresh supply and plopped down on the bench to sip it. Just how far would a man go to stay competitive?

Bianca took another sip of ale and rubbed her feet. She'd done a lot of walking and it had been a long day. As she ran through Nimble's answers, she began to wonder who this Poncé de Lyon was. Well, she thought, there was no end to the chin-wagging in Southwark. It wouldn't take long to find out.

A loud scrambling outside drew Bianca's notice, and Hobs bolted through the open window with his ears flattened and his fur on end. He scurried toward the corner to hide behind a large pelican retort.

"What frights you so?" she said. "You have an infinite life, yet you still find reasons to run."

Meddybemps popped his head through the open window and she nearly dropped her mug when his loud voice called her name.

"Cuds me, Meddybemps! I nearly lost my drink down my front. I've no other change of clothes."

The streetseller apologized. "I'd not expected you to be so tightly wound."

"I suppose it comes with John being gone."

"Have you word from him?" Meddybemps stepped inside and removed his cap, avoiding Bianca's kirtle dripping on the floor.

"Nay, he just left. But I hear they are being sent to the northern border soon."

Meddybemps dragged a stool to the table and sat. He could think of no words to comfort her and remained respectfully quiet.

"Henry wants to grind the Scots into dust. He fears the northern border, especially if France strengthens their friendship with the Earl of Arran." Bianca expelled a long, wistful sigh, then smiled. "I suppose you have come for some remedies to sell." She got to her feet and brought down jars from a shelf. "These are for ague. I made the concoction with the meadowsweet you brought."

Meddybemps admired her work. "The lowlands reek with sitting water. Stagnant marshland begets nuisance insects and ague. I've seen it so. These will sell quickly. You'll need to make more soon." He gathered several jars in his arms and carried them out to his barrow with Bianca doing the same. They lined the bottles and packed them tightly to keep them upright, and Meddybemps threw a blanket over the whole lot.

"Meddy," said Bianca, helping him tie down the cover, "have you heard of a man named Poncé de Lyon?"

An eyebrow lifted and Meddybemps's eyeball jittered. "Pray tell, why do you ask?"

"Does he live in Southwark?"

Meddybemps snorted. "Live in Southwark? That is a question for which I have no sure answer. Likely, the ponce would live apart from his office."

"Is he a wealthy man?"

"Assuredly. The ponce might even rival the king's coffers." Meddybemps bit his lip as he tightened the rope on his cart. He secured a knot, then stopped and grinned at Bianca's bewildered look. "My dear, you have lived in this unsavory borough for well over a year and the ponce has escaped your notice?"

"Is he French?"

"Could be."

"Why do you not say? Is it a secret? Forsooth, just tell me!"

"You truly do not know?" Meddybemps snorted and shook his head.

"Apparently, Constable Patch doesn't know either."

"Patch doesn't know much of anything. Least of all, anything about this ward." Meddybemps helped himself to a drink of Bianca's ale. He wiped his mouth on his collar. "The ponce, or shall I say *a* ponce, is a cock bawd, a panderer. There are any number of them in Southwark. And a Poncé de Lyon hails from our curly-tongued foes across the sea."

"Is he a particular man, or just a name given to one such as he?"

"I think the latter. These men profit off the trulls and keep to the corners of the night. There are plenty in your chosen ward, but unless you travel in their circle you would not know for certain who they are."

"Do you know any who are French? It might be a start."

Meddybemps finished off Bianca's ale. "One comes to mind. Only because I have had some . . . awareness of him. But I cannot say that he is your chandler's man. Then, too, the fellow may be leading you astray. You'll need to root out the truth, like a pig on a truffle."

"I wonder if Jacoby Nimble just threw us a rotten fruit."

"Ha! You'll find plenty of rotten fruit in the stews of Southwark."

Bianca didn't respond to Meddybemps's tart remark. She declined chastising him for his own licentious behavior that resulted in his catching the French Pox years ago. If she had not produced a salve to dab on his lesions, on *his* rotten fruit, he would be in far worse health.

The smirk on Meddybemps's face fell away as if he knew what she was thinking. He turned serious. "Maude Manstyn owes a certain debt to a Frenchman. He oversees her stew and keeps them out of trouble. Or, in trouble—depending on how you look at it."

"And Maude Manstyn's stew is near the Clink."

"Aye, it is at that. You can find her easily enough. Look for a sign painted with a red bull and follow down the side of the building to the back stairs."

Another question sat on Bianca's tongue. She could no more ignore it than ignore her fear that he was involved in murder.

"Meddy," she said, hesitating. "On the night of Leadith Browne's murder, did you tell her to be quiet or you'd stuff her mouth?"

"I did."

Bianca felt the color drain from her cheeks.

"Did you stuff her mouth with meadowsweet?"

"*That* I did not do."

Without another word, Meddybemps took up the handles to his cart. She wouldn't get another word out of him. She didn't even try. He pushed his cart down the alley and turned the corner, leaving Bianca staring after. When she blinked out of her woolgathering a chicken stood at her feet ready to cross her threshold. She waved it off, went inside, and shut the door.

A sharp pain shot up from her womb and she lowered herself on a stool until it passed. She wondered if they would have a son. It felt strange thinking of the possibility. Whether they had a boy or a girl it mattered not, though men had the advantage in this world. If she were to have a daughter, she wondered how the girl would navigate life. Would she be kind and generous like John? Who would she favor?

Her thoughts drifted to young Timothy Browne, having just lost his mother. The boy's father didn't seem particularly bothered by the loss, but she wondered how the boy fared. Living with a father who drank until he was numb and who earned his living as an alchemist was a sad existence for a young child. Tomorrow she would look in on him and take him a meat pie.

Dikson Browne replaced a wallboard, tapping it carefully back in place. He had spent all the money Jacoby Nimble had given him, but the alchemist needed more. Besides, the chandler made it clear that he supported him in his endeavor to create the coveted glowing element. What wasn't clear to the alchemist was— for how long would Jacoby Nimble be patient? Browne could not tell—the chandler was a bit of a riddle. But considering the man's level of interest, Browne sensed he could bide his time, pretend progress, and wring every last penny out of the man.

However, Dikson Browne always took for granted what he should have been grateful for.

Dusk was upon him, and if Browne wanted to enjoy his envisioned night of cavorting he would need a couple of crowns to pad his pocket. He galloped down the stairs to the bottom floor and looked about for Timothy. Mayhap the boy was out finding a meal on his own. Timothy was growing up fast without his mother to coddle him. Apparently Leadith's death had bettered the both of them. Anticipating a memorably orgiastic evening, Browne drew the door shut behind him, delighted he did not have to bother with putting together a meal.

He practically pranced his way across town toward Jacoby Nimble's shop. Along his route, apprentices stepped from establishments to hang lanterns beside the doors to aid pedestrians and ward off the dark. Never had a lantern's glow interested him before, but the alchemist now passed each light with a studious eye. "Imagine London as a town where the sun never sets," he said aloud in wonderment.

He promised himself that after he got more money, he would wait a goodly amount of time (at least a couple of days) before asking the chandler again. Even though Tim and he had not found any more glowing stones in Albern's room, from the looks of it he figured it would not be long before Goddard created more. Then he could deliver on his promise and have enough money to leave London for good. He had to admit—Albern Goddard was an industrious man. But, he reminded himself with an arch smile—*he* was the more clever.

At St. Laurence, Browne turned down the lane and noticed that Nimble had not hung out a lantern. What if the chandler was not there? Then he'd walked this distance for naught. Nearing the shop, he paused next to the window to peer inside. To his relief, several candle holders were in use, putting on a show of ambient light, and the chandler looked absorbed in his work.

Without a thought as to whether the business was closed or whether he might be intruding, Dikson Browne pushed open the street door and strolled inside. He predicted the chandler would be keen to see him. "Master Nimble," he said. "A good eve to you."

The chandler looked up from his task and stared at him. "The shop is closed. What brings you?"

The alchemist had not expected so curt a greeting. "I have made some strides in achieving our goal. I came here to tell you about it."

The chandler straightened and his eyes flashed with skepticism. His foul mood surprised Dikson. He thought the chandler would welcome any news to his favor. Nevertheless, Browne gibbered on according to his plan. "I have created the base stone from which the element can be derived. It is a momentous accomplishment. I did not think I would have gotten so far, so quickly."

"It has only been a day." Jacoby Nimble raised an iron ring dripping with soft tapers and tied it off. He watched the wax dribble down their sides.

Smug in the belief that Nimble would give him whatever money he needed once he understood how close he was to extracting the glowing stones, Browne launched into a convoluted explanation that no one, including himself, could possibly make sense of. But the inclusion of alchemical terms and processes did sound impressive.

Nimble turned from his candles and gave the alchemist a hard stare. "Your process means nothing to me. When will you be finished making the glowing element?"

"When?" Dikson Browne made a face indicating that this was a thorny question. "It is impossible to say. Alchemy is an unpredictable art."

The chandler took a step toward Browne. "I did not pay for unpredictability. You told me that you discovered the element. Surely you can estimate its completion."

Browne explained that repeating a process in alchemy was fraught with challenges. "Sometimes one might get the temperature wrong. Or an ingredient may not be of the quality needed for transmutation to occur. Creation is a tricky business." Seeing that the chandler's expression did not soften, Browne attempted humor. "Why look on our Holy Father, sir. Why would he create fleas to bite our ankles and make us itch?" He laughed, but his mirth was met with silence from the chandler. "Even God errs on occasion."

Jacoby Nimble circled in front of the alchemist so that Browne's back was to the hearth. "Why have you come here, Master Browne? I suspect that there is something more on your mind. You would not have walked so far only to tell me that you are close to creating the stone."

"Forsooth," blustered Browne, "how perceptive of you." If humor could not charm the man, then perhaps flattery would. "You are an astute man of great intelligence. It is true I did not journey all this way with only the news that I am close to creating the element. It is not my nature to trouble a man if it is not important—if it is not crucial to this juncture in the process." He drew himself up and attempted sincerity. "I am in need of more material."

"Ha! More material." Nimble crossed his arms. "What sort of material?"

"Well, sir," said Browne, stalling until he had thought of something. An explanation came to him. "I am in need of silver to create alkahest—a solvent that can reduce luminium ore into its primordial water. This is a necessary gate in creating the element."

"Silver, say you? That is a costly necessity."

"I agree it is an expensive request, sir. But I assure you that I can go no further in the process without it."

From the expression on Jacoby Nimble's face, he did not appear glad to hear this. "Yet you wear a fine, new doublet, I see," he said. He stepped toward the alchemist and ran his hand down the smooth velvet, admiring it.

Browne, disliking the man's close proximity, took a step away. He felt his calves growing warm from the fire and vat of wax. Browne glanced down at his recent purchase and realized too late that he should have worn his old doublet.

"This, sir? Why . . . it is not so splendid. I wear it on occasion."

Nimble's expression remained cheerless. "I have had a disappointment, Browne. As an alchemist, you are familiar with the cruel flame of misfortune?"

"It is common in the dark art." Dikson's gaze skittered around at the room and his heart began to pound.

The chandler took another step, further encroaching on Browne's precious space. The alchemist could not retreat toward the large kettle or else he'd be in it. As it was, he stood dangerously near and feared catching his netherhose on fire.

"I have given you more than I should have," said Nimble. "And yet, you ask for more." He leaned in, so that Browne was forced to bend backward as far as he was able. His roundness hindered his flexibility and he hit his head on the suspended iron ring, sending it swinging. The drying tapers caught on his hat and dragged it off his head. Browne instinctively turned toward the kettle to try to catch his ten-shilling topper.

Just that fast, the chandler closed the remaining space between them.

Unfortunately for Dikson, his hat danced off his fingertips and dropped into the wax. The chandler pressed against him and Dikson feared he would follow the way of his cap. Instinctively, he grabbed hold of the kettle on either side.

Alas, the iron vat should not have been touched. His damp hands sizzled and he cursed gustily as the metal branded the skin on his palms. If that was not punishing in itself, Jacoby Nimble took hold of Dikson's hair and forced his face to within inches of the bubbling wax.

"I am not the fool you take me for, Browne. I will not be gulled for your gain. You think to squeeze every last penny from me." He pushed on Browne's head so that his nose met the bubbling wax. Browne screamed from the pain.

After a moment, the chandler yanked back Browne's head and spoke into his ear. "And then through your conjury, through your fraud, you will miraculously bring forth the stone that you so wrongly stole."

Browne sputtered and spewed. "I swear. I know not of what you speak!"

Ignoring his protests, Jacoby Nimble pushed the alchemist's face into the kettle so that the man's eyelids and his entire face were submerged. Browne's arms flailed. His legs kicked. He bucked and struggled, but the chandler held him fast.

"There is only one fate worse than being a liar," said the chandler, finally lifting Browne's head. "It is being dead."

CHAPTER 21

The next day, Bianca stopped at Borough Market to buy a pie for Timothy, then continued on across the bridge. She wondered if she would find the boy home or instead be faced with his father, or worst of all, neither of them. In which case, she'd have to tote the meat pie on her errands rather than risk dogs eating it if she left it on the stoop. However, her concerns were waylaid when young Timothy answered the door.

"Good day, boy," she said. "I've brought you some proper food." She offered him the pie. "I can't imagine you've had much more than bread of late."

"You are kind, my lady," he said, eagerly accepting the fare. He stared at her a moment not knowing what to do.

"Is your father home?"

Timothy shook his head. "I don't know where he is. He didn't come home last night."

Bianca thought Dikson's drink had probably laid him flat somewhere, but she didn't mention it.

"Go on," she said, nodding over the boy's shoulder toward the interior. "Eat before your father gets hold of it."

Timothy hesitated and Bianca asked if she could come in.

"Oh, aye," he said, apparently glad to have some company.

He took a bite out of the crust before he'd even made it back to the table, then sat and hungrily devoured the rest of it. Bianca thought maybe she should have bought a second one. She found him some drink, then searched through a cupboard and collected a few shriveled sticks of dried meat.

"Have you any relations who look after you?" Bianca sat opposite on the bench.

He shrugged and took a long sip from the mug. "I have an aunt," he said.

"Do you see her much?"

"Not of late. I don't think she knows Mother is dead."

"Your father didn't tell her?"

"He doesn't like her. I used to go with my mother to visit her, but they had a tiff the last visit."

"Your mother and her sister argued?"

Timothy nodded like it sounded right to him.

"What is your aunt's name?"

"Alice."

"Why did they get upset with one another?"

The boy scratched his nose. "Mother was saying how she was going to make a lot of money soon. And Alice didn't like it."

"How was your mother going to make a lot of money?"

"She was going to sell some glowing stones."

Timothy took a bite of dried meat and chewed it like it was a leather hide. He washed it down and wiped his mouth on the back of his hand.

"Glowing stones. Now that's a wondrous thing. Did your father create them?"

"Nay," said the boy, starting on another stick of dried meat.

Bianca sensed Timothy held a secret. One he kept uneasily quiet. She ran her eyes around the interior and saw the makings of a white witch's craft. "Did your mother make those glowing stones herself?"

Timothy shook his head.

"Then where did she get them?"

He hesitated, then said, "From an alchemist."

"Ah! But how did she know he had glowing stones? Someone very wily and clever must have found out about them. I wonder how she would be privy to such news?"

"I told her," said the boy, proudly.

Bianca rested her cheek on a fist. "You? My, you are clever. How did you learn about them?"

Timothy glanced around like he might get in trouble if he told. Seeing the door firmly closed and knowing that it would creak loudly when opened, he relaxed a little. "I followed a puffer to his room." He shrugged. "I had nothing else to do. So I climbed to a high window and watched him."

"Did you expect to see a sorcerer conjure something fantastical?" Bianca's eyes opened wide. "These puffers are a cunning lot."

"I seen him play with a vial of glowing light. 'Twere like a wild animal it was. And he was tryin' to tame it. It would glow bright and flames would flicker and then he would smother it. But the stone did as it pleased. It burst into sudden flame and caught his beard afire."

"Forsooth! What happened next?"

"I thought the room was going to catch fire. I didn't want him to see me, so I left straightaway."

"And you told your mother?"

"I got home late to supper. She liked it not if I am not by." He smiled regretfully. "If when she called I did not come."

"So, you told her where you'd been?"

Timothy set down his food and got to his feet. He turned around and lifted his shirt, revealing a significant purple and green bruise running the width of his back. The kind of mark that came from a strap. He dropped his shirt and sat down.

"I told her and she didn't believe me. She said the devil would snip my tongue if I didn't stop lying."

Bianca imagined such a story would be difficult for any mother to believe. However, Leadith was married to an alchemist, so she would expect the sometimes bizarre discoveries associated with its practice. Perhaps Leadith came to remember that.

"But you convinced her," said Bianca.

"She wanted to see for herself. So I showed her the room and she even climbed to the window and had a look for herself."

"She believed you then."

"Oh, aye, she did. She was sorry she'd beaten me." He stopped chewing and his eyes grew moist. He wiped his nose, then resumed eating.

Bianca felt for the boy. He had lost his mother and only had an unsympathetic, unproductive sot of a father to love him. Timothy was left to fend for himself. She hoped the aunt would assume his care and be an improvement.

"And so, she got hold of the stones. How did she manage it?"

"One day I told her about the stones, and the next day she had them. She told me not to tell anyone. I didn't. But Father found out anyway."

"Did he want them?"

Timothy nodded. "I think so. They got into a row over it."

Bianca sat a moment thinking. Dikson Browne never mentioned the stones when she and Patch had questioned him, but, she realized in retrospect, neither had they brought them up. Browne said he had followed Leadith to Southwark to beat her for her lascivious inclinations. If he cared so much as to argue over the stones, then he probably wanted them. A sick feeling came over her. Had they believed Dikson Browne's story too quickly—that he'd been stopped by a man with a red cap? But even that was corroborated by Meddybemps.

"Perchance have you seen a man with a red cap come by of late?"

"A red cap?" Timothy made a face and a shoulder jerked up and down.

"A red cap and the man's eyes are a bit different."

"I'm not always here."

"I see, of course not," said Bianca. She tucked some loose strands of hair back under her coif. "A man named Jacoby Nimble came by asking after your mother. Do you remember what he looked like?"

"He were tall," answered Timothy.

"A little tall or a lot tall?"

The boy shrugged. Probably every man seemed tall to a young boy, thought Bianca. "Had you ever seen him before?"

"Nay."

"Is there anything you remember about him? Maybe something unusual?"

"He had a strange voice."

"Strange? How so?"

"He just said different words."

"The words he used were strange to you?"

The boy nodded. Bianca thought a minute. "Did ye ever follow your mother on her errands?"

Timothy had a look like he would have the stuffing beaten out of him if he admitted it.

"I used to follow my mother," confided Bianca. "I often didn't know what to do with myself. So I would follow my mother on her errands without her seeing me. No harm in it."

Timothy seemed glad to hear that he wasn't the only one who stalked his parents. "I seen her stop at a rent a couple of streets over. She had words with a woman there. I heard my mother ask to come in, and she refused her. It made Mother angry. At first she was talking low and then she was yelling."

"What did she say?"

"She called the lady a drabbing, hot house cow. And I thought to myself, she doesn't look like a cow, why did she call her one?"

"Sometimes adults confuse their animals."

Timothy nodded in agreement. "I left. I didn't want her catching me."

"So your mother never saw you watching her."

"Naw, I was too quick."

Bianca smiled. Her parents' rent was two streets over from Trinity Lane. Possibly Leadith and Malva had had words. She ran her gaze around the room, wondering if Dikson would remember to feed the child on his return. "I'm going to stop by again soon," she said. "I'll bring you another meat pie."

"What if me father's here?"

"Well then, I'll bring two."

Bianca left Timothy and, being in the neighborhood of Lambeth Hill, went to visit her mother. By now, Albern would have left for his room of alchemy, which would allow her to speak with Malva in private.

After knocking, the door cracked open and Malva peeked out with one eye, and scowled. "Another visit so soon?"

"I want to talk with you," said Bianca, slightly irritated by her mother's sarcasm. Then again her visits were not so frequent as to be expected.

Malva searched her face, then looked over Bianca's shoulder into the road. "You bring anyone with you?"

"Of course not. Can I come in?"

Malva reluctantly offered the door and turned away to walk across the room. Every step seemed measured, slower than usual.

"Are you well?" asked Bianca, concerned.

Malva eased herself onto the bench at the table. "Your father and I had a discussion." It was then that Bianca saw her mother's left eye, swollen shut and blackened.

"You needn't try to soften what happened. He beat you."

Her mother took a sip from a bowl. From the smell of mint and fennel it was probably a soothing infusion of some kind.

"What led to this?"

"Whenever he is frustrated, I am a convenient sack to punch."

"He's still riled about his missing element?"

Malva's brows flicked in answer as she took another sip from the bowl balanced on her fingertips near her mouth.

"He blames you for the missing stones," continued Bianca. A part of her felt sorry she had gotten involved in this whole sorry mess. She shouldn't have told Albern about Leadith or that she believed the woman had swallowed the *lapis mortem*. But her father was not naïve. He would have sniffed out some version of the story, and it still would have ended with Malva being blamed.

"Mother, I know that Leadith Browne had words with you. There is no use in denying it." Bianca paused, hoping her mother would tell her what had happened.

Instead, Malva lightly pressed a finger to her swollen eye and winced.

Exasperated, Bianca continued. "There are too many coincidences linking you to the missing element. Leadith found out about it from her son and she schemed to get her hands on the glowing stones. I do not know whether you sold them to her or not, but I do know that they were in her possession the night she was murdered. And she must have swallowed them rather than let someone else have them."

Malva closed her eyes and tipped the bowl to her lips. "There are things I will not tell you. Understand that."

"Mother, I need to know what happened so that I can protect you."

The bowl came down hard on the table. "Protect me?" Malva looked quizzically at Bianca. "I am not asking for your protection. It is not a mother's privilege to ask it from her daughter."

"But I am offering it." To Bianca, the unspoken divide between what a mother allowed her child to know about her life and what a mother knew about her child's seemed like a needless and now a dangerous guise. "Do you not see that there are so many pieces to this that conspire against you? I refuse to sit idly by knowing that you are keeping the truth from me. The truth can be ugly and you may think I should not hear it. But Cudso, Mother, do not treat me like a fool."

"You confuse respect with being treated like a fool."

"It is not respect if you fear that I will love you less."

Malva smiled ruefully and shook her head. "There's no making you see, child."

Bianca recoiled at the word "child," knowing that it was the reason for her mother's silence. If her mother refused to talk, then she would have to piece together the story from what she knew. She lowered her voice.

"Mother, you are forcing me to tell you what happened as I understand it." She bit her lower lip, wishing her mother would just save her from blundering and making connections that should not be made. When she saw that Malva remained reticent, she took a breath and began.

"Leadith found out about the glowing stones, and she saw an opportunity to make money. You've told me she was a poor healer and I know that you thought very little of her. But is there more to just your disliking her?" Getting no response, Bianca pushed further.

"I know that Meddybemps and Leadith knew each other intimately once. Did that enter into this? Or is it merely a coincidence?" Bianca searched her mother's face, which remained unreadable.

"You believed the stones posed a danger to our family. You said that Father's plan to return to the king's good graces was a fool's errand. The last thing you wanted was for him to draw attention to himself and to our family. He could have looked elsewhere for compensation, but he was determined to win the king's favor."

Bianca paused, looking for signs of accord in her mother's expression. Malva's eyes flicked to the side, then refocused on her.

"So, when Leadith came to you about the stones, you saw an opportunity to be rid of them. Perhaps you even hoped Leadith and her husband might use them to curry favor with the king—and if it should lead to their ruin or success? So be it. Either way, it was not your concern and it would prevent Father from involving himself with the king again.

"So when he fell asleep, you took the key to his room of alchemy and you unlocked it. Either you took the vial of glowing stones or you let Leadith in to take them. Afterward, you locked the door. You replaced the key in the pocket of Father's jerkin. Only you replaced the key in the wrong pocket. And he noticed."

Bianca paused and stared at Malva, who was focused on a crack in the table.

"Later, you regretted giving her the stones. And you wanted them back."

"I did not want them back."

Their eyes locked. So, she had gotten part of the story right. Bianca thought a moment, then went a different direction. "Father confronted you and he demanded that you return the stones."

Malva took another sip from the bowl and said nothing.

"Was it by chance that you saw Leadith trying to sell the vial of glowing stones at the Dim Dragon Inn? Or did you know she was going to be there and you needed to get the stones back?"

Bianca's mother set the bowl on the table. "This is where your story ends," she said. "I'll not listen to another word of speculation." She rose from the table and glared down at Bianca. "I will thank you to leave now." She crossed the room to the front door and opened it. "Be gone."

CHAPTER 22

It was late in the day when Nye Standish hurriedly locked a cabinet at the sound of someone entering his shop. He had already shuttered the window and was readying to close when William Thomson's distinctive accent preceded him. The Scot commented on the lizard mounted on the shopkeeper's table.

"Ye 'ave a name for it?" he asked, grinning with enviably straight teeth. He seemed jolly and the apothecary relaxed a little.

"It is a strange pretension when a man names a reptile as if it were a companion," replied Standish.

"Piddle, I see no harm in it." Thomson glanced around. "I see no one else to keep you company."

Standish eyed him curiously. He *had* from time to time spoken to the reptile about certain matters, but he didn't care to confide this to his customer. He changed the subject. "I have your tisane." He excused himself to the back room to retrieve it.

With his headache nearly gone, William Thomson thought the world a grand place once again. He whistled as he took in the apothecary's herbarium, noting the array of herbs drying and all the little jars neatly lined in rows on the shelves. Standish kept an organized shop, unlike Leadith Browne's pother of a room with its plants strewn about on tables and chairs, stuck in her hair and in her teeth, and the sharp smell of vinegars and moldery plasters made of fermented foodstuffs. All the time he wondered if he didn't leave feeling worse than when he had come in. But she had readily made the medicine for his ague and never squawked against it. She was a lass who cared not so long as she got paid.

However, Nye Standish was a more exacting fellow. Perhaps it was a guild requirement having to uphold certain standards and pretense. It seemed the city was full of professionals flouncing about self-importantly in their weighty gowns and chains of office.

Anyway, he would soon be going home. And the tisane would last him until he got there.

Nye Standish returned carrying a stoppered bottle and set it on the table in front of his customer. The Scot popped the cork and ran it under his nose. "It smells like I had hoped."

The apothecary lifted a shoulder, indifferently. "I should be curious to hear if it helps."

"I have no cause to doubt," assured Thomson. "If ye made it as I wanted."

Nye Standish looked skeptical but a brief smile appeared, a polite smile that one might reserve for a child in front of its parents, or for someone you wish to be rid of. Thomson noticed its insincerity. He wondered if the apothecary had ignored his request to include meadowsweet. So he asked, just to be sure.

"I made the recipe as you wanted," said the apothecary, snippish. "However, I truly doubt its efficacy. No doubt it was a waste of my time, but I did your bidding and included the meadowsweet you brought." Standish swept imaginary dirt off his counter. "Now if you would kindly pay so that I may get back to my work . . ."

Thomson found Nye's change in temperament insulting. He resented not being taken seriously—it was a sore spot for him. Didn't the wazzock realize just by looking at him that he could snap his fool neck in one try? The ache in his head began throbbing so that his patience and generosity grew in short supply. Thomson's eyes narrowed as he attempted to control the kind of reaction that might get him clapped in stocks.

Instead, he chose a more effective and less debilitating method—intimidation. He wanted to see the man squirm—if only for a little. "I was asked about your interest in Leadith Browne's stones the night she was murdered."

"I have nothing to hide," said Standish, indignantly, but his bluster barely covered the worry surfacing on his face. Wondering if Constable Patch had inquired, he asked if it was the lawman.

The Scot shrugged. "Ye neglected to say how angered ye was when Leadith rejected your offer to settle for less money."

"The woman baited me, then turned me down for her amusement. The strumpet overstepped the proprieties of one so lowly born."

Thomson's newfound dislike for the apothecary doubled at the mention of those "lowly born." To the Southrons, the lowly born included Scots and women in general. It probably included the majority of humans walking the earth.

Thomson dropped the remedy into his sporran. "Ye didn't say that ye had threatened her upon leaving."

"Threaten? I did not threaten her!"

"I suppose it is a matter of opinion," said the Scot. "Though, I recall ye wished God would overlook her greed. There was some heat in your words."

"You misunderstood me, then."

"Did I?" Thomson patted the badger head flap of his pouch. "After leaving in a rage I remember ye returned. Ye looked upset, I thought."

"I forgot my meadowsweet," defended the apothecary.

"Ach!" Thomson slapped his forehead. "Ye forgot your meadowsweet? So that is why ye returned?" He shook his head as if he should have guessed. "Interesting, that is. Because when Leadith Browne's body was found, her mouth was stuffed full of it."

The apothecary paled. Thomson had hit a spot so soft he could see it melting. He grinned with his damnably even teeth and his gaze shifted off the apothecary. He caught sight of something . . . something of interest.

Thomson's gaze returned to the apothecary. In that brief second, the Scot thought the man looked like Meg of Meldon turned to stone. Thomson held his smile for another second, then let it fall. "Ye took exception to the chandler winning the stones. I wondered then, as I wonder now, what would an apothecary want with glowing pebbles?"

Indignant, Standish answered, "I wanted them to make a medicine."

"A medicine? What medicine could be made with something so . . . fiery?"

Standish's jaw clenched so tight it ached. His instincts told him this conversation was not to his benefit.

Thomson continued. "Leadith swallowed the glowing pebbles. Can ye imagine that?" He shook his head in disbelief. "Would her insides shine so bright that ye could see her liver? Could ye see her heart beating? Or could ye see through her stomach and see what she ate for breakfast?"

Standish snickered, thinking the man completely serious and utterly ignorant.

"Ach. But a healer, such as yeself, ye want to make a medicine. I just cannae see that it could be used to help people. Not when"— his eyes rose to meet Standish's—"the stones could be used to far greater effect."

The apothecary stared, wondering what the Scot had in mind. He attempted a conciliatory voice. "Since the stones have been lost, their purpose will never be known or understood. Not unless someone else succeeds in creating them." He cleared his throat. "They being lost, such as they are."

Thomson's jaw dropped. His head tilted; then he guffawed as if Standish was an irrepressible wit. "Lost? Ye think them lost?"

"I do, sir."

"Naw," said Thomson. "They be not lost."

Standish stole a glimpse at the window, wishing he had left it unshuttered. All over London, pedestrians hurried home against a descending night. Surely someone might happen by in need of a last-minute remedy? He cursed himself for neglecting to hang out a welcoming lantern.

"At first," said the Scot, "everyone thought Leadith Browne gobbled up the stones. But she didn't eat all of them." He paused, studying the apothecary's face whose eyes had grown large. "I saw a man leave an alley where Leadith's body was found. Was it you? I wonder, because ye returned to the Dim Dragon looking disheveled. Truth be, I've never seen ye so rumpled." He made a face. "I suppose I could have been mistaken. But we both know why ye looked so frowzled. Ye think it is a secret, but it is not."

Standish tried salvaging his dignity. "There is ruin in making suppositions."

"Certainly someone shall be ruined," the Scot agreed.

Standish found no humor in the man's quip.

"So, a fellow exits an alley," said Thomson. "It piqued my curiosity. I had to see for meself. Tsk, what I saw was not so pleasant. Poor Leadith had breathed her last."

He then leaned across so that his face was within inches of Standish's. "Let us not pretend. It is a tedious game." He straightened, then smiled again. "I found, as did ye, sir, that there were no glowing stones in that alley. Pfft—they were gone! And neither were they in Dikson Browne's rent."

"I do not follow you," said Standish.

"Your feigned ignorance grows tiresome, sir. I say that in warning. My patience is quite fragile of late." His gaze lowered to the mounted lizard and he ran a finger down its spiky spine. "So, says I to meself. Leadith Browne must 'ave eaten all the stones." He stuck out his tongue expressing how unpleasant that must have been.

"Then, I heard about ye telling the constable that the chandler arrived to the waterfront after ye. I wondered, why would ye say that? Unless ye wanted to see Jacoby Nimble questioned."

"It is the truth! Sir, you are a liar and a fabricator befitting those of your ilk."

"Those of me ilk?" replied Thomson. "Exactly *who* are my . . . 'ilk'?"

Standish took a step back.

Thomson appeared earnestly disappointed in the man. "I was about to commend ye for turning the attention upon a man ye despise. Ye successfully managed to remove him from his shop so that ye could search it while he was being questioned."

"You do not know that."

"I can read ye, sirrah. I saw ye come to the Dim Dragon in high spirits. It is not very like ye. A man who is usually sullen does not smile easily . . . unless he has cause for celebration."

"I do not know what you mean."

"Something made ye happy. So did ye threaten Nimble, or did ye steal the stones from 'im?"

"Sir, your story astonishes me. I do not know what you mean."

"Then what were ye so hurriedly locking just now?"

"Hurriedly locking? I was merely attending to a cabinet." Standish set his jaw. He wasn't about to let this man get the better of him. "You . . . have accused me of threatening a fellow professional, Jacoby Nimble. I can only say that you have the imagination of a scoundrel."

"Ye insult me again," said Thomson, maintaining his composure even though his head now throbbed like thunder clattering over the Highlands. He casually moved a hand to rest on his knife. "When I walked through the door a wee bit ago, I saw ye close a cabinet door and hurry to lock it."

"Hurry? You overstate what you observed."

Thomson's eyes traveled to the heavy oak repository to which he was referring. "That one," he said, tipping his chin toward the offending cabinet.

The bulge in Standish's throat traveled up and then down as he swallowed hard. His head turned toward the cabinet and in the fading light of the day he saw what William Thomson saw.

Standish's mind wildly sought an explanation. Surely he could think of some excuse, some distraction to divert the man. But fools wish not to be seen as such, and it vexed the apothecary that a Scot had exposed his duplicity. He wished to escape the discomfort that came with being awkwardly divisive. He had failed. And he had done a colossal job of it.

When he turned back to Thomson he was met with the man's inscrutable grin . . . and a knife tickling the tender skin of his throat.

"Open that cabinet, sir," said Thomson, who smoothly came around the table while keeping the blade trained on the apothecary's thin hide. When he reached the other side he turned Standish toward the closet and held the blade against his neck. "Sir, I'll not be condescended to. Let us be quick."

"The key is in my pouch," offered Standish, cooperating.

"Then we must remove it," said Thomson. He pushed Standish up against the shelves of jars, upsetting several that crashed to the floor. Seeking the purse, Thomson reached around the apothecary's waist, grabbed hold of the leather sack and with a forceful yank, pulled it around and removed the key.

Now, with the object in hand, he needed the man out of his way while he worked the lock. He thought he might tie Standish up, but since the apothecary seemed like a reluctant fighter, Thomson forcefully knocked him aside just to remind him of his place and to save time.

The apothecary struck the worktable, reached for its top, missed, and fell to the floor.

The Scot gazed down, almost pitying the poor fellow for his clumsiness. He returned his knife to its sheath. These professional types usually lacked the necessary mettle to fight respectably. Still, he thought, as he watched Standish wallow in pain, he did not want to be interrupted; so for added assurance, he kicked him in the stomach.

While Standish drew up his knees and gasped for breath, Thomson worked the key in the cabinet's lock.

The door swung open.

A blazing light filled the room. Thomson quickly shielded his eyes, impressed that the element's brilliance seemed even more vibrant than he remembered in the tavern.

Squinting through his spread fingers, he tried to determine the number of stones in the glass vial, but the light's intensity made it difficult for him to look any longer than a couple of seconds. However, the glow was mesmerizing, and he became momentarily captivated by it. Such a thing of wonder, he mused. Its ferocity seemed otherworldly. He reached for the vial but found himself rudely interrupted.

The delayed pain of his nose being sliced caught up to a perceived wetness on his upper lip that ran into his mouth. His eyes watered and he tasted blood.

Through his blurred vision he saw Nye Standish brandishing the stuffed lizard. He had pulled the reptile off its mount and was sweeping it back and forth frantically. The creature's sharp spine had made for an effective weapon as the blood streaming down Thomson's chin and neck proved.

William Thomson's head began to roar, drowning any speck of composure he still possessed. He drew his dagger and, with a terrifying cry, charged the apothecary and drove its tip through the man's wrist.

Standish dropped the lizard.

To be sure Standish had learned a lesson, Thomson gave the blade a vindictive twist, then removed it.

These Southrons with their snide remarks and condescending attitudes needed to learn to stop provoking their brothers to the North, thought the Scot. Thomson watched Standish clasp his wounded wrist. He sighed. If he couldn't eradicate the whole lot of them, then he could at least rid humanity of one particularly odious and thoughtless prig.

Thomson did resist the urge to mock the man for the whimpering, which was quickly beginning to grate on him. Instead, he grabbed hold of Standish's doublet and pushed him forward, marching him around the corner into the back room.

A faltering candle threw a wavering light in the small pantry.

There was a chair and table on which several mortar and pestles sat. The cloying smell of rose and lily burned Thomson's nostrils and turned his craw. He'd rather have endured the stink of South-wark's Morgan Stream than these flowers with their syrupy-sweet scent.

"Sit," he demanded, forcing the apothecary into the chair.

"What are you going to do?"

"Don't ask," said Thomson; then he punched him in the jaw with a swing that would have felled Gorgeous George at the bear garden. "That should keep ye from nammering on."

If Nye Standish's whimpers had previously irritated Thomson, then the fellow's shrieks now drove him mad.

All he wanted was for the roar in his head to stop—and for the apothecary to quit his pathetic mewlings. The racket built to a crescendo in Thomson's brain. He took up the candle and looked round at the walls closing in on him. He wanted to stuff the man's mouth to keep him quiet, but what could he do with flasks and pans?

"Clamp shut your mouth, man! Let me think!"

But Standish continued to whinny.

Thomson glanced at the apothecary and brought the candle closer for a better look. The man's jaw hung at an unnatural an-gle, and a mix of blood and drool flowed down his pretty doublet. "Bah, your jaw is askew." He grabbed Standish's chin and gave it a yank to straighten it.

"Cannae ye shut your mouth for Christ's sake?" he said when Standish's screams and gurgles doubled. "I'll not have ye carry on like that!" But the apothecary was inconsolable.

Spying a pile of cloths stacked neatly on a shelf, Thomson seized one and rolled it into a tight coil. He kicked Standish in the gut and while the man was doubled over, he pulled his wrists behind his back and tied them together. As soon as he let go, Standish toppled to the floor.

"Ah, ye wibbling rutter," he said, thoroughly disgusted. "Some-times there's just no helpin' a man."

CHAPTER 23

Most men slept content in their beds. However, there were a few who, for whatever reason, resisted sleep and the illicit caress of a breeze blowing across their worried brows. They thrashed in their beds, disturbed their spouses, rose to gape out the window at the Queen Moon holding council in her celestial court. Alas, the queen would forever be regal—and indifferent. She never troubled over her subjects, never offered advice for their pitiable requests. In time, fretting souls had learned the futility of asking. Instead, they learned to take comfort in admiring her patient presence.

A young man rose from his spot on the ground and stepped between snoring members of his troop. A large oak stood majestically at the edge of the field and he went to it. He leaned against its ancient trunk and peered up through its gnarled branches at the starry sky—the same sky that his beloved would see if she were awake. But he hoped that she slept peaceably.

John picked up a twig and stripped its bark down to the fibers. This was his last night in London. One more day of preparation and they would move under cover of dark, North, to the borderland. Would he ever lay eyes on his city again? He tossed the peeled stick aside and wondered if he would see Bianca again. Would their child ever know his face? The thoughts of a young man on the cusp of battle are long.

His days had been filled with discipline and learning how to fight with a pike. The officers impressed upon his rank that their ultimate duty was to protect the archers. Resentment toward the revered troops brewed among the more pedestrian ones, but no one mentioned the disparity. Instead, it was understood by knowing glances and clenched jaws when reminded. A kind of honor or camaraderie stitched these men together and made them fierce. On the field, their loyalty to one another would far outweigh the perceived disrespect that was lobbed their way.

John had learned to keep to his own. Even though Roger, the cocky archer at the Dim Dragon, continued to mock him whenever they crossed paths, John kept his temper. John knew that in the frenzy of battle he might see his chance to permanently put an end to the rascal's groundless taunts, vengeance and war being one and the same.

But look on how he'd changed in these few days since leaving his previous life. His mind, plied with the thought of killing, wrestled with his own mortality, cycling between the two like a cog turning a millstone . . . grinding relentlessly. Would its tenacious hold on his every waking moment stop once he returned home? Or, would death be his only release?

He'd never been farther than the village of Dinmow, and his time there had not been pleasant. In the effort of finding a link between a series of deaths associated with St. Vedast Church and the untimely demise of Boisvert's new bride, Bianca and he had traveled the uncertain road north of Aldersgate and had incited the rancor of an entire village against them. Upon their return, he vowed he would never again leave the comfortable confines of London's city walls. But now he had no choice in the matter.

The sound of an owl distracted him and he craned his neck

trying to spot it through the limbs of the oak. A second haunting call drew his gaze to the branch where it sat, and he stepped away from the trunk to better see it. Depending on the species, an owl could foretell one's fate. Emitting a low curse, John identified the bird as a common owl, a bubo, known to inhabit graveyards. Disgusted, John returned to his blanket on the ground. He picked it up and wrapped himself to lie down again, but he would find no peace in this night's sleep.

Beneath the bridge, the Rat Man stood in his boat watching a wherry launch from Old Swan stairs. He should not have been able to see anything more than the wherry's lantern and perhaps the faint outline of the boatman and passenger crossing the water. But an unexpected glow seeped from the seams of the seated man's doublet. For whosoever was being ferried to the opposite shore, that man had in his possession something that made the Rat Man's heart pound, what little remained of that grand muscle in the specter's withered chest.

His green cat-like stare did not waver from the unsuspecting passenger and with darkness providing sufficient cover, he eased his boat into the current and followed the wherry to the other side. It landed near South Gate and the man disembarked, taking the stone steps two at a time until he reached the top. There he paused, as if sensing being watched. He cast a suspicious glance over his shoulder, then disappeared behind a building.

The Rat Man blinked.

He drifted for a while in the shallows and surveyed the row of inns lining the South Bank. Only a few lanterns winked from the windows, and he saw the façades grow dark as lamps were extinguished in turn. Even London's wayward playground desired a rest from its fanatical merrymaking.

The slam of a brothel door and the long sighs of lovers faded, replaced by the creak of branches against buildings and the high-pitched twirr of crickets in the fields beyond Paris Garden. Even the Thames had a voice if one was quiet enough to listen.

Its gentle lapping against pilings and stairs, the squeak of a rope stretched by a mooring, a swan shaking its head and spreading its wings, then settling again.

As the Rat Man listened, his ears heard the sound of one whose partner lay awake with an anxious mind. She cried out in her sleep, her whimpers mistaken for sounds of content by her purring cat. She felt her lover's angst and in a deep unspoken world she went to him.

For the line between real and imagined does not exist in dreams.

The Rat Man needed her as much as John did. The time was near and he had to insinuate himself into her consciousness. So he focused on her mind, and he crawled into it.

Bianca twitched as if she'd been pinched. Startled, she let go of John, and he fell away from her, tumbling through space as if dropped from a cliff into a bottomless well. His body became smaller to the point of disappearing. She dropped to her knees and reached a hand after him. But there was no preventing their separation. Sorrow leveled her. She felt as weak as a blade of grass bending in the wind.

The Rat Man observed her grief. A tenuous sensation—was it empathy?—tugged at his heart. For he, too, was familiar with the ferocity of loss.

The Rat Man knew that nightmares and dreams exist as much in the imagination as they are made of it. There is a kind of amnesia that occurs upon waking. A person may not remember the story, that fleeting phantom of a tale lived moments before. But the message succeeds in planting a seed. Whether the message is nurtured or grows wild and untended is not a conscious decision. The wraith understood this and he played the opportunity to his advantage.

If he revealed his physical self he would risk losing her to fear, or . . . perhaps . . . revulsion. Bianca's trust had to be earned.

He had been sending her dreams of water and drowning, and

fire, since Albern crossed the bridge seeking her help. Such dreams of water often haunted a woman with child. Did such nightmares spring from a forgotten memory of living in our mother's womb surrounded by fluid like a fish? Well, no matter, mused the Rat Man. A dream of water served his purpose.

For the River Thames would be his soul's final battleground. And comparing mankind's necessity of a watery birth to his watery grave seemed perfectly appropriate.

So the Rat Man wove Bianca a nightmare. He infused it with just the right touch of terror. And in that nightmare he would let her sense his presence.

As Bianca reeled from her devastation, from her loss, the wraith reached into the bottom of his skiff and lifted a leather-bound book to his knee. He opened the cover to the first page and ran his skeletal hand under the inscription. The ink had run and faded, but he could still see Ferris Stannum's scribbled title—*Occulta Dei et Naturae*—Secrets of God and Nature—the respected alchemist's journal. The wraith had saved it from ruin, fishing it out of the river beneath the bridge. He had once believed that it held the recipe for creating the elixir of immortality. Perhaps it did. But sense and desperation had prevailed. He didn't want to live forever. His forever had been long enough.

He flipped through the pages, finding what he wanted, then stopped to admire its simplicity. Every alchemist knew the symbol's meaning; however, he was sad to find it faded. He took a lump of charcoal—the remnants of a fire in Southwark that had spewed its charred embers into the sky, that had pelted the river with black rain—and traced out the figure. Satisfied, he then circled the object with a pointed fingernail and teased it from the page.

The daughter of an alchemist would know. The daughter of an alchemist would understand.

He held the piece of vellum to his lips and he gave it a kiss. Then holding it over Bianca's bowed head, he let it go. The symbol scissored back and forth, slicing arcs of air until it landed gently at her feet. She bent to pick it up.

An open cup. The alchemical figure was one with which she was familiar—

The Hessian crucible.

Crucibles were wombs of discovery. Into them an alchemist poured his hopes, but to create a desired outcome one must possess honorable intentions. The intense fire of examination awaited these little receptacles; either success or failure awaited the traveler. It was always one or the other.

Bianca understood her journey. Her womb was her crucible, and it contained her love for John and his love for her. The test was to see if the two were equal in strength and veracity. Through the fire of time, this child would be the amalgamation of their life together, born of their devotion to one another and their desire to sustain that devotion.

Was it the Rat Man's plan that she found strength in this reminder and pressed the symbol to her heart? She kept the vellum there and stood on the edge of the abyss. Beneath her was infinity. The darkness no longer frightened her. The divide between her and John was expected. It was a necessary test. It was surmountable.

The Rat Man's lips drew into a pleased smile, for she had been receptive to his message. No longer worried that she would reject the sight of him, Bianca would make an acceptable crucible for his final quest while believing it to be her own.

She would only sense a vague familiarity when the time came. No fear, no revulsion would doom his plan. She would not remember him upon waking.

Confident that he could insinuate himself into her dream, he spoke to her in a voice no louder than a beech leaf fluttering in a drift of air. He had once done the same, a year before. She had only heard his disembodied words and had attributed them to her imagination, which on that particular night had been racing with jittery apprehension.

He said then, as he said now, three simple words: "*Fortes fortuna iuvat.*" Fortune favors the brave.

Is it not true? Fear leads to ruin. What man can achieve his noble cause when he is occupied with doubts? To agonize is to be insecure. And insecurity is an insidious form of self-loathing. But a man who conquers his fear, who sees fear for its power to defeat, will achieve much through strength of character.

So the Rat Man sailed his wherry into the emptiness over the crevasse and willed Bianca to open her eyes to meet his. Still clutching the vellum to her heart, she blinked them open and stared.

She took in his thin gray skin stretched taut against the bones of his skull. His frayed wool cape billowed in an absent wind, his luminous green eyes returned her gaze, and his pointed teeth opened to let a tongue flick the air between them.

She stared in fascination. She drank in his monstrous appearance. And the Rat Man was pleased.

A strange familiarity passed between the two; it was as if they shared the same soul. But that could not be. The wraith puzzled that they should be so similar of mind.

For a fleeting second he thought how simple it would be to exchange lives with her. Let *him* be the one to walk the streets of London one more time.

But he knew that was impossible. He had lived too many years in this hellish purgatory to ever want a second chance at life. Breathing, feeding, defecating was not so desirable that he wanted to repeat years more of it.

Still, as he lingered there in Bianca's dream, he felt her longing for John. What a magnificent wash of joy it was! He had worried that Bianca would be the one to shrink in fear, but now it was he who felt distress watching her. This forgotten elation born of love startled and confused him.

As much as he wanted to shun that long-vanquished part of his heart, he could not help but glory in it. He told himself that he did not deserve, nor could he allow this kind of emotion to consume him. There were matters to attend. Besides, a greater satisfaction awaited him. He shook himself free of Bianca's blue stare and regretted as much as welcomed doing so.

Making the sign of the cross, the wraith sailed away from Bianca's nightmare. He left her to finish her sleep in peace and returned to his cavern beneath the bridge.

As he looked out, admiring London in the night, he remembered the man he'd followed earlier, the man with the light hidden in his coat. He breathed in the air still marbled by the man's passing smell and let it sit on his tongue. The man had unfinished business, he could taste it. The Rat Man knew he would return to London. The fellow would not be long in London's inglorious companion city.

With a smile of gratification, the Rat Man anticipated his time was at hand. He would watch. And he would be ready.

CHAPTER 24

Bianca woke with a start. Her alchemy room sat in grainy darkness and she got up to open the window. A breeze pushed into the room riding on moonbeams that streamed over bottles and stillheads, washing them in lapis blue light. Bianca leaned against the wall next to the window and blinked up at the crystalline stars. She marveled over why they glittered and wondered how they got there. When she was small, Malva had told her that the stars were *opalus* gems that angels hung on the tapestries in heaven. Neither of them had ever seen one of those precious stones, but word circulated about the king's fondness for them.

It had taken Bianca a while to fall asleep. Her mother's harsh words earlier in the day kept repeating in her head. She had no explanation for her mother's sudden anger except to believe Bianca had gotten too close to the truth. Yet the truth still eluded her.

Her thoughts ran to John and she wished she might see him one more time before he left. This would be his last night under a London sky for a while. Her breath caught at the thought of him never returning to sleep under it again.

Hobs leapt to the windowsill, demanding attention, unhappy

he should be ignored. She stroked his back, and when he'd had enough he escaped out the window to join a parade of creeping creatures outside their door.

Bianca absently watched her cat skulk down the alley; then she searched for the Queen Moon, who must have dipped behind the bridge. A tinge of malaise slipped into her stargazing, like a premonition of impending harm. She reasoned that the feeling was normal, that any young mother might grapple with self-doubt, facing a changed life.

Matters aside, she knew she would not sleep with her mind churning so. Setting up a distillation or tinkering with one of her medicines did not appeal to her. As a young girl, she had often delayed assisting her father in his room of alchemy by collecting plants along the river in the early morning, hours before London stirred. She considered doing the same now, but there was not yet enough light by which to see. Still, a walk through the fields beyond Paris Garden might settle her anxious mind.

A chill rattled Bianca's spine and she realized that once again she had soaked her night smock with sweat in her sleep. The other had dried from a few nights before, so Bianca shrugged out of the damp one, letting it pool at her feet. As she bent over to pick it up, she became aware of a new heaviness in her breasts. She pressed her fingers against one to gauge its tenderness, and as she palpated the muscles and the skin stretched taut, she noticed a strange mark over her heart. Puzzled, she bent her neck to try to see but could not manage the awkward angle. She attempted to rub it and what looked to be charcoal came off on her fingers.

"What is it?" she asked. But the night tends to keep its secrets.

She rummaged about for one of her newer alembics and, dipping a corner of her smock into a bottle of sal ammoniac, polished the surface until it shone. A beam of moonlight streamed through the open window and she positioned the metal in front of her like a mirror.

There upon her chest, imprinted directly over her heart, was a cup—a crucible. She felt a twinge of disquiet and traced it with a finger. The mysterious symbol smudged on her skin. To her dismay, it took several minutes of rubbing before it disappeared.

A rudimentary recollection—perhaps the fragment of a dream—came to mind. She wondered if her pregnancy had caused her to walk in her sleep and, without knowing it, to draw a crucible over her heart. Pregnant women often behaved unpredictably, and this could be entirely plausible. The explanation also suited her. At the least, it calmed her a little . . . though she still felt a bit uncertain and wondered if this, too, might be a dream?

The warm night felt clammy against her skin. She finished dressing, taking her time lacing her kirtle.

With her hair stuffed under her coif, Bianca left her room in Gull Hole and walked to the main road running across Southwark along the river. A gap between two inns revealed a reflective sheen upon the water; ripples of silver waves scattered the moonlight into bands that undulated and rolled. A lone ferryman crossed in the distance.

The sky began to brighten and the horizon took on a faint copper burnish. Deep overhead, the stars lost their crisp detail and began to diffuse into a matte lustered sky. She stood a moment, willing herself to see beyond Bridewell Palace to the yard beyond, where John slept, awaiting his orders. Unfortunately, she was unable to see into the courtyard or fields of the encampment.

Bianca moved on. She turned down Broadwall to enter the fields past Paris Garden. Even before catching sight of the public greens, she could smell the cloying scent of meadowsweet gone by.

Across the way, the archery butts reminded her of John's fateful accident with his bow. If she could go back in time, she would insist that John practice his archery.

Now they both would pay the consequences.

As she walked on, her body felt heavy and slow from weariness. Her feet became heavy as if shod with lead shoes. Beyond the meadowsweet she spied an inviting grassy knoll. She made her way there, sat upon the mound of matted grass, and leaned back on her outstretched arms. Her feet ached. She removed her shoes and spread her toes in the soft, cool grass. Breathing in the morning air, she closed her eyes and listened to the crickets and then their sudden collective silence. A moment passed, then they began chirring again. It became increasingly difficult to resist stretching out. She lay back and blinked up at the still-dusky sky and a dreamless sleep finally found her.

On any given morning, as the sun broached the horizon, the citizens of London began to stir in the early hours. A day took its time to start. But those who reveled in the dark of night, who coveted its black cover, hurried to finish their deeds, then receded into hiding. Alas, once day had reached full bloom, corpses would appear in the city like weeds between cobbles.

Bodies—the victims of intrigues kept secret by the night—cropped up in alleys, lay sprawled on streets, in beds, upon church steps, and fields. And in the Thames.

Depending on which side of the river was closer, or which ward a corpse washed up on, the constable of that precinct would undertake retrieving, identifying, and handling a victim's disposal. If animals had been included, a constable would do nothing else but dispose of bodies all day. But, fortunately for the constables, animals were not their responsibility.

Constable Patch irritably woke to an insistent rapping on his door that roused him from his bed. He dragged himself down his stairs dressed in his night smock, his knobby knees peeking just below the hem, and freed the latch. His hair askew, his face pale in the morning light, Patch stared out at his summoner.

His minion stared back. "There's a floater wedged by way of the Falcon Inn stairs, sir."

Patch cursed. "Why are ye after me so early? The cock hasn't crowed."

"Pardon, sir, but it has. I would have waited, but the body is causing some ado."

"Why?" queried Patch. "Is it someone we know?"

"We cannot tell."

"Been in the water a bit?"

"Nay, it is fresh. But its face . . ."

Patch tilted his head. "Its face . . . what?"

The lackey seemed incapable of words to describe it. "Sir, ye should just get there as soon as ye can."

By the time Constable Patch made his way to the waterfront, a group of people had gathered, all looking toward several muckrakers out on the flats. The mudlarks had risen early to scavenge at low tide and one of them had discovered the body. It was caught up in a loose piece of netting that had snagged on the pilings of an abandoned pier. They had cut it loose and the body now lay in the mud, sand fleas and flies buzzing about, a lump visible from where Patch stood. The constable surveyed the flats and, seeing everyone at least ankle-deep in muck, hollered for the men to bring the body over. Far be it for him to spoil his shoes.

One took hold of the arms and another the legs. With the other muckrakers leading the way, they carried the body toward the stairs, the fishnet trailing behind, cutting a furrow in the squidgy thick. When they arrived at the stairs, Patch ordered everyone back, and the men struggled up the slippery steps to deposit the corpse on the landing.

"God's wounds," said Patch, staring down at the thing. "Find Bianca Goddards!"

It wasn't the songs of robins, or the bump of a bladder ball, or even the matin chime of a distant church that woke Bianca the next day. It was that, finally, her mind was given the relief it needed. She woke on her own and sat up with the urgency of someone momentarily confused. It took her a minute to realize where she was and for how long she had slept. Around her, children played and couples strolled by. The South Bank bustled with activity. The sun had reached its height.

Bianca rubbed her face and picked up her coif. She shook it out, then covered her hair. Though the morning had gone, she would make the most of what was left of her day. She brushed herself off and, with renewed determination and a loaf from market to nibble, set off for Maude Manstyn's.

Nearing the Clink, where debtors shared squalid quarters with murderers and vagabonds, Bianca quickened her step. She, too, had spent time in the place thanks to Constable Patch, whose conditional trust fluctuated in accordance with her ability to remain useful to him. On more than one occasion he'd benefited from her quick wit, as it was the source for his advancement out of Southwark—neither of which bothered her in the slightest. But now that he was back in his old stomping grounds, the sooner she could solve Leadith Browne's murder and be rid of him, the better.

Bianca followed the street running alongside the prison wall and avoided looking at the slit windows, where the sounds of atrocious suffering and madness seeped. Though she skirted wide of the fence, where prisoners begged for food, their shouts still unnerved her. Few would ever again know the feel of grass beneath their feet as she had just enjoyed. Death through disease or starvation would be their only escape. She kept her head down and pushed her memory of the Clink from her mind.

Opposite a storehouse she found a red sign of a painted bull and turned down the curving lane, where only one building had a flight of stairs that led to a second-story access. The neighborhood had a tame and lethargic quality during the middle of the day. No bawds called from the windows or loitered at the corner to lure reluctant customers to sample the selection. A woman dressed in a modest kirtle and simple headrail exited a door and turned to pull it firmly shut.

"Is this where I might find Maude Manstyn?" inquired Bianca as she scaled the last few steps.

The woman, who'd not noticed her, startled. She surveyed Bianca before answering. "It is," she said, tilting her head with curiosity.

Bianca smoothed the fabric over her slightly rounded belly. "I wish to ask a few questions of her." She wondered if the woman had assumed she was there seeking employment.

Still facing Bianca, the other woman reached behind and opened the door, calling over her shoulder for someone to fetch

Maude. "There ye are," she said, closing the door again, and she left Bianca on the landing.

Bianca watched her gallop down the steps and disappear around the corner before realizing no one was coming. She knocked at the door and when that went unheard, or ignored, she lost patience. It was a brothel, she reasoned; what was the sense in being polite? She tried the crossbar and let herself in.

She had taken only one step before a strong odor of sweat and white musk—a popular aphrodisiac—stopped her in her shoes. Her stomach balked at the combination and it took her a moment to adjust well enough to ignore the nauseating mix.

The dim interior hid a multitude of sins, both human and of the construction kind. This stew was not in one of the more sturdy buildings in Southwark. She felt movement over the top of her shoe and saw a mouse scurry into hiding.

It often followed that the quality of doxy could be inferred from her residence, and Bianca concluded that Maude Manstyn's establishment sat on the fringe of respectability, struggling to survive. For a moment, she thought no one was home.

But the creaking floorboards announced a grimacing woman walking through a hallway, her unkempt hair as wild as a mockingbird nest. She wore a thin smock that left nothing unnoticed.

"What is you about?" she asked Bianca suspiciously. The heel of a hand rubbed the sleep from her eyes and her smock shifted, exposing an immodest nipple.

"I wish to speak with Maude Manstyn. Is she here?"

The woman scowled at Bianca and opened her mouth in a loud bellow. "Maude! They is someone to see you!" She smiled coyly, pleased to have startled the visitor. With a satisfied smirk, she retreated on grubby feet.

There was a slam and then a creak. Bianca stared down the dark hall. A husky voice preceded a figure moving toward her with a slight hitch in her step. "It's a wicked hour to come calling. What is your purpose?"

Faded blue eyes with soft pouches below looked filled with

years of weariness and want of sleep. Maude Manstyn had lived a hard life, first as a doxy and then as a mistress of the game. Though her curves had rounded with age, here was a perceptive woman who'd learned to survive by her wits instead of her swives. Now she played a different game—she could have others suffer the raucous abuse; all she had to do was keep the rooms filled and collect the money. No doubt she employed a brute to dispense with customers who didn't follow the rules.

"I'm a friend of Meddybemps," said Bianca. She saw a flicker of recognition soften Maude's face at the mention of his name. "He told me where to find you."

"He did, did he? And why must I be found?"

"By chance, do you know a man named Jacoby Nimble?"

Maude Manstyn crossed her arms. "How does it help me to answer you?"

Bianca resorted to exploiting their common acquaintance. "Meddybemps has a fondness for you . . ." she began.

Maude snorted. "The jack has a fondness for everyone."

"For cert," said Bianca. "However, he may soon be in some trouble."

"I don't know anyone who isn't. But he has a particular talent for finding it."

"Answering a few questions might keep him safe."

"Keep him safe? Who *are* you? Why do you care what happens to that brittle-boned skate?" Though her words sounded sharp, Bianca suspected that underlying her disapproval was an affection for the man cultivated from years of acquaintanceship.

"I care because I depend on him for my livelihood. My name is Bianca Goddard."

"Goddard, ye say?" she mused. "I've heard that name." Her eyes slid off of Bianca to a hole in the wall, then back again. "Ye shouldn't lean so heavily on the rake. He's nearly gotten the stuffings beaten out of him on more than one occasion. Mostly by cuckolded husbands."

"Meddybemps's indiscretions are not unknown to me."

"How do ye depend on him? Why do ye care?"

"I make medicines that he sells at market for me."

Maude's face suddenly brightened. "I know who ye is!" she said. "He speaks of ye often." She looked Bianca up and down. "I know all 'bout ye."

Bianca shifted her weight, wondering just how much Maude Manstyn knew. Did she only know that Meddybemps sold her medicines, or did she know about her father's reputation? Or, did Manstyn know about her mother's affair with the streetseller? Bianca wished to avoid mentioning Malva in all this if she could possibly manage it. She had a difficult time reading the woman and judging whether Maude approved or disapproved of her, so she tested the waters.

"I'm hoping to find out some information surrounding a woman's murder," said Bianca. "Specifically, a woman named Leadith Browne. Her body was found in an alley near the Dim Dragon Inn."

"Leadith Browne ye say?" Maude sniffed as if she knew full well of the woman and had an opinion. "I heard about that murder. Strange thing it were. The air glowed green above her." She squinted and made a face. "Surely the wench was up to no good— her soul hovering there before being cast into a fiery hell." She gave Bianca a questioning look. "What has her murder got to do with us? We don't have any business with her."

"I'm sure none of you had anything to do with the murder. Why would you? I'm not here to accuse anyone of mischief."

"Well, if word didn't travel so quick in Southwark, we wouldn't have known about it. We only just found out." She sounded defensive.

"I'm sure you had no cause to see this woman dead. I'm here because Meddybemps told me you might know a person called Poncé de Lyon."

Maude studied Bianca and considered whether to answer her. "I might," she finally said.

"Your business with the man is not my concern. But is he in the habit of lending money?"

Maude stalled in answer. "To whom?" she asked.

"Specifically to a chandler named Jacoby Nimble?"

"I don't know the comings and goings of the Poncé. But, aye, he has his dealings. I have not seen him of late."

"Have you an idea where I might find him?"

A grin spread across Maude Manstyn's face. "My dear, the Poncé is not one to be found. And certainly not by the likes of an innocent such as you. He shows himself only when he wants."

"But if you were to need his help, what would you do?"

Maude looked down at her nails and picked out a sliver of dirt. "He knows. He just knows."

Bianca began to think she'd get nothing out of Maude Manstyn. She brought the conversation back to Jacoby Nimble.

The bawd spread her fingers, still inspecting her nails, then rested a hand on her hip. "I do know the chandler. He is often in Southwark. However, his tastes do not include my house of women." She seemed to resent this.

"Your clientele includes professional types?" asked Bianca, touching on what might be a sensitive topic.

"We get a few," said Maude.

"But Jacoby Nimble did not visit the night of Leadith Browne's death?"

"He was not here." She met Bianca's eyes. "Though, we did have a man of professional standing attend our establishment that night." She said this, Bianca supposed, so that she might think better of the place.

Bianca considered how she could get Maude to tell her who. Obviously, the madam knew when to keep quiet, but the sly smile on her face made Bianca think the woman enjoyed knowing that men of virtue and men of money were not one and the same.

Given the seamy surroundings, Bianca wondered if Maude had once enjoyed better circumstances with a better-paying clientele. Perhaps, thought Bianca, Maude might welcome an opportunity to even the score, if only just a little.

"There were several men interested in Leadith Browne's offerings at the Dim Dragon that night," needled Bianca. "Men of some wealth." If the woman knew anything more, Bianca hoped that her sense of justice, or perhaps her bitterness, might loosen her tongue. "If you know anyone who may have been to the Dim Dragon Inn that night, then came here, it might be helpful in proving Meddybemps's innocence. Understand that I will leave you out of this. I will not use your name or mention that I asked you."

Maude took a step closer, closing the gap between them. Bianca could smell her breath as soon as she opened her mouth to speak. "As I said, there was another who happened by. He came here from the Dim Dragon." Then she added, with a look of disgust, "As is his habit." She gave a slight snort. "Rare is the man whose depravity clings to my mind." Her lips pressed together and her rheumy eyes watched Bianca.

"And is this man a frequent visitor?"

"He is." Something compelled Maude to tell the story of their association. Perhaps she felt an explanation would atone for some past grievance or lapse in judgment. The woman had a responsibility to keep her ladies safe, and when a madam of the game failed to protect her "family," then blame could weigh heavily on her shoulders.

"It came about innocently enough," she began. "He first arrived here on orders from the Bishop of Winchester when the bloody flux spread through the stews like melted butter. It ran through the borough unchecked. A piteous time it were. The bishop wanted the ladies treated." She said as an aside, "He was losing money." She nodded knowingly. "No one would come to Southwark if they chanced leaving with cramps and their stools running as putrid as the Fleet. My wenches got a healing draught of wormwood and within a few days they were of sturdy constitution."

"The man was a physician?"

"Nay, not a physician."

"An apothecary?" guessed Bianca. Then reading Maude's face, suggested, "Was it Nye Standish?"

Maude didn't confirm that it was, but Bianca could tell by her stifled smile she was right.

"My mistake was in thinking it would benefit us to cultivate a friendship. We didn't have the means to pay him in coin." She paused to see if Bianca understood. "I must take care of my assets."

The unwelcome aftermath of their trade was well-known to Bianca. She had often been covertly sought by bawds for her healing salves to ease itches and, on occasion, had provided a philter to deter unwanted fetuses from thriving. She preferred the money earned from the medicines vended by Meddybemps, but she never turned away a woman in need who knew where to find her.

Maude continued. "But we didn't expect the price we had to pay."

Bianca would have preferred not knowing what that price was, but Maude told her.

"The man cannot know his pleasure without choking his tart near to death."

"There is a simple prevention," said Bianca, thinking the solution obvious. "Teeth."

"Sarky girl," quipped Manstyn. "It is not the mouth of which I speak."

"Nye squeezes her neck?"

Maude nodded. "The fellow has strangled all of my wenches. One of these days he will go too far. And then, I will have a body to bury."

"I'm surprised you have avoided it thus far. Haven't you a keeper? Someone to post by the door?"

"Does it look as if there is money for one? We look out for each other. When the apothecary shows, at least two of us stand outside the door, ready to pull him off."

"Why not refuse him?" But as soon as she suggested this, Bianca realized her naïveté. Any money was needed money. She regretted asking.

Her irritation surfacing, Maude answered, "If we could make do without, we would. As it is, our survival is at risk by me telling you."

"It may feel as if you are risking your livelihood," said Bianca.

"But understand, you made the right choice. Goodness has a way of filling a void left by fear."

"I'm not so young as ye. I haven't the years in front of me to see it be so. But I've grown weary of the skate. I want him to face judgment while I'm still alive to see it."

Nye Standish's incident at Maude's on the night of Leadith's death might explain his disheveled appearance. He claimed he'd walked to the river, then realized his meadowsweet was still at the inn. He had never mentioned a visit to Maude's. His strangling women while docking them was significant. Bianca remembered the bruising on Leadith's neck and began to wonder if it could have been caused by the apothecary.

"Did you notice if Nye Standish had any meadowsweet with him? Perhaps he mentioned it?"

"Meadowsweet?" Maude scowled. "What has meadowsweet to do with it? I think I might have noticed if he'd brought my wenches flowers."

"What do you remember of that night?"

"Only that he arrived in a foul humor. The girls take turns in their service with him, and the doxy who was to do him refused. She said he be so stormy she feared what he might do to her."

"Did anyone . . . attend to him?"

"Oh, aye. We made her take her turn. Bucked her up to do her part. We promised if he got out of hand we'd stop him." Maude scratched an itch on her arm. "And like she feared, he grabbed her throat. I thought he'd nearly kill her. It took five of us to drag his feverish, truculent self off. And if one of my ladies hadn't set on him like a wild boar, I'm afraid to think what he would have done. None of us stopped her giving him a thumping and a few helped hold him down." A satisfied smile lifted Maude's expression. "We think he understands his bounds now."

Bianca considered Standish's violent behavior. Leadith Browne had sustained telling bruises of strangulation. Granted, the apothecary's perversion was reprehensible, but if he could find pleasure in strangling a woman, could he also be excited by slicing her?

"I see now that Master Standish is not the man he appears to be. Such a man relies on others to keep his secrets, but he does nothing to assure that the secrets are never told. His reputation is at risk. No doubt he has plenty of enemies, and it is only a matter of time before he is exposed, or worse. But now I must bid you a good day." Bianca nodded in deference to Maude Manstyn and turned for the door.

"Ye say you are a Goddard?" asked Maude, and Bianca stopped in her steps.

She faced Maude. "Aye, it is my name."

"Your mother is Malva—a white witch."

"Aye." Bianca's insides went suddenly hollow.

Maude nodded knowingly. "I remember Meddybemps talking about her. There's nothing he wouldn't do for her."

CHAPTER 25

Having spent the morning dispensing his cronies to chase around after Bianca, telling them where to go to try to find her when they came back empty-handed, then straining his brain thinking where else she might be, Constable Patch had just about given up. He wondered if she hadn't met an untimely end, herself, when the least likely man in his entourage arrived at the ward's quarters with her in tow. By then, Patch had calmed down from the morning's urgent duty. Sometimes, identifying bodies, especially victims of gruesome incidents, required more time and expertise than could be found at six in the morning.

They'd moved the body over to St. Mary Overie, and so long as Patch didn't have it under his nose it could stay there however long he needed it to—within reason. Now with the arrival of Bianca, he would have to pick up where he'd left off and take care of the whole unfortunate matter.

"You sent for me, Patch?" Those blue eyes of hers had always unsettled him.

"We has a body I want you to see." Never mind that women were not usually consulted in such matters. Patch didn't feel the need to shield her from the morbid results of murder. To Patch, Bianca was more like an entity. And she was an observant one at that.

"I hope yer dinner is settled," he said, leading the way to the church. He told her he had been summoned early, that it had been a matter of some urgency to remove the body out of public sight. "This is a queer one."

Bianca refrained from questioning him on their short walk, preferring instead to draw her own conclusions without the input of Patch's opinions, which he was all too willing to usually provide. To her astonishment, the constable remained uncharacteristically quiet.

Upon reaching the stone steps leading down to the lower levels of St. Mary Overie, Patch took a rushlight from a holder and solemnly made his way through the cavernous underbelly of the church. They reached an alcove lit by rushlights and tallows, where the sexton, hearing them approach, looked up from his work at a trestle and squinted in their direction. An exterior opening provided a small square of natural light and the inadequate means by which the smoke and stink could escape.

"Hiram," said Patch. "We came to view the body."

The sexton had been in the process of mixing aromatic herbs with which to stuff the body of a dead cleric. As Bianca's eyes adjusted to the haze, the outlines of several corpses lay on tables behind him, stripped of their clothing. Hiram would have several graves to dig.

The sexton eyed Bianca with curiosity and Patch made an attempt at introduction. "She is of some use to me in this matter," he added in response to Hiram's questioning expression.

"As you wish," said the sexton, putting aside his mortar and pestle. He went to a body, the only one, in fact, that was covered. "I've seen plenty, but none so strange." With a final glance at Bianca, he pulled back the blanket.

Patch had already seen the pitiful corpse and was more interested in Bianca's reaction. Bianca, for her part, managed not to flinch; however, her stomach somersaulted in revulsion. The victim had suffered a severe burn to his face. The skin had sloughed off, revealing patches of swollen musculature, fascia, and bone. The eyes had been blinded, one, glazed in a white stare, the other as viscous as an uncooked egg. No recognizable features were left to identify him. No lips surrounded his mouth so that his tartar-stained teeth protruded in a silent, twisted scream. Bianca noted that he wore the garb of a merchant, a middle-class professional, but his shoes were ill-fitting and worn, making her wonder if perhaps the shoes had been taken by the perpetrator and replaced with this shabby pair.

"Are there any wounds on his person?" she asked, regaining her calm.

"None readily apparent," said Hiram. "Truth be, I did not disrobe him to look."

"Can we turn the body?" asked Bianca.

The sexton shrugged. He grabbed hold of the shoulders and rolled the corpse onto his stomach. Of particular interest was an area where the skin still adhered to the skull, leaving a patch of graying hair.

"The victim was restrained to receive his punishment. His head was held in place," said Bianca. She stepped closer and ran her eyes down the man's back, then down his legs. She caught a whiff of something distinctive, but she couldn't place it. There was no indication of stabbing, no cut or rip in the man's clothing. Grabbing hold of the collar, she pulled down the neckline of the doublet and examined the skin of the victim's neck. The clothing was still damp and once she finished, her fingers felt slippery.

They rolled him back over, and after studying the man's face—which was beyond recognition—Bianca suddenly got within inches of the man's front.

The sexton exchanged a glance with Patch, whose nebbishy lips quivered.

Bianca scratched at a spot on the wool with her thumbnail. She straightened, rubbing her fingers together. "It's wax," she said, and showed Patch. She then ran her hand over the doublet. "The wax is the same color as the wool. In this light, it is difficult to see it."

Bianca thought a minute, pressing the wax between her fingers, sniffing it, and thinking. "Ah," she said, her face suddenly brightening. "I fear I am slower to reason of late. The man was dunked in scalding wax and held there. That explains the untouched bit of flesh at the back of his head." She caught sight of some redness and blistering on the palm of one hand and checked the other. "His hands show that he must have held something hot."

"But if his face was dunked in wax, why do I not see it on his face?" asked Patch.

"He was held there long enough for the skin to peel away." Then reading the constable's blank expression, added, "Like boiled chicken. Furthermore, the damp fabric smells of linseed oil and is slippery to the touch. I suspect that whoever did this used it to try to remove the tell-tale signs of wax. Then again, he could have submerged the man's face in hot oil."

Patch scowled while tugging his chin hair and staring at the victim. His expression changed as an idea occurred to him. "We've seen this rascal before," he said, looking up at Bianca.

"Think you Dikson Browne?" she said, coming to the same conclusion. "But he is wearing the suit of a merchant."

"So he is," said Patch.

"Either someone switched his clothes, or the man came into some money. When last we saw him, he didn't appear to have a penny to his name," said Bianca. "Which makes me wonder about a change in fortune." Bianca laid a hand on his coat. "And the residue on his doublet brings to mind a fellow who deals in wax and oils."

Though it was late in the day, shops had not yet started to close. Nimble's chandlery was lit from within, and the light escaped through the beveled glass windows, on the cobbled lane outside his shop. Inside, the candle holders were attractively displayed with burning candles, the flames flickering with easy ambiance. Neither Patch nor Bianca saw the master chandler, but it did not deter them from inquiring of his whereabouts.

A young apprentice arranging boxes greeted them.

"We be looking for Master Nimble," said Patch, taking on an officious tone.

"He isn't here."

Bianca stood aside, scanning the room. Her eyes settled on the large vat of wax and the suspended metal ring of dripping tapers.

"When do ye expect him back?" demanded Patch.

The apprentice shook his head. "I do not know. He did not tell me."

Bianca walked over to the wax kettle while Patch continued asking questions. Her eyes found nothing suspicious. She saw no large quantity of dried product caked on the floor. Just the small drips of single candles.

"How long has he been gone?" asked Patch.

"I cannot say exactly," came the reply. "I think it was well before the vespers chime, but, truth be, I don't pay any mind. Sometimes I have no idea how fast the day moves."

Bianca lingered near the kettle. "Perchance are you required to keep the shop clean and in order?" she asked over her shoulder.

"He expects it of me. But I've been home with a fever of late and am behind in my chores."

"When was the last time you cleaned the floor?"

"It were this morning. The master had tipped the kettle by accident. It took me the better part of the morning to scrape the wax off the floor."

Now that his apprentice was over whatever malady had afflicted the youth, Jacoby Nimble left him with a list of tasks and sought repast at the Crooked Cork. There he sat at his usual table near the window, mindlessly observing the view of street traffic filing past while downing his third tankard of ale.

He struggled to keep his red-rimmed eyes open; it had been a long night. The lure of bed skittered just out of reach. Even if he did succumb to the seductive allure of his pillow, he knew he would not sleep. When a man's mind boils with unanswered questions, peace is difficult to achieve.

When the serving wench collected his empty vessel, he ordered up a pottle pot—why waste time waiting for her to bring another tankard, when two quarts would do fine? Nimble shoved a closed fist up against his cheek and stared glumly out the window.

Here sat a man who thought it far more important to demand a transgressor to atone for his sins now, rather than wait for the scoundrel to beg mercy on judgment day, when he probably wouldn't get the pleasure of seeing him grovel anyway. It did not matter that he, too, had transgressed. To Nimble, turning the other cheek was a coward's way.

Besides, there was nothing worse, thought Jacoby Nimble, than being a pigeon.

The wench returned with a pottle pot and waited for him to riffle through his purse for a coin. It was impossibly dark in the ordinary; the place was lit with tallows of poor quality, and his eyes were not as good as they once were.

Jacoby Nimble took a sip of his drink, then sighed. He had not succeeded in his objective, and the Crooked's ale did nothing to numb his misery. Nimble waved off a pretty maid who thought she could cajole a smile, and maybe a coin, out of him. He thought back to his interview with the constable. Though he had blamed Dikson Browne for trying to play him, the constable's comment about Nye Standish did not sit well. He'd never thought much of the apothecary. He knew all about his deviant whoring. The Poncé took exception to men who abused his trulls. Whenever Standish appeared at the Dim Dragon, he grudgingly allowed the man to sit at his table because he was one of the few professionals who frequented the inn with any regularity.

He had mistaken the measured persona of the apothecary, judging him to be a fellow of some taste, who wished for indulgences beyond his means. Nimble's mistake was in excusing the frustration that comes with that kind of pent-up desire—the brutal treatment perpetrated on women whether they deserved it or not—as understandable in a world where privilege was most often given and not earned.

He should have known that such a man is capable of duplicity.

His comment to the constable placing Nimble at the waterfront after the apothecary had left for London, his face unmistakably and brilliantly illuminated, evidenced the man's sly maneuvering. The more Nimble mulled that particular point, the more indignant he grew. Apparently, Standish had visited the constable to amend his original story. And while being escorted to Southwark for questioning by the irascible lawman, his chandlery had been burgled.

Jacoby Nimble finished only half his pottle pot before getting to his feet.

Nothing would do but to confront the botanical canker blossom.

As the sun set and the men readied for their long march North, John sullenly gathered his belongings into a blanket and tied it to his back. The weight of his brigandine and sallet helmet on a warm evening would make for a long journey. He eyed the officers and cavalry with envy; even the lot of the lowly provisioners in their cumbersome wagons, prone to losing wheels and getting stuck in the mud, seemed preferable to walking.

He looked toward the Thames and Southwark, at the dusky horizon and skyline losing its colors and dissolving into a steely blue outline. In his mind's eye he saw his beloved talking to Hobs and painting a leaking connection on an alembic with colophony. She would be busy concocting a medicine to keep her mind off worrying about him. He smiled ruefully, wondering when he would see her again. *If* he would see her again.

No one seemed to know how long it would take to reach the borderland. The Scots were a wild and unruly people, a formidable foe, resistant. Why else would Henry dispatch an army to subjugate them? John had never seen the horrors of combat; he had never killed a man.

"When you are in battle," a seasoned soldier advised, "the man who hesitates to kill will die."

John thought long on this, and as much as he wanted to believe he could execute when the time came, a part of him feared he was probably a man who would hesitate.

CHAPTER 26

Constable Patch stood outside the chandler's shop, disappointed. "I suppose our only hope of talking to Jacoby Nimble is to stand here and wait for his return." He cast a sidelong glance at Bianca, underwhelmed at the prospect of loitering with the maid. In spite of his appreciating her keen intellect, Patch still harbored a general dislike for Bianca, or rather he did not completely trust her. Anyone with her kind of shrewd insight knew how to manipulate people, and he could never be sure if he wasn't being hoodwinked.

Bianca put a hand to the small of her back, arching it, then rubbed an ache lodged in the base of her spine. "As I think about Jacoby Nimble's questioning, I noticed you gave away the goose."

"Say ye?"

"You told Jacoby Nimble that the apothecary, Nye Standish, had recognized him on the waterfront, and that Nimble had left after him. We haven't learned the truth in Nimble's delay. Perhaps he visited with the Poncé, but I have not found or discovered who that phantom rogue is. Poncé de Leon seems little more than a convenient excuse for anyone who needs one. Have you ever met him?"

"Well," scoffed the constable. "I don't have to sees him to know that he exists."

"There is too much of that kind of thinking."

"How now? I've seen a few more years than ye, and I venture to say I've lived in the borough longer than ye, too. There's no call to be insulting."

"Methinks we might warn the apothecary that the chandler might take exception to his statement. Look on what he did to Dikson Browne."

"It's not definites that Nimble was the man who murdered the alchemist," said Patch, surprising Bianca with uncharacteristic restraint.

"When one sees a turd in the road, don't think a bear did it."

Constable Patch snickered. "I suppose we'll accomplish nothing standing here. Lead on to Nye Standish's."

Patch followed Bianca down the lane, then moved in front of her when they exited on a main thoroughfare. He should be leading the way to Bucklersbury Lane, not she.

The last light of day rapidly dwindled and was all but gone when they turned down the apothecary's street. The two found his door secured and the shutters closed. No welcome lantern hung at the entrance.

"The man has closed for the night," said Patch.

Bianca knocked on the door anyway. While they waited for an answer, a customer joined them.

"I've come by three times and his shop has been closed," complained the man. "He said he'd have a balm ready for me today." The man pointed to a swelling on his neck the size of a crab apple. "'Tis the King's Evil."

Constable Patch winced and took a step away from the fellow while Bianca went to a shutter and firmly pounded on it.

The customer spoke. "Are you a constable?" He looked Patch up and down, his eyes taking in the smart doublet.

"I am," said Patch, but he was in no mood to gloat, so left it at that.

"This is not usual for the apothecary. Standish never closes. The man never takes a day for himself. He cannot afford to."

Getting no response, Bianca tried the shutter, prying it back from the window enough to peep inside. "The shop is completely dark. He is not here."

"The king no longer lends his healing touch to those like me. My scrofula grows by the day. What am I to do?" He looked explicitly at Patch, expecting an answer.

"Wells, the king is busy these days," said the lawman, distractedly.

Aggravated by Patch's indifference, the man pushed Bianca aside to see inside for himself. After confirming the shop was empty, the man forced open the shutter, splintering the wood at its hinge. He'd sized up Patch and deemed him lazy. The man wanted his salve.

Instead of chastising the customer, Patch pushed him aside and couldn't get through the window fast enough. He came around to the door and unlatched it.

"We need a light," said the customer, stalking over to a wall sconce. He began working at the wick with a firesteel.

Appreciating the fragrant medley of drying herbs, Bianca breathed in the confined scents of Nye Standish's shop. But her nose caught the smell of something foreign, something with a rank undertone. Her eyes followed Patch as he disappeared into a back room while the customer lit candles along the periphery.

A clipped, high-pitched scream echoed from the back, sending a jolt of alarm down each of their spines. "Od rabbit it," cursed Patch. "Bring me a light!"

Bianca snatched a candle and hurried to the constable.

"God save us," repeated the customer, arriving behind her.

The three stared aghast. Tied to a chair was the body of Nye Standish. His head lolled to one side, exposing a stab wound to his neck. The frilled collar of his smock was saturated along with the front of his doublet. His jaw hung at an unnatural angle so that his mouth gaped as if in bewilderment. Indeed, the dead man's expression mimicked their own.

If the apothecary's unfortunate end was not in and of itself cause for surprise, then the victim's lacerated nose and stuffed lizard sitting on top of his head certainly was. Glinting in the candlelight, the lizard's glassy eyes stared accusingly at them as if they were the authors of this terrible crime.

Bianca recognized the lizard as Standish's stuffed companion, but the creature still managed to evoke a menacing message. The customer approached cautiously.

"I realize they both be dead," he said, reaching a tentative hand toward the lizard, then removing it. "But this little beast looks like he could bite."

"It appears the murderer used it to rake his nose," said Bianca, noting the lizard's spiky spine covered in blood.

Patch grimaced and took the candle from the client to better examine the neck wound. "A deliberate stab. It's deep. I've gots to alert the constable of the ward and tell him he has a body."

Several pesky flies had found the apothecary and were investigating his wound and open mouth. Bianca looked around for something to throw over him, and the customer retreated into the main shop.

"So's who do ye suppose did this?" asked Patch.

"The chandler comes first to mind. Standish succeeded in making us consider Nimble in Leadith's murder and he appears responsible for Dikson Browne's demise. Mayhap the chandler took issue with Standish for incriminating him."

"Come, come!" exclaimed the customer in the main room. Bianca looked at Patch and they both hurried to see what was at issue. They found the man in front of the shelving, apparently searching for his remedy in the hopes of finding it. "Look," he said, pointing to a cabinet whose door hung open.

The man turned his serious face on them. "It's gone. It's been taken!"

Patch raised a shoulder. "What has been taken?"

"The stones. The glowing stones."

"Standish had them?" asked Bianca.

"Oh, aye," said the man, nodding adamantly. "Nye was studying them when I walked in. He swore me to secrecy. I thought it a strange curiosity. A product of his experimentation. He said it would make a miraculous medicine, but he needed privacy until he understood its nature and how he could best use it."

"The stones were not lost after all," said Bianca. "They have changed hands, and we have a man willing to kill to possess them."

"Jacoby Nimble," said Patch. "He's the last man standing."

As much as Bianca wanted to blame the chandler for Leadith's murder, they had no definitive proof that he was responsible for her death. It was possible he could have found Malva's lost knife, then used it to murder her when she refused to give him the stones. He could have stuffed her mouth with meadowsweet; after all, he used the herb to scent his candles. If he *had* murdered Leadith, it would explain why he arrived to the waterfront after Standish. It might also explain Dikson Browne's room being ransacked. Perhaps he believed Dikson was in possession of the *lapis mortem*.

"Ye stays here," directed Patch. "I shall summon the constable of the ward."

The customer returned to the shelving and continued hunting through the bottles and jars for his remedy. Bianca returned to the back room and continued to search for something to cover Standish's body.

On the table was a pan with a square of linen tied around its rim. At least she could use it to cover his head. She released the twine and shook out the herbs drying on top when she noticed something on the floor next to the chair.

She bent over and picked it up. "Another ball of stone." She rolled the small sphere between her thumb and finger, then pulled the other one from her purse to compare the two. They had similar carvings but were not identical. Wondering if perhaps the customer knew what these perplexing little objects might be, she went out into the main shop and asked.

The man was standing on a stool, searching through the bottles on the uppermost shelf. He finished reading the labels on the bottles, popped a cork to sniff one of them, expressed delight at having found what he wanted, then climbed down. Bianca dropped the stone ball into the palm of his hand.

"Ah!" said the man, interested. "Methinks it is a petrosphere."

"A petrosphere," repeated Bianca. "What is it used for?"

"They harken back to ancient times. Their purpose has been forgotten along with the people who carved them. But it is lucky for the person who finds one. It's a talisman against evil." He turned it about, studying the designs. "See you here, each side has a different pattern etched on the knob. My guess is that they may have rolled them like dice. Used them as an oracle; maybe the patterns mean something depending on how they land."

"How do you know this? Have you seen one before?"

"In Peebles. Scotland."

Bianca took back the stone and dropped it in her purse with the other. Its discovery got her thinking.

Having found his remedy, Standish's customer edged toward the door, making an excuse to part ways. No amount of persuasion could convince him to stay just a little longer and he left Bianca alone in the herbarium to wait for Patch. With a lit lantern in hand, Bianca returned to the back room and took a moment to study her surroundings. Odd how she had fished a petrosphere out of a puddle in the alley where Leadith's body had been found, and now she had found one under the apothecary's chair. She removed the round stones and held them side by side, contemplating. The significance of the carvings were lost on her. But as she stood there thinking, more important than the cryptic meaning of the unique spheres was their point of origin.

Scotland.

This was the night John and his company of soldiers were leaving for the border. With her thoughts redirected, Bianca stared at the apothecary's bloody front. She knew now who she must find.

She glanced toward the other room, torn between waiting for Patch and the need to pursue her hunch. Her annoyance with Patch multiplied as she considered leaving the body unattended. What purpose did it serve her to stand there and wait? After all, he couldn't be killed a second time. The damage had been done.

Behind her, the lamp threw her shadow across the floor and up the opposite wall. It had grown completely dark outside. Her decision made, she extinguished the lantern and left it on the table next to Standish. She turned, assuring herself that Patch did not need her, when she heard the sound of the shop door open.

Bianca expected to hear Patch call, but no greeting announced the arrival. All she could distinguish was the door creaking closed and the deliberate sound of footsteps.

CHAPTER 27

"Master Standish. Be you here?"

Bianca recognized Jacoby Nimble's voice. Where was Patch? Apparently nowhere near, else the two might have passed on the street.

The chandler stepped in front of the shelves and took hold of a candle that threw a hulking shadow against the opposite wall and through the doorway to the back room.

Bianca held her breath and stepped backward to the small worktable behind the body of Nye Standish. She took hold of the stuffed lizard and crouched.

"Ha!" said the chandler as if something surprised and amused him. "Where be your scaly friend?" There was a silence as if the chandler was scanning the shop. Listening.

Bianca felt her face flush. She hoped the apothecary's slouched corpse might block Nimble from noticing her under the table.

"Standish?" the chandler called again. The light from his candle pushed into the back room and the rush crunched softly underfoot. "God's TOOTH!" came a sudden cry. Bianca watched his legs stop in front of the chair. An arm went to remove the cloth covering the apothecary's face. Bianca hardly breathed as she imagined him staring for a long moment.

"I see someone has blemished your depraved countenance, sir," he said, finally. "Its corruption must have been born of some outrage that you no doubt inspired." The chandler bent so that he was face to horrible face with his deposed nemesis. "I am not surprised. Your arrogance and your contempt for nearly everyone . . . is your undoing." He paused. "I came here to have a word with you." He chuckled softly, as if remembering a quip only he was privy to. "And I shall still have my word."

Bianca heard a slow intake and exhalation of breath.

"*I* resented your meddling. *You* resented my wealth. I believe that it was you who went to that incompetent constable and told him a tale to your benefit. So I was wrong. It was not Dikson Browne who snatched my element." Nimble paused. "Nay, it was you." Sounding like a disappointed parent, he continued on. "And that constable, so dim of wit, believed every word, every utterance that you fabricated. What a wily fellow you be. They hauled me all the way to Southwark for questioning. And while I was waylaid in that depraved ward of iniquity, you took my element. I should have saved my ire for you."

Jacoby Nimble arranged the cloth over Standish's ghoulish head and stepped back. "And now, someone did you over. I'm sure that you've created a bevy of unhappy acquaintances. Whoever treated you thus must have been greatly offended. They did a thorough job savaging you."

Bianca heard him breathe, heard the tap of his finger on a dagger. Her legs cramped from supporting her weight in such an awkward angle. Where was Patch? Where was the constable of Cheap Ward? Then she heard the crisp *sha-wink* sound of a rondel blade leaving its metal sheath.

"Get up."

There was no mistaking to whom he was speaking. Bianca remained low and crouched. She kept her tongue. Biding time was her best weapon.

Nimble's feet came around to the side of the table and Bianca scurried backward, putting distance between them. She now struggled to stand, her thighs protesting from the lack of blood to her legs.

"Dikson Browne's daughter," he said, watching her get to her feet. He swiftly advanced and thrust his dagger under her nose. "But I think not."

Bianca inched backward and Nimble closed the gap. "I am curious, what brings a young woman to visit a dead apothecary? Should I thank *you* for Nye Standish's demise?" A bemused look replaced his menacing one.

Bianca ended with her back against the wall. She kept her eyes steady and focused on Jacoby Nimble's face.

"Who *are* you? Dikson Browne and his whore of a wife could not possibly have spawned a maid so handsome as you."

But Bianca refused to answer.

"Why do you seek Nye Standish?" he demanded. "I doubt your being here is mere coincidence. I saw you near the constable's when he brought me in for questions. What part do you play in all this?"

"We know you murdered Dikson Browne."

Nimble appeared astonished. "Me? Why say ye?"

"We found wax on his doublet, and I know there was a spill in your chandlery."

"Spills often happen in my trade. But to assume I murdered the alchemist is bold. There are few citizens in London who don't have dried wax on their sleeves or front."

"That, I grant you. However, I know you had business with Browne. You were seen at his residence on Trinity Lane the day you were to meet Leadith. Your interest is the glowing element. Just as it was Nye Standish's interest. In other words, your presence here is not a coincidence."

The side of the chandler's mouth turned up as if this was an incredible tale.

"Standish told Constable Patch about the evening when Leadith went to the Dim Dragon Inn. He said you left before he did and that you arrived later on the waterfront, after he was onboard a wherry."

"That is not significant."

"Except that he claimed you had a substance that illuminated your face with a fulgency beyond any common candle or lantern."

"Your proof is anecdotal."

"You had in your possession the element. But I wonder why you went to Dikson Browne's residence twice in one day?"

"Twice? Such nonsense."

"Did you seek to engage Dikson Browne and see if he had more element?"

"I admit that I employed him to make me more."

"Was it you who ransacked his rent?"

"I know nothing of his rent being pilfered, nor did I visit him twice in one day. But the man was playing me."

"And on the night Leadith was murdered, what delayed your departure from Southwark?"

"I already spoke to the constable regarding that. I was seeking additional funds."

"And with those funds, did you seek Leadith to pay her, or to murder her?"

"Foolish maid. I am not bound to answer you."

"Nay, but what business have you now with Nye Standish?"

"Ha! I came to speak with him—not to murder the fellow." The chandler made a little circle with the blade of his dagger. "But I do wonder," he said, dropping the coy tone in his voice. "What do you take such care to hide behind your back?"

Bianca's mind became a jumble of thoughts. For as much as she disliked Constable Patch, she wished him there now. John's image flashed before her and the gnawing question of whether she'd ever see him again bit at her heart. Had the chandler killed Leadith? Certainly he was behind the alchemist's death, and from the intensity of his appraising pale eyes, the man could be contemplating a similar fate for her.

With a shriek, Bianca brandished the stuffed lizard from behind her back and lunged for Jacoby Nimble. She slashed his cheek with the reptile's sharp spine. Its scales, as menacing as any blade, as sharp as an executioner's ax, flayed open his skin.

The chandler staggered and his eyes widened in astonishment. He put a hand to his face, then turned his sight on his wet, bloody fingers.

Bianca barely gave pause. She broke past Nimble, bolting for the door, and shoved the small table in his path. She was nearly there when he caught her up by the arm and pulled her back.

"Nay, I won't let you leave without inflicting the same punishment on you," he said, and he threw her against the seated apothecary.

Bianca tried to prevent tripping over the seated corpse and dropped the reptile. She stumbled, upsetting the chair—the body toppled onto the floor, and she along with it.

The chandler stepped over her, one hand pressing a bloody napkin to his cheek and the other holding the dagger. Bianca rolled onto her back, catching sight of the lizard just out of reach.

Jacoby Nimble glared down and their eyes locked. He threw the napkin aside and Bianca got to her elbows. The heat of fear hung in the air between them.

Suddenly, Bianca walked her elbows back and got to her knees. She reached for the lizard, but just as she got it Nimble's foot came down and pinned her hand.

"You won't do that again," he said. He lifted his shoe off her throbbing hand and kicked away the lizard. Grabbing the back of her kirtle, he then lifted her over the floor like a bundle of wood and dropped her well away from the stuffed reptile.

Bianca tried to break her landing, but she fell awkwardly. The wind was knocked from her lungs. She gasped and the chandler pressed his knee into her back, flattening her against the floor.

Bianca tried to scream, but Nimble's crushing weight constrained her ribs.

"I am not a vain man," he said. "But I take issue with being cut on my face. Because of your unkindness, I will spend the rest of my life explaining this scar." He seized Bianca's thick black hair and yanked back her head. "It is only fair that you should spend the rest of your life doing the same."

He pressed his blade against her cheek, then slowly drew it across her skin.

Constable Patch finally found his cohort in an inconspicuous office tucked beside a soapmaker. Two previous inquiries had taken him on a circuitous tour of the ward from Mercers Hall to the conduit, leading him, finally, to a questionable residence, where he was informed that he could find Constable Minot down a set of stone stairs on the side of the building.

The night proved to be an overly warm one, and the partly opened door allowed for a bit of air. Light spilled from the interior and Patch trundled down the stairs but was momentarily stymied by the unrestrained and heated moans of docking.

Patch drew up short, disgusted. But Patch was a man deprived of sexual gratification on a nightly basis by his petulant wife. So, softening his steps, Patch crept down the stairs and peeked around the corner.

Constable Minot had his back to the door and the white cheeks of his buttocks trembled like chicken fat in a bowl. His weapon drawn, he thrust repeatedly, oblivious to everything and anyone.

Patch watched with mounting envy.

The woman—he assumed, because he could only see her white legs beneath Minot's alabaster ones—seemed to enjoy being fubbed off facedown across a table that rocked and creaked in rhythm to the constable's foining.

Their intercourse seemed to take overly long, but this might have been only because Patch savored every jiggle, every sordid detail, envisioning himself in Minot's place. Finally, Minot erupted in an arpeggio of high-pitched trilling, mimicking a young maid's sighs of ecstasy. Patch—horrified at the feminine vocalizations coming from the constable—shook out of his vicarious pleasure and gaped at Minot like he was from France.

Minot, still panting, pulled up his hosen and began attaching them to the stays of his leather jerkin. The woman was the first to spy Patch and her shifting eyes gave him away.

Constable Minot, unperturbed, turned a placid eye on his voyeur. Noting the popingay velvet and shiny brass buttons of Patch's doublet, Minot recognized him as a fellow constable and invited him in.

"Would you care for a dram of Spanish sack? I obtained it from an Iberian in exchange for letting the man operate without a license," he said, unconcerned. "This is a ward of wealthy merchants and there are certain perks to being constable here." He smiled.

Constable Patch took an immediate dislike to the man's casual manner. "I've gots a matter of importance concerning a murder in your ward," he said. "The apothecary, Nye Standish, has been brutally killed in his shop. I suggests ye bring yeself and a few deputies to expose of the body."

Minot blinked. "A murder, ye say?"

Patch frowned, wondering if the man was stalling for time or completely incompetent. He decided on the latter. "I'm on to a man who is the likely cockpit."

"Mean ye, a man running a gambling operation?"

"Gambling? By troth, man. This has nothing to do with gambling!"

"Ye mentioned cocks."

"I did not."

The woman finished arranging her skirt. "Does he mean 'culprit'?" she asked her paramour.

Patch scowled. "I haven'ts the time to tarry. There is a murderer abouts and I need your help!"

"My dove, duty awaits me," said Constable Minot wistfully to his wench. He tucked his chin in deference and poured himself another sip of sack.

Patch's lip curled. He wondered if he should inform the man of his civic duty to spur him into action. Deciding Minot could use the reminder, he launched into his signature pratdoodle.

But Minot suddenly whisked past and scaled the steps, stopping at the top. He called down to the startled constable. "Are ye with me, man?"

Bianca's flesh burned under Nimble's blade. Blood flowed down her cheek. Instead of crying out in pain, she felt numb from its intensity. Resisting and thrashing would have made him more frantic, more inclined to cut deeper. She held his wrist, applying force away from her face, which countered him digging into her skin.

When he finished, he shoved her away. He wiped his rondel with the already bloody napkin, then tossed it to her. "Take it."

Bianca reached for the cloth and got to her knees. She pressed it to her face, wincing from the sting.

"Be grateful that I only cut your cheek." Without a second glance, he returned the blade to its sheath and made for the other room.

Bianca got to her feet and looked for something to wield. A heavy clay mortar lay on the floor. She snatched it up, felt its weight in her hand, then hurried into the main shop just as the chandler reached the door.

Before he had time to turn, she hurled the mortar at the back of Jacoby Nimble's head and hit him square on.

The chandler reeled from the blow. He blinked, straining to open his eyes. His hand went to his head as he crashed against the wall.

Rather than wonder if he would fall, Bianca ran forward and with all her might, pushed him.

Nimble dropped to one knee and flung out an arm, swiping at Bianca. He caught hold of her kirtle, but Bianca, now with the advantage, wrangled free. Snatching up the heavy mortar, she swung it at the chandler and struck him in the temple. Nimble fell forward on the herbarium floor, insensible as a lump.

Chapter 28

"Ye didn't have to kill him!" exclaimed Constable Patch, staring down at Jacoby Nimble, whose body lay in a quiet heap. He stepped over the chandler and Constable Minot followed. "Now what am I to do?" he said in exasperation. "It appears ye is up to yer old tricks, Bianca Goddards. But this time ye can't save yerself from the noose."

"He's not dead. And I suggest you bind his wrists and ankles while you have the opportunity. He'll be none too pleased when he comes to."

Constable Minot nudged the chandler with the toe of his shoe, eliciting a low moan. "He's not dead," he confirmed.

"Ye's lucky, this time," said Patch, removing a length of rope to tie Nimble's wrists. He looked over at Bianca and did a double take. "Yer face! Ye is sliced!"

"He took issue with me slashing his face."

"Ye need something to cover that. Ye's a sight to see."

"I haven't time." Bianca edged toward the door and Constable Minot and Patch rolled the chandler away from it. "For cert, the chandler is Dikson Browne's murderer," she said. "But he did not kill Nye Standish." She put her hand on the latch. "I've a sense who is to blame for that." She opened the door while saying over her shoulder, "But I haven't time to explain."

"Where to, Bianca Goddards?" called Patch as she exited into the lane.

But her answer was lost in its slam.

The wraith of the Thames watched a fellow waterman ferry Bianca across the river to Southwark. Every manner of conveyance dotted the water, lanterns gleaming, boats tacking this way and that, all busily shuffling citizens from London to their favorite playground. The night air wafted warm and humid, a welcome change from spring's peevish temper that could overheat one day, or chill one's bones the next. The Rat Man stood in his boat next to a starling beneath the bridge and licked the air. He tasted the trembling thrill of opportunity, the thrumming heat from Bianca's pounding chest.

His ability did not include reading the future or knowing how it would unfold. But he could sense the fervid feelings, the intense emotions of one whose fate was linked with his.

Bianca.

Her priority was John.

She held him foremost in her heart. She would gamble her life to save his.

Could the wraith have confronted the thief on his own? He had seen the man skulk down to the waterfront and hail a ride across. With rapt attention he followed the man's progress to Southwark. He even willed that they "shoot the bridge" and pick *his* particular cavern. In the dark, they would be confused. Others would say it was their imagination—which would have suited him. Alas, his fellow wherrier dropped the man shy of the bridge, and the river was too heavily traveled to risk intervening without some sort of cover.

So he watched, knowing that this night his redemption was at hand. And he would be waiting.

* * *

Bianca disembarked and wended through the short lanes to her room of Medicinals and Physickes to fetch her knife. She cut across a cemetery to save time getting to the Dim Dragon Inn. She knew of only one place where he could be. And she hoped she wasn't too late. With her determined gate and crimson cut across her cheek, no miscreant dared provoke her.

As she neared the tavern, she could hear it humming with activity. A lantern on a hook lit the sign of their dragon mascot overhead. Instead of throwing open the door and drawing the curious notice that usually came this time of night, she hurried around to the back of the inn and entered through the alley door.

Goodwife Frye was ladling bowls of stew and was the first to see her. "Mary be, what happened to your face? Is someone after you?" Her eyes slid past Bianca toward the dark alleyway.

"Nay, Goodwife. I didn't want to be seen by your clientele."

"Well, it will be a while before that heals and people stop asking. It's still seeping." She found a towel and dabbed at Bianca's cheek. "Who did this?"

"A man who has something to do with the missing stones. But the wound isn't why I don't want to be seen."

"Who do you wish to avoid? Is it Leadith Browne's murderer?"

"I cannot answer just yet. I am certain, though, that the man is involved in a murder, and his intent may prove deadly for our king's army."

"And he be here? Among us?" The goodwife's voice rose with alarm. "This night?"

"Possibly," answered Bianca. "Is Cammy working?"

"Has she something to do with this person?"

"Not at all. I merely wish to speak with her."

The alewife's shoulders relaxed. "The girl is always working," she said, returning to filling bowls of soup. "She is with the clients."

Bianca stepped to the wall partitioning the kitchen from the dining area. She slowly tipped her head to see into the tavern.

Customers lined the trestle tables, taking every available space. Cammy and one other serving wench tended the patrons. Bianca also spied William Thomson.

The Scot nursed a tankard, staring into his mug, distracted and slow to react to a friend's jest. Bianca studied him for a moment, then sank back behind the wall. She had also seen Mackney and Smythe. They sat at a trestle a discreet distance from Thomson.

"Goodwife, Constable Patch should be here soon."

"Is there to be an arrest?" she asked.

"It is my hope," said Bianca.

The words were barely out of her mouth when Cammy walked into the kitchen.

"Bianca," she said in surprise. "Why are you not in the tavern?" Then noticing her friend's face, said, "O me, what happened?"

"I need your help," said Bianca, taking her aside in confidence. "I think William Thomson killed the apothecary. We found Standish stabbed in the neck."

Cammy drew in a sharp breath. "Was it Thomson who cut you?"

"It was Jacoby Nimble. Patch is with him now, but he should be here any minute."

"Be you sure that the Scot murdered the apothecary?"

"I am nearly certain of it. Standish had the glowing stones and now they are missing. I believe Thomson has them."

Cammy looked toward the tavern room. "Do you think he hides them on his person?"

Bianca shrugged. "What concerns me is what he plans to do with them."

"Pray tell, what do you presume?"

"Remember all the talk about the king's army moving north to the border? He was involved in that discussion. The man is a Scot living in London, yet he remains fond of his homeland. Also, I found two talismans of Scottish origin near Leadith's and Standish's bodies. It is a notable coincidence."

"Do you think him a spy?" asked Cammy.

"I think him a man who puts his country's interests before England's."

Cammy's expression changed to worry. "The army is moving north tonight. Roger and John . . ."

Their eyes met, neither mentioning what could happen if the Scots got hold of the *lapis mortem*.

Cammy spoke first. "Bianca, I cannot stand here prattling. We must prevent him from hurting anyone else. We must think of Roger and John." She boldly started back into the tavern, but Bianca took hold of her elbow, catching her up.

"Content yourself," said Bianca. "I do not want to approach Thomson before Constable Patch gets here. The man is dangerous and I should not want to see anyone harmed."

"The clientele here are a rough breed; they can help us."

"If Thomson is in possession of the stones he could create a screen of smoke and escape. Worse, he could burn down the tavern. Though I would think that his primary interest is in getting the stones to his brethren ahead of the king's army."

"I shall tell everyone of his intent. There isn't a man in that room who would let him escape."

"*If* they believe you. He is well liked. His friends will defend him and he would make you look like a fool."

"Have you a better idea?"

"Go to Mackney and Smythe and tell them if Thomson makes to leave they must stall him."

Goodwife Frye spied the two huddling together across the way. "What do you plan?" she asked. "I should like to know if my patrons are in danger."

With a tip of her chin, Bianca urged Cammy back into the serving room. She turned to the alewife. "I do not want to alarm you. But a murderer must be confronted. Constable Patch is on his way. Understand, though, that it is not my wish to cause a disturbance in your establishment."

"Who? Tell me who be this culprit?"

Bianca hesitated, but realized the goodwife should probably know. "I believe it is William Thomson, the Scot."

The goodwife's chin dropped. "I thought him a man glad to be in London."

"I think it unlikely," Bianca said in a low voice. "Speak not a word to anyone. Surprise is our best weapon."

Bianca ignored the questioning stares from the kitchen help and returned to the partition to watch Thomson. She had just reached the wall divider when Cammy came barreling into the kitchen, inadvertently knocking into her.

"He's gone!" she cried. "Thomson is gone!"

CHAPTER 29

"Could he be in the alley?" Bianca hoped his absence was only temporary.

"Plucking roses?" Cammy shook her head. "His table said he had left for the night."

Without a word, Bianca burst into the tavern and scanned the room. William Thomson was no longer sitting with his crew of friends. Curious eyes stared at her marred face. She wasted no time asking where he might have gone but strode to the tavern door and threw it open.

It took a moment for her eyes to adjust to the dark. She looked up the lane, then down it. William Thomson was nowhere in sight. Her fear was that he could be heading back to London. There was the possibility that he was returning to his quarters for the night, but what if he was following the king's army to the border?

She ran toward the waterfront, hoping to catch him before he caught a wherry. On Tooley Street she looked past the South Gate in the direction of the nearest set of stairs. A few pedestrians populated the road, mostly men who had tired of their recreation and were ready to return home to their soft beds. She failed to recognize Thomson among them.

Frustrated, Bianca hurried up the road, straining to see through the murky dark. She turned toward the dock near St. Mary Overie, searching for Thomson among the gathered men waiting their turn for a ride, then continued toward a landing beyond Winchester House. Ahead, a lone customer watched a boat approach, and she recognized the familiar figure. Quickening her stride, she was within yards of him when she felt a hand on her shoulder.

Bianca whirled, her heart a lump in her throat. "Cammy!" she hissed. "What are you doing?"

"I promised John I would take care of you."

Bianca pulled her against the walled enclosure of Winchester House, letting the building's shadow afford them cover. "Go back to the inn. If Patch arrives, tell him I've gone to the encampment. We must warn the king's army."

"Let me tell them."

Bianca shook her head adamantly. "Cammy, stay here. Wait for Patch and tell him where I've gone."

"I'm going with you."

Bianca protested, but her argument was clipped by the sound of a wherry scraping the quay. She held out her hand warning Cammy to silence. William Thomson spoke to the boatman, his lilting brogue carrying across the way.

"It's him," whispered Cammy. The whites of her eyes were as round as quoits and reflected in the faint semblance of light. "What should we do?"

Bianca craned her neck and saw Thomson step on board the wherry. The bench creaked from his weight.

"I'm going after him," said Bianca. "But promise me you'll wait for help." Bianca stepped out of the shadows to hail the boatman, but in those brief few seconds, the boat had traveled well away from the stairs. The boatman poled them smoothly into the current, and it swept them a distance too far to turn back.

Bianca's shoulders slumped as she watched them trek toward

London. No other passengers remained at the stairs. William Thomson was the sole rider onboard a single skiff.

Cammy joined her side. "There are no waiting boats. They are all occupied and headed for London."

"And the bridge is closed," said Bianca, seeing no one beneath the Stone Gate.

Dejected, Cammy sighed and walked along the river bank while Bianca continued watching Thomson's progress across the river. The boatman cut a course next to the bridge, making the wherry bob, when suddenly Cammy began shouting.

"There! Do you see it?" She pointed at a boat tied to a short pier.

Encouraged, the two raced along the river toward the diminutive dock, but within steps of it they drew up short, stopping to gawp at the barely passable structure. It was a shaky creation with warped and buckled planks laid haphazardly across charred cross members. Whoever owned the vessel didn't lie awake worrying that his boat might be stolen. Navigating the perilous mooring without falling through and landing in the water was deterrent enough.

"I doubt it is taken out much," said Cammy.

Bianca approached the rickety set of stairs and tested the bottom step with her foot.

"Let me," said Cammy, but Bianca sprinted up the steps to the landing.

She looked down at her friend. "We've no choice but to try to take it." She reached a toe forward and gingerly applied pressure, listening to the creak and give of the wood. "Some of these planks are stronger than others."

Cammy dutifully followed, suppressing her fear of water, concluding that if she had to she'd prefer tackling Bianca to safety on the derelict structure to fishing her out of the river.

Bianca lifted her kirtle, freeing her feet from tripping on its hem, then dropped into a crouch. She told herself she wouldn't have so far to fall and might even be able to cling to the pier if she felt a plank give way. She held her breath and inched forward.

Despite the need to hurry, Bianca made painfully slow progress. A couple of boards bowed precariously, threatening to break. She got down on her knees to reach out for the next sturdy crosspiece. In the distance, the skiff carrying William Thomson still bounced in the quick water beside the bridge.

"I think you have lost your good sense and I am a fool to follow," complained Cammy, whose legs shook worse than the rotten slat on which she stood. "Even if we do reach the boat, we don't know if there are oars. A fine predicament that would be."

"You needn't fret, I spy a pair in the bottom of the hull." Bianca crawled opposite the vessel and sat. "The boat is in better condition than this pier."

Dangling her legs over the vessel, Bianca gathered her skirt in her lap, then dropped off the dock. A loud *whump* followed as she awkwardly landed in the hull and the boat began to rock and tug at its rope. Her knee had hit the gunwale on the way down and it throbbed angrily, making her curse as she tried to steady the boat. After a moment she found her sea sense and the boat slowed its rocking.

Cammy leaned out and called from above. "Are you hurt?"

"Not at all. The boat is a bit wobbly, though." Bianca clambered to the stern and lifted the oars into their locks. "Are you coming?"

The bottom of Cammy's shoes hovered overhead, and with a shriek the kitchen wench dropped into the hull beside Bianca. Another round of cursing and rocking followed, then the two got under way, Bianca in the bow and Cammy zealously rowing them free of the mooring.

In their favor, years of farm labor had thickly muscled Cammy's back and arms, and she took to rowing with an affinity that would have impressed, and no doubt shamed, most sailors. They sped through the water like they were gliding on ice and Bianca barked which way to go, sometimes impatiently paddling with a broken piece of pier to help spur them on.

As they approached the middle of the river, a brume had begun to settle on the surface as if the water wished to become the sky. At times they did appear to merge and Bianca worried that a thickening murk would confound their mission. She urged Cammy on and her friend complied, paddling faster and covering more distance with every stroke. Ahead, Thomson's boat sailed dangerously close to the starlings and looked to be buffeted by the crosscurrent of water flowing through them.

"We've nearly caught them," shouted Bianca, willing their boat forward as if she could travel the final distance just by wishing it.

But a shrill voice inside her head questioned her resolve. What if she was wrong about William Thomson? She had no proof that he had killed Leadith Browne, only the desperate and self-serving hope that he was to blame. And, if she cared to admit it, the petrospheres might be a mere coincidence and have nothing to do with him. She didn't know for sure whether he had dropped them. So what, exactly, *did* they prove? If they belonged to him, they only meant that he might have visited Nye Standish's and Leadith's murder scene—*not* that he was responsible for their deaths.

Then, as if to further unsettle her, she and Cammy found themselves enveloped in a fog that draped the river in ribbons so opaque that they lost sight of their quarry. Even more disconcerting, Bianca could barely see Cammy rowing furiously, barely three feet away.

"Stop!" cried Bianca. "I can't see!"

Cammy lifted the oars from the water, welcoming the chance to catch her breath. Bianca surveyed the water and listened, sound being the only clue that could warn her of what was close by.

Cammy's breathing drowned the gentle lap of water against their hull and muted the conversations and laughs of others passing in nearby wherries. The boat rocked gently; it rocked uncertainly, but Bianca knew the current was about to change. And when it did, it would pull them toward the bridge, suck them right under its arches, where the churn and foam could sink them.

Though the night air was warm and heavy, Bianca shuddered from a sudden chill. She rubbed her goose-fleshed arms. A sense of foreboding unraveled what was left of her confidence and she looked up at the sky, hoping for a constellation to set her course, but all was gray mist; droplets of water refracting random light.

"Which way?" asked Cammy.

"Wait." Bianca feared the stroke of an oar could send them faster into the churning water beneath the bridge. She looked for a shape, a form, an outline of a boat, or even the hulking architecture of the bridge, anything to help determine their bearings.

Then, an opalescent glow, white and luminous, caught her eye.

"Do you see it?" she asked. "Do you see that light?"

Cammy tried following Bianca's outstretched arm to where she pointed. "'Pon my honor, is it the element?" asked Cammy.

"If it be someone's lantern it is remarkably bright." She studied the gleaming orb, trying to determine if it was the element and if William Thomson was holding it. But the undulating fog absorbed the light, dispersing and subduing it in waves. She could only see the glowing beacon, not what it revealed. "My friend, if you have the strength and are willing, get us there speedily."

Cammy took up the oars and they were off again, slicing through the water. Waves broached their gunwales and soaked their feet, but neither gave it a thought. Cammy had a knack for the sport; she adjusted the boat's angle and made up the time they lost. Through sheer strength, Cammy made the little boat fly.

Bianca sat in the bow like a carved figurehead, the water spraying her face, stinging her wound, her sights fixed on the mysterious glow.

She had no plan, only the desire to stop William Thomson. If she had given it more thought she might not have been so brave. However, Cammy's unwavering belief in their endeavor bolstered her own. Bianca didn't consider that she might fail, though in her heart she knew it took more than just goodwill to succeed. It would take a bit of luck, too.

As they neared the glowing orb, the waves began rolling crossways and sideways. Cammy struggled to keep the skiff moving forward, but the closer they got, the more turbulent the water. They breached a particularly high swell that lifted Bianca out of her seat. Around them, the smell of the Thames filled their lungs. The stink of mussels and dead fish, the putrid graveyard of river bottom churned to the surface and permeated the air around them. Bianca's condition, insistent and unaccommodating, reminded her of her folly. She leapt for the gunwale and clung to it, losing the contents of her stomach to the noisome river.

Cammy could only watch in sympathy as her friend leaned over the side. She battled to keep the boat from swamping and pointed it closer to the light, waiting for Bianca to settle.

At last Bianca wiped her mouth and got back to her seat. Still hunched over from her nausea, she held on tight and urged Cammy to row. Her face was as gray as the river in day. They were nearly upon him.

A pair of green eyes glowed from beneath the bridge. The wraith of the Thames watched from his cavern. A kerotakis and alchemy journal lay in the bottom of his boat. Having plied these waters for so long, he knew every nuance of his mistress river. He knew her varied moods, the subtle change of color that reflected the sky and the elements. And like any solicitous lover, he catered to and indulged her every whim.

He stood in his skiff, head erect, his cloak covering his person— a figure indistinguishable from the dark underbelly of the bridge's arch, but for his eyes. And then, they were easy to miss. Easy to dismiss if one had consumed too much drink, or blinked and the wraith looked away. From here the Rat Man measured the strength of his mistress's sighs, her heaving breaths fostering waves and restless motion.

An inexperienced boatman played into his hand, carrying William Thomson perilously close to the roiling water of the bridge abutments. The Rat Man could not have hoped for a better scenario if he had orchestrated it himself. A chuckle rose from the pit of his being. And behold—Bianca was close behind.

Soon he would leave this purgatory to which he had been condemned. Would he miss his mistress Thames and Lady London and regret leaving them to forge their own fate? He'd only been able to do so much. And now he was tired.

The king and his courtiers, the moneyed merchants and nobility would continue to ignore the suffering masses and consider them irrelevant. This, thought the Rat Man, was uncharitable; after all, who would fight their wars? Wealthy officers paid for their positions and garnered the glory and recognition that was earned by their underlings, their soldiers. And what was a soldier's reward? If he was fortunate, he would return with his life. But those who died would only be remembered for as long as their loved ones missed them. Their bodies would rot on the battlefields, their bones plowed into soil by a farmer's harrow.

This inequitable distribution of power would continue for as long as mankind existed. 'Twas the foundation of civilization and always would be. However, there is nothing that doesn't benefit from balance. There is no system, no government that wouldn't improve because of it. But, he mused, noble intentions will always bend from the weight of gold.

The Rat Man sighed, weary of this world and of the purgatory he had been forced to endure.

He wished his end. He held no delusions that there was any place more desirable to go. If heaven and hell were his only choices, then he was content to let God decide which he deserved. His only desire was for his soul's resolution. Even if there was nothingness—an eternal silence void of color, smell, and taste—he would gladly accept that as his final rest.

Within him dwelled the souls of lost potential, the aborted hopes of those taken too soon, taken from the earth by a malevolent pestilence. His hubris had been his undoing, and now he dared to hope that his soul had been suitably cleansed.

If he could release those lost souls and end his haunting, his purgatory, and *their* purgatory, then could they, too, find rest? He could not give them back their lives. What more could he do for them? But if one last act of sacrifice could save hundreds more souls—living souls—from an element, this *lapis mortem*, whose evil intent had not yet been fully realized, then was it not worth the effort?

Surely, if he succeeded, the wraith had earned his end.

* * *

He was too angry to notice a rowboat lurching toward their stern. William Thomson cursed his boatman, struggling to steer his craft through the rolling swells. Too late, he questioned the man's judgment. Too late, he regretted getting onboard with the lone boatman waiting at a landing where no one else bothered to go. Just, too late.

Thinking himself more capable than his captain, the Scot stuffed the vial of glowing stones into his purse and snatched the man's oar, then threw him aside to take command of the stern. He dug the paddle deep to port and pulled the boat away from the massive bridge to free them from the turbulent water. But his effort did little and his concentration was so great that he did not hear or see Cammy and Bianca approach through the thick fog.

"William Thomson," yelled Bianca.

"Sir, a lady calls to you!" shouted the boatman, pointing.

The Scot turned his head to see them near. "Ah, so it is." Again he dipped his paddle and attempted another broadside pull, but instead their boat tipped awkwardly and a wave nearly swamped them.

"Stay, sir!" yelled Bianca, while Cammy drew their boat alongside his.

The two hulls clacked together, jarring everyone onboard both vessels. It was a dangerous position, but Cammy instinctively understood the play of water. With a sweep of her paddle, the boats collided a second time, wrenching the Scot's oar from his grasp. Pinched between the sides, the paddle stood upright and could not be freed.

Thomson cursed, but just as fast the bobbing boats separated and the oar toppled into the water like a fallen tree.

He reached for the floating oar. His purse dangled from his waistline, the light from the vial of stones glowing conspicuously. As Thomson leaned over for the floating oar, Cammy dug her paddle into the river and with a mighty pull bumped their small craft into the wherry yet again, this time crushing Thomson's hand.

"Devil take thee!" screamed Thomson, trying to shove away the offending boat.

Bianca, with no thought of her earlier nausea, stood up, crouching to keep her balance, then leapt onto his wherry. Putting her years of cutpursing to use, she grabbed hold of Thomson's purse and sliced its strings.

The Scot swiped at Bianca and missed. His anger turned to fury, and he rocked Cammy's boat enough to free his trapped hand. Despite Cammy's efforts to keep her boat against the wherry, they separated. Her bow caught in the current and she fought the pull of the bridge, leaving Bianca alone with Thomson and his boatman.

Thomson held his injured hand. "We can avoid more unpleasantness if ye give me that," he yelled over the sound of rushing water. His face showed his pain, but he endeavored to remain calm.

"Considering that you stole them, that is a bold request," shouted Bianca. She maintained her distance from the Scot as the wherryman scrambled to the other end of the boat and cowered there. "I believe your intent is not a noble one, sir."

"Honorable? Ye know not of what ye speak."

"You seek to use the stones against the king's army."

"You've never seen the atrocities your king has wrought on my people. There are no rules in war. It is kill or be killed. But you waste my time. Hand over my purse and I shall let ye live."

"Did you kill Leadith Browne for these stones?"

"Nay. Verily, I liked the woman. She made my medicine."

"But you were in the alley where she died."

"I searched the alley for the glowing stones, but Leadith was already dead. Alas, I didnae find them."

"So you ransacked Leadith's rent."

"They were nae there, either."

"We found Nye Standish's body at his herbarium."

William Thomson smiled. His teeth glinted in the faint light. "The man was a pompous, intolerant cullion who hated anyone not English. Why should he possess the stones?"

Another wave hit the wherry and broke over the side of the gunwale. Both Thomson and Bianca fought to keep their balance.

"Lassie, ye are cut," said Thomson, once the wherry settled. He gestured at the slice across her cheek.

Bianca resisted touching her wound. She kept her arms out to her sides like a rope walker, her knife in one hand, the sack of element in the other. The Scot's face twitched with a thought. Bianca wondered what that thought was when suddenly he lunged for her. She leapt backward and her calves struck the crosswise seat. She grabbed on to the gunwale to keep from falling but was suddenly jarred from their wherry being bumped. The vessel tipped and water gushed over the side. It swirled around her feet and swiftly rose above her ankles. The force was too great. Bianca fell into the river.

CHAPTER 30

Bianca gasped from the frigid water enveloping her body. Her skirt ballooned with trapped air and the terrible shock of realization set in. Green murk and indigo bubbles churned in front of her face. The faint outline of a boat's bottom appeared within inches, nearly hitting her head, and she reached for it—but the smooth hull spurned her grasp and floated away.

Then Thomson was upon her.

He grabbed Bianca from behind and pulled her backward, grappling after her wrist. She still held the pouch like she believed she needed it to survive, but the fierce need to breathe took over. Bianca pushed her hand in the Scot's face and wrestled free of his grasp, clambering to the surface.

"Bianca!" screamed Cammy, spotting her.

Bianca desperately fought to keep her head free of the choppy current. The rowboat swung around, and she saw the flat bottom of the overturned wherry disappear into the fog. There was no sign of the boatman.

But the sodden weight of her wool kirtle pulled her down again. She slipped below the surface and felt her body sink. Bubbles escaped the tent of trapped air and rose in an effervescent stream disappearing overhead.

Again, she struggled for the surface, and again she felt the unwelcome grip of William Thomson. This time, he seized her leg.

Though muscular in build, his experience in the water was no better than hers. He could not swim any better than she, and while obtaining the bag of glowing stones had been his first thought on falling into the water, merely surviving now took precedence. His hand firmly on her calf, he yanked her down and began climbing her torso with the intent of using her as flotsam to stand on. His body rose to meet her face and they were eye to wild bulging eyeballs.

She thrashed and pushed his hands off her shoulders, then struck out for the surface with a furious kick. Thomson followed and made a second attempt to steal the bag of glowing stones. The two wrestled underwater in a slow pavane, each trying to use the other as a foothold.

The Rat Man watched the contest from his cavern under the bridge. His intent had been to bump their vessel and prevent William Thomson from taking the stones. Instead, they'd both gone in the water. He hoped Thomson would sink from his woolly garb and inability to swim. But the Scot had proved stronger and more cagey than he'd expected.

Now the Rat Man was faced with a dilemma.

The two were as tangled as vines. How best to separate them so that he might finally take possession of the element? If he dared to maneuver his boat close enough to hit the man, he risked striking Bianca instead.

A woman's cursing drew his attention, and he saw Bianca's companion row valiantly against the current in an effort to save her friend. Mayhap he should let her intervene.

Cammy rowed with the might of an army. Indeed, she did have the army's best interests in mind (namely, Roger) as she threw her back into every stroke. Over her shoulder she saw Bianca's arms out of the water. Relieved to see her friend still alive, Cammy took several strong pulls, then looked a second time. Instead of Bianca, now William Thomson surfaced. She feared the worst for her friend and, with shaking hands, rowed even faster.

She veered into their general area and lifted the oars out of the water. The boat drifted and her eyes searched the surface. She saw no sign of either of them. No bubbles, no clothing, nothing. Again the little vessel met the uncertain current and began to rock. Perhaps both Thomson and Bianca had been lost. With an audible sigh, Cammy leaned over the side and scanned the water one last time. She stifled a sob, when suddenly she heard thrashing and gasps. Off her stern, she saw Thomson and Bianca struggling, not so much in the hopes of killing each other as just to survive.

Cammy brought the boat around and, positioning the craft behind Bianca, shouted for her to grab the paddle. Bracing its stem against her side, Cammy held firm and Bianca lunged. But she landed shy of the stick. She began stroking her way forward, racing William Thomson for the paddle.

Unfortunately, Bianca could not match his strength. Thomson got to the oar first and Cammy, horrified that she was about to rescue him instead of her friend, levered the oar from his grip. She freed the paddle from its lock and wielded it like a cudgel. The Scot barely knew what happened when Cammy brought it down, full force, bludgeoning him.

The look of dismay was short-lived for the Scot. William Thomson fell back, his eyes wide and now unseeing. The fight went out of him. He slipped underwater as if it had consumed him, swallowing him whole.

Like angel's wings, Bianca stroked her arms in an arc to overcome the heavy drag of her clothing. She rose incrementally toward the surface, but just as strong was the mulish force of water tugging her down. Her lungs ached for breath, her chest swelled to the verge of bursting. She fought to keep her mouth shut. She willed herself to resist the urge to take a breath.

A kick sent her upward and, still clutching the pouch of glowing stones, she swept her arms down and broke the mirrored edge of water. Her chin lifted. She took a gulp of life giving air and, unfortunately, a measure of river water along with it.

Again, the river tugged her under. Her eyes wild, she glimpsed William Thomson slipping to the depths beside her, his mouth open, his eyes frozen wide, and his arms motionless.

She kicked and felt herself lift, but she could no longer control her body's desire to cough. Her chest heaving, she finally gasped. The river flowed down her throat, burning her lungs like fire. She thrashed, but now it was only the wish to move her legs. Try as she might, there was no movement. She could no longer command her body.

Her chest convulsed, and water filled her mouth and lungs. She struggled a moment more. Confusion set in. Her vision compressed, shrinking as if she were looking through a pinhole.

So this is what it is to die, she thought. An excruciating pain thwarted her efforts to fight, but then it began to subside and she became wrapped in peaceful calm. Time lengthened. Time became irrelevant. The drum of her beating heart softened and slowed, like feathers falling on snow.

A dream of the child in her womb flitted through her mind. How strange that life begins in water. How strange that life—her life and that of her child—would end in water. Together this is where they would die, bound for all time.

She would never know the soul that she and John had created. A pain of regret pinched somewhere deep inside of her; a sorrow for leaving this life with so much left undone. But then, as much as we think we are and wish it so, we are not our own masters.

The Rat Man heard Cammy pleading for her friend to grab her oar. When Bianca did not surface, the wraith stared at his mistress river and muttered a curse. Had he not been this river's devoted subject? He only asked that *his* existence be finished. Why did she desire Bianca Goddard's to end?

Abandoning his wherry, he dove into the water.

His green eyes glowed, lighting his way through the silty depths. Ahead he spied a listless shape and swimming closer saw that it was the Scot. He understood the man's reasoning for pursuing the stones, but, he thought cynically, matters of state are not decided by a man's single effort.

The bottom of Cammy's boat drifted overhead, the blade of a paddle extended to aid Bianca to safety. But Bianca was nowhere within range. Looking directly beneath him, the wraith saw nothing, not even the top of Bianca's head or an errant bubble rising to the surface. She must have sunk like a rock.

He descended toward the river bottom like a feeding carp, still searching for the alchemist's daughter. His desire to release all the lost souls to their final rest did not include adding Bianca to the list. If she should still have in hand the purse of glowing element, then all the better. Down he went. Down to the depths.

At first he did not see her floating silently suspended in time. He swam opposite and stared at her face. Bianca's eyes were open and unblinking. Her loose hair waved gently in the undercurrent. How serene, how peaceful she looked. One arm rested easily, slightly extended. The other arm was bent across her chest. In her hand was the stolen bag containing the element.

The Rat Man untangled the strings from her fingers and freed the purse. Her fingers resisted his taking them, and as he stared into her eyes he saw a flicker of life still in them. Her soul had not yet left.

Seizing her arm, the Rat Man pulled her to the surface, speeding through the water as if it were air. Though he could have granted her the mercy of a tranquil death—for who knows how tortured a future death might be?—he knew she was destined for a greater purpose. He could not wittingly commend her soul to its earthly end. Maneuvering her just below the paddle, he stretched out her arm to lay it on the blade.

Her friend responded with shouts of encouragement. *The poor dear*, thought he, *human nature is ever hopeful*. But lo, had he not a measure of humanity left? Why else was he trying to save Bianca?

Cammy's hand broke the water and reached for Bianca's arm to haul her up. She would not succeed without his help. A lifeless body weighs twice what a breathing one does. The Rat Man pushed Bianca out of the water so that there would be no second attempt to get her out. Cammy took hold of her armpits and with a mighty tug landed Bianca in the hull of the boat. For a fleeting second, Cammy would think she was stronger than she thought.

There was nothing more the Rat Man could do. He had gotten her into capable hands and whether she lived or died was not his decision. It was hers. His deed complete, he prepared to leave this world.

With a final glance, he saw Cammy working to save her friend. He slithered back to his wherry beneath the bridge and in that dark recess dragged himself partway out of the water. Clinging to the side of his boat, the Rat Man dumped the vial of glowing stones in his skeletal hand. His palm began to smoke, but it mattered not. He welcomed the feeling of pain.

In the bottom of his wherry lay the kerotakis and book of alchemy retrieved months earlier. At the time, he had believed they would lead him to his final redemption. Before abandoning them to the river, Bianca had pursued creating the elixir of immortality—not because she had wanted to bestow immortality on her dying husband, but because she thought that if she stopped short of the final stone, it would yield only what was needed for health and healing.

She had been wrong.

Once an alchemist himself, the Rat Man could not bear to see another man's life work lost to posterity. He'd fished the journal out of the river and then thoroughly studied its contents. But Ferris Stannum's work contained only recipes designed to impart life, not to end it. And so, the journal, as far as the Rat Man was concerned, was useless.

The wraith took one last look at London. Her future would be determined by her people. Only time would tell whether she would be remembered for her beauty or for her filth. He smiled ruefully. Everything, everyone is similarly judged. Taking one last breath of earthly air, he tossed the element into his mouth and the stones settled on his tongue. They sizzled and smoked. Then making the sign of the cross (in case God was watching), he tried to swallow.

Albern Goddard's creation was evil. Nothing good could be salvaged from his element except, perhaps, its ability to bring the wraith's unnatural existence to an end.

Smoke seeped from between the Rat Man's pointy teeth, and the stones melted a hole through his palate, but he continued to hold them in his mouth like a lozenge. He relaxed his jaw for air to enter his mouth and the stones sparked. They flared and burst into flames.

The pain was so intense, his desire to stop the burning so strong, that he fell back into the water to spit them out and extinguish the fire. But the damage had been done. The Rat Man sank below his wherry and the river carried him down.

His was not the flesh of man, but the bizarre amalgam of bone, lost souls, and restless imaginings. He was born of his own hubris; created when he believed he could prevent death and save those who had died prematurely. Instead, he had become the vessel of their anguished cries. He was their crucible.

Even the worst physical pain could not compare with the despair he'd suffered for all this time. So intense was the emotional debt he'd been given that he welcomed depuration in whatever form it took.

"*Eluit me,*" he cried, desiring to be cleansed. "*Adducere mihi in finem.*" He fervently wished his end.

The stones coursed down his throat, vaporizing his peculiar flesh and burning his bones like aged timber. A thousand lost souls rode his muffled screams to the river's edge and escaped into the night sky, rising through the shroud of fog to a realm of infinite stars. In this unfathomably ancient celestial serum they would find their long-desired peace.

And, in the end, the Rat Man's God took pity on his wretched soul and gave him what he so desperately wanted. His purgatory ended. His soul was cast free of his earthly costume and it followed the lost souls on a journey to the stars. His worn corpse settled to the river's gravelly bottom, where it would be covered in layers of silt and sediment, forever entombed. And forever forgotten.

CHAPTER 31

The first thing Bianca saw when she opened her eyes was the intent stare of two green glowing orbs. Her body shuddered in panic, her muddled brain worked in confusion until she realized she was no longer underwater, but lying in her bed in her room of Medicinals and Physickes. The eyes belonged not to some illusory entity with mysterious intent, but to her immortal cat, Hobs.

The feline had kept watch over her for these days since she'd been carried there by Cammy and Tendle from the Dim Dragon Inn. Her mother, Malva, had tended her, occasionally relieved by the concerned tavern wench who had promised John she would help Bianca when the time came.

And the time had come.

Still groggy from her days of unconsciousness, Bianca extended her hand for Hobs to rub his chin against, then reached for Cammy, who gripped her weak palm and clasped it between her two.

"You've had quite a few days," said Cammy, reassuringly. "Rest. Do not strain yourself sitting up." A smile of relief eased her furrowed brow. "When you are ready I shall get you some broth."

Bianca swept her gaze around the room, its familiarity comforting. It was a mystery how long she had been there, yet she didn't feel ready to learn the details. She was still sorting through the scraps of memory that came to her when she closed her eyes.

The suffocating panic of not being able to breathe would haunt her for years, but for now she was aware enough to know that she was safe. She wondered what other frights would snap at her heels when she least expected?

She moved her legs beneath her bed linens, the sheets feeling cool against her thighs. Her nose woke to the smell of smoke and savory beef broth. Hobs flopped beside her, content that his mistress was awake and that she could raise her hand to stroke him.

Bianca was resting easily, listening to the sounds of Cammy across the room, when a wave of pain suddenly gripped her womb, twisting it angrily. The sensation of wet between her legs brought her to sitting. She ran a hand down the sheet and touched her skin, saw her fingers covered in blood.

She was staring at her fingers when Cammy crossed the room carrying a bowl of broth.

Cammy froze in place and read the devastation on Bianca's face. She hurried to her friend and wrapped her in her arms.

It was a while before Bianca stopped shaking. Her grief was quiet and sorrowful. Her tears were heavy and silent.

"You lost the child two days ago," Cammy told her. "You are not quite healed. It will take some time."

Bianca nodded and wiped her nose with her sleeve.

"Allow yourself to grieve, but then you must get on with it." And Cammy took care in helping Bianca inch to the edge of the bed and stand. She wiped down her legs and smock, then stripped the bed of its soiled linen. When finally Bianca was settled, she sat next to her and made sure that she took some soup. "Foremost, you need your strength."

"Were you here when it happened?" Bianca asked, surprising herself with the sound of her voice croaking free of her throat.

"Your mother was."

Bianca took another sip. "What did she say?" Her voice sounded like strange bleating.

"What is there to say? Such things happen. It is nature's will."

"Not God's?"

"I've raised enough cows and animals to know that nature is a woman's realm. She does as she likes whether God agrees or not."

"Did Malva know I nearly drowned?"

"Bianca, you did drown. I don't know how you survived being underwater for as long as you were. It is unnatural."

A faint impression of helplessly sinking, then of being propelled through the water coursed through Bianca's mind. She thought on it, then decided the fantastic recollection was probably the invention of having nearly died.

Cammy went on to tell her that she had pulled her from the river and that she had pushed on her chest to expel the water. Bianca had sputtered and begun breathing, but she had been unresponsive since that night.

"William Thomson drowned," said Bianca, remembering his lifeless body floating beside her.

"His body was found later, beneath the bridge."

Again, Bianca grew thoughtful. The spectacle of an unearthly being surfaced in her mind's eye, and she struggled to recollect exactly what it was. Its presence would stalk her for the rest of her life, and she would continue to feel both gratitude and confusion in equal portions whenever the memory surfaced.

"Tell me everything since that night," she said.

Cammy obliged, recounting Bianca's rescue and how the patrons of the Dim Dragon had come to her aid. "Roger and John have moved on from London. I don't know when we might see them again," she sighed. "But they won't suffer the element being used against them." She patted Bianca on the leg. "We have done our part for the king's army."

"Does Meddybemps know what happened?"

At the mention of the street vendor's name, Cammy's tone changed. She became curt. "He came by," she said. She collected the empty bowl and disappeared across the room. When she came back Bianca was ready with a question.

"Something happened," she said. "What do you know?"

Cammy hesitated, sensing there would be no avoiding it. She pulled a stool close to Bianca's side and spoke in a confidential tone.

"This Meddybemps," she began. "He wears a red cap, does he not?"

"He does."

"And his eyes, the directions that they point . . . it is not usual."

Bianca nodded.

"He arrived when your mother was caring for you. I will say he seemed of good intention. He expressed concern and sat by your side. Your mother and I did some chores; then he stood to take his leave." Cammy wound an apron tie around her finger, fiddling with the string before continuing.

"I do not say this to be unkind, but your mother's disposition . . . she is not . . . demonstrative. Or so I judged her when first she came around. But when Meddybemps arrived, she became visibly ill at ease. Like she felt the pricks of a hundred needles.

"She saw him out and the two continued talking in the lane. Forgive me, but I could not stop my curiosity. I lingered near the window. He embraced her and at first I thought him reassuring her, for they both care for you, I could see that to be so. And given that you had lost the child, she must have felt the grief that she knew you would feel once you learned what happened." Cammy looked down in her lap, smoothing her apron against her thighs. She glanced at Bianca before continuing. "But no, that was not why he was comforting her.

"He tenderly stroked her face and he said that it was their secret. That she need not worry. No one would ever know. Not even you."

"Me?"

"Aye, Meddybemps said your name. Then your mother drew back from him. 'But she suspects,' I heard her say."

Bianca sat up straighter in bed. "Did Meddybemps answer?"

Cammy nodded. "He said, 'I told her I did not stab her. And that is where it will end.'"

Bianca's level stare unnerved Cammy. She showed no outward

sign of dismay, insult, or even outrage. Eventually, she dragged her gaze from her friend and focused on some far-off spot only she could see. "I would like to rest now," she said.

Later, when Cammy left to go to market, Bianca got to her feet and unsteadily made her way to the jake. She padded to the alley door and opened it, checked the water level in her rain barrel, a daily habit that always managed to comfort her. Standing there in her modest rent, she heard the faint cluck of the neighbor's chickens, smelled Morgan Stream, felt a breeze through her window, and watched the herbs twist on their strings. Never had she felt so alone.

Her room of Medicinals and Physickes had always been her refuge. The drying plants, the stills, the chattels of her industry gave her an endless source of inspiration. Her mind constantly ran through a catalog of smells and the healing properties of plants. She spent hours pondering how best to draw upon their strengths and combine them effectively. But the loss of her child, of their child, sat heavily on her mind.

She blamed herself for the loss, but how could she have prevented it? She could not stand idly by while William Thomson used her father's element to destroy John and the king's army. Their child's death was a sad consequence. There was no other way to think of it.

And if John returned, would he forgive her? Would he think she willfully contrived the miscarriage? She had the means to do so with her decoctions and he knew it.

Bianca dragged herself back to bed, stared up at the rafters for a moment, then pulled the sheet over her head.

The faraway chatter of voices grew louder and Bianca heard Cammy ask if she was well enough to take visitors. The request set Bianca's thoughts in motion and they began to order themselves.

"Certainly," she answered.

"It is Patch," conferred Cammy. "I can send him away."

"Nay," said Bianca. "I should like to speak with him."

Her friend raised a skeptical eyebrow. "Let us prop you up, then." Cammy rolled a blanket and supported Bianca's back enough to make her comfortable. "If he overstays give me a nod and I shall escort him out."

In a moment, Cammy returned with Patch. He had removed his cap—out of respect? wondered Bianca, but no—it was more likely that the room was overly warm and probably his head was drippy.

"Bianca Goddards," he said, looking a bit unsure. "I would say ye've lost yer color, but then ye never had much blush to start." He stood at the foot of her bed and looked all around him. "I sees ye been taken care of. Even that hideous scar on yer face seems to be healing. Ye be lucky to have a friend so loyal." He peeped dubiously at Cammy standing near, keeping a close eye on him. She looked as though she could squeeze his skinny little neck with one hand and that she relished the idea of doing so.

"Are you here to assure that I am not dead, or is there some other purpose to your visit?"

"Wells, I thoughts ye might want to know what all happened while ye were indisposed."

"I do." Bianca ignored the erratic way some of her words sounded too loud while others disappeared behind intent. Her voice was still weak. "Is Jacoby Nimble in custody?"

"Oh, aye. He is in Newgate. We wish to make his murderous neck as thin as a wick at Tyburn, but he admits to nothing. Ye left us in a hurry that night, leaving Constable Minot and me with his insensible self." Patch mopped his forehead with a napkin, then continued. "We thoughts we could tease a confession out of him, but he is guarded and keeps his counsel. What, exactly, did he say when you was with him?"

Bianca laid her head back and closed her eyes. The memory of their visit to the apothecary's shop crawled out of the corner of her mind. She remembered the lizard, its spiky scales red with blood. Patch licked his bottom lip expectantly as she began.

"I was alone in the back room with the body when I heard Nimble enter the shop. He called for Standish. The customer had left and I didn't know when you'd return, but I thought you would not be long. I hid under the table.

"Nimble was surprised to find Standish dead and he had his say as if he needed to dress down the apothecary. He didn't know that I heard every word.

"He commended Standish for successfully casting blame on him. He said he had been wrong to blame Dikson Browne for stealing the stones from him. That he should have saved his ire for Standish."

"Wells," said Patch. "I believe that is as close to a confession as we will get out of him. Are ye willing to swear to it?"

"Aye, Constable."

Patch tucked his cap under his arm. "Methinks ye should have told us where ye was going when Minot and I arrived. Perchance it might have prevented yer current predicament."

"I did tell you. And this is not a predicament, Patch. Only a temporary inconvenience."

The constable snorted. "So sayeth the waylaid maid. But ye was after the Scot—William Thomson. Yer friend, here, told me so."

"While I waited for you, I found a small stone sphere on the floor near Standish's body. It was similar to one I had found in the alley where Leadith Browne was discovered. Standish's customer identified it for me." Bianca described the size of the stones and the markings, for surely now they were lost. "They were relics of an ancient people who once lived in Scotland. The spheres are coveted as talismans of a sort. Though they could have belonged to anyone, my mind went to the only Scot who entered into all of this. And when I remembered the conversations at the Dim Dragon about King Henry's plans for Scotland, I knew I had to question him."

"So's ye thinks Thomson murdered Standish and took the element."

"I know it to be so. Thomson as much as admitted it."

Patch tipped his head in satisfaction. "It all falls into place." He gestured at Cammy. "She tolds me about the struggle ye had on the river that night. It could have ended worse than it did."

"However we can be thankful that the element is lost and will do no harm sitting at the bottom of the river."

"I suppose ye is right. I am sorry I never gots to see this fantastical element that caused all this whobub."

They each seemed to ponder this for a moment, then Bianca spoke.

"Dikson Browne's boy—Timothy," she said. "What has happened to him? He can't live by himself on Trinity Lane."

"Naws," said Patch. "He has an aunt who has taken him in. A smite better circumstance than living with that sloshed metal mangler."

Cammy brought Bianca a wedge of cheese and bread. She sat on the bed and encouraged her friend to eat.

"There is still one lingering question we have yet to solve," said Patch. "It is the murder that started this whole matter. Who killed Leadith Browne?"

Bianca stopped chewing and gulped down a lump of bread. "The Scot killed Leadith," she said. "William Thomson did it." She ignored Cammy's stare boring into her.

"Hmm," said Patch, raising his brows. After a moment he seemed to agree with the answer. "He dids seem to know a lot about that night." With a quivering smile of satisfaction, Patch set his cap upon his head. "All the better the rustic knave ended as he did."

Cammy waited until the constable was out the door and around the corner before speaking. "You surprise me. I thought you were scrupulously honest."

"I have no scruples lying when it serves a greater good."

"*Your* greater good."

"Everyone has their own sense of justice."

"You're letting a murderer go unpunished."

"Don't be so quick to say it. No one escapes their misdeeds, even if their intentions are noble. I have no illusions that my deceit will someday catch up with me." Bianca threw back the sheet and sat on the edge of the bed, offering her explanation. "Some men have privileges that you and I will never enjoy. We did not choose to be born to a farmer or to an alchemist. The monied nobility and merchants have the advantage of wealth and influence to protect themselves and their families. But I have only my wits to take care of mine."

Chapter 32

Though her room of Medicinals and Physickes seemed painfully quiet without John's and Cammy's near-constant presence, it came as a relief to Bianca when finally she was well enough to resume life concocting medicines and tending to matters on her own. The privacy afforded her the chance to sort her thoughts.

The inkling of something dark still lurked deep in her subconscious. Unable to understand or identify her disquiet by day, she would sometimes wake at night with a start, prickling with unease. She'd sit and stare across the room pondering her peculiar dreams. Dreams so real, so vivid that she wondered if they might be memories.

Bianca snipped a bunch of meadowsweet and *Nepeta* to make more remedy for ague. No doubt, Meddybemps would eventually come calling and she needed to replenish her usual salves and balms. Without John's stipend from Boisvert her money would soon run out.

As if Hobs could read her mind, he left when she began her chemistries and later returned with a dead mouse, which he proudly presented.

"It has not quite come to that," she told the great hunter, picking up the limp creature by its tail. "I know how delectable you find them. By all means, enjoy the fruit of your labor." She flung it in the alley and as Hobs ran after she heard a call from out in the lane.

It was the first Bianca had seen Meddybemps since she had come to.

"Good morrow!" exclaimed the streetseller when they met at the door. "The prodigy walks, has color in the cheek, though a thinning scar across it, but by all counts is a mickle bit better than when last I inquired."

"I am improved." Bianca bade him enter. "I am working on my salves for market."

Meddybemps stepped into Bianca's aromatic quarters and was pleased that the smells were not offensive, but rather soothing compared to her usual creations. "Know't I am relieved that we shall soon be collaborating as before."

Bianca hesitated in her steps. "Not quite," she said pointedly.

"Pray ye?" Meddybemps sensed Bianca's displeasure, but perhaps he was wrong. He did not ask her to explain, preferring, instead, polite accord to bristly explanation.

But the room held only the two of them and Bianca would not blithely ignore what sat between them like a brimming chamber pot.

She wanted an honest and direct answer, and dropped all pretense between them. "You killed Leadith Browne," she said.

At first Meddybemps sought to deny it, but then he realized fabricating another lie would do more harm than their friendship could withstand. His response was a not so simple silence.

"I am not naïve about you and my mother," Bianca prompted. "But I had asked for you to leave her alone."

"By my troth, I did not go against your wish."

"It appears that you did."

Meddybemps removed his cap and ran his hand through his scant hair. "She sought me."

"You should have graciously refused."

Meddybemps shook his head. "I could not. I still care for her . . . and for you."

"Now the consequences are more dangerous than if you had done nothing."

"It is a risk I willingly take." Meddybemps hoped Bianca would leave it alone, but she tipped her head, waiting for him to explain. There would be no patent understanding until he voiced his reasons. "Should I have left your mother to suffer Albern's hand? Leadith threatened to stir the pot with me and your mother in it. Your father is not a man who would have ignored her story. He is not a man who would allow himself to be the victim of her gossip. Albern will not be made a cuckold. Do you imagine he would allow himself to be publicly embarrassed a second time? To be forced to ride skimmington through the streets of London? Leadith threatened to tell all and then some. What exactly, say you, would your father have done?"

"I cannot know how he would have reacted. My father is an unpredictable man," said Bianca.

"Your father is a ruined man," said Meddybemps. "He cannot walk down the lane without hearing the whispered accusations of treason. He would rather see your mother dead than suffer another humiliation."

"Aw! Then Leadith's rumors are founded?"

"Nay, they are not. I have left your mother alone since when you asked it. And that I speak in truth. But Leadith was a conniver. She saw a way to profit from your father's element. She intimidated your mother, threatened to spread lies and to shame Albern. That is how she got the stones."

"Could you not have contrived to get them back? Was murder your only choice?"

"And when would it have ended?" posed Meddybemps. "I gambled your mother's life for hers."

"But to brutally cut her?"

Meddybemps stared at Bianca in frank astonishment. His complexion changed from its usual pallor. "I would never brutalize the woman, or any woman. No matter how much I despised Leadith Browne, I did not mutilate her."

If Bianca had learned anything, the balance between right and wrong was often subtle. Circumstances both personal and external lead to one's perception of justice. Bianca did not admonish Meddybemps for choosing as he did, nor, after she thought about it, would she think less of him. He, too, was taking care of his own.

Either Jacoby Nimble or William Thomson (or even Dikson, for that matter) must have observed Leadith swallow the stones, and after finding her lifeless body sought to retrieve them by slicing her. Bianca chose to believe this, because the thought of her beloved friend committing such a heinous crime was too horrible for her to accept.

But she knew that she and Malva were the beneficiaries of his decision.

Going forward, she would now bear the burden of his awful secret. And it was one she would take heed to never betray.

Poppy replaced spent meadowsweet in the fields beyond Broadwall. The flowers were like hundreds of miniature jesters, each clad in exuberant reddish orange costume, all flirting with the first heated gusts of summer.

Bianca admired their merry display. The sight coaxed a smile to her face for the first time in weeks. She tipped her face toward the sun and felt it melt away the last of her melancholy from this irascible spring.

She'd visited her father at his room of alchemy and told him a Scot had murdered Dikson Browne's wife, hoping to steal the coveted element and use it against the king's army. The business about Malva's involvement she kept mum and suggested Leadith's son had spied him with the element and that the Brownes had schemed to steal it. She assumed her mother could defend herself against Albern's accusation of the missing key placed in the wrong pocket. Their argument was no longer hers, and the apathy which this family had for one another further deepened.

Malva visited Bianca the day after her conversation with Meddy-bemps. Neither mentioned the obvious. Instead they talked about whether burdock root could be combined with red clover to make a purging tea that would thin the blood and help one tolerate the occasional blistery days that would surely come with summer. They parted on amiable but guarded terms, each keeping the other wondering. Sometimes opinions needed more time to mellow.

As days turned to weeks, Bianca often visited Cammy and sat with her friend in the off hours at the Dim Dragon Inn, sharing news about the king's forays into Scotland and Boulogne.

Both fervently wished for their lovers' return, and until that day came would satisfy themselves with genuine hopes and cherished memories.

Bianca bent to collect a posy of the sanguine poppies, though they might last only a day in water. She'd take some to Cammy, who would be reminded of her country home. For the humble flower calls to mind remembrance, and though fleet of pleasure, its message lingers long in a young maid's heart.

GLOSSARY

bandy ball—a kind of field hockey

barrow—a two-wheeled hand cart used by street vendors

batlet—a stick used to stir and beat clothing when washing

beck—constable

bloody flux—dysentery

brigandine—armor jacket

caput corvi—"head of the crow," an alchemical term for the color black

carl—country person

codswallop—nonsense

colophony—tree resin, sometimes used for sealing vessels airtight

cove—a man, person

crapulous—sick from too much drinking

Cross Bones—graveyard for indigent women

cruck house—a desirable type of construction with arching trusses

cullion—base fellow

curber—a thief who uses a hook on a line or a curved stick to steal items from open windows

destrier—a stallion warhorse ridden by royalty and lords

docking—sexual intercourse

drabbing—whoring

drabs—whores

Earl of Arran—regent of Scotland in 1544

elflocked—tangled

Elle est ton oiseau à farcir.—(French) She is your bird to stuff.

Eluit me. Adducere mihi in finem.—(Latin) Cleanse me. Bring my end.

Et j'ai une grosse carotte.—(French) And I have a big carrot.

executor—executioner

foining—thrusts

fubbed off—fucked

gaumless—vapid-minded

giglot—a loose woman

gudgeon—credulous, gullible

gulled—duped

hot house—a brothel

Je vais tu voir bientôt.—(French) I will see you soon.

ken—alehouse

kerotakis—an apparatus used for sublimation

King's Evil, the—also scrofula—the swelling of neck lymph nodes caused by tuberculosis

lead fume—lead oxide obtained from the flues at lead smelters

madam of the game—a brothel madam

Mais puisque vous êtes ici.—(French) But since you are here.

malmsey-nosed—color of a strong red wine

Meg of Meldon—Scottish legend of a woman turned to stone for dancing on the Sabbath

Mouldwarp—from the *Prophecy of Merlin*, in which a ruler or king would at first be greatly praised by his people, then would suffer being cast down by sin and pride

mushrumps—mushrooms

nebbishy—weaselly

nidget—coward

opalus—opals

ordinary—a place to eat and drink

palliasse—straw mattress

pigeon—dupe

pillock—a stupid person

plucking roses—urinating

Pope Joan—a card game

posy—bouquet

pottle pot—a vessel holding nearly two quarts of ale

quoit—curling stone

rawgabbits—gossipers

say—lightweight fabric made of wool and silk

scrofula—tuberculosis of the lymph nodes

scrumpox—impetigo

scut—softer version of "shite"

skimmington—the act of putting a cuckolded man on a donkey to ride backward through the streets

Southrons—Scottish name for British

stampers—shoes

starlings—bridge supports

stew—a bawd house

tetters—a skin disease

tilly vally—nonsense

trulls—whores

wazzock—a fool

whobub—hubbub

wibbling—talk incessantly

writhled—shriveled

AUTHOR'S NOTE

Creating a believable world set in sixteenth-century England comes with its own particular set of challenges. I give a great deal of thought about interspersing period words throughout the text; it is not my intention to lose or irritate the reader. Part of the joy I find in writing stories for this period is that I love the language and find it colorful.

Readers who have gotten this far in the series know that the stories are somewhat whimsical and that I add fanciful elements not based in reality. This is because I enjoy wondering about that which is only sensed and never seen. Tudor England sat on the cusp of modern society, where folklore and superstition still influenced the collective mind-set. To my way of thinking, it makes sense to mix these beliefs together in the hopes of creating a more natural portrayal of the period.

I spend a great deal of time researching the history of Tudor England and the various topics that I write about. Be that as it may, at times it is difficult to find agreement among historians and sources, and I will have to choose how I will write about a topic. Granted, this is a work of fiction, but historical fiction must first be grounded in reality, then allowed room for creative interpretation. I wish to clarify at least two things with which I took creative liberty.

The glowing element, the *lapis mortem* around which this story is centered, is loosely based on the element phosphorus. Chemists will know that "the element" that I describe does not accurately behave like the true element. The discovery of phosphorus is attributed to the German alchemist Hennig Brand in the seventeenth century. All alchemists toyed with urine—the golden stream—to try to find the philosopher's stone. It is altogether possible that an earlier alchemist could have created the element; however, the secretive nature of these men and their discoveries makes it difficult to confirm.

When I first started researching, I came across artifacts called petrospheres—small, carved stone balls. Some five hundred of these have been found throughout Great Britain but are primarily attributed to the late Neolithic Pict culture of Scotland. There continues to be a great deal of speculation as to what, exactly, they were used for. Originally, I imagined them to be about the size of marbles; however, later I realized the smallest were around 70 mm (2.75 inches)—considerably larger than a child's marble. I decided just to go with my original mistake; it didn't make sense for Bianca to tote around a stone that big.

Finally, a brief mention regarding the shame of skimmington. In the sixteenth century, the term refers to a punishment reserved for cuckolded men. The husband—forced to ride backward on a donkey—was paraded through the streets to the derision of onlookers. Throughout much of history and in Tudor England, women were regarded as undisciplined and wanton by nature (arising from the doctrine of original sin), and therefore needed the guiding discipline of a husband or father (usually in the form of beatings). A cuckolded husband was viewed as remiss in his duty to control the lustful yearnings of his unfaithful wife.

ACKNOWLEDGMENTS

I wish to thank the following people who contributed their expertise, time, and help in the creation of this book (any mistakes are purely my own): Pamela and Gale Rhodes, Andrea Jones, Tracey Stewart; the patrons and staff of Walker Memorial Library in Westbrook, Maine, for allowing me to commandeer their quiet rooms; the Glickman Library in Portland, Maine; my family and friends; the unsung heroes at Kensington who work on behalf of this series, Fred Tribuzzo and John Scognamiglio—whose name I can now spell and correctly pronounce.

I would be remiss if I did not mention the readers and librarians who have reached out and pointed me in new directions while offering enthusiasm and appreciation for this series. We have in common a love of reading and story, and I am forever grateful for this support.

And thank you to anyone who takes the time to leave a review. Now more than ever, new authors depend on those reviews and word of mouth to help get the word out in this increasingly crowded field. Whether the review is positive or negative, it means someone has been moved enough to voice an opinion. And that is always a good thing.

Connect with Us

Visit us online at
KensingtonBooks.com
to read more from your favorite authors, see books
by series, view reading group guides, and more.

for sneak peeks, chances to win books and prize packs,
and to share your thoughts with other readers.

facebook.com/kensingtonpublishing
twitter.com/kensingtonbooks

Tell us what you think!

To share your thoughts, submit a review,
or sign up for our eNewsletters, please visit:
KensingtonBooks.com/TellUs.